Band of Six:
Demons

BRETT KELBERRY

DEDICATION

To my Family -

For the examples, the encouragement, the tolerance and the love
that molded me into who I am today.

Thank you.

1.

On the northern outskirts of Hollingston, where civilization began to give way to the forested hills, a wagon rolled to a stop. The driver sprang from the buckboard and wrapped the horse's reins around the post of the low, picketed fence. Not that the sinewy mare was any threat to run. The horse was too tired to bother nibbling at the strands of long grass that grew by the fence posts.

The driver walked around to the back of the wagon and jumped into the bed. Fishing through the straw, he uncovered the two things he'd hidden there. One was the tool of his trade – a well-worn, broad-headed shovel. The other was a body, sewn into a white billy-cloth bag.

Just a child. Other men may have gone sentimental at the thought, but to a gravedigger, the smaller the body the smaller the effort required.

Hefting the bagged corpse over one shoulder and resting the shovel on the other, the gravedigger jumped from the wagon bed and strode into the graveyard. He whistled while he walked, angling towards where he planned to bury the body. Some folks had issues with walking through a graveyard in the somber darkness of night. Some would have shuddered over superstitions of the resting dead. The gravedigger knew better. He'd worked with corpses all his life – they'd never voiced a word of complaint against the living. Any digger worth his shovel knew that if you planted a man deep enough the first time, you'd never need worry about him again.

Towards the back of the graveyard, behind a low cresting hill, the gravedigger slung the body off his shoulder. The small corpse landed heavily in the grass and rolled to a stop on the leveling slope. It was an area far removed from the road and the other graves – one that wouldn't be disturbed by those who came to visit. It was the perfect location for a grave that wasn't supposed to be there.

1

He looked over towards the shrouded bag and shook his head. *Another child.* The gravedigger would have given his left eye to know where Master Rice kept finding all of these children to bury – but Rice wasn't the kind of man who appreciated inquisitive employees. The instructions he gave were specific – the body was to be moved in secret, late at night, buried in a graveyard on the fringe of Hollingston in a spot where no one would likely look.

It was the same instructions he'd received for the past five small, dead bodies.

The shovel head bit easily into the earth. The soil was loose, easy to work on account of the frequent spring rains. A rectangular-shaped pit emerged, his years of experience with the shovel incurring no wasted motion. He tracked the dimensions as he worked – length, width, depth – measuring with a discerning eye. Rhythmically the work continued until at last he was satisfied. Pitching the shovel head-first into the graveside mound of upturned earth, the gravedigger turned to fetch the billy-bag. He grabbed it with two hands, swinging it backwards to gain momentum for the throw …

He dropped the bag and stepped away, face ashen and his throat tight. He licked at his lips as he stared at the stark white bag lying in the grass a few paces in front of him. It must have been a trick – an illusion of the mind! Merciful Domus, it was this forsaken hour of the night! But he could sworn – he was almost certain – he'd felt the body stirring in the bag.

The billy-bag remained motionless. Feeling somewhat the fool, the gravedigger smiled and wagged his head in disgrace. Was he really losing his nerve? After hundreds of bodies? He shook his head. The body had shifted already – he'd been boiling heaving it, hadn't he? Of course the body had probably slid around, bending at the knees or the like! It was explainable!

Despite the sound reasoning rolling though his mind, the gravedigger didn't go directly for the bag. He first fetched his shovel. Gripping the handle near the head, he cautiously approached the body and prod at it. Two times, then thrice. The digger shook his head. Mighty disrespectful to treat a body this way, but his heart was still thumping madly in his chest …

The billy-bag came alive, squirming in the grass like a fat, albino worm. The gravedigger panicked and cursed aloud in his fright. His hands slid down the length of the shovel instinctively, and he swung the blade against the possessed corpse with all his strength. The blow connected, but had no effect on the writhing corpse. As the digger backed away her heard a ripping sound.

The bag split open.

Darkness emerged.

The digger stumbled backwards over the mound of graveside dirt, almost tipping into the waiting pit. He landed roughly in the grass, but managed to quickly scramble to his knees. He let out a fearful scream as he swung his shovel at the terrifying creature bearing down on him. His efforts did nothing to slow the beast. It raised dagger-sharp fingers that seemed to lengthen in the moonlight and the gravedigger cried out again.

The scream cut off abruptly and silence returned to the graveyard.

2.

The Eight Flagons tavern in the waterfront district of Hollingston had developed a distinct reputation. Though it had a bar and a scattering of isolated tables, it wasn't that kind of tavern. No one came to the Eight to drink or to smoke or to seek out some other form of escape. There were no games of Tens running in the corners. You came to the Eight Flagons to discuss business – or you made it your business to be elsewhere.

The Eight Flagons was a marketplace, operating in the buying and selling of illicit deeds.

For some, the mere existence of a place like the Eight would have raised questions. Certainly such an operation had not escaped the notice of the constabulary! Why was such an establishment tolerated? Why was it not shut down, the patrons arrested in bulk?

Billick could picture in his mind the kind of individuals that would ask these questions – people not personally acquainted with the dark workings of a civilized society. They could not understand that a criminal element would continue to exist – regardless of having a centralized location. And they would not understand the necessity of such a marketplace. The government would never shut it down. The government was the most regular client.

The room quieted as Billick entered, every eye in the tavern making a quick assessment of the newcomer. Billick was not a stranger, and their attention returned to the secret matters discussed in low whispers. Each table in the Eight was small and isolated with a single lantern a fixed overtop it. By design, the lamp gave light poorly, the radiance barely extending the full area of the table. It allowed the men to remain hidden in the haze of shadows, free to conduct their criminal business.

Janns, the barman, watched him from the lighted nook at one end of the room. He nodded as Billick approached. "Billick," he said as the distance narrowed.

"Janns." With as many times as he'd come to the Eight Flagons, Billick had never carried a conversation with the barman that had consisted of more than their names. They were two men cut from the same mold, really. The hardness etched into the face and into the eyes of Janns marked him as a former soldier; a hardness that hadn't faded with the graying of the barman's hair. It wasn't hard to picture them sharing a bottle as they swapped stories of their service on the front-lines – but they never would. That was something one did with friends. And neither one of them had any use for friends.

The barman reached behind him and gave two solid tugs on one of the many cords in the nook. Each was attached to a small bell in the back rooms where those seeking additional privacy conducted their negotiations. It wasn't ten seconds before the door to the largest of the rooms opened slightly and a familiar man slipped into the aura of light supplied by the nook's twin lanterns.

Hennessey had a wide, optimistic and utterly disarming smile. It was the same smile perfected by the hundreds of hawkers in the Wellington District. The smile tended to distract attention away from Hennessey's other notable feature – his eyes. His eyes carried a signature intelligent cruelty; they seemed better suited on a predatory beast than on a finely-dressed man. However pervasive Hennessey's smile, Billick had never witnessed it reach his eyes. Truly, Hennessey was a dangerous man skilled in making you forget how dangerous he truly was.

"You are late," the shorter Hennessey accused Billick. "Not that I expected anything different from you, not after so many year working together. They're already here." Wrapping an arm around his back, Hennessey began to shepherd him towards the backroom door. While there was nothing about his line of work that Billick truly enjoyed, these meetings that Hennessey arranged were truly torturous. Hennessey took care of all the periphery details – he contracted the work, laid out the specifics, and collected the payments. The arrangement suited Billick well. Yes, Hennessey took an overly generous cut of the profit, but Billick didn't have to meet his clients.

And yet, from time to time, someone would request to meet the infamous Billick. They would demand an opportunity to meet with the man they were hiring. Hennessey hated these conferences as much as Billick did – for he knew that Billick could not hide his contempt for the people who paid for his services. Why should they desire to meet him? Why, if not to see a man with no soul? Why, if not to try and glimpse the stain of the murders on his hands? Hennessey theorized their clients did it to feel a closer connection to the murder they were contracting. Murder, if it was anything, was always personal.

Hennessey paused at the doorway, and turned to look up at him. The smile was there, though the eyes spoke of minimal confidence. "Left your sword at home? Good." Per Hennessey's request, Billick was only sporting his large serrated field-knife. The clientele grew nervous at any overt display of steel. "Try to make a good impression this time. Oblivion take you, if there was ever a client to try to behave for – this is the one." Billick cast a silent, stony stare at the intermediary. Billick knew who they were meeting with – the young Lord Northing. He would be Baron over the land once his father passed on – and some rumors claimed he'd re-establish the crown.

A future King, perhaps. Still, Billick was not a muzzled bear, brought out to dance for the crowd. Fawning over the client was Hennessey's job.

The optimistic smile pleaded. "Just … try?" Sighing, the man backed into the doorframe.

The private room was not large, but measurably better lit than the tavern floor. A rounded table in the center of the room sat surrounded by velvet-cushioned chairs, and was lorded over by a hanging lamp. Only one of the chairs was occupied – by a sandy-haired youth in his early twenties. The youth was handsome, well-groomed, and his clothing was expertly tailored. But he was not the client. It was obvious. Billick had seen too many men like him before – they wore their position in life as plainly as they did their shirt. This man was a companion; he was a noble's attendant. He was here for moral support.

Billick smiled to himself. Moral support – for hiring a killer.

The other man stood at the far side of the room, his back to them, making a show of examining the molding on the fireplace mantle. The hood of his dark riding cloak was down, the need to obscure his identity having lost out to the overwhelming demand to show his face. While ego played a part in it, this was a matter of ownership. This nobleman needed to feel a connection to the killing he was about to order.

5

"I appreciate your patience, sirs," Hennessey warbled to their guests as they took their seats. "Let me present my colleague, Billick."

The lackey at the table nodded towards Billick. "You come highly recommended."

"There isn't a better assassin-for-hire on the island," Hennessey assured.

"Master Rice assured us of the same," the sandy-haired youth continued.

"Ah yes, good Master Rice," Hennessey mused happily. "Why, I believe I have lost count of the number of jobs we've done on his behalf. Twenty now? No, that seems low. But never a miss on a job. Never a delay. The results, as promised, every time."

The youth's eyes flickered to Hennessey. "Do you plan to do all the talking for him tonight?"

Billick spoke before Hennessey could respond diplomatically. "Do *you* intend to for *him*?"

The man at the fireplace gave a half-turn, exposing the lower half of his face. He was smiling. "Well said, Master Billick."

Even if Hennessey hadn't told him their client was a Northing, Billick would have known it by now. The family resemblance was unmistakable, as was the pretentious air behind the voice. You could almost smell the entitlement on him. "Care to ask me your questions yourself, Lord Northing?"

Hennessey looked very uncomfortable. He liked to stay in firm control over these encounters, which only happened if Billick did not engage in an abundance of talking. "What I think he means to say is ..."

"Tell me, Master Billick, why should I hire you?" the nobleman asked, cutting Hennessey short.

Hennessey looked to him, wordlessly pleading for a tactful response. Billick declined to oblige him. "Because, young Lord Northing, if you thought you could kill a man yourself, you wouldn't be here."

Hennessey's eyes winced, although his enthusiastic grin didn't fade. The nobleman flinched ever so faintly at the perceived slight; his fingers constricting in their interlaced grip. Only the lackey failed to keep his emotions transparent;

his face a complicated compilation of sincere shock and feigned outrage. Billick guessed that the companion was probably debating what response his Lord expected of him – a verbal barrage against the insulter, or perhaps a flash of steel? Billick guessed that the sandy-haired youth was also contemplating what the consequence of any such action against a man of Billick's reputation would be.

The nobleman turned fully this time, the light from the hanging lamp illuminating some of the fine features on his face. "A truthful answer," he said at last. "I eat my fill on a nightly basis – yet I don't soil my hands planting the crops. I wear the finest clothes the markets can offer – yet I don't rub my fingers bare at a loom. Why should this be different? If I want someone dead …" He held up his hands, palms forward. "… why should my hands get dirtied?"

"Well said," Hennessey complimented. "An opinion I rather agree with …"

"But you could kill a man?" Billick pressed.

That wiped the smile from Hennessey's face. His eyes bored daggers into him from a distance. The nobleman shrugged. "If I had to …" he mused.

"But you don't?" Billick observed.

"No he doesn't," Hennessey jumped in.

It was notable that the young Lord Northing did not respond. "You might not *have* to," Billick explained, "but that doesn't change the *wanting* to, does it? Otherwise you wouldn't be here." The nobleman lifted cold eyes in Billick's direction, and they spoke volumes. "Someone made you angry – crossed a line. And now you *want* to end their existence – you *want* them to pay with their life. But the *want* isn't enough. If it was, you'd have seen to it already." He gave a jerk of his head towards the seated lackey. "Or you would have ordered him to do it, if you thought him capable of it either."

The nobleman's companion was at a complete loss for how to act. Billick wondered if the two men hadn't rehearsed the meeting beforehand. The sandy-haired sycophant appeared ill-suited for improvisation. Or perhaps he'd forgotten how to have an original thought altogether.

"What I think my friend is trying to say," a dejected Hennessey intervened, "is that we are ready and willing to supply you what you *want*, good sir. You give

us a name, you give us a deadline, you give us any special considerations –
weapon of choice, amount of suffering …"

With disciplined grace, the nobleman took a seat next to his companion. "His
name is Malcolm Humes. He owns a small tavern on the corner of West Harper
and 5th."

"I know him," said Hennessey. "I don't like Malcolm much, either."

The name didn't register with Billick – but his targets usually didn't. Billick
kept to himself, stayed cloistered in his room in the city. But Hennessey –
Hennessey seemed to know everyone. It was especially true for those who
mingled in the morally gray aspects of society.

He hadn't noticed himself doing it, but Billick found himself scratching at his
right shoulder with his left hand. His upper arm felt irritated. He flexed his
fingers and lowered them below the table.

"When do you want it done and how?" Hennessey asked.

The nobleman shrugged. "As soon as possible, and I don't care. The result is
all that I'm after."

The intermediary smiled. Hennessey liked working with an empty canvas. "As
soon as possible it is. He does, as memory serves, have a family. A wife.
Children."

The nobleman searched for any additional meaning in the comment. "Is that a
problem?"

Hennessey shook his head warmly. "A problem? Hardly, no. Billick has no
prejudice based on age, gender or creed. In fact, his first true murder was a
child …"

"What's wrong with your arm?" The question came from the nobleman's
companion. It brought the focus of the group to bear on Billick. He retracted
his hand from his upper arm – not remembering having reached up to scratch at
the irritation a second time. He could feel the skin burning under his shirt –
begging for relief. But that wasn't the only thing.

He was overcome with the feeling that he needed to be elsewhere.

"Just an itch, I'm sure," Hennessey down-played the distraction. Then, perhaps noticing the sweat that began to bead on Billick's brow and the flush to his face, he amended his analysis. "Or, a spider bite ..."

"I'm fine," Billick mustered through gritted teeth. He looked to Hennessey. "Finish the arrangement."

The intermediary needed no further prompting. Negotiating the price was one of Hennessey's fortes and one of his passions. As he opened his mouth to start the process, the noblemen acted first. He tossed a bag of coins onto the table; the loose drawstring keeping all but a few from spilling out. One rolled and clattered to a halt close to Billick. It was gold. He lifted the coin; rubbed his thumb against the coolness of the metal.

"If Master Rice is to be believed," the nobleman said. "That should more than cover your usual fee."

Money brought out the worst in Hennessey. Billick could see the man fighting the urge to finger through the bag and calculate the sum. Hennessey's eyes lingered on the bag for a second longer before he freed himself from the allure. "I trust it shall," he said. "I believe we are all at an agreement, then."

The nobleman, however, was not finished. Billick met his gaze, as the young man opted to voice his question. "Don't you want to know why I want him dead?"

It was not the first time someone had asked Billick that question. He always gave them same answer.

"No."

The nobleman marveled. "You don't care what he did?"

"It doesn't matter." The burning sensation intensified. He clenched the coin in his fist, trying to sap its coolness. He had to leave. He had to go north ... why north?

"It doesn't matter?" The nobleman repeated. It was always the same. It was what people like this young lordling and his lackey, people who had never taken another man's life, what people with some portion of their soul left intact couldn't quite grasp.

"It doesn't matter," Billick replied. "He's guilty. If not for what you're condemning him for – then for something else. Maybe even something worse." It was the truth. "Everyone is guilty of something, young Lord Northing. Everyone. And that makes everyone worthy of death."

The pain became unbearable. He turned his head – to the north – and felt something there. Something calling for him. He needed to go to it. He needed to go.

He had no choice.

The nobleman spoke. He had to feel justified. "He cheated me," he began, but got no further.

Billick stood up.

The lackey got unsettled. "Where do you think you're going?"

Billick glared at the seated youth – and wondered if his eyes reflected any of the insanity he was feeling. The sandy-haired man wilted under the look. "Out," he answered, and headed for the door.

"What, now?" Hennessey said angrily, standing.

"Now!" Billick growled back. He was through the door before anyone else could say another word. Janns the barman stood alertly behind the bar. He was fingering something just below eye-level, something that Billick couldn't see. Something special for when a patron stepped out of line. He let Billick pass, and the murderer-for-hire cut a straight line for the door.

As if sensing his intention, the pain began to ebb.

The door of the Eight Flagons closed on its hinge behind him, and Billick stood alone on the tavern's lamp-lit porch. Reaching across his body, Billick forced up the sleeve on his right arm. In the night-washed light of the lamp, Billick examined the flesh on his upper arm. The skin rose in a discolored hue – angry and swollen. It worked all the way around his arm.

A marking - one solid band.

3.

From his lofty vantage point on the roof, Ethiere watched the approaching constable.

He watched; and he thought about boots.

They perplexed him. He could not fathom why anyone would want to wear boots. To be fair, he'd never owned a pair. He'd never even had the opportunity to try a pair on. He could only go off of what he observed – and his observations on the boots of the man below painted a very disagreeable picture.

For one, the boots did not bend naturally with the feet. The constable did not appear to be bothered by this; he appeared to be walking just fine. While the boots seemed to allow some movement from the ankle, it appeared to be limited to a strictly up and down motion. Ankles could rotate marvelously, but the boots seemed to impede most of that motion. And the toes? Toes were marvelous for the finding purchase against the bricks of a wall, yet the boot seemed to lock them away altogether!

And what of the noise the boots made? Ethiere had heard the constable approach long before he'd spied him. The hard soles of the boots made murderously loud noises every time they touched against the cobblestones. You'd never be able to sneak around in footwear that announced your every step.

The constable paused at the mouth of an alley and looked vacantly into the shadows on either side. The act made Ethiere grin. Had the man convinced himself that merely staring into the darkness satisfied the demands of his job? Was it possible to espy a man hiding in the deep shadows from twenty paces away? The constable turned slightly on his heel and went to check on the next alley. As he walked, the light from the lantern he carried caught the polished shine of his brass boot buckles.

Perhaps that was the reason, Ethiere conjectured, why people owned boots. They wore them just to show other people that they could afford to wear them.

The constable, satisfied with what he'd not seen, continued on his round, his boots pounding out his exit.

Ethiere scratched at the back of his head. Maybe when he finally cashed out with Master Hat he'd buy himself a pair of boots. Nice boots – black with a high gloss and silver buckles that would sing in the moonlight. Fantastic, gentlemanly boots. He would buy them, he would. But he still couldn't imagine he'd ever wear them.

The leather pads he wore were much too comfortable.

They were simply constructed – a piece of leather on the bottom, a piece of leather on top and stitches around the edges. A hole at the top fitted with a draw-string so you could tighten the pad around your ankle. They were comfortable, reasonably durable, and not the least bit restrictive. As Ethiere stood up, he could feel the curve of the individual roof slates under his toes. In a boot – well, Ethiere imagined you'd not feel much of anything except the boot.

"You've got that look on your face," the girl at his side said. Kari was three years his junior and unquestionably his closest friend in the entire world. "You're thinking again."

Ethiere smiled.

"Do I want to know about what?" Kari asked.

"Probably not," he answered. "You ready?" The question had a sobering effect on her mood. Kari folded her arms beneath her breasts and pouted at the street below. Ethiere sighed to himself. "What? How much longer do you propose we wait? Another hour? Another pass from the good constable? Morning?" The last earned him a slight uptick of a smile at the corner of her mouth. To her credit, Kari replaced the pout immediately. "Might be intriguing, going for it in daylight …"

"You're not the least concerned, then?"

Ethiere batted away the question. "On a nice, easy job like this? Come on, Kari, how much more routine could it be? Either one of us could pull it off alone."

"That's what the others thought." The statement was bleak, and very unlike Kari. "Nice, easy job."

It was inevitable that the conversation would steer this way. Kari was worried. Their friendship aside, she'd invited him to accompany her this evening because she was scared. She had no desire to suffer the same unknown fate as the others in their crew.

"Master Hat is looking into it," Ethiere tried.

Kari harrumphed. "I'm sure he is." Recent events had soured her opinion of their benefactor. Despite losing multiple members of their tight-knit Gang in the past two months, Hat was not altering their plans. He was still sending them out on jobs; still taking the same risks. It made sense to Ethiere. While the losses were unsettling, what else was there to do? They still had to eat. "You really trust him?"

The question was pointed. Ethiere was number two in the group, only second in leadership to Master Hat. His opinion and word carried a boulder's weight with the more junior members of the Gang. He carefully considered his response. "Well, I don't distrust him." He rubbed at the back of his head, wondering if that was more or less the same thing. He looked Kari directly in the eyes. "Do you trust me?"

The girl looked away. The answer had never been in question. "You know I do."

He reached out a hand, placing it gently on her shoulder. "You know I'll never leave you. And I'll make sure that you don't disappear, either," he promised. Kari leaned back against him. Ethiere let the moment continue. Kari was of the age now that a friendship like theirs might blossom into something more. Neither of them spoke of it; the moments like this made it less important to use words. He grinned; it was time. "Now, isn't it about time we fell off this roof?"

Kari whipped her head around and stuck out her tongue. Taking a step forward, she shifted her weight to let her momentum carry her down the incline of the slated roof. Ethiere followed suit, pushing off slightly with his leather pads and starting his slide towards the looming edge. The slide was still a rush – even after all of the years. The uniform buildings of Wellsford Park were a mere two stories tall – high enough that a fall wouldn't likely kill you, but would still manage a hideous number on your knees.

At the last second, just as Ethiere's toes reached the edge of the slated roof, Ethiere rotated his body a half-turn and reached with outstretched arms. The storm gutter was waiting for him. It shuddered under the sudden impact of his additional weight, testing the strength of the bolts that held it in place. Hanging by his fingers, Ethiere looked to his right. Kari hung in similar fashion no more than two arm-lengths away. She started to sway, rocking her legs in a controlled pace, before letting go. She landed safely on the ledge that divided the two stories of the building.

To any normal person, the series of moves Kari had just completed would have caused a lot of hesitation and a great deal more concern. With the same ease, Ethiere lowered himself onto the ledge. To him and Kari and any other member of the Children's Gang – this was simple. This was how they played.

Every member of the Gang had more or less all had the same story. Deprived of parents at an early age. Living on the streets. A starving belly and a dearth of generous hearts. This was their circumstances when they found the gang ruled by Master Hat. He was the closest thing Ethiere had known to a parent since the plague had claimed his entire family at age five. Hat provided them a place to sleep and regular meals. And he taught them how to play.

Thievery, at its core, was nothing more than a child's game. How to climb the handholds the decorative bricks walls provided. How to perform the rooftop acrobatics. How to move through a crowd without being noticed. How to pick crude locks. How to lift a coin purse without alerting the owner. Learning it all was a mere matter of recital – of practice. Any child could learn to do it.

There was a click and the glass-paned window on the second story swung open. Kari stowed her pick triumphantly and swung a leg over the sill. Ethiere followed after her. The layout of a Wellsford Park building was ingrained in their heads. They could navigate their way through the entire edifice in pitch darkness. They'd learned exactly where the support beams under the floor were strongest and not likely to creak. Being quiet was a game too.

The night-dark room was being used for storage, there were wooden shelves laden with boxes topped with thin layers of dust. Silently, the two of them crept towards the stairway as if someone had painted footprints on the floor for them to follow. Down the stairs they went, Kari moving with the grace of a dancer. Ethiere watched her as he followed – and another thought struck him.

"Can you dance in boots?" he whispered to himself.

Kari turned on a heel and raised an eyebrow. She was intrigued, albeit skeptical. He could tell by the curious half-smile. "Dancing? You were thinking about dancing?"

He shook his head. "No. Boots."

Her light-colored hair tousled as she shook her head too. "I should have known."

As their whispers faded, they surveyed the ground level of the apothecist shop they'd just broken in to. What exactly an apothecist did, neither of them knew for certain. Usually Ethiere could perceive the value of the items Master Hat sent them to fetch. Jewelry, gems, silks, coins; these were the staples of their profession. But recently, Hat was only interested in apothecist shops.

This one, like the others, had rows after row of shelves in the storefront, each bearing an assortment of stoppered glass bottles or pouches with cinched draw-strings. The air of the apothecist shops always smelled strange, though Ethiere could not place the odors his senses picked up on. Ethiere held up a bottle – not able to tell if the glass was blue or if it was the liquid secured inside.

"Bottles, bottles and more boiling bottles," Kari muttered. What the bottles held was a topic of frequent debate among the children of the Gang. Master Hat wouldn't say – he only warned them against drinking anything. It didn't matter to Ethiere. One theft was just the same as the next one. "I wonder who comes to buy this stuff?"

Ethiere picked up a miniature bottle. "People who aren't very thirsty?" he guessed. He padded his way to the storefront window and dug the folded scrap of parchment from his pocket. By the faint moonlight, he examined the drawing that Master Hat had made for them. The three bottles in the picture were larger than any of their counterparts on display – but that was normal. Master Hat liked to provide them with pictures that plainly showed the detail. Ethiere examined the characters on the label of the drawing.

It was in these moments that Ethiere wished he could read. He was sure he could learn. He was bright – Kari said so. Everyone said so. He could recognize some of the characters as ones he had seen in the past – on signs and the like. It irked him to think that the letters withheld a secret from him – their meaning locked tightly away by his own ignorance.

There was no time to learn now. His hope of an education had been slim as a child. Second son of Degan immigrants. His father a dockworker. When the plague took his parents and siblings, that hope had died completely. He'd learned the lesson quickly and early in life. Aspiration was futile. Dreams went unfulfilled. Life was bigger than you were and you at the mercy of Fate.

He'd come through alright. He had a family in the Gang. He enjoyed being able to play in Wellsford Park. Maybe when he cashed out with Hat he'd hire a tutor. Maybe.

"I think I found one," Kari called out softly. Ethiere turned and she gently tossed the tapered-necked bottle in his direction. "See if it matches."

Angling the parchment towards the moonlit window, Ethiere compared the bottle to Master Hat's request list. The bottle was unmistakably the right shape and shade of grayish-green, and most of the characters on the front matched … "Are there any others like this?" he asked, stuffing the sheet of parchment back into his pocket. "The ending on the label has a few differences."

"Toss it back, then," Kari replied.

Ethiere complied – and continued with his own search. His eyes focused on a squat, blue-shaded bottle with a thick cork stopper, and he smiled. If his memory served, the characters on the label were a match . . .

The pain hit him with staggering intensely. His fist clenched in agony at the same moment that his hand made contact with the bottle. The spasm sent the bottle teetering into those it stood next to – giving the quiet of night a tiny concerto of jostling glass. Ethiere brought his arm down, and clutched it protectively with his left. It quivered violently – even with the extra support. He felt his face flush; his skin erupting in perspiration.

In an instant, Kari was at his side. All of the nervousness she'd displayed on the rooftop was back in full measure. "Ethiere? What happened?"

He looked to his friend – he could see the fearful concern in her wide eyes. But he couldn't answer her questions. He didn't know. He only knew it felt as hot coals were branding his right shoulder. He had never felt pain quite so inexpressibly severe. Had he been poisoned? He'd not touched any of what the bottles held …

He looked back to the window – and was captivated by the moonlight.

He needed to get out. At the moment, nothing else mattered.

He pushed himself away from the shelf with his left hand, using the momentum to stagger across the storeroom floor. The boards beneath his feet groaned under his weight, but he didn't care. Master Hat's games were the furthest thing from his mind. His inflamed right shoulder hit the door first, but the door held strong under the added security of three steel locking pins. The pain seemed to abate just long enough for him to use both hands to pull back the first of the heavy pins …

"Who's down there?!" came an angry call from upstairs. The moan from the top step of the staircase announced the shop-owner was coming.

Kari was at his side again, her nimble fingers working at the third bolt while Ethiere focused on the second. Both came lose at near the same instance, and the door relaxed inward on its hinge. Ethiere yanked it open, as he and Kari fled the shop.

"Thieves!" he heard the shopkeeper cry out. "Help! Thieves!"

Rounding a corner, Kari's hands shot out for familiar handholds on the bricks and she began to scale the building. It was what they had been taught. They were to find higher ground. The constables and the soldiers would hunt after them – but not one of them had ever considered chasing a thief to the roof …

Ethiere ran by.

"Wait!" he heard Kari call. "Wait, where are you going!?"

He did not stop to answer her – he wouldn't have known what to say. He was purposefully leaving her behind, and he knew Kari would not understand. With everything that had happened recently to all the others – to disappear ….

"Ethiere!"

He'd promised he would never leave her But without any knowledge of what was happening, Ethiere couldn't allow his friend to follow after him. Kari might hate him for it, but he cared about her too much. He wouldn't risk dragging her into this.

Whatever *this* was.

This was life. It had a sadistic way of reminding you that you were at its mercy. What you wanted couldn't matter less. You were a mere leaf on life's raging river – it would take you where it wanted until it tired of toying with you and swept you under for good. He ran, and the pain eased with each stride. Life was leading him along, the river it chose.

It was taking him north.

4.

The human body is infinitely complex. Without a solitary thought, the body regulates its temperature through sweat, creates its own energy through digestion, disposes of its own waste, draws its own breath and circulates lifeblood through the whole being. The common man would be baffled by the intricate chemical processes that happened continually within his own internal organs.

Once you had studied the science behind the physical body, it was a mystery that man managed to live at all.

As complicated as the body was – it was dwarfed by the mind. The body was the vessel of the mind, the craft that carried the consciousness of man through the paths of mortal experience. There was a constant battle for supremacy, an individualistic and unseen war between body and mind. The body sent a barrage of signals – hunger, thirst, pain, fatigue; assaulting the mind with its myriad needs.

The common man succumbed. The common man lived cravenly – his mind dulled in slavery to the demands of his own flesh. The common man found no purpose in life beyond that of keeping his body sated of its needs.

Kashif was no common man.

The Arcan scientist sat completely still as another solitary drop of sweat gained momentum as it rolled down his glistening forehead. The fingertips of his brown-skinned hands were nearly a ghostly shade on account of the pressure he exerted on the arms of his chair. He took slow, measured breaths, counting seconds, demanding obedience from his mortal coil.

Yet his body panicked. His lungs screamed for deeper draws of air. Despite the intensity of his focus, Kashif could feel his heart quickening in his chest. Contrary to the calming message his mind forced upon his limbs, he could feel the muscles in his arms and legs tensing – ready. Ready to leave. Ready to go.

With a purposeful pace, Djemal was back by his side. His countryman tapped lightly on his jaw, and Kashif complied by opening his mouth. The younger apprentice made quick work of fishing the glass disk from its spot inside Kashif's cheek – where Djemal had placed it minutes before. Holding the disk eye-level, the other man took a reading from the mercury.

"You're temperature has risen again," Djemal noted aloud as he scribed the data onto the ledger. "Another degree and a half in the last ten minutes."

Kashif didn't bother with a response – choosing to remain tightly in control. Instead, he opened his mouth again, allowing Djemal to reinsert the disk. After doing so, the younger man stuck his two longest fingers against the large vein in Kashif's neck. He could feel his pulse beat against the pressure of Djemal's fingers. As he counted in his mind, the younger man offered additional observations. "Your pupils are dilated. The pain is increasing, yes?" Kashif answered by dipping his head in the slightest of nods, careful not to disturb the fingers at his throat.

Pulling his fingers away, Djemal recorded the new measurement. "You are unable to control your heart rate, yes?" It was an innocent observation, but it sparked a nerve with Kashif. While the comment was true, it was an insult to a man of Kashif's status within the Scholastad caste and to the man that had trained them both. He could feel the knot of irritation – his stinging pride – bubbling within him. It was a distraction to his focus. With ease, he banished it from his mind.

Its disappearance left him with nothing besides the agony building up behind the wall of his self-control. It swelled, an oncoming tidal wave rushing at a dam.

"You should drink," Djemal suggested.

He had done it again – and once more, completely without guile. Kashif turned his head slowly to glare at the younger apprentice. His body pleaded for water, for relief from the burning fever that ravaged his skin. His body cried out in *need*. To drink would be to give in. To drink would be to succumb.

"No," he whispered with rasping intensity.

"Your body is losing water …" Djemal adjured.

"No!" he repeated, voice rising to a threatening tone. Djemal heard the warning behind the words; the younger man's face said that he would not force the issue further. "Take another sample of my blood," Kashif ordered.

Djemal hesitated. "Another?"

"Whatever has gripped me," Kashif answered, filtering the pain from his voice, "has introduced rapidly escalating symptoms. You would do well to evidence these changes. Take another sample."

The younger scientist wasted no time in complying. Djemal was excellent student of the Scholastad caste arts, meticulous in his studies, a fast, albeit unimaginative learner. He carried a natural love for proof, and as such held facts and measurements and posits in an almost reverential light. He returned with the lacquered box of spines and the siphon syringe.

Djemal procured a deep blue needle from the box. Made from the spines of the sea-dwelling nettle urchin, nature had provided them a better tool than man could have ever crafted. The hollow spindle, when attached to the siphon that would provide pressure, worked as the perfect instrument for drawing blood. Djemal dipped the tip of the spine quickly into the two small jars kept within the lacquered box – the first a cleansing agent, the second a numbing agent with low potency.

There was a momentary sharp bite on the skin of Kashif's forearm where the spine was inserted, which was blanketed over by tingling warmth.

His left leg began to shake, an unbidden embarrassment. He tried to force the leg still, but his body fought back with rich and frenetic signals of its own. *We must go! We must leave! Now!*

It was all Kashif could do to remain seated when the large door to their laboratory was thrown open. It was as if his legs saw the avenue of escape and were determined of their own violation to take it. Lord Baron Northing stormed in through the door in a thunderous mood – no doubt his reaction to hearing of Kashif's affliction. Marooke – the final and most senior of the Arcan party – trailed the nobleman only slightly. He alone reported to the Lord Baron, and as such had elected to convey the news himself.

Kashif watched the eyes of his mentor and master, hoping for answers. Marooke was numbered among the greatest of the Scholastad class – the foremost living expert on the human organism in Arca if not the entire world. It was the reason Lord Baron Northing had hired them. Despite the recent conflict, Northing had hired three Arcans. He'd wanted the best. And Marooke and his two apprentices constituted the best.

Northing stalked towards Kashif, alert blue eyes capturing everything in a moment. "Alright then, show me." Djemal withdrew the spine as Marooke slipped past the Lord Baron and pulled the sleeve clear of Kashif's right upper forearm. Even against his dark brown skin, the perfectly shaped black band stood out clearly.

Northing needed no more than a glance. The Lord Baron turned away in disgust. "Boiling luck," he cursed.

"This is the Banding, yes?" Marooke asked.

"There hasn't been a recorded Banding in some twelve years! Twelve! And now it comes? It comes and it steals away one of my Arcans?" Djemal busied himself at his working desk, labeling the small bottle of blood with the time in was extracted. The youngest Arcan grew noticeably quieter in the presence of the cold, confrontational Lord Baron. Was it reverence of the man's authority, or the knowledge that his man had launched the war against Arca not sixteen years ago?

Northing turned on Marooke. "Can you treat it?"

The gray-headed mentor frowned. "Can it be treated?"

"You are the man of science!" Nothing glowered. "You are the one who has studied the body all of your life. You were touted as second to none in expertise on the physiology of man – and you ask *me* if it can be treated?

Marooke stood calmly in the face of the tempest, arms folded behind his back. He tolerated Northing speaking to him in such a manner – but only because Northing was a product of the unrefined Tollian culture. No one in Arca would dare to adopt such a tone. "This *Banding*, as you and your people call it, is foreign to us. Never before has an Arcan contracted this condition. Never before has one Banded set foot on Arcan soil. Never before has the Scholastad had opportunity to study one so afflicted."

Through a tensed jaw, Kashif managed a question. "What ... is it doing to me?"

Northing eyed him without compassion. "It is forcing its will on you," he answered. "It will keep raising the level of pain, incessantly torturing your body, until you relent. And you will relent, eventually. No one can resist the Banding once the magic has a hold of them." The nobleman turned back to Marooke. "He is lost to us. He's just one of the unfortunate six now. He'll go where the Banding takes him, and that's one less Arcan working towards our agreement."

"We did not do this ..." Marooke said evenly – which to the best of their knowledge was true. While the scientific mind allowed for the chance that Kashif may have touched something to initiate the onset of the disease, the odds were highly unlikely. Reason would state that if one of the Arcan's contracted the condition – all of them would. They ate the same food, walked the same corridors, handled the same instruments …

Why had the Banding afflicted him – and none of the others?

"I did not say that you had," Northing replied. "What I am saying, Marooke, is that you are no longer abiding the conditions of our contract. Blame is of no relevance. I paid for three scientists of your order, and am I left with only two. I have lodged you in my own manor, supplied you with a bevy of the rare substances your experiments have demanded, and you have yet to deliver anything in six months! What chance of success is there with only two of you now?"

Marooke turned a glance to Kashif, who felt awash with shame. If Northing's words were true, the pain he could not overcome was more than he could be expected to bear. But Marooke preached absolute control of mind over body. Banding or not, magic or not, he would see this as failure. "Is he lost for certain?"

The nobleman shrugged. "For now. After that, who knows? The Banding could take him for ten days, ten months or ten years for all we know. He may never return. Surviving a Banding is not guaranteed. Only one in two generally survives the quest."

The gray-haired Arcan frowned to himself. "We must accept this loss then. We must let him go."

Kashif thought to protest, but his entire being clenched in one agonizing seizure at the idea of staying still another hour. Whether he liked it or not, he was losing. There were no meditative chants, no relaxation techniques, no tranquility poses that could drown out the all-consuming crisis the Banding was putting him in. He would succumb, and it would be soon.

"What of the research?" Northing demanded. "What of my result?"

"You have been informed of our progress," Marooke answered.

"I'm not paying you for progress," the Lord Baron snapped.

"And we are not a people that will waste time in frivolous efforts," Marooke clarified, remaining decidedly calm. "Need I remind you, when you hired me, you admitted that the problem we delve might not yield a solution. But I accepted the challenge you posed. Believe me, Lord Baron, I would not have accepted employment of you had I thought the effort in vain."

Northing paced away. "It is the result I need. It is only the result I care about."

"You will have your cure," Marooke promised. "Science will unlock the answers you seek. I feel we are closer than we might realize."

"Words," Northing muttered. "Of what worth are mere words?" The nobleman turned back to eye Kashif. "Tell him to leave, before he injures himself. He's no good to either of us anymore." Without another word, the Lord Baron stalked towards the laboratory exit in the same heated rage he'd entered with.

Kashif swallowed hard, wetting his scorched throat. He was free to go.

He realized he was standing. He could not recall when, exactly, that had happened. The pain was still present – it was still intense – but even standing, even that paltry bit of progress had earned him a small relief. He looked back at the arms of the chair – and could plainly see the divots where his fingernails had bit into the wood.

"Lord Baron?" Marooke said, stopping their benefactor in the doorframe. "Tension exists been our peoples, though the war is a decade dead. You know what Kashif will face outside the walls of your manor – an Arcan alone among your citizenry." In truth, the prejudice wasn't exclusion to those outside the manor walls. Several of Lord Northing's own staff were not subtle regarding their hatred of the black-skinned race they'd lost a war to. "He is a resource, Lord Baron. A good scientist. It would benefit you to have him survive."

Northing weighed the request. "I will see to an escort," the man said at last. Adding no details, he disappeared from the room.

"Djemal, a bag!" Marooke called out once Northing was gone. The junior apprentice responded instantly with the pack. Djemal must have been stealthily stuffing the pockets while Northing had vented his frustrations. And, from the strain on the canvas seams, it appeared Djemal had spared nothing. The bag hung like a bulbous growth on the younger man's back.

"I'm certain I have not forgotten anything," Djemal assured as he handed the back over. He leaned in. "The samples I took, as well as the ledger, are on the bottom. I've included several vials for additional samples, as well as several basic solutions with which to run analysis. Such sensitive work shouldn't be performed in the open …"

"He will be fine, Djemal," Marooke assured.

"Note everything ..." Djemal adjured, but the raised hand from Marooke silenced him further.

Marooke stood before him, the mentor appraising his pupil. "We know nothing about this Banding as an affliction," the old Arcan said. "But we have heard about this Banding as a curse. You will be led to what you need to find, that is a certainty. What happens when you find it...?" Kashif understood what his superior left unsaid. "Use your head," he continued. "Those that you travel with will most assuredly not be of our kind. Be wary, for they will hate you. They will hate you for a past they cannot change and cannot forget. Be careful, and rely on your intellect. You have an advantage – use it."

"I will," Kashif answered.

"And should it come to it," Marooke added as Kashif reached the laboratory door, "you can see to it that they are placed in the path of danger first. Let them take on the needed risks. Allow them to be the sacrifice. In the eternal plans of the Architect, you have significance."

It was the truth. He represented generations of hard work, of sacrifice, of creation. Those that shared his affliction would be a rabble, misbegotten, only an afterthought in the eternal schemes of the Architect. Their lives would take on a greater meaning simply by being allowed to die in his stead.

"You have a purpose ..." his mentor assured him.

"And they do not," Kashif finished. With a deferential bow to Marooke, he adjusted the large bag on his shoulder, and walked out into the lamp-lit corridor.

5.

"Father?" she called out softly into the night. The call was hesitant, and it betrayed her uncertainty. She was still not sure she wanted her father to hear her; wanted him to come. Sarah clutched at the well-worn quilt, hoping to draw clarity as well as comfort. The hour was so late; he would be so tired. Much too tired to be bothered by something so ... so ... childish. She was nine now, far too old to trouble her father with silly feelings. And yet ...

"Father?" Sarah called out again, a little less timidly this time, albeit a little more sheepishly. She was not sure whether she was relieved or disappointed when she heard him stirring in the bed across the room from hers. Within seconds, he was standing over her, alarm written on his weary face.

His face was always fatigued, Sarah thought to herself. It was as if he stored all of his worries in the dark circles under his eyes; his pressures in the down-turned corners of his mouth.

"What is it, Sarah? What's happened?" His voice carried not a shred of bitterness, not a trace of anger. There never was – despite it all. There was only concern – deep, abiding concern that could only exist between a father and his daughter. "Have you injured yourself?"

It was the question he most often asked. It was the question she was least qualified to answer. "No, Father. I don't think so."

The anxiety drained from his face, leaving only the deep-rooted weariness behind. "Then what is it?" he said with genuine patience. "Why did you call for me?"

She lowered her eyes and ran her fingers along the sewn ridges in the quilt. What was she to say? Perhaps it would be best if she just let him return to bed …

The feelings welled up inside of her again.

"Sarah?" her father asked.

"I need to leave, Father!" The words escaped her mouth, even as she tried to keep them in.

Her father rubbed a hand against his tired brow as he entered the room. He carefully felt for Sarah's legs before taking a seat at the foot of her small bed. "Leave? In the middle of the night? Leave and go where?"

"I don't know," she answered honestly. Sarah let her head turn of its own accord, and she found herself looking in the same direction she had been for the last several hours. There was something … something to the northwest.

He sighed – which was followed by a cavernous yawn. "Can we talk about it in the morning?"

"Yes," she said meekly, and the urgent feelings flooded back with renewed intensity. Her father began to rise and she reached out to grab his wrist. "No. No, now!"

Her touch reawakened the alarm in his eyes. In one motion he pulled her hand from his wrist and placed it to his cheek. Quickly he was back sitting on the bed, his hand reaching to feel her brow. "Mercy from Domus, you're burning up! Your skin is on fire!"

Sarah's right hand clenched to a fist around the border of the quilt. She felt fine – but that wasn't telling. She always felt fine. Sarah did not know any other way to feel.

The Physicians called it the Numbness.

Sarah had never once experienced the sensation of physical pain.

It was unfathomable to some. Goodwidow Maybee, who rented her upstairs room to them, wasn't convinced it was true. Never knowing the hurt of a stomach ache, the tenderness of a sprained joint, the sting of a burn – to those who had experienced such things, the Numbness must have sounded like a gift from Domus himself. But Sarah knew better. And so did her Father.

She was a risk to herself. She could accidentally cut herself on something sharp – and would never know unless she saw the blood. She could break a bone and would not be able to tell unless she noticed the bruising on her body or the awkward way the limb behaved. She was at constant risk of sickness – she could not tell when she was too cold. It was the same with heat – her body didn't know to cool itself. Her body didn't know how to sweat. Like tonight.

Her body was cooking itself, and she was none the wiser.

"We need to cool you down," her Father said as he ripped the quilt off of her. "We need to fetch for Physician Forsyth. We need … we need ice. The Goodwidow's ice-chest …"

Sarah shook her head, "No … no, I just need to go."

Her father scooped her out of bed with arms strengthened by years of toiling, manual labor. "Hush now," he whispered. "I'll take care of you." Cradling her in his arms, he carried her to the stairway. The single dot of a lit candle waited at the bottom of the narrow flight of stairs.

"What is the matter?" the Goodwidow asked in the warble of her age-faltering voice. "The girl again?"

"A fever," her father said, taking the stairs two to a stride. The Goodwidow had to back up quickly to keep from being run down. "We need the Physician." He gently set Sarah into a reclining divan in the old woman's parlor. "I'll run for him – please, keep her cool. Ice. Anything." He exited through her front door before the Goodwidow had a chance to respond.

She stepped forward at her arthritic pace, setting the candlestick on the table next to the divan. Goodwidow Maybee clutched her herb-pouch to her nose – she was as nervous around disease as any of the others who'd survived the plague. Still, she placed a wavering palm against Sarah's forehead and watched her suspiciously. "Honestly can't feel that?" she questioned after a pause, and hobbled away. Sarah knew she wasn't seeking an answer – only to reemphasize her suspicion that this was a ploy for attention.

Regardless of her doubt, Goodwidow Maybee returned with a cloth rag and a basin of shallow water. Sarah applied the dampened rag to her own forehead while the old woman looked on. Sarah could only assume the water was cold – she could not sense its temperature. She could only feel the wetness against her skin.

It was some time later that her father returned. She heard the physician's single-horse wagon pull up in front of the Goodwidow's house. Her father rushed through the door and was instantly at her side. "How is she?" he asked the widow.

"She hasn't complained," the old woman answered. Physician Forsyth rapped politely once on the open door frame before entering. Sarah liked him. He had an honest face – one you intrinsically trusted. Sarah had known him all her short life. Never once had the physician tried to coddle her – or lie about what she could expect from the disease. Never once had he discounted the notion that there could be suffering, even without pain …

Forsyth peeled the cloth from her brow and set his own palm against her skin. He nodded, conjectures confirmed and rinsed his hands in the basin. "You've come down with something terrible, my little patient," he said.

"So it seems," she answered.

He nodded again and knelt to be at her eye-level. "You've been out of the house, perhaps? New places?"

The question agitated her father, and he looked at her expectantly. He didn't approve of her going out. There were too many unknowns, too many risks. He worried about her when he went to work – worried that he wouldn't be there to take care of her. Worried of what might happen if she snuck out of the upstairs rooms while he was out …

"No," she said truthfully. As much as she hated the confinement, she hadn't disobeyed. She wouldn't betray her father's trust. "Not since the last holiday service."

Forsyth grimaced in thought. "Visitors, then? Come to see you? Or the Goodwidow, perhaps?"

"No," Sarah answered. Who would come to visit her? Sarah spent all of her time upstairs. Outside of those people she saw at the services, she had no friends, no acquaintances. No one that would drop by to check in on her. Nor did the withdrawn Goodwidow entertain guests. "The last person to see us here, Physician, may have been you."

Forsyth remained pensive. "Hmm. Your father told me that you woke him up?"

"Yes."

"But, of course, not because of any pain …"

"No."

"Then how did you know you were sick?" Forsyth queried.

Sarah lowered her eyes. "I didn't."

The Goodwidow guffawed and took another deep sniff of the herbs in her pouch. Forsyth ignored it. "Then why wake your father, Sarah? Could you sense there was something amiss?"

She was reluctant to express what she'd felt with the physician. But she trusted Forsyth. He wouldn't have asked the question if it wasn't important to his diagnosis. And as silly as it sounded, perhaps her feelings were a symptom of the disease.

"I … I had to get away from here …" Sarah offered meekly.

"Get away?"

"I felt like I needed to be somewhere else."

Forsyth eyed her warily. "Where, Sarah?"

She sat up in the divan and pointed. To the northwest. As odd as it sounded, she knew that they could blindfold her, spin her around until she couldn't tell up from down, and she would still be able to point to that exact spot to the northwest. Whatever it was, Sarah was more aware of it than of anything else in existence.

The physician drew nearer. Her father must have noted his concern. "What? What is it?"

Forsyth very carefully rolled up the thin fabric of Sarah's nightdress sleeve, pulling it away from her right shoulder. Grabbing the candlestick from the table, he held it close enough to her arm to provide them light enough to see. An angry welt, dark and puffy, rose in a perfect ring on her skin.

"Mercy from Domus," he father whispered. "It can't be. It just can't be."

Forsyth dropped her sleeve and took a step back. He turned an apologetic, consoling eye to her father. "I'm sorry, Henry. I truly am. There is nothing I can do." He looked back to Sarah. "I don't understand how, or even why – but your daughter has been Banded."

6.

In theory, the Cahills could afford to travel anywhere in the world in comfort. Greer had ridden in enough carriages in her lifetime to accept that no amount of wealth could make a long journey bearable. You could overstuff the cushions – but you couldn't take the ruts and rocks out of every road. You could shade the windows – but you couldn't stop the incessant sun from making the cabin-box temperature feel like a brick-hodder's furnace.

Worst of all, nothing could be done about the horse smell. Not if you enjoyed breathing.

The carriage went over another uneven patch, causing the heads of the three passengers to bob and weave in perfect unison. Sophie, Greer's lady companion, was still trying to keep up the pretense of working on her newest cross-stitching. It was comical watching her try to align her threaded needle over the exact spot on the hoop where the next stitch was designated. The carriage reeled just enough – even on the mostly level patches of road – that the needle's point danced around like a wicked stinging insect. Sophie was more likely to stab herself in the arm than make the correct pass with the thread.

Still, Sophie persisted. Cross-stitching was her *hobby*. Ladies and their companions were expected to have hobbies – and a long trip had time that demanded to be killed by one.

The companion caught her watching. She flashed a winning, toothy smile and held the hoop aloft to display her work. "It's going to be a bird, Lady Greer!"

There were just enough stitches in more or less their correct spots that Greer could identify the shape of the bird – but enough were misplaced that the creature looked grossly, unnaturally unhappy. Had Merciful Domus fashioned such a misshapen beast, he would have immediately destroyed it in an act of holy pity.

"Perhaps you'd like to rest from your work for a time," Greer suggested kindly. Emotions were like dresses in her closet; Greer found herself able to slip in and out of them on a whim. It was necessitated by the pomp-and-gesture world she lived in. She spent a majority of her time with Sophie – that is what companions were for. But in truth, she barely tolerated the young woman. She accepted her company as a custom of nobility – something that couldn't be gotten around or avoided.

There was no part of Greer that cared a whit about Sophie. She would not be shocked in the least if Sophie didn't care for her either.

Sophie's concentration returned to the hoop. "Oh, once I get started on one of these, I simply can't bear putting it down!" It was a very Sophie statement – overly expressive and blatantly cheerful. Sophie was as good at acting her role as Greer was at acting hers. No one – no one sane – was as eternally mirthful as Sophie. No one. Sophie spoke every sentence as if she exhaled rainbows.

Her feigned enthusiasm was at its peak today. It always was whenever they were in the presence of Greer's father.

If there was one thing that Lord Baron William Cahill did not lack – it was presence. He seemed to fill the entire carriage – everything that was not explicitly Greer or Sophie was the Baron. He did not do so in a loud or over-bearing fashion – that was not like him. Her father was shrewd – it was the best word Greer had ever found for him. He was shrewd and strategic and always in control.

Perhaps, thought Greer, that is what 'presence' really was – the level to which others saw you unquestionably in control.

Her father had not spoken for most of their journey – which had begun in the small hours of the night. Instead he varied between a state of meditative half-sleep and a wordless, unrelenting scrutiny of his daughter. Greer was poised enough – trained enough – to not falter under his interminable examination. If the Baron would perchance turn his gaze on Sophie, the young woman would probably vomit.

But knowing her companion, Sophie would probably manage to vomit sunshine – or potpourri.

There was a sudden rippling feeling that emanated from Greer's core – a pulse that went out in a wave and ended with a tingling feeling on her extremities. Her father's head moved just slightly – perhaps sensing that something was happening.

"We need to stop the carriage," Greer announced.

Her father didn't require a reason – didn't need to discuss the decision. He reached behind him and rapped three distinct knocks on the wooden panel. Instantly the driver was heard calling for a stop; the horses whinnying against the sudden tension on the reigns. The carriage slowly lost momentum – and finally rocked backwards to a stop.

Sophie had momentarily forgotten her cross-stitch. The feigned smile was still plastered on her full lips, but her eyes betrayed a high level of uncertainty. This was all very unusual – all very strange to Sophie. It would have been in character for Sophie to announce how happy she was that they'd stopped – except Greer knew her companion wasn't happy they had.

Sophie didn't know why they'd stopped. And there was no guarantee it was a good thing.

Greer frowned. Sophie was not sure what to think – now that her mistress was Banded.

Boots hit the road and seconds later the carriage door swung open, the driver ducking into a formal bow. Her father gave her one last reflective look, slid off the cushioned bench and exited the carriage. Greer followed him out.

It was late morning, the sun full and vibrant in the clear sky. Greer's eyes fought against the sudden intrusion of light. It had been dark when she'd entered the carriage. Her backside and shoulders ached from the eight or nine hours they'd ridden – but she was curiously not fatigued.

Her father's guards stood at the ready – as was expected. Captain Reed's brass buttons burnished in the light, and his uniform looked crisp. It seemed hardly possible that the senior officer in her father's private guard should look so well-kept after following the carriage on his horse for the entire journey. Though senior officer, Reed was only in his late twenties. His body should have been able to bear the journey better than someone longer in the tooth.

"Captain?" her father asked.

Reed saluted. "Lord Baron. We passed a ruined fountain a few hundred-paces back. There were people there, but we could not determine an exact count as we passed. Our maps show nothing else in the area – we are still a half-hour at best from the Wizard's College. I sent pairs scouting in each direction, nonetheless – just in case."

The summary was satisfactory. "Good," the Baron answered. He turned back to her. "Well?"

Greer instinctively turned back in the direction they'd just come from. It was back there. Whatever she'd been driven to go towards – it was back there. She just knew it.

Her father assessed her body language. "Captain, go secure the fountain." Reed saluted again, and turned heel at a trot to issue the orders to his men. Reed was – in a word – precise. It was the primary reason her father had promoted him to such a prominent position at such a young age. Baron Cahill offered Greer an arm. "Still feeling the urge to go through with this?" he asked.

"We both know it won't allow me to stop," Greer answered. She remembered the pain at the onset – especially on her upper arm. She'd screamed loudly enough the Sophie had come running from her room next door with the guards. She remembered kicking and screaming as they held her still for the house physician to examine her. No, the Banding wanted her here. Even at the suggestion of turning back, the darkened band of skin on her upper arm throbbed in warning.

It was the fountain. She was as certain as an entirely uncertain person could be.

There was a particular pace that people of the noble class walked at. Her father had mastered it – it was a part of him. The measured pace perfectly blended the urgency of having an important task immediately on-hand – and the casualness that said it would wait until they arrived. Sophie, cross-stitch hoop still in hand, followed in tow.

Just as Captain Reed had reported, the fountain was ruined. There was no movement of water through the higher levels of marble – some appeared cracked and chipped. The stone itself was weathered, and while once pristine white, moss and mold had blotched the color with patches of orange and green.

A dead fountain. This is what had beckoned for her.

Reed and a majority of his men were milling around the fountain area. There were three strangers in the clearing with the fountain. All men, two sat at opposite ends of a toppled marble pillar, with the third stopped mid-pace behind the fountain. As with most of Reed's men, Greer's attention went instantly to the brown-skinned foreign sitting on the fallen pillar. An Arcan! She'd never laid eyes on one before. The war with Arca – one her father had agreed to initiate – had ended thirteen years ago. The two nations were at peace now. But an Arcan …?

Greer had grown up on stories that painted the Arcan's as the spawn of Oblivion on earth.

Captain Reed met them at the edge of the road. "Just the three of them, Lord Baron. The fellow with the Arcan is wearing Lord Northing's colors."

"And the other?" her father asked, watching the side-burned man as he was eclipsed by the dead fountain.

"Not with the other two – or so says Northing's man."

As she watched them, Greer felt a connection. Not with the one Reed identified as one of Northing's soldiers, but with the other two. She did not know either man – had never seen either before – and yet she knew them. They were familiar … familiar, but not …

"They're Banded too," she said to herself.

"You can tell that?" asked her father. "Just by looking at them, you can tell that?"

Greer felt drawn to them. The side-burned man raised his head in her direction – and Greer knew that he recognized her as well. Not a face – it was not a face to recognize. But it was a feeling. A commonality. A bond.

A bond through the Banding.

The feeling grew stronger with each step – so much so that Greer suddenly found herself able to detect a new presence. There was a third! She turned her head quickly in the direction, the newfound sense pointing out the hidden watcher like a lodestone. She watched the foliage – and was sure she saw a shape shift in the greenery.

"Your soldiers missed one," the side-burned, broad-shouldered man said to her. Defensively, Reed put a hand to the sword-hilt on his hip, his eyes trying to follow where Greer watched. This elicited a short, derisive laugh from the broad-shouldered man. "Better grab your steel. Skinny Degan boys are a dangerous lot, after all…"

Reed shot the man a withering look, but did not respond.

"I sense no others in your party are Banded?" asked the Arcan – the preciseness with which he pronounced the words not fully masking his accent. "I was given to understand there will be six…"

"There are always six," her father muttered to himself. He placed a firm hand on Greer's shoulder and turned her away from the men. She felt her cheeks flush slightly. The Lord Baron was exerting control over the situation. It had taken her years to see it clearly – to see his subtle manipulations to maintain his power in the moment. The world was his dog – and he kept the leash taut.

He was who he was, but it made Greer angry that she let him do it to her – knowing it was happening.

"The three we know of this far," he said to her conspiratorially, "do not inspire a high degree of confidence. The side-burned man has the look of a criminal, if I don't miss my guess. And an Arcan? A boy hiding in trees?" He trailed off, allowing his sentiments to settle. "Unless the last two fellows in the Band turn out to be professional soldiers – well-disciplined – I can't feel confident of your safety."

"Father ..."

It was hardly a gesture, a slight raise of the arm, nothing threatening about it – but it was all he needed to do to cut off her response. She turned her head away.

"Even if they are Dragoons or Lancers ..." His pause commanded her attention, and she complied by casting her eyes back toward him. "...even if they are, this would still hardly qualify as a group able to keep you out of harm's way."

She shook her head slightly. "I can't not go. Not even you can get me out of this."

The shrewd eyes of her father mulled her words. When he spoke, his words were without humor. "There are very few things in this world that are unalterable, daughter. Power and authority open doors locked shut. And when those fail – the lure of gold will pry others open. And if gold fails ..."

He didn't finish. She didn't desire him too. A man that couldn't be persuaded or bought could always be persecuted or broken.

"In any case," Lord Baron Cahill said, "I will not see you – my daughter – as a fatality in the Band's deadly game."

The hush in the clearing was suddenly encroached on by the steady gallop of horse-hoofs. A pair of Reed's men returned, their horses at a trot, escorting an open-bed, mule-hitched wagon. The man driving the wagon looked forlorn and lost, his shoulders hunched as if he were trying to squeeze himself out of view. It was his passenger, seated to his side on the buckboard, who garnered everyone's attention.

His robe was pewter gray, wide at the wrists, loose around the neck and descending to the ankles. Around his neck hung a stole, denoting the mantle of his office. The rich purple silk of the stole was riddled with insignia and symbols that climbed the fabric like ivy up a cobble wall. The man stood on the buckboard and gazed over the watching throng.

At that moment, Greer realized that her father was no longer in unquestioned control. Still, the Lord Baron Cahill was the first to speak, albeit secretively, for only her to hear. "Greer, it looks like your Band has a wizard."

35

7.

It wasn't even his coat. His mother had thrust the rich-brown coat into his arms during the delirium of the previous night. In all likelihood, the coat belonged to one of his father's patrons – some sot too drunk to realize he'd left it behind. Somewhere, someone was waking up with red eyes, sour breath and a missing article of clothing.

It was a nice coat – it really was. It didn't fit him right, as one might expect when a grown man's coat is being worn by a thirteen year old. It sagged down, bunched around the elbows, and hid all but his fingertips in the sleeves. The collar was rakishly upturned, the top of which came level with his earlobes. He could hunker down into the coat to where his eyes were barely able to spy over the tops of the lapels. Dominic could slide so low, he couldn't see anything at all.

To where, it seemed, nothing could see him either.

"We're getting close," the girl next to him whispered. He glanced sideways at her over the collar. The girl – Sarah – kept talking to him even though he wasn't obliging her with any answers. She didn't seem to care. What's more, his silence didn't seem to strike her as odd – she just accepted it and jabbered on as if all conversations were supposed to be single-sided.

Dom would have refused her offer for a ride had he felt he could. But when the wagon had rolled past him on the outskirts of the city, he'd *felt* her. It had been the gray hours of the morning, right before the sunrise. Dom hadn't even seen her riding in the back of the straw laden cart. But he'd felt her – as surely as if they'd collided at full speed.

She'd felt him too – her reaction had proved it. Sarah had called for her father to stop the wagon and had invited him up. It was the feeling – that new sense of connection – that ultimately had landed him next to her in the scraggily straw. Dom still wasn't sure if he'd made the correct choice.

The girl chattered on in her innocent monologue. "You can feel it too, can't you? How close we are getting? You know what I'm talking about, right? I don't think I can rightly explain it – but you understand right?"

"Things will become clearer," said the wizard from his seat on the buckboard. "Soon, that is. From what we are told, the others are not far now."

As if matters couldn't be any worse, there was a wizard with them. A real one. The girl had glimpsed him walking the road and he too had received an invite to join them. A wizard. Only great fools sought to spend time with wizards! Dom's face hadn't ventured out of his collar in the last hour since the old man had joined them.

It only seemed to be getting worse. First the chattering girl. Then a wizard. Then horseback soldiers demanding to know their business. Yes, only getting worse.

And yes, he could feel it too. They were getting closer to whatever was summoning them. Just before the cart stopped, Dom knew they had arrived. A wide smile spread across Sarah's face and she turned on to her knees to peek over the buckboard. Dom took the opportunity to slide down deeper into the straw.

"Aren't you excited?" she asked him.

He was decidedly more terrified than excited. But he was used to living in a state of watchful fear. He was lamentably comfortable there.

The cart shook as the wizard stood and spoke. "I am the wizard Algius of the Sixth Circle, wearer of the Amethyst Stole. I have come to hail the Band as it is newly forming. As it has happened countless times before, so it happens today. A gathering of those chosen. Six, and always six. Banded on the arms. Bonded in their aims. A perfect six, possessing as a whole the attributes, the skills and the heart to defeat the evil that has escaped the depths of Oblivion. I hail you – the Band of Six; involuntary heroes one and all. May Merciful Domus grant you the grace equal to your task!"

"And what task would that be, wizard?" The questioner was an older man by the sound of the voice. An older man presumptuous, powerful, or stupid enough to talk back to a wizard.

Algius shrugged. "How should I know?"

The response was met with scoff. "I was under the impression that wizards knew everything concerning magic," the older man quipped.

There was no immediate response, and for a moment Dom wondered what expression showed on the old wizard's face. He almost considered it worth venturing a look. They said when wizards grew angry, the air around them crackled with sparks of light. But instead of ire, the wizard offered a brief chuckle. "Everything? No, I'm afraid not. We only know enough to be wise, Lord Baron Cahill. Just barely enough."

The wagon creaked as the wizard shifted in the cart. Dom swore he could feel the man's eyes latching onto him. "Come, children. Out of the cart. It's time." Sarah was quick to stand – enthusiastic to comply – which elicited a terse rebuke from her otherwise silent father.

"Wait, Sarah," he commanded. "Let me come around and help you."

There was a small wince of embarrassment from the girl as she looked his way. Dom pretended not to notice it. "I can do it ..." she replied.

"Let me help," her father repeated sternly, coming around. Sarah waited without further argument, keeping her eyes downcast. Carefully, her father helped to lift and lower her from the wagon bed – as if she was made of precious, thin glass ...

A burst of light flashed across his vision and the world plunged into muted, dark colors. Everything before him was drained of its vibrant shades, leaving only dusk-toned hues of various grays behind. He could still see shapes, outlines – the strong arms of Sarah's father, his hands firmly on her hips, the flecks of straw as they fluttered away from her dress. It was deathly dreary – all of it – except for the swirling auras of emotion that pulsated in the core of each person.

The ball glimmering in the center of Sarah's father roiled; a current of somber eddies. Other emotions would momentarily emerge in faint strands, only to be engulfed by the grief as soon as they appeared. Dominic, in that moment, knew exactly what Sarah's father was feeling. He saw the aura, and could immediately share in the all-consuming sadness of the man.

Sarah, on the other hand, was a beacon of pure excitement shining like a miniature sun. It radiated from the center of her aura in throbbing, rippling waves. Like the white cap on a tidal wave, the energy of Sarah's pulses was tinged by the other emotions – embarrassment, and a touch of anger.

Dominic didn't know how he did it. He had gained some control over the ability; but not completely. There were times, like now, when it came unbidden. His mother said it was a talent, a blessed gift from Merciful Domus. It was his talent, but Dom had never seen it as anything but a curse.

Another outline loomed overhead. "Have you forgotten how to walk, son?" the wizard asked. His core was vibrant, brilliant in its intensity. The sheer glow of the orb nearly blinded Dom to the layers and patterns of congealing emotions underneath. They were more complex than anything Dom had ever seen in anyone before ...

The light flashed across his vision again – and it was over. The wizard, standing high above on the buckboard, looked down with a knowing smile. The smile distressed Dom, as nothing was more important to him than keeping his cursed talent a secret. Especially from wizards. As Dom slid himself over the side of the cart, the wizard continued. "Will the Banded move towards the fountain – please? Yes, thank you. And, yes, that does include you in the tree. Yes, you, young man. Yes, I really can see you up there. To the fountain, please."

The fountain looked old. It was definitely man-made – carved and constructed – but to Dom, it appeared as a natural part of the clearing – as natural as any of the trees or rocks or tall strands of mountain grasses. It was broken down, the tiers eroded and cracked, but the imperfections in the stone only seemed to enhance the indigenous quality of the fountain. Dom leaned over the first tier, catching his broken reflection in the shallow, stagnant water. A water-bug skated across his reflection, stirring tiny ripples in the otherwise calm surface.

There was a rustle of leaves, and Dom looked up just in time to see a figure drop down beside him from the branches above. The young man landed neatly in a crouching position, and offered Dom an impish smile as he rose to his feet. He was Degan – that much was obvious from his dark, curly hair and tan complexion. Dom's father never had anything nice to say against Degans. Said the entire lot of them where idlers, beggars, drunks and thieves. Dom sidled a half-step away from the young man.

"Lord Baron Cahill, please step back with those non-Banded," the wizard called out.

The white-haired Baron leveled a steady, emotionless gaze towards Master Algius. "Are you telling me that I can't stand next to my daughter?"

"I believe I just did," the wizard answered as he adjusted the long purple stole around his shoulders. Their behavior was something Dom had observed before many times in the gamblers at his father's tavern. Every gesture, every glance, every word was meant to test the opponent. Every answer, every reaction, every hint was meant to be analyzed, considered, and dissected. And once an exploitable weakness was found ...

Baron Cahill moved away from the fountain without further remark and went to stand with a cluster of his soldiers. And then, there were six of them. Even keeping his eyes down, Dom could see they made for an odd group.

Algius walked down the line, looking each of them over carefully. Dom ducked into his lapels as the wizard passed him once, and then again on the return. Dom didn't like the way the wizard's eye dug into him – as if thumbing through the layers of his soul. Algius said nothing until he stopped in front of the tall, dark-skinned Arcan.

"Scholastad?"

The Arcan deigned him with a slight nod.

"Area of focus?"

The Arcan answered without hesitation. "The human body."

The wizard frowned and wet his lips. It was obvious that the answer was not to his liking. He wended his way down the line once more. He stopped at the far end, before the side-burned man.

"You're going to need him," the wizard muttered softly. "The Arcan. You'll have to keep him alive." The brute's jaw clenched and his eyes glowered. Algius moved on.

"Lady Greer Cahill," he said, addressing the nobleman's daughter. He paused for a moment, dipped his head into a respectful bow, and then continued.

"That's it?" the Lady questioned, her cheeks coloring.

The wizard's progress halted, but he didn't turn around. "There is more there than you realize." He stopped before the Degan youth next to Dom. The wiry young man stood tall and met the wizard's eyes. Algius took his time, inspecting the young man's clothing. His footwear – sewn leather slippers – seemed to attract the most attention. Finally, the wizard took the Degan youth by the shoulders. "You know what you'll have to do," he said. "You already know none of the others will."

The words were cryptic to Dom, but the curly-haired youth nodded as if he understood. The wizard released him, and Dom was next to incur the wizard's gaze. Surprisingly, he said nothing. There was only a subtle, conspiratorial wink as he passed. Dom felt his stomach twist. Winking wizards! What did that mean?

Sarah was the last to receive a personal appraisal. She was not hiding her eager impatience well. As he stopped in front of her, the aged wizard sank to a knee, bringing them even at eye level. Sarah smiled; Dom sensed the same free-flowing exuberance he'd dealt with during the cart ride. Algius did not speak immediately; indeed, he seemed to be carefully choosing what to say. When he did speak, Dom wondered if the emotion veiled behind was clear to anyone else but him.

Sadness.

"What is your name, my dear?"

"Sarah!" the girl responded.

Algius swallowed. "I do believe, Sarah, that you are the youngest person ever to be Banded." Rather than draw any concern from the statement, the young girl beamed proudly. The wizard matched her grin, though his was rueful. "You, dear Sarah, must be very, very special indeed." He patted her cheek in a grandfatherly manner and rose to standing again.

The wizard took three steps back and looked them over once more. "You are the six chosen," he intoned. "I had wondered what I might say to you. I wondered who you might be. I had hoped that in meeting you, the words which I could impart would be clear to me.

"You have been taken from your families, uprooted from your daily lives. You were chosen for whom you are, but what you were no longer matters. Your work, your kin, your passions and preferences – these disappear now. From this moment on, there is only the Band. There is only the task before you. You have already felt the unspeakable forces that compel you to action. Until your task is complete, you are bound, slaves to your assignment, until the evil you hunt is dead … or you are. Until then, none of you will be free again.

"We do not know why those chosen are chosen. We do not know if we can attribute this to Merciful Domus or some other force of nature. But the Banding never selects incorrectly. You can know with a certainty that your inclusion in this group is vital to the Band's success. None of you can accomplish what needs to be done without the others. You come together as strangers – diverse and different. If any of you are to survive this task, you must unite. You must learn of the capabilities and talents of your companions. You must learn to trust them with your life – and they, in turn, must learn to trust you with theirs. If you don't, if you can't – you will collectively fail. And make no mistake – failure in your cause equates to death."

The tall man with thick sideburns spoke up. "Enough talk. Give us the task, wizard, and let us get on with it."

"What evil are we to face?" asked the brown-skinned Arcan.

The wizard smiled – and Dom thought he saw the same swirls of complex emotion in the simple expression. "I've already managed to bore you with the instructions, have I? So much for tradition! Very well. Your task? It is not given me to know what you are to face. It is not my role to give you your assignment. I am only here as a witness – because things like this should not go unnoticed. They should not go unremembered." He extended a hand towards the fountain. "The Banding brought you here for a reason. It had a purpose in mind with this location, with this fountain. If you would know your task, may I suggest you reach in and touch the water."

There was a collective moment of hesitancy among the six strangers, as they glanced back into the algae-filled pool behind them. The perfectly placid water stared back at them.

Dom heard a small splash beside him. Sarah leaned over the edge, her fist submerged. She was the first. Dom and the others watched to see what would happen. Nothing did. The water settled.

"It will probably take all of you," the wizard said. "Unity, if you recall …"

The young man from the trees waited no longer. The side-burned man was close behind. There was a slight, skeptical pause before the Arcan complied, and then there was just two. He and the nobleman's daughter. She was looking to her father, who stood with an unreadable expression amidst his horsemen. What was wordlessly communicated between them escaped Dom, but she eventually sat on the edge of the fountain stone and with all the grace of her station dipped her hand into the water.

All eyes were on him now. Knowing this, Dom chose to focus on his reflection in the pool. He grimaced, knowing that no matter how high he pulled up the coat's collar, this wasn't going away. This wasn't going to stop. He couldn't just disappear. He couldn't just hide.

They would find out eventually.

"It's okay," the girl beside him whispered.

With reluctance, Dom tugged up the long right sleeve of the brown coat, bunching the fabric further up at his elbow. Slowly, his fingers came into view – and then his hand – and then his wrist …

Someone gasped. The flesh around his wrist was raw – bruised and bleeding. Just looking on it again reminded him of the pain. Ashamed, Dom closed his eyes and thrust the injured hand into the tepid fountain water.

Immediately, the water sprang to life.

8.

Very few things could cause Billick to startle. It hadn't always been that way. But he'd seen extended service in the military – had served in three separate campaigns. The Sixth Lancers had seen the worst of the action amid the snows of Dullot Pass. They'd been among the units to storm the beaches during the Bay of Chalase landing. And that had been followed by the three years fighting on Arca. Billick had watched men he stood with on the sentry line suddenly take an arrow to the chest – or to the head. He'd run at fortress gates while arrows hailed down on him and his comrades-at-arms. He'd seen what an Arcan war machine could do to a formation of men.

After a time, it ceased to be startling. The extreme became commonplace. The fear inducing moments were just part of the routine. Some people – those lacking such experiences – called it a *hardening*. They looked at a returning soldier and they said the war had hardened him, made him more steel than flesh.

It wasn't so. The constant exposure to terror didn't change how terrorizing it could be. It only taught you that fear did nothing to help you. Fear did nothing to save you. You learned, eventually, to not expend energy on something as trivial as fear.

When the timid boy down the row finally stuck his hand into the water, the result was instantaneous. The once-still water began to agitate as if in a super-heated cauldron. The water roiled and bubbled and hissed, coming alive at the touch of the six.

And then it stopped.

Looking down the row, Billick saw that the others of the Band had withdrawn from the fountain. All, except for one. The little girl, who couldn't be any older than ten, had wide, concerned eyes. But her small fist was still firmly enveloped by the settling water.

Though averse to doing so, Billick studied her. Perhaps it was the feel of the water against his skin. Perhaps it was the age of the little girl, or maybe her stone-still reaction to the unexpected. Something in that moment dredged up long-buried memories, and with them came unwelcomed emotions he'd long ago exorcised from his being. He looked away, but it was as he feared. The haunting past lingered in the stillness of the fountain water.

"That was interesting," the wizard said. "Nothing to be concerned about, to be sure. All part of the process. If you would all please continue. Please, all of you, touch the water and learn of your task." Billick tried his best to ignore the wizard. He was a man with a fancy title, a colorful shawl, ambiguous statements and nothing more. Billick had known many such men in his lifetime – they were most often the kind of men that employed him. They were men that spoke and ordered and demanded; because they lacked all capacity to *act*. Billick had no respect for such men.

The others of the Band, at the insistence of the wizard, returned their hands to the fountain's pool. Once again, at the moment that all hands were submerged under the surface, the water began to churn. This time, however, none of the six hands were pulled out.

There was a rushing sound – like a hollow wind – and a gurgle – and the fountain came to life. With a choking sputter, water began to splash from the second tier over into the bottom, and then from the third tier into the second. With one final struggling belch, the water erupted from the pinnacle of the old fountain in a fine, misty spray. The mist showered down lightly over the entire fountain, the tiny beads of water spreading as they caught the afternoon sun.

And somehow – by some magic – something dark materialized, moving through the vaporous haze. As it took shape – limbs, a head – Billick realized what he was seeing …

This was the enemy. This was his victim.

It moved with stalking, limber strides; lower legs fashioned in a crouching, near-animalistic form. The arms were longer than a man's – lean and sinewy – and the fingers … Billick tried to study the fingers, but they seemed less defined in the mist. The ends faded into nothingness before he could determine if the creature bore claws or not.

The apparition turned, giving Billick a clean look at its face … and Billick saw the creature didn't have one. It appeared as if someone had placed an oily black cloth over a man's face, completely negating the sockets of his eyes, the shape of his nose, the definition of his mouth. It was all smooth, nothingness …

The creature grew larger, as if coming towards them. To his side, the Cahill noblewoman panicked and fell back. Just as before, all action in the fountain stopped. The waters sunk, the mists ceased, and the afternoon sun annihilated what remained of the haze from the air. The creature disappeared completely from view.

Billick pulled his hand from the pool. He'd seen what he needed to see. He knew what he was after. The fountain had given him a prime opportunity to study his opponent before he faced it. He was rarely afforded such an advantage – not that he needed one.

There were soldiers already to the side of the noblewoman, helping her to her feet. She begrudgingly let them do so, assuring them she was fine.

"What was that thing?!" demanded the Lord Baron Cahill of the wizard.

The wizard, his back to the Baron, muttered something under his breath with a sigh. "Shall I give it a name, Lord Baron?" He turned his profile to the man. "Does its appellation really matter? You each saw just as much as I saw. You know just as much of the creature is as I do. I know nothing more than what I've told you – that demon escaped the bonds of Oblivion that have kept it locked away from the world. Now it is loose. It is a threat. And it needs to be dealt with."

The wizard turned a slow circle and faced the crowd standing away from the fountain. The girl's father, the Arcan's guard, Baron Cahill, the soldiers and the Lady's companion. "If history is any guide, this Band will gain a company. Many seeking adventure will join, follow and commit their lives. They are not necessary. They are fools. But they are acceptable. There are others who should not be permitted to stay in the company of the Band. It is those of you who share a connection with one of those Banded."

45

Algius addressed the group as a whole, but Billick was certain he was addressing only one man in particular. Lord Baron Cahill crossed his arms over his chest and frowned. He must have sensed it too. "You may believe you are only there to help," the wizard continued. "You may believe you are there because of love. You might swear to me that you will not interfere. I promise you, you will not able to stop yourself. You will rise up, you will act, and your actions might eliminate all hope of the demon being destroyed. So please. Please. I beg you to heed my words. Leave the Band be. Go back to where you came from. Go home, and pray to Merciful Domus that your loved one will soon be returned."

The wizard turned his gaze back to the Band and dwelt on each of the six in turn. Billick saw the seriousness in the old man's eyes. "I have nothing more to offer you – nothing more to say. I have given you your charge – the burden now rests on you to fulfill it. I wish you speed, safety and success. Most of all, success."

It was an abrupt adjournment. Perhaps the wizard was wiser than Billick had suspected. He had given them what they needed, and was now stepping aside to let them go and do.

Billick brushed roughly past the Arcan on his way back to the fallen pillar, purposefully knocking the man back a step. The dark-skinned foreigner didn't respond, but kept his gaze resolutely on the fountain. From behind he heard the young man from the tree exclaim, "It didn't have eyes! What kind of creature can exist without eyes? Do you think it can see?"

Billick reclaimed his spot behind the fountain, but found it too close to the others to allow him the space he needed to think. He could still see the milling groups of people; hear the speculation and trepidation in their conversation. The Cahills stood at the center of it, father and daughter forming a tight inner circle with the whimsy companion and the leader of the guardsmen close at hand. The nobles were arguing – albeit in very reserved tones and limited gestures, but only the Lord Baron seemed to be talking.

"They don't know what it is. They don't know what it can do. How can I justify letting you walk off with – with what? One brute, an Arcan, and three children? It is madness to think that you six would be able to fend off that demon – let alone defeat it!"

"Father …"

"No, Greer. I've made up my mind. Captain Reed and a select number of the guards will accompany you. I have to have someone I can entrust your safety to while I fix this ..."

"Fix this? Fix this how?"

"You needn't worry about that. You will stay with Captain Reed and he will keep you alive. You keep yourself out of harm's way, and this will be ended before you know it."

Billick scratched at his stubbly chin. So they'd have additional men courtesy of the Lord Baron. While Billick wouldn't discount the advantage of having extra swords on hand, the soldiers would be a setback. Captain Reed would make them a setback. He knew what kind of soldier Reed was just by watching him. Reed would assume he was the leader. His men would march to his tune; and he would expect the rest of the Band to fall in line.

Billick wanted to leave them all behind. The soldiers. The other five. He'd go off alone, find the thing, kill it and be done with it. There was no reason to involve the rest. He cast a glower at the dark-skinned Arcan. The wizard thought the Arcan was important? Needed to be kept alive? Billick harrumphed. He'd spent three years killing every Arcan he crossed paths with. This one was nothing like the muscle-bred warriors he'd faced on the plains, but that didn't matter. Billick would sooner swallow his foot than trust a boiling Arcan!

And the others? The leather pads gave the Degan lad away as a pick-pocket. What good would a thief be against a monster? The pampered noblewoman? She'd nearly fainted at the first appearance of danger. The timid boy with the bleeding wrists? The little girl too naïve to know she should be frightened out of her mind?

The horrors of the past returned as he thought of the girl, and he forced them back into their broken graves. The other five were all useless. Every one of them worthless. Billick didn't need any of them.

"Sir?" Billick hadn't been aware that anyone was behind him, and turned abruptly. The little girl's father took a long stride backward out of fear, his hands wringing uncomfortably at his waist.

"What is it?"

The man licked his lips, but still refused to meet his eyes. "I'm so sorry to disturb you, sir. So sorry. But – I ... I don't know what else to do, who else to turn to ... The wizard said ..." Billick followed the father's eyes as they strayed to the base of the fountain where the young girl sat, talking to the thief. "My daughter ... I'm worried about her safety."

Billick had long since forgotten how to feel pity. "You should be," he surmised.

"Of course, of course I am. It's more than just that, though. It's my Sarah. She isn't like you and me. She's not like other children. She ... she doesn't feel pain. At all."

Never felt pain. It explained her reaction at the fountain; she lacked fear of danger because she'd never known the threat that danger possessed.

"She hurts herself, on accident, and she doesn't know that she's done it. She'll cut herself, or break something, and she won't be any the wiser that it happened." The father drew a step closer. "Please, sir. You are the largest. You are the strongest. They'll listen to you – the rest of them will. Sarah will listen to you – I'll tell her to listen to you. You have to limit her. She doesn't understand her limitations – how could she? She'll put too much strain on her body – she's won't be able to take care of herself."

"She'll have to learn to." Billick knew his answer was harsh, but it was reality. He knew exactly why he'd been Banded – and there was nothing in the wizard's cryptic words that implied he'd spend any time with Sarah. "Tell your daughter to run, tell her to hide, tell her to stay out my way. If she does that, just maybe she'll survive this."

The father paled slightly. The truth could be hard to confront. Billick spared the man the other thoughts running through his mind. Why was little Sarah included? What use would a small girl be against a vicious demon? Was she merely there to vex him, a new canker to aggravate his deadened soul?

The answer had to be in her inability to feel pain. How could that be utilized? Sadly, the only answers Billick found to that question involved using the girl for bait. She wouldn't be able to feel the sting of death; perhaps it would absolve the others of some guilt.

The father gathered his emotions and made a final appeal. "Please, sir. She's my only daughter ..."

"I'm sorry, Henry." Neither of them had seen the wizard near; how much of the conversation he had overheard, Billick couldn't say. "It will be hard to bear, but for the time, she is not yours anymore. She belongs to the Band of Six. She must leave you, her devoted father, to fulfill the duty to which she is bound."

"She is just a little girl …"

The wizard demonstratively pulled on his purple stole. "Sarah's involvement is not by accident! We do not know much about the magic behind the Banding – but this much is for certain: the Banding makes no mistakes. She is a very special girl, she has a very special purpose. The exact purpose, Merciful Domus willing, will be revealed to us in time."

The man shook his head. "I … I can't just leave her …"

"You must!" declared Algius. "And you most certainly can. In fact, I find myself in need of your assistance. I must trouble you for a ride back to the College." Billick smiled at the blatant manipulation. This father would be just the type to interfere out of love, and the wizard appeared ready to drag him away from the fountain by force. "Come, Henry, we'll need to be going soon."

"Actually," interjected the Lord Baron, walking into the conversation, "I was hoping that you would accept the comforts of my coach, wizard. I can get you back to your college in a quicker, more …"

The wizard didn't wait to hear him out. "No, I must decline …"

"There are things we need to discuss …" Cahill clarified.

"All the same," the wizard repeated. "I must decline." He turned his eyes to Sarah's father. "Say your goodbyes, Henry. I'll be waiting."

The Lord Baron stared down the unhappy laborer. Poor fool, caught between noble blood and a wizard. He latched his gaze to his shoes and sidled off to find his precious daughter. Cahill targeted the wizard next, but Algius was not so easily cowed. The Lord Baron had calculating eyes, almost exactly like Hennessey's. While both men carried the same intensity, Baron Cahill lacked the touch of cruel insanity that infected all of Hennessey's actions. Cruel or not, Billick could see he was looking at a man accustomed to getting his way. And he would crash down like a tidal wave on anyone brazen enough to impede his path.

"You will hear me out," Cahill averred.

Algius conceded the point. "Probably true, but not now. Not here. I'm needed back at the Wizard's College."

"Then I will follow you there," the nobleman promised. "I have business at the College as well." He gave a sidelong disapproving frown to Billick before striding back to his soldiers. Billick looked to Algius. The wizard's face was expressionless, but Billick could almost hear the man chuckling. In one move, the wizard would be removing the terrified father and the all-important Baron from the board. He nodded a farewell, and left to fetch the wagon driver.

Billick listened with one ear as Cahill laid out his instructions. "You've chosen your men?"

Captain Reed nodded. "Myself and four others."

It satisfied Cahill. "My daughter's companion will accompany you as well." This earned a high-pitched gasp of shock from the blonde woman who was waiting in the wings with the soldiers. There was no way the Baron could not have heard her – he apparently didn't care. "You'll do everything in your power to keep her safe." It wasn't a question, it was a demand.

Reed saluted with confidence. "Of course, sir. She'll come to no harm."

"I'll return as soon as I am able. Leave me word on the route so we can follow. I expect the Band will not travel too quickly in my absence." His eyes shifted to his daughter, then returned to Reed. They burnished with a farewell warning. "Keep her safe."

Reed nodded. "On my life." Lady Greer rolled her eyes.

Blessedly, the fountain clearing began to thin. The wizard sat next to the red-eyed father on the wagon's buckboard. Sarah stood up on the fountain's stone ledge, waving until she could see them no longer. Cahill's coach and accompanying riders followed close behind. And it was time.

Billick stood. "I'm leaving," he said, and turned to face the road back south.

Captain Reed turned on him. "Just like that?"

"I don't have any reason to stay," Billick answered.

"Nor do I," agreed the Arcan.

Billick made it a point to turn and glare at the dark-skinned man. He didn't want anything – including support – from the Arcan. Prejudice from the citizens of Tollia wouldn't be anything new to the foreigner, but Billick was more than just prejudice. He'd bled on Arcan soil. He'd seen their society. He hated everything that Arca represented.

Reed crossed his arms. "Off you go then."

"Shouldn't we stay together?" Sarah asked, her concern evident.

"We should," agreed Lady Greer. "None of us have a reason to remain here."

Reed, it seemed, had expected his charge to be part of the opposition. She was probably doing it just to spite her father. He remained steadfast. "We should have a plan …"

Billick harrumphed. "The plan is to kill the demon. The end." The snide comment won him a toothy smile from one of Reed's men, a bearded fellow with a crossbow.

"We need to understand our resources," pressed the Captain. Billick saw what Reed was attempting. The longer he kept the group at the fountain, the further they would be from the demon. Unfortunately, Billick was in no mood to stall. The wizard had been quite clear – he was trapped in this Band until the creature was dead. He'd have to endure an Arcan, a self-important Lady and children for a time – but he was not willing to extend that time any longer than necessary.

"Stay if you elect to, Reed," Lady Greer answered. "I'm going with him."

Captain Reed looked around the clearing for support. He was left lacking. The only other members of the Band weren't even adults. Valiantly, the Captain tried once more. "Do you even know where you are going? Do you even know how to find this thing?"

In unison, each member of the Band stuck out their arm, pointing in the exact same direction. South by south-west. Billick just knew. He didn't know how he knew – just like he didn't know why he was being drawn here. But he was vaguely aware of a presence to the south – and he knew that presence was the demon.

The unquestionable agreement of the six pointing fingers could not be disputed. Those not of the Band shuffled in uneasy bewilderment at the display. Reed, back straight and jaw firm, took an inventory of each finger and conceded the point. "Lead on."

9.

With patience and precision, the string was lowered deeper into the wedge of rocks, completely submerged under the glassy surface of the pool. The hermit sat on his haunches, content to let the mosquitoes float around his face as he listened to the croaking of the river frogs. Slowly, he let the string drift to the left – further up into the tight wedge …until he felt it. An ever-so-gentle tug against the string.

With practice, the hermit placed his own tension on the string. Not much – not enough to pull the bait completely out of reach – but just enough to convey the message: *if you want it, you'll have to fight for it harder than that.* The next tug on the string was firmer, and the hermit matched the intensity. When the third tug came, the hermit was ready. He pulled up on the string with all of his strength.

The large crawfish, claws clamped protectively onto the flesh-flecked quail-bone bait, dangled from the string. The hermit raised the creature to the level of his eyes – and grinned at his catch. "In the bucket with the other unfortunates!" he sniggered as he wrestled the crawfish off of the bone. He had three now – and large, meaty ones too. Certainly enough for a supper. A kingly supper, when you were only feeding one!

Successful, he dropped the large crustacean into the bucket. The other crawfish were at the edges, trying to feel for an escape route. The hermit shook his head at them. "Tis how it goes, lads. Everything is food, when its time comes. Birds eat the frogs, frogs eat the flies, flies eat at me – they do. By the size of you three brothers, it would seem that you've eaten off others very well indeed."

He stood. "No shame, remember. Your time came, that's all."

The smile slowly left the hermit's face. The frogs – they'd gone silent. Unnaturally silent. The frogs only did that when they sensed a predator close at hand. The hermit switched the bucket to his left hand and he drew his serrated hunting knife with the right. A wolf? A bear? Most of the predators knew this was his part of the woods – his territory. They'd always left him alone …

The hermit stopped. It wasn't just the frogs.

The mosquitoes were gone as well.

The entire forest was still. The hermit tightened his grip on the knife. "Eerie in my bones, my brothers," he whispered to the crawfish. "Deep eerie in my bones!" Out of the corner of his eye, he thought he saw a form amid the forest foliage shadowed by the afternoon sun, but it was gone before he could focus on it. He cursed his eyes for cheating him – a child this deep in the woods?

It came at him swiftly from his side – a rush of darkness in contrast with the late afternoon sun. There had been no time to react. The hermit fell to the ground – dropping his knife. The bucket splashed into the pool. The struggling hermit looked up into the face of the predator pinning him.

He saw nothing but empty blackness.

He drew a quick breath in panic – and felt the black creature's fingers burrowing into his chest. There was bitter agony – and he knew he was going to die. *Tis how it goes.*

He screamed – only once – and the forest pool returned to a still and stagnant quiet.

*   *   *   *   *

Edgar Hardy was not a man who failed to collect on payments he was due. So it was with most of the laborer class – they could be late to their duties every morning and find a good excuse to sleep in on Holydays but they would sooner catch the plague or wade through Oblivion than miss compensation. Master Gideon Rice counted on this fact. He frequently withheld the promised boon from those he contracted with until they reported back to him that the job had been successfully completed to the standards he expected.

Rice served as the personal liaison of the Northing household to the criminal element of Hollingston. The position, of course, did not officially exist. Lord Baron Northing would deny such an untoward association – although each and every Lord Baron in Tollian employed a man like Rice. Official recognition didn't matter; official sanction did. Those that dealt at the back tables in the dark rooms knew who Rice represented. Everyone knew Rice demanded sterling-quality work. No one argued; they also knew of sizeable quantities of wealth at Rice's disposal.

When Edgar Hardy missed their arranged appointment, Rice assumed the worst. In his business, the worst was well-defined and easily summarized as *the unknown*. There was a litany of things that might have happened to the hapless Edgar – and all of them could be handled and addressed once the specific circumstance was discovered. But until it was, while it remained a mystery, Rice could not plan, he could scheme. He was rudderless when in the doldrums of the unknown.

He set out to find Edgar. Rice could think of only one place to look for the missing gravedigger. Mounting his horse, he set out on a tour of Hollingston's graveyards.

As he approached the second stop on his circuit, he immediately knew he'd found the place. Two constabulary carriages were parked alongside the fence, next to a horse and wagon that could easily be Edgar's. Rice lashed his reins to the post and strode purposefully into the hills of the graveyard.

The constables were gathered in an obscure corner of the yard, deep in conversation with one another. The chief was onsite, luckily someone that Rice had an understanding with. Some men were gifted with the talent of looking the other way – that talent alone had made this chief a particular wealthy man. When one of the other constables moved to intercept, the chief waved him away. "Let him see the body," he instructed. The officers parted, and Rice got his first look at the mangled corpse.

Gideon Rice was no stranger to dead bodies, no man in his employ could afford to be, but he'd never seen remains like this. Edgar's arms were crisscrossed with deep gouges, a meager defense against the feral animal attacking him. The claw marks seemed too large to be a wolf. A bear perhaps? Rice would have expected a bear attack to be bloodier. Aside from a few dried streaks on Edgar's arms, the entire scene was virtually blood free. Edgar's remains look shriveled, a dried husk.

Rice tried to tell himself this was a good thing. He was no longer facing the unknown of Edgar Hardy's whereabouts. But he faced a new unknown – and one far greater. He'd need to determine what had butchered the poor gravedigger.

The chief waited at his shoulder. "Friend of yours, then?"

Rice stared into Edgar's ashen face and knew he'd not divine the answers on his own. "I want everything – all that you've found that might be relevant to the murder. I want written descriptions from your constables of the crime scene. I want the body readied for transport – and I want it preserved in its current status to the closest extent possible. The House of Northing will be taking the investigation from here."

One of the constables walked past, a ripped and empty billy-cloth bag in his hands. Rice frowned. This was an unknown he'd not solve on his own. He only hoped that Lord Northing and his Arcans would be able to provide the answers he needed.

10.

They made for a decidedly peculiar group. Picked out by Fate. Individually selected, if the wizard was to be believed. Forced together into an impromptu and unnatural cohort. An improvised family.

As a member of the Children's Gang, Ethiere had a very loose interpretation of families. New children, fresh from the streets, were adopted and accepted without question. Older children would settle up with Master Hat, cash in their share of the takes, and disappear to start a new life in a different city. The Gang family was constantly changing, but it was united in a way that the Banding magic could not duplicate. Each child of the Gang knew loss – and they were bonded by their emotional need to have one another.

It was only the afternoon of their first day together, but Ethiere didn't see this Band of Six coming together in that way. The side-burned man had plainly spelled out his desire to be left alone. The Arcan – the first man of that nationality the thief had ever laid eyes on – was already ostracized from the group. The dark-skinned man seemed accepting of this fact and thus far had remained aloof. The noblewoman was fascinating to Ethiere, as anyone born to wealth might be to a boy who'd lived in poverty, but her cadre of guards were keeping her well isolated from the "lesser" citizens in the party.

Ethiere kicked at a stone and watched it scramble up ahead of him on the roadway they traveled on. An odd group, to be sure. Was he honestly supposed to believe this was the work of some all-knowing, all-seeing being? That they had been hand-selected for some special reason? That Domus or some other grander God knew them personally?

As nice as that sounded rolling around in the young thief's mind, Ethiere's eyes could not ignore the proof laid out plainly before him.

There could not have been six more random people chosen for the Band. A mixture of genders, ages, even nationalities. It was as if Fate's hand had fished around in the pockets of the universe and just happened to snatch them up. How else could it be explained? Their Band had a thief, a cheerful little girl and a boy with ugly rope-welts on his wrists. They were vital in fighting off a faceless demon? They would be instrumental in the downfall of an evil cunning enough to have escaped the bonds of Oblivion?

It was amazing that the wizard had made it seem even remotely possible.

It was much easier to believe that this was what life truly was – a series of random events, unconnected, unable to be controlled or anticipated. They just happened. There was no forethought, no oversight, no grand plan. Just things that happened. A leaf floating along the river. It was easier for Ethiere to believe he'd run into a terrible eddy. He'd have to accept that this might be the eddy that ended his unfortunate existence.

Even thieves knew the stories of the Bands. All of them – every one of them – suffered casualties. Success for the group still could mean death for certain individuals. And knowing his luck …

Ethiere pushed the fatalistic thought from his mind, kicking the stone off into the road-side underbrush as he continued his steady pace forward. He scanned the party once more, spread out in a line on the country road. Six strangers – completely different from one another in all ways but one.

They all seemed to prefer to walk the path fate was pushing them down in silence.

All – except for one …

"My name is Sarah." Walking several paces behind them, Ethiere had a perfect view of the attempt the girl was making to talk to the side-burned man. She took two or three steps to every one of his in an effort to match his pace, and waited expectantly for a reply. When it became clear that an answer wouldn't be forthcoming, she opted to prompt for one. "What's your name?"

A visible tension in the side-burned man's body language suggested that he didn't speak to young girls very often. His response was as terse as allowable. "Billick."

"Billick," she repeated. "Billick. It's nice to meet you Billick."

"Did your father put you up to this?"

The direct question puzzled the girl. "My father?"

"Did he tell you to talk to me?"

There was no debating the innocence. "No …"

He eyed her sideways, a shaded look that spoke of cynicism.

Sarah didn't notice. "Do you live in Hollingston as well?"

Billick's side of the conversation came with a decided lethargy. If the conversation with the little girl was inevitable – the side-burned man thought to at least control the pace. "Yes."

"By yourself?"

"Yes," he answered, and turned on her quickly. "Why do you care?"

"Why wouldn't I?" Sarah wondered aloud. Ethiere had to smile. The girl was completely blind to Billick's verbal cues and body language. She was disarmingly genuine.

She switched subjects. "What do you do?"

"Do?"

The girl brightened, and Ethiere knew why. It was the first response from the unsociable man that wasn't distrustfully attacking and actually invited further talking. "For a living," she clarified. "My father is a groundskeeper. What about you?"

Billick looked down at the girl again, taking measure of her. Strange as it was, Ethiere got the distinct feeling that the question had made the man uncomfortable. Had it been the question – or the questioner? He went back to focusing on the road. Ethiere found the man intriguing in a very dangerous manner. There was heaviness in his eyes. Deadness to them. It fascinated the thief, seeing it there, and the girl unwittingly poking at it. Was there a soul hidden away somewhere in those lifeless eyes?

"Surely you do something," she pressed against the stony silence.

His face hardened. "People pay me to do terrible things."

"Terrible things?"

"Think of the most awful things one person can do to another." The man paused, allowing Sarah's imagination time to work, and then continued in a growl. "That, little girl, is what I do."

Sarah's pace rapidly fell off. The gap between her and Billick widened, and neither of the two seemed unhappy about the fact. When his own pace put him side-by-side with the girl, Ethiere could see the little girl's face was pale, her brow flexed in worried contemplation. He wondered if he shouldn't say something to take her mind off of whatever dark thoughts Billick had placed there. As it turned out, he didn't need to.

"My name is Sarah," she told him. She started with that introduction – and didn't stop.

Ethiere smiled. Kari liked to talk too. About anything and nothing – just talk. Perhaps that is what girls did when there wasn't really anything else to do. Ethiere didn't mind. He found it easy enough to answer Sarah's questions and still think about other things. Plus, after some time, he grew curious to see how long she could go before she ran out of things to say.

Currently, they were discussing trees.

"Do you climb a lot of trees?" she asked.

"No, not usually trees," he answered.

"You climb other things?"

"Buildings mostly."

Sarah's brow wrinkled. "Why?"

He decided to flip the question on her. "Well, why not?"

It gave her pause. "Well … it's dangerous, I suppose. Clear up on top of a building – couldn't you fall?"

"Of course. You could. But that's hardly a reason to not do it. There was never any height worth getting to that didn't have some risk of a fall attached to it."

He turned to look at her. "You've never climbed before, have you?" She shook her head. "I think you'd like it."

"I would?"

Ethiere smiled again. "Of course you would. Everyone would. Climbing buildings is one of the best kept secrets in Hollingston. People who know tend to stay silent on the matter. We want to keep the roofs to ourselves. It would be terrible if they got too crowded."

He paused as she smiled while imagining it. It was interesting – Ethiere had never thought about roofs before, he'd never realized how much he believed what he was telling the girl. More for his benefit then Sarah's, he tried to think of the best way to describe it. "The world is a very different place when you are up higher than everything else. When you are down on the ground, where it's swarming and noisy, it is really easy to get lost. But not up high. Up high, there is space – there is sky. There is always a view of the horizon – of the sunrise or the sunset." He shrugged. "You get a different perspective on things, really. You aren't lost or crowded, like those on the street below. It's just an illusion, but you can almost pretend you are actually in control."

"I like to watch people on the streets – from my window," Sarah said. There was still a smile on her ever-cheerful face, but this one was different. This one was sad. "It's one of my favorite things to do – to sit up on the edge of my bed and watch them. I pick someone out on the street and I follow them along until they disappear and I wonder to myself where they are going. Who are they going to see? What exciting plans have they made to be rushing on like they do?"

"Why do they wear boots?" Ethiere added off-hand.

Sarah's nose crinkled in a smirk. "Boots?"

Ethiere grinned at the reaction. Apparently girls never thought about boots. "You can dance in boots," he told her.

"I suppose you can," she answered. "So what did you see when you were up in the tree?"

"Hmm?"

"While you were up there – looking down on us. Getting your 'different perspective'." She giggled. "Were you picturing us dancing?"

He shook his head. "No – just watching. Like you do at your window. Trying to guess who people are – figure a little of what they are about. See what they are like when they don't think anyone is watching."

"And what did you see?" Sarah asked.

He looked at her. What should he tell her? Of the Arcan that pricked his own arm with needles to draw out blood? Of all of the strange things that must be hidden in that large pack he carried? Of the tension that had erupted between Billick and the Arcan as soon as they'd seen one another? Did he tell her just how dangerous he thought Billick was, of how well he matched the crueler men that lurked in the shadows of Hollingston? You learned to size people up as a thief. You needed to know who was dangerous. There were some people who would curse and yell if you picked their pocket. There were others that would save their breath – and hunt you down. Billick seemed like one of the latter. Ethiere did not know a thief in the Children's Gang that had enough rocks in their stomach to pick the pocket of the side-burned man.

Or should he tell her about the nobles? Ethiere stole a quick glance behind him. The Lady Cahill and her blonde-haired companion were riding side-saddle as the horses walked at a leisurely pace. He'd tried to absorb every moment of the nobles' activity once they'd arrived. He was fascinated by them – people with power and gold. People that wielded influence and resonated with importance. He was fascinated by them – in truth – because he didn't know what it was like to be one. To be important. To be powerful.

Powerful enough that you didn't have to be concerned about anyone other than yourself.

Sarah waited for an answer but Ethiere still didn't know what to give. Did he tell her of her father? Of his grief? Had she noticed it when he had said his brave goodbye with a gentle hug and she'd promised she'd be good? Had she not seen – as her father had – that this was the end? Or of the boy she came with – the boy that shied away from people – that even now was hunched and cowering in his oversized coat.

He looked at the little girl again. Or should he tell her about the innocent little girl – the girl too innocent to realize what was happening. The little girl that hadn't yet realized that there was less to be excited about than there was to be terrified of. The little girl that hadn't yet realized that the Arcan, the dangerous man, the noblewoman and all of the soldiers at her command – all of them combined didn't care one brass button about what happened to her.

"Well?"

"There were a lot of leaves in the way," he lied.

--- * --- * ---

They'd told him to wait in the alley. There'd been a plan – and Ethiere had done his part. He'd made an obvious grab for the merchant's coin purse – obvious enough to attract the attention of the two nearby constable deputies. He'd led them on a mad dash through the crowded Hollingston streets. He'd escaped; crowds were much easier to slip through for a stick-figured six-year-old. He'd circled around and planted himself in the predetermined spot where the others were supposed to meet him.

Four other boys had used his distraction to raid a corner vendor's fruit stall in the absence of the deputies. They'd promised him a portion of what they managed to take.

Ethiere clutched at his knees as he sat in the filth of the narrow alleyway. He rubbed his legs, not because they itched or were cold. He rubbed them because it took his mind off of the gnawing hunger in his belly. He'd not eaten since yesterday morning – and that had only been a molding crust of bread thrown out by a baker. He rubbed his knees because it was better than crying.

He'd been waiting since noon. It was now well past sunset. He'd watched the shadows on the wall opposite him grow longer and longer as the day dimmed to night. He knew they weren't coming. They had no reason to come for him. The take was greater divided among four mouths versus five. They had no need to come for him. There were more than enough plague orphans roaming the Hollingston streets nowadays.

And yet he wanted to cry anyway. He'd allowed himself the hope that maybe they'd accept him. That they'd take him in and help him survive. It had been all he'd hoped for since the plague had swept through the docks and claimed his entire family. He'd hoped, despite knowing there was a long day in a lonely alley ahead of him.

The insistent hunger eventually drove him out of his hiding spot. He had no destination in mind – his nose caught an alluring aroma on the breeze and he followed it. The vendor's cart was small, crowded up against the large stone building behind it – but his meat pies smelled heavenly. Even across the way,

Ethiere could heard the sizzle from the portable hearth. His stomach twisted and groaned – sensing the nearness of the food.

Haloed in the moonlight, Ethiere could see the vendor was watching him. The man was short with a stocky build, with a fleshy but otherwise ordinary face. He held a long-bladed pie knife in his right-hand – a warning to boy he perceived as a thief. There was a tipping point in the young boy's mind – and desperation out-shouted the pleas for caution. On weak legs, Ethiere padded across the street, towards the meat-pie cart. The vendor eyed him the entire way.

There was a momentary pause – one last chance for him to decide against the act. He swallowed hard against the knot in his throat and stretched out his fingers. A passerby said something to the vendor, momentarily distracting him, and Ethiere's hand went up. Moonlight gleamed off the moving knife ...

Striking like a viper, another hand caught his before it reached the pies. The momentum of the newcomer completely turned Ethiere around, pulling him up the street. "I need a word with you," said the teenage boy as they plowed forward. "Perhaps several words if your brains are wax." Ethiere had never seen the boy before. He glanced back at the meat-pie cart. The vendor was still watching – but he'd set the knife down.

Ethiere was dragged another block before he spoke. "I don't know you."

"True," said the lad with a crooked grin. "And if I was any later, you'd never have known me or anyone else ever again. Get it?" The boy nodded his head. "You must have rocks in your Degan stomach. Yep rocks. Know how I can tell?'

"No ..."

"Cause nobody that doesn't have rocks in their stomach dares try to rob Old Murry, especially when he's already tagged you for it. Guts made of stones, for sure, until Murry slices them out of you. Isn't pretty. And none too smart. Gotta have rocks in your stomach – and candle-wax for brains." They made a sudden turn down a side-street. "Just saying how lucky you are I came along." As an afterthought, he added. "I'm Carl."

Ethiere rubbed at the back of his head. He felt like his brain was still a half-block behind him, trying desperately to catch up. "Where are we going?"

"A place I know," was the cryptic answer. "You'll like it there."

"I will?" He fought down the hope in his heart. This was too good to really be happening.

"Oh sure," said Carl. "You look like you could use a good meal." His mouth wound into the crooked grin again. "Mind you, when I say good it isn't Murry meat-pie good, but that's a tough hedge to hurdle, if you follow me. But it's food, and even if your tongue gets offended your belly will welcome it gladly."

"Food?" Was there a chance?

"And a place to stay," Carl added. "A warm place to sleep – out of the rain and all. Lots of other kids to play with. Quite a few Degans. We play lots and lots of games."

Ethiere pulled his hand free and stopped in the alley. The move surprised the larger Carl, who turned around with a questioning eyebrow. Ethiere fought the urge to just stay silent, to just keep following the boy and hope for the best, but it had been a long day of waiting. Hope was thin. "Why are you doing this?" he demanded. "Why are you being nice to me?"

Carl acted as if the questions were strange. "Why?"

"You don't know me!" Ethiere said. His six-year old frame trembled as tears welled in his eyes. "You have no reason to want to help me! Why?"

The jovialness left Carl's face. The teenager still smiled, but it was a knowing, compassionate smile. "Because I was little and alone once," he answered. "Because I was hungry and cold once. Because someone older found me. Someone older looked out for me. And I promised him that when I was the older one, I'd be just like him. I'd be just like him and look out for the small ones. Follow?"

Ethiere could tell Carl meant it. "I follow."

Carl nodded and the crooked grin reappeared. "So you're coming, right?" he asked and held his hand out.

Ethiere took it without hesitation. "I'm Ethiere."

As they walked, Carl leaned a long arm across his Ethiere's bony shoulders. "Ethiere, huh? Okay. Come on, then. Let's go fill that stomach of yours with something besides rocks." Carl laughed at his own joke, and settled into a smile. "Something tells me you and I will become really, really good friends."

--- * --- * ---

"Leaves?" Sarah wouldn't have it. "You had to have seen more than just leaves."

He nodded. "Alright, then," he sighed. "If I must." He paused again – as long as he thought she'd allow him before sticking him with a sharp elbow to the ribs. "When I was in the tree, I saw that you and I and possibly that quiet boy that hitched a ride in your cart … I saw that we are going to become really, really good friends."

The wizard had seen as much. None of the adults in the Band would give Sarah and the silent boy a second thought. Ethiere would have to do it. He was the older one now. He'd repay Carl's kindness.

Sarah's face blossomed into a surprised joy. "Really?" she exclaimed. "I'd like that." Unexpectedly, a short spell of silence came and the conversation ebbed. Ethiere hid a smile and began counting the number of seconds in his head.

"His name is Dominic, by the way," she broke in before he got to eight. "I think he prefers to go by Dom – well, I asked him, but he didn't really answer me. But Dominic sounds like such an older person's name and Dom seems better suited for a boy, don't you think? I hope he would have said something if he didn't like people calling him Dom – because that's what I called him …. I called him … the entire …"

Ethiere glanced at the girl as her stream of thought grew jumbled. "Sarah?"

Her legs buckled. Nimble as he was, Ethiere was unable to move fast enough to keep her from crashing to the side of the road.

11.

Out of the corner of his eyes, Kashif saw the small girl falter and fall to the ground. The wiry young man she'd been speaking with for the last hour was quickly at her side, calling her name and attempting to rouse her. The entire procession, including the mean-tempered man at the forefront, stopped amid the commotion. Kashif was shocked when he didn't immediately opt to keep walking.

Kashif had been relegated to the middle of the traveling Band and had spent the entire walk as if on his own island. The Lady Cahill and her men traveled behind him; a surly soldier with a sizeable crossbow served as an immediate barrier to the women in his wake. Captain Reed was the only one of Lady Greer's party to move forward to assess the situation with the little girl. "What happened to her?"

"I don't know; she just collapsed mid-sentence!" the young man said. They'd rolled the girl to her back, which appeared to be the extent of what they knew do to for her. "She's hit her head."

"Is it the plague?" Greer's high-voiced companion fretted aloud. Kashif found the Tollians to be a disease-conscious people; understandable given their experience with the localized epidemic that had annihilated the docking districts of Hollingston. It had not been uncommon to see Lord Baron Northing's attendants carrying poultices of crushed herbs on loops around their necks. Men and women alike were quick to cover their mouth and nose with a handkerchief should anyone cough or sneeze. As a man of science, Kashif found some of their practices – and more notably, the absence of others – laughable to say the least.

"My squad surgeon went with the Lord Baron," Reed muttered to himself. As the captain raised his head to scan over the rest of the group, it was plain to Kashif that he was the sole qualified expert in the matters of health and body. Yet he resisted the thought of moving in to examine the condition of the fallen girl. How would the others expect him – the Arcan – to act? Would they perceive a proactive gesture as an overstepping of his bounds? Their behavior thus far suggested they preferred him isolated from the rest of the group – a lone one surrounded by a Band of five.

"Her father told me this would happen," the side-burned man said. The utter lack of compassion in his voice did not come as any surprise. "She's a liability to herself. She can't feel pain."

The revelation, even in the simplistic terms in which it was delivered, immediately put everything into perspective for the man of science.

This girl was Refaid.

--- * --- * ---

"I have another question." The man sitting across from him leaned forward studiously, the fingers of his hands pressed together like a jagged row of mountain spires. His hair was course and very short, and it was mottled with gray in very much the same way lichen grows on stone. "Did you ever harm any of your brothers at the dohourn?"

At nine years of age, Kashif felt dwarfed by the imposing man. There was nothing separating the two of them but open air. Kashif did not like feeling so exposed. He was standing in the middle of the room while the men sat around him and his legs were beginning to burn with fatigue. Still, he endeavored to keep his back straight and his eyes forward. The old women of his dohourn had taught him that he mustn't wilt when he stood before the men. Not that the grandmotherly caretakers had ever witnessed the Sifting process, but they had been the only founts of wisdom Kashif and his twenty-seven brothers had ever known.

"Harm?" he echoed.

"Hurt them," restated the man. "Perhaps by accident, even. Or perhaps because you felt they deserved to be harmed ... "

Kashif rolled the question around in his weary mind. Each of the men had interviewed him in turn, asking their questions. What answer did this old one desire? Was this a test to see if he was overly aggressive – or perhaps too passive? Did they want to see if he could control his emotions? Did they want to measure his judgment in meting out punishment to those who'd wronged him?

Was there a right answer at all?

Kashif selected his response. "I don't believe I have."

His answer earned a thoughtful nod from the questioner – and another question. "What circumstances warrant the harming of another boy as acceptable?"

Kashif again tried to swallow down the lump lodged in his throat. Many of the boys in his dohourn had speculated what the Great Sifting would entail. All that the old women had been able to tell them was that the Procession of Ten would open the gates of their community at their ninth year and escort them away. Ten men – a ruling Magistad, two wizened Scholastad, three Ballistad warriors and four of the mercantile Industad. These would represent the first true men the boys had ever seen. The women knew nothing of where the men took the boys – or what exactly would be done with them. All they knew is that the Sifting decided what role each boy would play in the overarching mission of the Arcan society.

That mission, simply stated, was to create the perfect man.

Abrim had thought the Great Sifting would be done in complete silence. The two of them had often stayed up late, wondering aloud at the process. Abrim had suspected the men would be able to look into your eyes and see your soul, and they would be able to determine which caste the Architect of Men would have you placed in. As he thought of Abrim, Kashif wondered how his fellow brother was faring. Was Abrim being asked the same difficult questions?

He tried to focus on the question, but his focus was spent. The Sifting process had seen him given physical tasks that tested his strength, tested his speed and tested his endurance. He was given puzzle-like games – twisted pieces of metal that he was instructed to take apart, or odd shaped blocks of wood that he was told to make fit together. He'd been given jars of rocks – told to quickly count some and estimate the number in others. He was placed in a dark room with a voice that incessantly carried on about subjects Kashif had never heard of – and then he'd been told to recite all that he could recall. They'd brought an ointment that had caused his skin to burn – a test of pain ...

"Kashif?"

"A boy doing harm should be punished," he answered.

There was another contemplative nod from the gray-haired man. Kashif guessed that he was a member of the Magistad caste. The others of the Procession deferred to the man – they spoke only at his bidding. He was a man that sat comfortably with the mantle of power on his shoulders.

"I am interested," the Magistad said. "Are there circumstances, you feel, that would merit a punishment of death?"

There was no part of Kashif that had ever conceived of killing another boy. Yet he found this question surprisingly simple. "Yes," he said. "When his actions work against the plans of the Architect. When his actions are limiting the progress of the Arcan nation. He should be killed – for the greater good."

The old man smiled. "Very well put, Kashif. I am impressed." He turned to look over his shoulder, and three or four of those in the semi-circle nodded their heads. He returned his gaze to Kashif. "The Architect of Man has given us the task of fashioning a race in his image – man perfected. We cannot jeopardize his plans being delayed even the slightest by those who do not bear the interest of all Arca in their hearts." The Magistad squinted at him and pursed his lips in thought. After a moment of reflection he began to nod again. "Yes, I do believe that the Architect has a special place set for you."

Kashif nodded, and for the first time during the interview allowed himself to smile. A special place! He and Abrim had spoken late into the nights of their highest aspirations – of being caste into the ranks of the Scholastad.

"I have just one more question before I leave you," the gray-haired man said, interrupting Kashif's dream. The world was suddenly a very serious place again. "I wish you to tell me, boy, why the Architect of Man – perfect as he is – creates some Arcans with obvious defects. Blindness. Deafness. Missing or weakened limbs. Why are such born among us?"

He was speaking of the Refaid – the incomplete. Those whose imperfections relegated them to the lowest caste of all – not even fit to be Dynad slaves. Those boys manifesting any physical or mental flaw were immediately removed from the dohourn – and as such, Kashif had little experience with the miserable lot. The suggestion the Magistad hinted at was blasphemous – the Architect did not make mistakes. If a man was created that way – it was the way the Architect saw fit. But as to their purpose?

"Could ... can they not be used to further the advancement of the nation?" he ventured.

The Magistad nodded knowingly. "This is a valuable thing to learn, Kashif. The deformed and the diseased can all serve a purpose towards our end. You have a very adept mind, one that reaches for meaning and seeks to understand. You will be a valuable addition to the Scholastad. You will learn exactly how we build towards the perfect man." He stood and once again turned to the gathered semi-circle. One stepped forward. "Does the Scholastad accept this boy as one of their own?"

"We do," the man answered. "I intend to take this one as an apprentice myself."

The Magistad nodded. It was done. "Teach him everything, Marooke."

Marooke folded his arms behind his back, and bowed his head as the Magistad and the others of the semi-circle departed. He stood in silence until the room was empty of all but the two of them. He then looked appraisingly at Kashif. "We shall begin your studies immediately. You have much to learn."

"What will I study?"

"Your primary focus will be on human physiology. As such you will need to learn our sciences of biology, anatomy, and chemistry. Before you begin on these topics, you will need a foundation of reading and writing. Advanced mathematical formulations will also be required." Marooke smiled. "My apprentice, you are already so terribly behind!"

Kashif was still in shock, his feet blindly following the Scholastad scientist – his new mentor! – to the door. He would be educated! He'd never hoped for anything greater! He would learn quickly – he'd apply every waking moment of every day to the pursuit of learning. And it would all be aimed towards building the perfect Arcan! He felt his pulse rising at the excitement brewing in his veins. It was undeniably ideal ...

A thought interrupted his euphoria. "What of Abrim?"

Marooke, hands still firmly clenched behind his back, continued on unabated. "What of him?"

Kashif sped to catch up. "Is he to join us? As a Scholastad?"

Marooke turned his head only slightly. "No."

The news was like a splash of water on the fires of his excitement – a sudden shock causing his joy to retreat. "But Abrim – he's intelligent. He's very smart ..." Kashif fell silent. What had become of Abrim then? A Ballistad? Abrim had never been one to excel at the physical competitions at the dohourn. An Industad? That would surely be a disappointment. Yes, Abrim would travel the world, but he too had hoped for an education ...

Marooke stopped at a balcony overlooking the terrace down below and beckoned Kashif forward. From the vantage point, Kashif saw twenty people milling there, each of them in the distinguished loincloth of the servile Dynad caste. Standing among them, looking scared and confused, was Abrim. Kashif could not believe his eyes. Abrim was Dynad? It made no sense, Abrim was intelligent, he was ...

One of the Dynad produced a hot iron from the stoker and advanced on the dazed boy. Two other Dynad took his arms and held him fast. The hot iron pressed against the skin on Abrim's back between the shoulder blades. Kashif cringed.

It was worse than he imaged. Abrim was not Dynad. Kashif looked to his mentor.

Marooke was watching the entire affair impassively. "Your fellow brother was indeed smart. But he was unfit for our caste – and all others. During our testing, we found that he has a weakened heart. We expected this might be the case – we've found a similar condition in half the males sired by the Arcan who sired your brother. The condition will not manifest until his sixteenth year – perhaps not until his eighteenth – but those with the defect do not generally live past their twenty-fifth year. Never to their thirtieth."

Refaid. Abrim was Refaid. He was imperfect.

"Do not concern yourself with thoughts of him any longer," Marooke instructed. "Men of our station do not waste thought on the Refaid."

--- * --- * ---

Scientific curiosity – not concern – set Kashif's feet in motion. Unable to feel pain. Unresponsive nerve endings. Kashif had read reports on such a condition, but had never seen a living example. It had ceased to exist on Arca over eighty years ago – the geneticists having eradicated the imperfection from the population.

Captain Reed watched his approach dubiously. "I have studied the human body my entire life," he told the military man. "Let me see her." He chose to explain his actions rather than just kneel next to the girl, if for no one's benefit besides the untrusting crossbowman behind him. Reed backed away, and Kashif, swinging the pack from this shoulder, took his place.

The girl was still unconscious, and aside from a small but bloody gash on her forehead, looked to have only suffered small scrapes. Kashif put his fingers to the artery in the girl's throat to time her pulse; then placed them on her chest to gauge her breathing. Every physical indication pointed to over-exertion, which made sense given the girl's condition. She wouldn't have registered her body's warnings of exhaustion.

The Arcan went for one of the small pockets on the pack, and was pleased to see that his guess as to where Djemal had packed the powdered chemicals was correct. He thumbed through the contents, reading the labels on the array of tiny glass vials. Selecting one, he removed the cork stopper, and shook a dash of the caked white dust onto his two longest fingers.

He extended the fingers below the girl's nose, and snapped. The dust billowed in a small controlled cloud that disappeared as she inhaled again. Her response was immediate – eyes opening wide to the intrusion of the waking salts. Her limbs startled, like one coming out of a dream, and she saw him hovering above her for the first time.

There was such a lack of guile in her eyes that it shocked him. Had no one told her of Arcans? Did she not know to fear the dark-skinned men? Had no one poisoned her mind with prejudice and hate?

She swallowed roughly and his mind returned to the business at hand. "Water?" he asked of Captain Reed. "She'll need water."

The Captain was uncapping his canteen as he came forward, and knelt next to Kashif. Strange as it might seem, Kashif's level of discomfort rose now that the girl was awake.

This was the first time in his life interacting with a girl. His childhood had been spent in the dohourn with other boys his age, raised by the elderly women. After his Sifting, his day-to-day living had involved interactions with only other men. Aside from the sessions for propagation arranged by the Scholastad geneticists, Kashif had not dealt with the feminine gender. It had been odd adjusting to the Tollian society, where women were allowed to freely intermingle with the men.

"Lay still," he commanded her. "You have hit your head and it will require stitching. Drink some water while I prepare the needle." To her credit, the garrulous girl didn't ask questions, and instead accepted Reed's help as he placed the canteen to her lips. Perhaps it was the ill-effects of the hard hit to her head, but her entire demeanor seemed to have changed. She seemed mortified.

Kashif found the suture kit within the pack. Normally he would have applied a little anesthetic to the area before applying the needle, but in the girl's case it wouldn't matter. She'd not feel the pain in either regard. He opened the kit and began to thread the needle when he caught the gaze of the young man. Kashif had overheard the talk of the others. They claimed the Degan youth was a thief. There was no mistaking the way the boy was staring at the pack; curiosity would demand he rummage through it.

Kashif realized he'd have to guard his pack very carefully.

The girl stayed silent and still as Kashif began to stitch the gash in her forehead. But the sinister side-burned man, watching from the distance, didn't. "What do you see when you look at her Arcan?" he goaded. "What do you see when you look at someone so far removed from your society's ideals?"

Kashif stayed quiet, not rising to the barbs.

"Does she count as a person to your kind?"

Another pass of the needle, another stitch over the wound.

"Should we tell the others what Arcans do to the physically and mentally imperfect?

Kashif made the mistake of looking up. He didn't make eye contact with the taunting man, but he saw the look in Captain Reed's eyes. And the questions springing up in the eyes of the thief. He had no answers for them. Not any that they would understand.

"Is she even worth the cost of the thread?"

Kashif finished his work. The girl was Refaid. She wasn't worth thinking about. But she was Banded, and even the Numb could serve a purpose towards an end.

12.

Sarah's fall disrupted the steady progress of the group. As the sun began to lower towards the horizon, they came upon the farming community of Tor Amon. There were only houses – no inns with offers of beds and meal, no stores that shelved supplies. Still, the farmers were a gracious lot. They produced a fair amount of food for the famished Band. The villagers only accepted a small amount of compensation at Greer's insistence. For lodging, they offered the use of a large barn for the night.

"It's a far cry from feathers," Sophie muttered to herself – or so she intended it to seem. Greer found her companion's lamenting asides were remarkably well timed for those exact moments when Greer crossed by. Sophie was doing everything in her power to subtly voice her distaste of their current situation.

The saddle had given her sores, the charitably offered supper had been too salty, the fruit had been overripe. Now she was venting on the makeshift bedding. Sophie had spent the better part of the last half-hour picking rogue pieces of straw from her blankets, as if defending her territory from an invading army. "We'll wake up with ticks, I know it."

"It's a single night," Greer reminded her. "We'll survive." She knew what Sophie wanted her to do. Given the word, Captain Reed and his men would expel some poor farming family from their home to allow her proper lodging for the night. Reed was in favor of the idea as well – citing concerns for her safety among the less reputable members of the Band. Though the prospect of a blanket over straw wasn't appealing to Greer, she wasn't going to give in.

The blonde companion pouted and flicked away another errant bit of straw. "Your father would never stoop to sleeping in a barn."

"A pity you aren't his companion." Greer hoped the retort would be enough to silence the parade of grievances for a time. She stood and surveyed the barn. Why was she so set on sleeping here tonight? She could tell Reed that she desired to stay with the rest of the Band, but that was a lie. She could tell herself that it was to irk Sophie, and that might be closer to the truth.

Honestly, Greer considered, the allure might be in the barn itself. She'd never slept in a barn before – it was completely below her station. Sophie may have unwittingly given her the answer. Maybe Greer was so keen on the idea because it was exactly what her Father wouldn't do.

Captain Reed gave her a quick gauging glance as she approached but did not break from addressing his men. He was outlining the plan for watch, detailing the rotation that would see her kept secure despite the presence of a murderer, an Arcan and a thief. Greer listened with one ear, but quickly grew bored. She didn't appear to be the only one. Sergeant Bostitch sat on a hay bale, blocky crossbow resting on his lap. His focus was entirely devoted to the Arcan across the way.

Despite the inconveniences of the Banding – which included an entire afternoon of riding side saddle – Greer had enjoyed her time with Reed's men. Though the Captain had tried to enforce a strictly professional decorum from his men, their personalities had begun to seep through the cracks. Sergeant Bostitch had a dry-humor, a quick tongue, and language entirely improper when in the company of a Lady. How Reed had squirmed at each of the Sergeant's off-colored asides! Greer had loved it.

Bostitch stirred. "Reed," he muttered darkly, and Greer saw the reason why. The Arcan was approaching. The tiny conversations throughout the barn hushed; something was happening. The Captain moved to stand between Greer and the foreigner. Bostitch moved a finger to the trigger of his crossbow.

"Bost, go check on the horses," Reed ordered. His subordinate scowled in knowing frustration and didn't argue. Corporal Neald caught his Captain's eye and accompanied Bostitch out of the barn door.

The Arcan looked at Reed and then around him, focusing on Greer. "I would speak with you." Greer did not wilt under his gaze, though it made her blood freeze. She'd never spoken to an Arcan before. She'd only seen pictures in books – pictures which portrayed them as more monster than human. In what few observations Greer had made of the man, he appeared to be culturally refined. His mannerisms and dignified behavior stood in far contrast to the villain Reed's men portrayed him to be.

"I would speak to the Lady privately," the Arcan added.

Reed shook his head. "We both know that isn't going to happen."

"I can speak for myself," Greer announced. She motioned with her hand to Reed. The Captain took a resigned breath and stepped aside. "A private audience will not be possible. Hopefully you understand why." The foreigner nodded, again managing to not steal a glance at the weapons. "The corner will be as private as arrangements will allow." Greer turned towards the area where she and Sophie's blankets were prepared. The Arcan followed.

Sophie, on seeing them approach, turned a sallow shade of white, muttered some excuse, and found somewhere else to be. As Greer reached the blankets, she became aware of how much straw she'd probably track onto Sophie's blanket. A pity, that. "Please sit down," she said, directing the Arcan to a bale of hay. Reed and his remaining men hovered at the outer edge of the bale ring.

"Thank you, Lady Cahill," the Arcan said. "I am called Kashif. I am of the Scholastad caste, a student of human physiology under the tutelage of Marooke." Greer was not sure if Kashif expected her to derive significance from the titles he had attached to his name; Greer did not think it was proper to ask. Nor was it necessary. Greer lived in a world of titles. The specific titles and accomplishments mattered little, but it grouped Kashif with all the others of the nobility who felt it necessary to bring them up. "I am in need of your assistance, and I didn't see anyone else I could go to."

"What do you need?"

"It is in our best interest to solve the Banding's riddle."

"Riddle?"

Kashif nodded. "The wizard suggested as much; that the six are strategically chosen. Tell me, have you studied the human body to any degree?" Greer shook her head. There were twenty-two specific Tenets of a Proper Lady that she'd been educated on since she'd learned to walk, but none of the dealt in heavy science.

Kashif appeared to have anticipated that response. "In my observations thus far, I find the condition of the Banding less and less mysterious. Allow me to explain. As with most things in the world, there are close parallels between the condition of the Banding and how the human body reacts to an infection. When a disease attacks, the body's response is immediate. It floods the bloodstream with agents designed to combat the sickness. When studied, we find that these agents are never constructed the same. They utilize the same basic components – individual proteins and cells – but the body organizes them in a precise manner, constructing them in a way specifically tailored to neutralize the threat. The agent is created as the perfect specimen to destroy the disease."

The Arcan's mannerisms reminded Greer of those displayed by her many self-important instructors when giving lessons. "You believe we are the agent," Greer summarized.

The foreigner nodded. "The world perceived a threat, diagnosed the danger, and created us as a Band to destroy it. We possess, within the totality of our skills, strengths and talents, everything needed to destroy our demon enemy. A perfect parallel." The Arcan smiled, his white teeth a contrast to his dark colored lips. "We are the parts, Lady Greer, but we must learn how we are to be constructed. We must determine what each of the Band will contribute, and deduce how they will aid us in defeating the demon."

"Easiest way to defeat something," interjected the side-burned man, "is to run a sword through it." The comment earned a chuckle from Reed's men. Greer hadn't been aware the murderer was listening in.

Kashif angled his body to address a wider audience, but his focus stayed with Greer. "If it were as simple as that," he disagreed, "this Band of Six would be comprised solely of skilled swordsman. It is not."

The murderer was quick with the retort. "If he's skilled enough, you only need one."

The Arcan did not respond, instead he slid closer to Greer on the hay bales. His voice dropped to a mere whisper. "You see why I come to you? He will not take this seriously. He will charge the monster, the rest of the Band following in his wake, and he will be torn to pieces. The key is the others."

Greer looked to the other corner of the barn, where the Degan thief and the two children sat. "The others?"

"They puzzle me," Kashif admitted. "A thief? Are we to steal from the creature? More likely he will be required to steal what is necessary to defeat the creature. I know nothing about the younger boy – I do not know that I have heard him speak. The little girl. She is Refaid ..."

"She is what?"

The Arcan struggled for the appropriate word. "She is incomplete."

"Say it again, Arcan," the murderer called out. "I don't think the others heard you clearly."

Kashif bent in closer, to the point that Reed looked uncomfortable. Thank Domus that Bostitch was out of the room, the crossbow would never have sat silently through the conversation. "You see why I need your help," he muttered.

"Tell us, Arcan!" the murderer egged on. "Tell us all about your boiling caste system!"

"What's a caste?" Sarah asked the thief.

The murderer rolled on. "Tell us, how many get the benefits you had versus how many are picked to be slaves!"

Kashif stood and faced the man who continued to interrupt the discussion. "That system you continue to malign follows the natural order of things. You look a hive of hundreds of bees. You look at a hill containing thousands of ants. Those systems not only exist – but they thrive. They are models of efficiency. Each insect knows his role and fulfills it to the best of his ability – to the betterment of the colony. It is the perfect system that you demean."

The murderer laughed.

"You demean it, though you live it in ignorance," the Arcan told him, then turned to address the entire barn. "You will all deny it, but you are already fixed in your castes. The nobility, the military, the servile. Fight against those labels – try it. See how far you can get. See how much effort you waste in your vain efforts. Do it – but do it after the demon is dead.

"We are a Band. We each have a role. We will each know our role – know our place. It does us no good to fight against who we are!"

--- * --- * ---

The music chamber was an undiscovered world. Her father's Chief Orchestrant was an obsessive man who strongly believed children did only one thing well – break things. As such, the chamber holding the collection of instruments was always locked – completely off-limits to "little imps".

That didn't mean Greer hadn't attempted to access the mysterious room before. Her companion, Bridgette, was remarkably clever, and the two of them often schemed up ways to get the door key off the uppity Orchestrant. The mustachioed man proved to be an opponent equal to their deviousness – as if he knew of the late-night plans they hatched to gain access to his sanctuary.

Today, however, they were being let in. The Chief Orchestrant's mustache bristled as he begrudgingly slipped the key into the lock. He wouldn't say it, but it was evident he disagreed with her father's assessment that eight years of age was old enough to start her on lessons. To be honest, Greer wasn't thrilled about the new opportunity either. While it would be interesting to begin her musical training – it was disappointing to know the room, once she was invited to be there, would never hold the same appeal.

As the door opened, Greer rushed to the center of the room and let her eyes take in everything they could. There were high-backed chairs and stands for sheets of music, arranged in a perfect semi-circle. The instruments sat high on shelves, resting on supportive braces. The brass horns burnished brightly, the polished wood of the stringed violins glowed, and in the back ...

Bridgette was already there, having rushed into the room behind her. Her honey-haired companion quickly scooped up the mallets, and was poised to attack the awaiting kettledrum. "That is not a toy!" bellowed the Orchestrant over the booming thuds Bridgette produced. Her companion managed a thunderous medley before the mustachioed musician stripped her of the mallets. Greer and Bridgette exchanged knowing smiles.

Headmistress Packer was the last to enter the room. "That is enough, Bridgette, thank you," she said simply. Bridgette curtsied and retreated back to Greer's side.

"These instruments are very expensive, Headmistress!" the Orchestrant reminded.

"The girls will be more careful, Guery," she assured, and the look she gave them made it clear she'd hold them accountable for the promise. "Would you please fetch the Lady's instrument?"

Guery waggled his mustache and pulled at his vest irritably before stalking off to one of the shelves. Greer felt a tingle of excitement in her toes. Headmistress Packer had told her she'd be receiving music lessons – but had not told her which instrument she would be learning. Greer glanced quickly around the room again, trying to guess what the Orchestrant was...

He turned, his fingers gently cradling a slender silver instrument. His face was solemn, as if he were bestowing on her a great treasure.

Except ...

The tingle in her toes died. "I don't want to learn the flute," Greer told the Headmistress. Of all of the instruments in the music chamber – she was to be given the smallest? She didn't even like how it sounded – so high-pitched and warbling. No, it was the wrong instrument for her.

"You don't?" Headmistress Packer asked. The Orchestrant snorted like he'd been personally insulted.

"No, I don't want to. I don't like it."

The Headmistress turned to look at the Orchestrant. "Alright, then. A violin perhaps ..."

"I want to learn the drums!" Greer told them. They looked fascinating – she wanted to make the booming rattles, just like Bridgette had. Or ... maybe the cymbals! She loved hearing their metallic crash during the private concertos ...

"Drums?" the Headmistress echoed in surprise. And then, she began to shake her head slowly. "No, dear, I'm very sorry. I don't think that will be possible."

Greer frowned. She didn't like being told no. "Why not?!"

It was the Orchestrant that answered. "Drums? Why, they are not an instrument for a lady!"

"Greer," the Headmistress clarified, "you know there are certain expectations of you, child. You are the daughter of a Lord Baron. You are of noble birth. A young woman of your station and prominence is expected to know how to ride a horse. She is expected to be able to cross-stitch and embroider. She is expected to be able to read – and to be versed in the New Age classics. And she is expected to be able to play an instrument, Greer. But not any instrument! You wouldn't see a high-class Lady puffing her cheeks out on a bugle! It wouldn't be proper if she were to attempt to play an upright bass! No, a woman's instrument is a reflection of her femininity. Like the flute. Or the violin. Or maybe the harp?"

"I should be able to play what I want to play!" Greer protested.

The standoff continued – the wizened Headmistresses on one side and the impudent nobleman's daughter on the other. Finally, the Headmistress held out her hand towards the Orchestrant, who obliged her by passing over the slender flute. "Very well, then, Lady Greer. I suggest you take your thoughts to your father. We should see if he has an opinion on the matter. Agreed?"

Greer nodded. "Agreed." Headmistress Packer dismissed them from the room, and Greer and Bridgette dashed away. With a giggle, Bridgette ran her fingers along the harp as she went by – earning another maddening shriek from the Orchestrant.

They spent the rest of the afternoon planning her argument. She and Bridgette walked the grounds of her father's estate, coming up with reasons why drums were superior to flutes. At the sunning rock, she had stood atop and delivered her appeal while Bridgette – doing her best impression of the Lord Baron – listened with a frown on her face. In as deep a voice an eight year old girl could muster, Bridgette pronounced their case as irrefutable. Confidence brimming, they went inside to wash and dress for dinner.

When they arrived at the dining hall, dinner had already begun. Her father and mother sat at either end of the table, with her brother and his companion on one side, and seats waiting for her and Bridgette on the other. Greer was anxious to launch into her appeal – when she became aware of the deathly somber mood in the hall. No one was touching the bowls of steaming soup that sat before them. Her father sat calmly, but Greer could feel the agitation rolling off him in great waves.

Without a word, Greer took her seat. No sooner had she done so then the butler scurried into the room, with the pale-faced Head Cook in tow. "As you requested, Lord Baron," the butler said with a bow.

The butler might as well have not existed; her father's attention was reserved for the heavy-set woman with the white apron. The Head Cook squirmed under the unwanted focus.

"My Lord?" the cook mumbled softly.

Her father pawed his bowl of soup towards the woman. "What is this?" he asked sharply.

"Soup, my Lord."

"Soup?"

"Tarragon soup," was the clarification.

Her father slowly lifted and turned the soup spoon, letting the broth trickle back into the bowl below. "Tell me, cook, did you follow the recipe for tarragon soup?"

The cook quivered. "My Lord ... "

"Did you follow the recipe!" the Lord Baron demanded.

The cook shook her head. "I'm sorry, Lord Baron. Truly sorry. I thought we had enough cream on reserve – I did! It must have spoiled during the night. I ... I used what we had – and tried to fill the rest with milk and a bit of butter ... "

Her father set his spoon down on the table. "Get this off my table," he ordered the butler, then refocused on the cook. "You should know this better than anyone – there are recipes for a reason. There is a right way to do things. If you tell me you are serving me tarragon soup, I want it to taste exactly like I know tarragon soup should taste!" His eyes swept out, encompassing those he shared the table with, but Greer felt like he was looking only at her. "If it is not put together the right way, it isn't befitting my time, attention, or table."

Shamefully, the cook and butler cleared the soup bowls from the table. The rest of the courses of the meal were brought in and eaten in complete silence. When finished, Greer excused herself and Bridgette from the dining hall.

Headmistress Packer found her in her bedroom. The gray-haired woman was carrying the silver instrument. "I take it that you spoke to your father, Lady Greer?" the woman asked.

Silently, the eight-year old nobleman's daughter crossed the room and took the flute.

--- * --- * ---

"You have to meet the expectation of your title," Greer said to herself.

"Exactly, Lady Greer," the Arcan nodded. It awoke her from her memories – she'd not meant for anyone to hear her speak. Kashif was smiling at her. "I knew you would understand."

She looked at the Arcan. He'd asked for help figuring out the others. Others – not including himself. Not including her. "And my role in this?" she asked.

"You are no doubt here to support the Band financially, as none of the others appear capable of doing so on any large scale. I assume your station brings with it countless acquaintances among the most influential people on this island; a boon which cannot be overlooked. Your presence has already brought additional soldiers to our ranks …"

Each comment was meant as a compliment, but Greer felt each hit her like a slap in the face. If Kashif was right – and she could not argue against him – then she didn't matter. In the grand scope of things, it hadn't need to be her with this miserable Band. It could have just as easily been any other noble.

They all followed the exact same recipe.

"There is nothing to understand, Arcan," the murderer challenged. "You want to assign people to roles? Categorize them? Fine! Do you know what I see when I look at our precisely chosen Band? I see five other people who have never had need to draw a weapon. I see five other people who don't know the first thing about ending a life." The sideburns became the framework for a devilish grin. "Have you ever taken a life, Arcan?"

He waited. Kashif did not respond.

"You go ahead and solve your riddle," the murderer spat as he angled towards the barn door. "And the Lady can be our coin purse. You can all do whatever it is you think you're here to do. But in the end, when it comes to facing that thing, there will be no mystery as to what will happen. I'm going to kill it. I'll kill the demon – because none of the rest of you is capable."

The chill that coursed through Greer's skin did not leave, even after Billick exited the barn. There was cruelness to his countenance; and he'd soaked the entire atmosphere with it. If anyone else was of a mood to continue talking, their faces didn't show it. "The others may confide in you," Kashif muttered to her as he stood. "Please see what you can discover." The Arcan picked his way between the hay bales back towards his corner of the barn. His exit prompted the unfortunate return of Sophie.

"These men frighten me, Lady Greer," the companion over-emoted. "The murderer especially."

"He wants to be feared," she answered bluntly.

"Certainly, Lady. Surely, though, it would be wise to find different lodging – perhaps one of the pleasant looking houses just up the road …"

"Sophie …"

"Certainly it would be of no trouble to Captain Reed …"

Greer was tired, and Sophie was only adding to her aggravation. "Reed and his men will stand watch while we sleep, Sophie."

Her companion nodded. "Oh, yes. I am sure they will … but knowing that murderer will be coming back? That he could be in the same room? I dare say that I won't sleep a wink."

"Then I'll inform Reed that you'll be capable of keeping one of the watches," Greer hissed, and Sophie's mouth closed into a petulant frown. "If you don't think you can condescend to sleep on the straw, then by all means, I absolve you from the responsibility of sleeping!"

Chastened but as of yet unconvinced, the companion sank to the blanket and began making a show of spreading it out and dusting off the bits of straw. Greer watched Sophie for only a slight moment before stooping to do the same. The more they beat on the blankets, the more Greer wondered if they were channeling their anger at each other into each exaggerated blow.

"I don't understand why you're doing this, Lady Greer," Sophie murmured as she lay down. "You don't belong out here, chasing monsters!"

In truth, Sophie was correct. But then again, Greer didn't know where she rightfully belonged.

13.

Martin might not have realized anything was wrong had it not been for Red. The aged hound had once been the stalwart patroller of their property – chasing off rabbits and visitors alike. But Red's joints weren't what they used to be, and the old dog devoted most of his time to the broad swaths of sunshine he enjoyed sleeping in. Red hadn't met them at the fence for years now. Seeing him, fidgeting with agitation behind the latched gate, quivering tail tucked firmly between his legs ...

"Poor Judith isn't going to say anything – not in front of her husband – but you can tell she's worried. It's been five months since their mule kicked Bertrand and his leg still won't support his weight. He's too proud to ask for help – but their apple orchard isn't going to harvest itself ..."

Martin put a weathered hand firmly on his wife's shoulder, a gesture that cut her observations short. Elsa was so perturbed with their neighbor's plight that she had not sensed the troubled state shared by her husband and the hound. Elsa was quick though; and her face lost a bit of its coloring as her eyes went to Martin. "What is it?"

"Don't know," he told her as he lifted the latch on the gate and slipped inside. She didn't attempt to follow him, which was a blessing. Red whimpered as the latch clicked shut and sulked at Martin's feet in a decidedly unhappy manner. The loyal dog looked longingly towards Elsa on the other side of the fence. Martin steeled his courage. "If I call out trouble, get yourself back to the Millers."

Elsa nodded, eyes brimming with concern. He smiled for her – a subtle affair that probably barely escaped the wrinkles of his face – and turned to face the house. Martin didn't consider himself a brave man. He certainly wasn't a fighter – he'd been too old when the Baron's had conscripted men for the Arcan War. He was and always had been a man of the earth – a farmer. A man of sweat – not of blood. But neither was he a coward. He'd put forty years of daily labor into this plot of land and there wasn't a man or beast on Tollia he'd let chase him off it!

Walking swiftly, keeping his eyes alert for danger, Martin maneuvered to the woodpile under the eaves of the large shed. With a tug, he freed the long-handled axe from the thick log it was embedded in. Martin felt reassured holding the tool. He was not a fighter, but there was nothing unfamiliar about the feel of the long handle against the skin of his calloused palms.

All signs from Red indicated the intruder was in the house. While the two-story structure was nothing when compared to the finer homes in Hollingston, it was the largest house on any of the homesteads in the Alben valley. Martin had constructed it himself. As he pressed towards it, Red grew increasingly anxious. He danced at the farmer's feet –warning of danger. Ten stride from the porch, the old hound's loyalty gave way to his fear. With a yelp he bounded back towards the fence and the waiting Elsa. Martin readjusted his grip on the axe and continued forward.

The farmer padded up the steps of the porch, expertly avoiding the warped spots that groaned under any amount of weight. With his left hand, Martin tested the door latch – and found it wouldn't budge. It was locked – just as they'd left it two hours before.

An unexpected movement to his left nearly startled him from his skin – but the curtain tossing gently in the sunset breeze presented no danger. It did, however, merit a closer look. Martin edged along the porch to the window and ran a finger along the casing. Thin, deep scratches marred the wood around the area of the window latch – clear evidence of how the intruder had entered their home.

Cautiously, Martin parted the wafting curtain and looked inside. While Elsa would have been a hundred times more adept at spotting anything out of place in her sitting room, Martin's quick perusal yielded nothing noteworthy. Nothing … except for the set of small, dirty footprints that disappeared around the corner and into the kitchen.

Martin muttered a quick word of gratitude to Merciful Domus and backed his way to the door. The footprints bespoke a small person – a child. A barefoot child! Hardly a threat to a grown, work-weathered man with an axe! A child had broken into their home by picking the locking latch on the window. Probably some orphaned waif, desperate for a meal.

The door lock clicked as Martin turned the key and the door swung open. Nothing but a child … and yet, Red was so visibly upset …

Martin's boots would not be silent against the floorboards as he crept through the sitting room towards Elsa's kitchen. He raised his axe to a ready position as he entered the kitchen, which was awash in the blazing colors of the setting sun. His ears heard her before his eyes found her. Her delicate, simpering sob gave away her hiding place in the corner behind the table. She sat, surrounded by the remaining crumbs of the loaf of wheat bread Elsa had left to cool. The tiny girl – who could be no more than eight years of age – looked up at him with sad, pleading eyes.

Martin relaxed his grip on the unneeded axe. "Elsa!" he called out with a firm, calm voice. "Elsa, dear, you'll want to see this!"

*   *   *   *   *

With effort, Elsa finally did manage to coax the girl from the corner of the kitchen floor she'd tucked herself into. His wife was well-versed in talking to children – having raised four within these very walls. Martin watched the girl's trepidation began to dissolve under the persistent, loving tone in his wife's voice. Timidly, their little intruder finally worked up the courage to reach for Elsa's outstretched hand.

"My dear, you are filthy!" cried Elsa as she drew the girl towards her. Martin, watching it all from near the stairs, saw what his wife was referring to. The girl's fingers were smudged with dirty smears, her nails encrusted with caked soil. Other bits of earthy debris fell to the floor as Elsa ran fingers tenderly through the girl's tangled brown hair. "We must get you in a bath!"

"Elsa?" Martin asked as his wife set a kettle to heat over the hearth.

"Fetch the wash basin, Martin," she directed.

Elsa's motherly instincts were in full control, but there was a conversation that needed to be had. "We should find out who she is …"

She responded with a motherly smile. "Hush, dear. She'll have time to answer questions when she is clean and comfortable. The basin, dear?" Martin perceived it was an argument he would not win. After fetching the wooden tub, he waited in his favorite chair in the sitting room as he listened to his wife sponge-bathe the young girl in the kitchen. Who was the girl? Thievery was not uncommon among destitute and abandoned children, but those usually plied their craft within the bigger cities where the crowds made it easier for a small person to disappear. Hollingston lay just across the hills, but Martin was hard-pressed to believe the frail girl had navigated the forested trails.

"See there?" Elsa stood behind the girl, hands on each shoulder. "Isn't she beautiful? All she needed was a good scrubbing off!" The girl, hair damp and tangled, wore one of the sky-blue nightgowns long outgrown by their youngest daughter. She stood stiffly, warily tense, and remained speechless. She seemed instinctively distrusting, having an expectation of endangerment, ever-ready to dart away. What kind of life had this poor girl known?

"Go have a seat in the sitting room, dearie," Elsa instructed the girl. "I'll fetch the comb and we'll work the knots out of your beautiful hair." The girl walked on light feet through the room, keeping a watchful eye on Martin. The farmer tried to smile, but knew it wouldn't lessen her cautiousness. Her first impression of him had him wielding a wood-axe. Martin stood and crossed the room to the stairs.

Elsa was only moments behind, and drew close to her husband as she passed. "She's had it rough, Martin," she whispered in a voice that wouldn't carry into the sitting room. "Poor thing is nothing but skin and bones. And there's a mean looking open sore on the back of her neck. It looks infected."

"We can fetch the physician," Martin offered. "But we need to figure out who she is and where she is from."

She cast him a withering look. "Is that really of the upmost importance? Whatever life she led before she picked the lock at our window was obviously a terrible one. Whoever is responsible for her care – if there is anyone looking out for her – has forfeited their rights to her as far as I'm concerned." Martin sighed. As he'd expected, his wife had already emotionally adopted the girl. "In any case, it's too late tonight. We've a bed for her upstairs – we can sort the rest out in the morning."

Deciding the conversation was over, Elsa moved past him into the sitting room. "I'll just sit here to the side of you, dear. We'll get those snarls out of your hair before bed." From the stairs, Martin watched his wife as she stroked the girl's hair with the fine-toothed comb. The girl sat obediently through the process, rigid as a board.

Elsa was right – there was no use in pursuing things until the morning. They could provide the poor girl with a warm bed, a nice meal and a safe roof. Martin had the distinct impression the girl hadn't enjoyed all three of those things in the same night very often. They'd keep the girl for the night. Still, Martin saw no need to wait with his questions.

"Do you speak?" he asked the girl. Elsa paused her combing long enough to level a disapproving stare in his direction. The girl remained silent.

"She'll speak to us when she's ready, Martin," Elsa declared with a reassuring pat on the girl's shoulder.

"I've no plans to ask her difficult questions, El. It wouldn't hurt for us to know who she is if she's going to spend the night. A name?"

"Martin ..." Elsa warned.

"Pennie." The girl's voice was high and reedy. The single word caused both the farmer and his wife to fall silent.

"Pennie, dear?" Elsa prompted.

The girl looked directly at Martin. "My name ... Pennie," she said timidly.

Martin nodded and smiled. The girl understood they meant her no harm. "We are glad to welcome you into our home, Pennie. You will be our guest tonight. You are safe. We'll take good care of you, so you don't need to worry. But Pennie, I can't help but wonder if you've run away from home. Perhaps you've a mother or father that might be worried about you ..."

"I don't have a mother ... or a father." She said it without sadness, as if stating just another fact, which made the simple declaration even more heart-breaking.

"I see," said Martin. "On your own then?"

The girl nodded.

"Pennie ...," he paused, deliberating how to ask the next question. "Has someone been ... hurting you?"

She nodded again.

Martin looked to his wife, her expression set. "Well, like I said, Pennie. You're safe here. No one is going to hurt you, alright? Don't you worry ..."

With a startle, the girl flinched and jumped from the couch. She rounded on Elsa like a wounded animal. His wife retracted her hands and looked apologetically towards the wary little girl. "I'm sorry, Pennie. You've got a large sore on the back of your neck that looks awful my dear. I'm sorry if I hurt you ..."

Pennie raised a hand to her neck, but Martin noted that she didn't touch anything towards the back of her head. The wound, he reasoned, must be terribly tender.

"I shouldn't stay," the girl said.

"But dear, it's already so late! It's dark out! We've got a comfortable bed upstairs; you'll be safe for the night ..."

"Not safe." Penny said the words under her breath, so low that Martin barely heard them. What had the poor girl been through? The farmer could see the debate warring inside her – of whether to stay or go. Of whether to trust or not. Penny raised timid eyes to Elsa. "I'm ... I am tired," Pennie said.

Elsa nodded immediately. "I'm sure you are. Sure you are." She stood slowly, disarmingly. "How about I show you to that bed, hmm?" The girl nodded and crept her way around Martin to the stairs. Elsa followed behind her – but Pennie kept a constant, safe distance between them. From the top of the stairs, Martin saw his wife give him a sorrowful stare, before turning to assist the girl.

Martin sighed. It was all adding up. Desperate girl. Under-fed. No shoes. The dirt on her hands, hair and clothing. Most likely abused. Most likely a run-away. Poor thing. There would be no rush to find who she was running away from. No rush to return her to the awful situation she must have endured. Martin could see it in his wife's eyes. Their youngest had married and moved away four years previously. It had been a long time since Elsa had had a child to care for in the home. She would find plenty of reasons for Pennie to make an extended stay – if only to fill that void.

His eyes were drawn to the window, to the latch Pennie had sprung to break into their home. Martin fingered the locking-bolt, curious if he himself would have known how to disable it from the outside. Strange girl. Strange circumstances. He heard a whimper outside and added another item to his mental list. Strange behaving dog.

The farmer opened the door. "Red!" he yelled. "Red, you and I both know that you'd rather sleep by the hearth tonight!" Martin held the door, but Red didn't

come. He heard the dog bay mournfully from the direction he'd last seen him –
by the gate in the fence.

"Strange dog, indeed," Martin muttered, and he shut the door.

*   *   *   *   *

Marooke stood back, hands clasped behind his back, and gave orders to Djemal.
He would have much preferred Kashif handle the autopsy of the gravedigger.
He'd mentored Kashif nine years more than Djemal. While the latter was fully
qualified at handling the measurements being taken, Djemal lacked Kashif's gift
of insight and natural creativity.

The apprentice was currently taking in-depth measurements for each of the
wounds on the gravedigger's body. Aside from the multitude of deep claw
marks, their examination had uncovered multiple puncture wounds along the
body's main trunk. "And?" Marooke asked, trying to hide his impatience as
Djemal recorded the figures into his ledger.

"You were correct," Djemal announced, not looking up from his book of
detailed notes. "Each of the puncture wounds is the correct depth to have tapped
into the man's main arteries." Marooke nodded. There had been no other
explanation for the utter lack of blood in the body. Something had drained the
gravedigger almost completely. The only explanation, Marooke had
conjectured, was that the creature had tapped each of the primary arteries in the
system. What purpose did it have for the blood?

Marooke nodded, and resisted the urge to pick up the instruments himself. If
this finding represented what he thought it did, he did not trust that he'd read the
details of the autopsy correctly. He could not risk his hopes biasing what he was
seeing. He sat down in his chair and pondered.

"Well?" To his credit, Lord Baron Northing had been uncommonly quiet for the
last hour. He'd stayed far enough back from the body to not interfere. Marooke
had almost forgotten the man was present – if it was possible to forget such a
commanding presence.

"We have gleaned what we can from these remains," Marooke answered. "I should prefer to keep them stowed away in an ice cellar if you can spare the room, just in case we need to examine it further in the future."

"What did you find?"

"Encouraging results," Marooke answers. "But we will need additional proof before my theories can become anything more than speculation. We must hope the creature strikes again." The three of them stared at the mangled corpse on the table, aware of how morbid the last statement truly was. "Additional victims will give us additional data. And it will lead us to eventually track and capture the creature itself."

"I will send men in every direction. Rice has as well-informed network of spies. A creature large enough to do that will surely draw attention."

Marooke flipped through the pages of an older ledger – one from the previous experiment. "The constables never found the body of a child?"

Northing shook his head. "Just the cloth bag."

Marooke felt the excitement welling inside of him. He kept his face passive. "Tell your men they are looking for a young girl. Ten years old."

The Lord Baron smiled wryly. "A girl?"

Marooke found what he was looking for and closed the ledger. "A girl named Pennie."

14.

The insistent rapping on the door awoke the wizard Algius from the meditative furlough his mind had departed on. The twist of dried marrowroot continued to smolder – sending up a thin column of pure-white smoke. There was nothing special about marrowroot. It was not a hallucinatory agent – not like some of the other wizards burned. Nor was it particularly fragrant, like the incense candles others used. Any strong smell, Algius found, served only as a distraction and hindrance to the meditative state he sought.

No, there was something particular about the marrowroot – something engrossing and at the same time supremely simple in the snaking thread of smoke it sent skyward.

The knocking sounded again, and Algius turned a tired eye to the door. "Yes, what business?"

The apprentice opened the door just enough to allow himself to slip through the opening – and smoothly closed it behind himself. Hartley bowed his head slightly in respect – showing a hairline that was just starting to recede. Only boys and teenagers adopted the title of apprentice outside the gated walls of the Wizard's College, but inside it was not so.

Hartley was in his mid-thirties. He'd earned the red-dyed knotted cord he wore around his shoulders nearly seven years ago. Before that he'd worn the unknotted cord of the Pupil. Hartley may have been introduced to the College as an adult, but he advanced at his own speed. In wizardom – the achievement of rank was not looked upon as a race or as a contest. Everyone progressed as quickly – or as slowly – as they themselves wished.

It was no secret, the further one progressed through the Circles, the less aggressively he went seeking the next.

Algius was a Wizard of the Sixth Circle, a Wearer of the Amethyst Stole, one of only three known living wizards to have seen what the Sixth Circle had to reveal. There was a Seventh Circle. But after the agony of the Sixth – agony that still caused him to weep even after three decades – he had no desire to venture into it.

Hartley coughed softly into his hand. "Master Algius?"

He'd let his mind wander off again. Algius frowned. The hour was late …

"Master Algius...?" repeated Hartley, a little more forcefully.

"I know he is still here," the wizard said, preempting what would undoubtedly lead to the apprentice's report. "I would hope that you would only choose to disturb me with news that is actually news."

Hartley grit his teeth, and for a moment the wizard allowed himself to feel pity. He had, after all, placed Hartley in the unenviable position of being the barrier standing against Lord Baron Cahill. It was like asking a wooden fence to impede the onslaught of hurricane-force winds. Hartley had come twice in the last two hours; evidence the apprentice was fast losing the battle to the imposing nobleman.

Algius had known Hartley would eventually fail. The only unknown was how much time exactly the apprentice would be able to buy him.

"He's not going to leave, Master," Hartley stated. "He insists on speaking with you, and Master, believe me, you'll not be able to wait him out." The apprentice shifted his weight on his feet nervously. "Surely it cannot be wise to make an enemy of a Lord Baron …"

The wizard couldn't have agreed more. Surely, it wasn't wise. It was very ill-advised. But prudence, in this instance, was completely beside the point. Algius looked at Hartley – and wondered if the battered fence might be able to hold out for even an hour longer. "You may tell him – again – that I shall be happy to see him when I have ample time to do so."

It was not the answer the apprentice had hoped for. "Master …"

"Is there anything else, *Apprentice* Hartley?" Algius over spoke him. He didn't need to hear Hartley's attempts to elicit some different resolution. The clipped tone he'd used in addressing Hartley by his title had hopefully reminded the man it wasn't his place to argue.

Hartley grimaced, but bowed his head again as he let himself out the door. As soon as the door opened a crack, however, Hartley was thrown aside. Two of Cahill's soldiers muscled into the room, flanked by the scowling Lord Baron. If Cahill had moved to surprise the wizard, he'd failed. Algius had known this moment was coming, sooner or later. Since he wasn't going to ever invite the Lord Baron in – and since he knew that the Lord Baron wouldn't leave on his own accord – Cahill barging into the room had been inevitable.

Cahill expected a response. What, shock? Outrage? Algius said nothing. He simply leaned back and stared at the nobleman through the thin wisps of marrowroot smoke. The Lord Baron took measure of the situation, and when he finally spoke, it was with careful control.

"We need to talk."

Algius smirked. "Tell me, Lord Baron: would you oblige someone their request had they just interrupted you in your private study?"

Cahill didn't flinch. "Do you leave all your guests waiting for endless hours in your lobby, Wizard?"

The marrowroot smoke curled ponderously through the air. "Only those that I did not invite into my home."

"I'm not one apt to wait for invitations." One of Cahill's men pulled a chair over for the Lord Baron to sit in – positioned in a place where the two men would be forced to stare at each other. Cahill took his seat without ever breaking eye contact. "You know why I'm here," he said. It wasn't a question.

"Yes, I do."

"Then you know I won't be denied."

"Yes, I know that as well."

Cahill's eyes flashed with a moment of anger. "My daughter's life is hanging in the balance – and yet you persist in avoiding me – in playing games. Why?"

Algius leaned forward. "Do you remember the man I rode with? The father of the little girl? I'm sure you do. There is a man – like yourself – who is unsure about how to cope with the loss of a daughter. She has been taken from him for reasons he cannot understand – but it happened nonetheless. But unlike yourself, that man is sleeping in his own bed tonight. I do not doubt that he mourns his loss – and will continue to mourn. But he is at home – where he should be. He understands little – but he understands that there is nothing he can do about the matter.

"You, on the other hand, are here. In my study. Demanding we talk. Why? Because you don't like knowing there is nothing you can do for your daughter. You don't like not being able to bend circumstances to your will. You are here because you will try to do something about the matter, Lord Baron – and I fear. I fear greatly that you will succeed in nothing but interfering with the chosen Band of Six."

"I will do more harm than help," Cahill restated.

"Yes."

"Because I don't 'understand'."

"Yes."

The Lord Baron studied him, eyes relentless in their intense stare. "I can accept that," he said at last. The words would have surprised the wizard …if that was the extent of the Lord Baron's reply. Algius knew better. He knew men like Cahill better. "You say I don't understand – fine, I don't. This Banding is magic – that's your realm of expertise, not mine. I may not understand, Wizard, and possibly you might not understand. So you claim. But you would have me believe that such is the end of the matter. In that regard, I know you are wrong."

"Am I?"

Cahill smiled. A knowing smile. "You are a Wizard of the Sixth Circle."

"So states my stole."

"That makes you one of the most powerful wizards in Tollia." Algius divined where the Lord Baron was leading with this, but Cahill continued over his attempts to interject. "One of the most powerful – and yet you return to your College. Lock yourself in your study. To what? Stare at smoke? Is that the way you choose to utilize your great power?"

It was the greatest misunderstanding non-wizards had about wizarding. Was he as powerful as Cahill claimed? Yes. His journey through the Sixth Circle had revealed to him magic that made the wisdom of the Fifth Circle seem paltry by comparison. But there had been more. With the immense power had come an equal burden of knowledge. Algius knew exactly what he was capable of doing – but he also fully comprehended the consequences attached to such actions. It was what their Order referred to as the Wizard's Balance. Those that understood magic the best, by choice, utilized it the least.

It was more than just a healthy respect. He and the two other Wearers' of the Amethyst Stole lived in dread of what they were capable of doing.

"You have great power." Cahill held out a hand, and one of his men filled it with a coin purse. The nobleman flipped it casually onto the table. The velvet fabric strained at the load of coins it held. "Release my daughter from the Banding."

Algius chuckled in bemusement. "Is that all?"

"Name your price," Cahill challenged.

"Keep your coin," he answering, stifling his laugh. "You'll not find a wizard in Tollia or anywhere who can undo the Banding magic."

Cahill remained undeterred. "Then allow me to hire you."

This idea was only slightly less ludicrous than the first. "Hire me?"

"To go after the demon. To kill it. I can't think of anyone more capable."

Algius never let his eyes drift to the coin purse. "I must decline."

The Lord Baron did not react visibly to the rejection – but then, he seldom reacted to anything at all. He only sat, observed – and calculated. "Perhaps you should reconsider …" he suggested. An overt threat clung to the suggestion.

"The answer is no," he answered plainly. It was an unalterable truth – those who try to solve problems by magic only end up creating more harrowing problems.

"Think, Wizard," Cahill pressed. "It is obvious! You should be the one hunting the creature. It should be a wizard. It should be someone endowed with great power. If that demon really has escaped from Oblivion, it needs to be dealt with by someone that can call down the Holy wrath of Domus - *not* by a Band of untrained children!"

Algius let his voice grow serious. "You honestly believe you know better?"

He could see it in the Lord Baron's eyes. He was arrogant enough to believe he did. The man redirected the line of questions, refocusing the attack on Algius. "Are you afraid of it, Wizard? Does the creature frighten you?"

"That is entirely beside the point."

Cahill pushed. "Does it frighten you?"

"I do not know whether to fear it or not," Algius answered. It was the truth. He didn't know what the evil creature was – what it could do – how it could be defeated. He simply didn't know. Frankly, he'd been pondering too many other questions about the demon to even begin considering if he should fear it or not. "It doesn't matter."

"It doesn't, now?"

"No, it doesn't," reiterated the wizard. "Because I, Lord Baron, was not Banded. There were six chosen – six with the specific abilities necessary to defeat the creature. Among those six, there were no wizards. Not one. What does that mean exactly? I don't know. But I know enough about the Banding to

95

know it doesn't make mistakes. If I was meant to confront that thing, the skin on my arm would be marked with the Band."

Cahill sat back, his mood deathly somber. "You," Algius pointed out, "don't have a Band around your arm either, Lord Baron. This is not a fight either one of us are meant to participate in." He leaned in. "Let the Band complete their task. Let your daughter fulfill her purpose."

"I know the statistics," Cahill answered, voice icing over. "On average only half the Band survives. You expect me to sit back while my daughter's life is in jeopardy? Should I just wait and hope she's one of the lucky ones?"

So the Baron knew the survival rate. It was something he'd specifically left out when he'd addressed the Band. "I plead with you, Lord Cahill. For your sake – don't meddle in affairs that are not your own."

The Lord Baron stood. "If your magic Banding didn't want me involved, it should have never taken my daughter."

Algius sighed. He'd not expected any different an outcome. It did not ease the disappointment.

The nobleman scooped the coin purse from the table. "I can see why you would be reluctant to fight. I can. You feel safe and secure, here within the gates of your College, surrounded by others of your Order. You've even managed to convince yourself that you have no responsibility in the matter – pawning that off to those that have been mysteriously Banded by the very magic you wizards claim to control. You believe that you can sit, and meditate, and wait – until the demon has been dealt with by lesser men. After all, the creature isn't waiting at your doorstep, right?

"Understand this wizard. If anything – anything! – happens to my Greer … If my daughter comes back marred in any manner, know this: I will come for you. You think you can wait out problems within these gates – I will show you that you cannot. You think you are safe surrounded by your brethren – I will bring men and swords and we will see how safe you really are. You think to hide? I promise you, Wizard, when I bring my wrath, you will long to have that creature coming after you instead of me!"

He stalked from the room, his two guards following in tow. With their exit, the small study suddenly felt very spacious. Algius peered up to the only other person still in the room.

Hartley was staring after the departed Lord Baron. His eyes spoke volumes.

A knot of disappointment rose in the old wizard's heart. "You know better ..." The apprentice shifted his eyes timidly back to the wizard, and then swiftly looked back towards the door. "I've taught you better. No amount of coin could make his proposal worth it, Hartley."

Without a word – without being able to meet his eyes – Hartley took two unsure steps towards the door, and then dashed out in a hurry. Algius frowned. He felt the tingle of things to come, the whisper of prophecy in his bones. "This," he told the marrowroot smoke, "can only end in death."

15.

When morning came, Dom wondered how much he'd really slept. The coat had provided a double bonus of keeping him warm and shielding his skin from the stubbly straw. He had been tired – but not as exhausted as he should have been. Not after the night he'd had before. Despite the fatigue, sleep had been fleeting. He'd dreamt of the creature – the faceless demon. He'd dreamt of it coming into the barn and ripping the soldiers and the others to bloody ribbons. He'd dreamt it had killed them all – every one – all except for him. And it'd sat, striping flesh from the dead bodies, laughing.

Laughing, and in a familiar voice asking, "Tell me, boy, what do you see?"

He'd spent the night, huddled in his over-sized coat, trying to avoid dreaming. Not because of the creature, not because of the carnage he'd imagined. But because of the familiar voice.

He startled awake at the sound of talking. The barn was brightening with the first rays of morning. He must have dozed off, curled up as he was. His hand hurt, and he opened his tight grasp to reveal his treasured pewter chain. The twin-circled emblem it bore had pressed itself onto the skin of his palm.

"What's that there?"

The question startled Dom, and he promptly shoved the necklace back into the coat's deep pocket. He didn't look up, but he could sense how close the thief was and the proximity made him terribly uncomfortable. He'd known this moment was coming – eventually. He'd overheard Sarah telling Ethiere about him during their journey here; he knew it was only a matter of time before the thief tried to talk to him. Dom began to panic. Of all people, he'd wanted to keep the necklace a secret from Ethiere. He was, after all, a thief …

"Sarah told me you don't talk too much," Ethiere continued. Uninvited, he took a seat on the closest bale of straw. There was an overt gap in the conversation – perhaps the thief was testing Sarah's observation. "How did you sleep?" Again silence. "You don't look any worse than the rest of us, I suppose. Sarah slept well though, really well. Apparently her Numbness blocks out the discomfort of straw bales."

It wasn't like yesterday with Sarah. The girl had babbled – on and on. She'd talked and she hadn't minded that he didn't participate at all. But Ethiere, he was waiting for responses. Dom could sense him watching for responses.

"How are your wrists?" Ethiere asked. From the corner of his eye, Dom could see that the thief was absently rubbing his own wrist as he asked. "Still hurt?" They did, but Dom wasn't about to say so. "You know, maybe we could get the Arcan to look at it for you. I didn't understand a lot of what he says he knows about, but he seems to have patched Sarah up well. Maybe he has something for wrists? His pack is awfully large …" The thief trailed off, almost wistfully.

It seemed as inevitable as the dawn: Ethiere would raid Kashif's pack.

Hand still inside the coat pocket, Dom grasped the pewter chain tightly.

"Those wrists – am I wrong in guessing that happened the night we were Banded? They look fresh enough." Dom slid his wrists deeper into the coat. "I know a lot of kids who come from situations …" Dom tensed and the Degan youth trailed off. "If you want to talk …"

"So what's your story, then?" Dom felt a bubble of frustration gather inside of him. Why all the questions? Why wouldn't the thief just leave him alone? "The Arcan thinks we're all pieces in some elaborate blacksmith puzzle, and I wager you're the piece that will stump him the longest. He'll not be prying any information out of you, that's for certain."

Ethiere smiled. "I've been around enough boys like you to know you have to be careful around the really quiet ones. Those are the ones who will surprise you, every time. Rest assured, I'm going to keep my eye on you. Once I learn your secret, I'm sure we'll find a way to put it to fantastic use!"

--- * --- * ---

There was only darkness in the small, windowless room. Unvarying, blanketing darkness. There had been voices – some time ago, how long Dom could not tell. His father. And his mother. Fighting. Or rather his father fighting, while his mother cowered and pled. He'd been able to hear them through the floorboards, but not anymore. Not for a while. Now, the only sound that invaded the hush was of ropes straining against the frame of the bed as he desperately fought to free himself.

There was only darkness – and pain. It had come on him so quickly, so spontaneously. It had come and it had never left. It had grown – swelling to agonizing proportions. Dom had never experienced such pain before. Only once had he heard described a pain as prolific as what he felt tearing its way through his core.

The Pain of the Irredeemable.

The Deacons taught with clarity: those who willfully and spitefully moved to thwart the will of Merciful Domus would, at death, be thrust into the gaping maw of Oblivion. There, they would suffer as only one forsaken by Domus could suffer, as their human soul was melted down and absorbed by the swathing river of pure vileness.

He'd wept at the onset of the pain – at his realization of what it meant.

He knew exactly why Merciful Domus was turning his back on him.

The thoughts flashing in his mind had confirmed it. He had to leave. He had to get out. The message was so absolute, so clear. Unless he left his current situation his soul was forfeit.

Dom had tried to leave. He had no desire to wear the chains of Oblivion.

Instead, he found himself bound by the ropes of his father.

"He's suffering," his mother had pled. "Can't you see? He's suffering!"

"He's not leaving," his father had answered. "Do you hear me?"

"Merciful Domus, he's your son!"

"You know what will happen if he's freed. You know he'll run. Is that what you want?" His father's voice had been angry. Loud and challenging. He'd been drunk – or at least drinking his way closer to that status. "You want another

son to leave? To not come back? Is that what you want?" He could hear his mother sobbing. "You want another son to run off into the night? You want another lost boy to plead to your Domus for, woman?"

"He's burning ... with a fever ..."

His father had spoken with unfeeling resoluteness. "He'll not be leaving." The next words had said all that needed to be said. "You know what he can do..." That was really what this was all about. Dom didn't try to pretend otherwise. This wasn't about Joshua leaving in the middle of the night. This wasn't about fearing the loss of a second son. This was about Dom's ability.

His father was only just beginning to explore the dishonest ways to use it.

To use him.

The memory renewed the anger in Dom's heart and he flexed again against the binding ropes. He arched his back in revulsion – of his father – of himself. Of what his father was making him do. Of what he was becoming ...

The handle to the door shook lightly and the door opened. Instinctively, Dom cringed. When his father was drunk ... A lantern swept into the room, the tiny dot of flame hanging in the air like a firefly. The soft orange glow only barely highlighted the delicate features of his mother's face as she bent over the bed. "Oh, my child ..."

"Mother? ..." His voice broke – cracked and dry and the rigidness in his body softened. She rested a hand gently on his forehead.

"It will be alright, Dominic," she assured. The lantern flame caught the metal of the knife briefly and he felt her attacking the ropes that held him. All the while she whispered soothingly to him. "It will all be alright." As the ropes fell free, Dom's mind was filled with the need to run. He had to leave. He head to get out.

Only the fear of his father kept him from bolting for the door.

She must have seen it in his eyes – the same fear that he saw often in hers. A fear they shared. "He is sleeping," his mother said. "The drink claimed him. I am sorry, Dominic, I didn't dare come until I knew he was absolutely out."

"I have to go, Mother ..."

"I know," she said sadly. "I know." He caught the glisten of tears in her eyes, but she smiled anyway. "It is hard for a mother to say goodbye to her sons. But Merciful Domus had wonderful things planned for Joshua and he has wonderful things planned for you, Dominic. Wonderful things." She took his hand and helped lift him from the bed. He winced at the pressure it placed on his wrists. Lantern in hand, she led him down the stairs ...

He spotted his father, sleeping at one of the tables. There was a tall, glass bottle clenched tightly in one fist. But he slept – not a muscle stirring. Regardless, Dom felt his heart sink to the depths of his stomach. If he did awaken? If he found out?

They made it to the door without issue. His mother turned the lock and the door presented an empty street crested by glittering stars. He could feel the urge to run – there was some place he needed to be. But his heart resisted the urge to leave.

He looked back at his mother. She was silently crying, but her smile did not waver. The additional light from the lit lantern at the door highlighted a discolored eye and a puffy split lip. Dom looked at her – and the stark realization came. "Mother, he'll know. When he wakes up, he'll know ... "

She nodded bravely. They both knew what the morning would bring – what he'd do to her. They'd both cringed under his enraged fists. "Come with me?" he asked.

His mother's eyes fled back to the table and the drunken man slumbering there. "I need to stay with him," she said softly.

"Mother ... "

"I love you, Dominic," she said softly, forestalling additional attempts to reason with her. A cool night breeze stirred the air, and they both shivered. Reaching back inside the door, she grabbed a coat and pushed it towards him. "Take it," she told him. "Every traveler needs a good, sturdy coat."

He obeyed. The pain arced through his body. He could not bear to stay. He could not stand to leave. He stammered forward, uncertain steps, and he heard her call.

"Dominic?" she said. He looked to find her reaching back behind her neck – unclasping the small pewter chain that she always wore. On the end of the chain hung two twin circles, perfect in their roundness, linked and fused

together. The Embrace of Domus. "Take this. Take this, so when you look at it, you'll remember me. You'll remember that I love you – just as perfectly as the Merciful One does."

She placed the necklace in his hand and he closed a fist around it. Without a word, he wrapped his arms around her and hugged her tight. She held him for a moment and then gently pushed him away. "Go, Dominic," she told him. "Go and do wonderful things for Domus."

He went, leaving the only person in the world he knew truly loved him standing, crying in the doorframe. He went ... but as he walked, he couldn't fight the notion that Merciful Domus was using him as well.

--- * --- * ---

Dom was to his feet so quickly, the Degan thief jumped back in surprise. Used. Dom was sick of being used. By his father, by Merciful Domus, by the Band of Six. Everyone thought they could have their way with him, to Oblivion with what he thought about the matter! The rush of anger coursing through his body caused his heart to race and his breath to draw ragged. Ethiere's eyes darted around, unsure what had caused the reaction and uneasy being the focal point of such escalated behavior. "Dom?"

He quivered inside of his coat, but the words wouldn't come. The words wouldn't have helped at all. Silence was better. Years at the mercy of his father's fists had taught him the value in facing torment in silence. Dom turned, unaware of where he was going, but knowing he needed to distance himself from the thief. He could feel the eyes of the others on him – Sarah in particular looking both concerned and curious. Let them wonder! Let them try to figure out his purpose! Let them try to guess at the curse he bore!

He wouldn't tell them. He wouldn't tell anyone of it ever again. Even if it meant the Band failed. Even if it meant he died at the hands of the demon.

He was done being used.

Dom charged the barn door, slid it open just wide enough to slip through, and escaped into the morning sunlight. Urged by his anger, chased by his fears, he continued to hear the voice of his father boil in his eyes.

Tell me, boy, what do you see?

16.

Kashif busied himself at the workbench fastened to the eastern wall of the barn. It was crudely constructed, the seams between the boards opening up with uneven gaps. But it was level – mostly – and provided a more stable surface than the bales of hay could offer.

He'd risen before the others of the Band –only the two men serving their watch over Lady Greer's camp were awake. As would be expected, Kashif garnered their full attention. The same could not be said of the one man Lord Baron Northing had elected to send as his guardian – one Corporal Murphy. The Corporal seemed resolute to perform his duties with the smallest sense of urgency allowed; Kashif did not doubt that Northing's man wouldn't mind if his charge got roughed up a little.

The morning had been gray, but the meager light slid easily between various slits in the barn walls. Kashif was used to rising early – his mind functioned best then. He'd realized mornings would be even more precious with his present company. Mornings would be the only time he might be alone.

With strict precision, he leveled off the top of the manganese-based powder on the tiny spoon he'd used to extract it from the thin lacquered bottle Djemal had packed. Satisfied with the measurement, he emptied the spoon into a larger vial that contained a sample of his blood. There was a small reaction when the manganese met the oxygen in the blood, and he promptly stoppered the vial. He paused in his work to hold the vial at the level of his eyes and watched as the chemical began to break the blood down into various strata of compounds. As he set the vial next to the two others currently undergoing different chemical evaluations, he could hear the general stirring of the Band behind him.

His time was growing short. Soon he would have to interact with them – again.

The reaction he'd received last night had not been positive; he'd not expected any different a result. He was the outsider. He was the dark-skinned man from Arca. He knew he would see their prejudices rise. The war may be over, but the hatred persisted. He knew they would fight against their roles – their places in the world. He knew his words – while correct and logical – would meet with biased-based resistance.

Tell us all about your boiling caste system!

Yes, they would all resist. The side-burned fighter represented the greatest problem. His attitude would be infectious; poison to the progress the others might make. That is why he'd tried to go to Lady Greer first and alone. He needed an ally – and she was the only other member of the party of an age and status that would be valuable. Had his conversation with her helped at all? She appeared to have cooled to his logic by the time their conversation had ended, but he could be mistaken. He did not know how to read the body-language of women. He'd never had a need to before.

But what could be done about the one called Billick? Kashif busied himself with another vial of blood.

There was a story told to young boys in the dohourn communities – a story about a fish that lived in a glassy lake. During the day, the young fish would look up through the shimmering water at the sun high above – and the wisps of clouds in the sky. At nights he would surface to gaze up into the infinite night sky, painted with speckles of stars. It was not long before the fish found his pond too crowded. His watery domain was too limiting. There could be no satisfaction with what he had. If only, he thought, I could swim in the heavens! Surely the vastness of the sky is the place for me.

So inspired, the fish began to jump. Starting from the bottom of the lake, building up speed as he rushed upward, the fish leapt and leapt. All the night long he struggled to swim among the stars. As morning dawned, the fish sped to the surface, broke the smooth plain of the water and pirouetted in the newly-risen sun. And as he marveled at his new surroundings, a kingfisher swooped down, catching the fish in his mighty talons and whisked him away. "Little fish," the proud bird said, "did no one tell you? You cannot rise above the place where you naturally belong."

It was a simple children's story; the message clear. To each their own place; to each his own duty.

The Tollians struggled against this principle – just like the fish. They always had their eye on the sky above them – on what those of a higher station enjoyed. They continued to fan the flames of childish fantasy, imaging one day – with work or with luck or with the help of the God they prayed to – they'd break through that invisible ceiling that held them firmly in place.

It was a ludicrous dream. How many dirt farmers and ware-peddlers ever found fame, fortune or glory? How many poor little boys grew up to be rich, learned men? How many handsome noblemen were willing to pull a title-lacking lass from her chores and spinning-wheel? The whole Tollian society reeked of inefficiency. It was an entire society of fish dying in a vain attempt to fly like birds.

Ethiere, the thief, was the prime example. Kashif was keeping an eye fixed on the rogue. He knew the gear-laden pack was too tempting a trial for one used to stealing what interested him. While Ethiere had made no attempt at the pack as yet, Kashif surmised the thief was simply momentarily distracted. The young man's attention was noticeably drawn towards the noblewoman, Lady Greer.

At first, he had attributed it to some trinket, some bobble of value that Greer had inadvertently exposed to the thief. Later, he'd wondered if the lad might be infatuated with the noblewoman, who was really only a handful of years his senior. But now, Kashif had a different hypothesis. Ethiere wasn't watching the noblewoman for the *woman*, but because of the *noble*. The lure of the lifestyle – the clothing and the attendants – must have enchanted the destitute young man like the stars twinkling in the sky had enchanted the fish.

Kashif's lips tightened to a knowing smile. Not five paces away stood the dedicated Captain Reed. The kingfisher was primed to swoop at a moment's notice.

A commotion rose behind him – from the least likely of sources. The quiet boy in the ill-fitting coat was standing in a threatening manner over the seated and somewhat astonished thief. Wordlessly, the boy made a mad rush to the barn door. The entire wooden structure rattled as the door was forced open and provided the boy with his desired exit. Kashif's attention was pulled from the disruption as he heard the sound of glass on wood …

A small white rat scurried across the final length of the workbench, tipping a vial as he went. In anger, Kashif swung a fist at the fleeing rat.

--- * --- * ---

There was little movement within the small cage. In the far corner, amid the flecked woodchips that covered the floor, a rat lay paralyzed – its spine arching backwards as if someone had failed in an attempt to bend it in half. The pus-like substance oozing from its eyes last night had crusted over. The small, angry red lesions flanking its skin could barely be seen through snowy white fur.

The other four occupants in the cage were huddled at the opposite end – a mass of quivering bodies. Like all of the Architect's lesser creations, they innately shunned the dying – but their lungs still drew breath. Kashif checked his ledger of notes. If the disease had been communicated to the other rats from the host, the first symptoms should have appeared at least three hours ago. Kashif watched the rats for several more minutes, taking in their appearance and behavior.

Marooke had anticipated the host rat would die today. His mentor was scarcely wrong with such estimations. Kashif walked back to the table to record his findings in the ledger he meticulously kept.

"And?" his mentor asked.

"Just as you thought it would be," Kashif responded. "The first is dead. Symptoms in the other four rats have yet to manifest." He quickly checked his math on the ledger. "This newest rendering of the disease held the dormancy period to approximately fourteen days. Upon the initial appearance of the lesions, the rat survived ... thirty-eight hours. That is comparable to the other fourth-generation hosts in our experiment."

"What do you surmise of the fifth-generation?"

"It is possible that the newest rendering of the disease has a prolonged dormancy period with each successive generation of carriers. If that were the case, the four rats might exhibit symptoms in the very near future." Kashif looked to his mentor. It was an honor to study under the undisputed master of biochemistry in all of Arca. "I do find that scenario unlikely. Our initial construct of this disease was to render it inert after several generations. I think we are seeing success with that objective."

Marooke leaned over the table, resting his chin on his balled fists. Finally, he made his pronouncement. "It is ready, then."

Kashif was caught by surprise. Ready? "Are you certain? Surely further testing ..."

Marooke turned in his seat, and Kashif quieted. It was not his place to question the practices of his mentor ... but it was his duty to share his thoughts and observations. Had he gone too far? He lowered his eyes and waited.

"Further testing would only yield results I am already confident of. We have done our work well. This is success, Kashif. You should smile."

Kashif nodded – and remembered to smile. A success! "Congratulations, Master."

Marooke held up a hand to silence him. "This is your success, Kashif – we both know that. Yes, I provided insights and suggestions from time to time, but you were the one that developed the structure of the disease. You were the one who designed which systems the disease would target."

"I would have never solved the dormancy problem without your help..."

Marooke lifted the hand again. "An old trick – now fully integrated into your considerable cache of knowledge. I am proud of you, Kashif. Arca is proud of you. The Architect of Man is proud of you too. You have risen to the role you were given, perfectly!"

Kashif could feel his face burning, embarrassed to be on the receiving end of such high praise. There was no higher compliment that could be offered than to perfectly fit your role.

Marooke peered into the rat cage once more. "The Magistad will be pleased. I had told them we would not be prepared with a viable disease for at least another month, but now they will be able to move up their timeline ..."
Marooke paused and turned back to Kashif. "You still do not know the purpose of the disease – why the Magistad ordered it created?"

"No."

"And you have never thought to ask?"

Kashif shrugged. It had never been important. "I assume it is for the betterment of Arca." Wasn't that the impetus behind all of their work?

Marooke studied him with intense consideration. His feet moved before his tongue, and he brushed past Kashif before he spoke. "Come, apprentice. It is time to learn the purpose your deeds will soon accomplish." Obediently, the student moved to follow his mentor. Kashif's curiosity grew as they left the compound of laboratories, heading south on the wide roadway. Market booths of the Industad lined both sides, swarmed by members of the servile Dynad caste making purchases as their duties required.

Kashif did not venture outside of the Scholastad compound very often. Marooke had three Dynad at his command – they were for fetching supplies or running messages. It was different – being among so many people after growing comfortable in the semi-solitude of his peers. Despite the mass of people, they were never pressed. The Dynad recognized them for who they were, and they respectfully provided an ample berth ...

Marooke stopped before a staircase that paralleled a tall stone wall. A thick-armed Ballistad stood directly at the base of the stairs, and Kashif spotted others with short-bows and spears walking the wall above. The warrior lowered his eyes momentarily at their approach.

"I wish my apprentice to see from the wall," Marooke said. The warrior nodded once, and called the arrival out to his associates above. Kashif watched the sinews and tendons in the warrior's neck contract and flex with each small movement. Ever so slowly, their race was ascending the path to perfection ...

Marooke took the stairs one at a time, and Kashif followed him up. "Not many outside of the Magistad and higher echelon of the Ballistad know what this compound holds. Very few of our caste are aware of its purpose. Today, you join those few." As his head rose above the sight-line of the wall, Kashif looked down into the compound, at the men milling below ...

They were white-skinned. Tollians. Their being within the vicinity of the city shocked him. The war had been over ... what had they told him? Six months? Seven? The Tollians had abandoned their campaign and had fled back to their islands disgraced. But down below were at least one-hundred and fifty ragged looking foreign soldiers.

"Our prisoners of war," Marooke announced as they gazed into the compound. "Those that the Ballistad commanders deemed worth holding and withheld from various experiments of our caste. The Tollians have sent many letters requesting their return. Recently, they have even sent diplomats to negotiate their release. Our leaders have dithered in their response, they have prolonged the discussions, waiting ..."

"For the disease ..." Kashif finished, and Marooke nodded.

"Some of the Tollian men have grave injuries. We have been injecting them with an addictive agent that dulls their receptors for pain." Marooke paused. "Many have formed a dependence on the injections. They beg for them ..."

Kashif felt cold inside – the pieces were coming together. "The Magistad will relent – they will release the soldiers to return home ..."

"The Tollians have boats waiting."

He looked to Marooke. "It is a fourteen day sail to Tollia from Arca," he guessed. "I am right?" His mentor didn't answer. Kashif didn't need him to.

"The disease will awaken from dormancy as ships reach harbor. It will spread through their cities for four generations before abating – enough to cause fear and panic without any hope of the plague returning to Arca. The psyche of the Tollians will be crippled, they will view the plague as a sign from their God. They will be less likely to return and resume their war with us." Marooke smiled. "You have done a great work for your people, for the Architect," Marooke reminded him. There was nothing different in what he said – the same laudatory words. But now? Now?

Now, Kashif knew their context. Ships would sail from Arca. Death would arrive in the ports of Tollia. "A great work," Kashif echoed, and he clasped his hands behind his back as he tried to suppress the haunting chill going up his spine. "I should be proud."

--- * --- * ---

The rat dove into a wedge between a stack of bales and the barn wall. Kashif watched the spot, daring the loathsome creature to return. There were things in his pack that could do wicked things to small animals.

"I think this fell."

Kashif turned to see Sarah standing behind him, lifting the vial from where it had fallen. She smiled as she held it out for him. "It doesn't look like it broke!"

He took the vial. "Thank you," he said. He walked past her to his workbench and sat. As he did so, he looked back toward the Refaid girl – and he realized that she wasn't going away. Furthermore, his protesting stare held no menace to her.

She was eyeing the vials. "Is that blood?"

"Yes," he said, returning his focus to his work.

"All ... yours?"

It was the tint of morbid curiosity to her question that caused Kashif to look back toward her. "Yes." He could see the thoughts firing in her brain, daring her tongue to frame the question. He sighed silently. "What is it?"

Her eyes flickered back to the vials momentarily before returning to meet his. "Don't … don't you ever worry you'll run out?"

Kashif felt the corner of his mouth curl upward. "Run out? Of blood?"

There was an innocent solemnity in the way she nodded. "My father always panics when he sees me bleeding. Whatever he's doing – he'll drop it immediately to come and hold a cloth over the wound. Back when I was littler, he used to carry me to the Physicians so they could sew up cuts he deemed too big. I don't know … by how scared he always gets; I just figured you couldn't spare many drops of blood." She looked at him with a thoughtful frown. "I think you are the first person I've ever heard of that lets blood out of his body on purpose."

He laughed. He'd supposed they'd only see a black foreigner. He was only partially correct. They saw him as the black foreigner that bled himself for pleasure. "Why do you do it?" she pressed.

He consolidated all of his reasoning into two words. "To learn."

"From blood?"

He smiled. "You would be surprised at what one solitary drop of blood can teach you – of the myriad secrets it holds." He turned and gently took one of the vials from the bench. "Already I am learning things. My blood is teaching me about the Banding – how it works. I have discovered that my blood chemistry has changed – and those changes may hold the key to additional discoveries. Such as, how the Banding is able to produce pain. Or how it is able to direct us – help us to understand the way which we must go." He reflected on the vial – the pool of clear fluid that was gathering towards the top and the darker sediment that was collecting at the bottom. "Certainly you must see the value in this – see how it is worth a vial of blood."

Lost in examining the vial, he was awoken from his inner contemplations by her surprising answer. "Would it help you to examine my blood too?"

The scientist in him jumped at the opportunity. The skeptic in him advised caution. "You … would do that?"

She actually giggled. "Well," she said, "I'm fairly certainly it won't be painful."

17.

Reed's man didn't see him. Billick watched him exit the barn and saunter over to the edge of the glade. The soldier proceeded to relieve himself only a half-dozen paces from where Billick had spent the night sleeping. The man spat after he'd finished, turned back to the barn – and must have caught Billick out of the corner of his eye. There was a moment of surprise, followed by chagrin.

"Sorry ... about that." The soldier looked toward the barn, then back to Billick. "We weren't sure if we were going to find you."

Billick stretched out his arms, feeling the soreness that came from sleeping against the trunk of a tree. "That so?"

The soldier nodded. "Thought you'd try to go get that demon by yourself. We figured you'd be half-way to wherever it is by now." The soldier's assessment was correct, Billick had tried to continue on last night, freed from the useless other five of his Band. But the pain returned after a half-hour down the road. Within fifteen minutes it became near unbearable, and he'd been forced to turn back.

Reed's man came closer, and sat against another nearby trunk. "The name is Bostitch."

"Billick."

"Fine looking axe you have there ... didn't see it with you yesterday."

A memento from his night journey, he'd stolen the axe from a farmer's woodpile. The onset of the Banding at the Eight Flagons had left him armed only with his knife. The persistent pain had prevented a quick stop at his small loft where he kept the rest of his arsenal, and the knife seemed inadequate against the predator he'd seen in the fountain. It was a solid weapon, and far preferable than begging a sword off of Reed and his men.

Billick kept the thoughts to himself. It was too much to hope that the soldier would decide to leave him be.

"Not to echo the boiling dark-skin, but you do look like you've seen a battle or two," Bostitch said. "You served?"

Billick nodded.

"Who with?"

"Sixth Lancers," Billick answered.

"Ah, Lancers!" the other man said. "Had a boy on our street that joined up with them, probably your era. Don't think he was Sixth division though. I want to say he was Third … but it doesn't matter. Never met up with a lad by the name of Hecke, did you? Freckled?"

Billick shook his head.

Bostitch bobbed his head. "Yeah, didn't think so. He never came back after Arca, so I heard." Bostitch reached into his trousers pocket and pulled out a flint. "Never did fight against the dark-skins myself – but me and Neald back there, we got as close as Jauda Reef. If the war would have lasted another week, I would have set boots on Arcan soil."

"You didn't miss much."

"I've heard stories." Bostitch produced a thin paper roll from his other pocket and set it on the ground. He whipped out his boot knife and set to work on the flint. Some of the dryer summer grass began to smoke, and Bostitch lit the roll on the failing sparks. His smoke lit, Bostitch crushed the smoldering weeds under the heel of his boot. He nodded to Billick and held out the roll.

"You smoke?"

--- * --- * ---

Billick sat on his haunches, crowding the only evergreen tree that grew atop of the small slope. Despite the blanket coiled around him, he could feel the icy chill of the snow seeping straight into his bones. His toes were numb within the confines of his boots – and they only lethargically obeyed when he tried to wiggle them awake. A giant shiver rolled through his body and the blanket shed the snowy layer it had gathered.

His first true campaign with the Lancers, and the weather had a better chance of killing him than the enemy did.

He was one of the youngest in the division; and as the youngest, he more often than not found himself given the third watch – the coldest of the night. Thinking of the other soldiers amassed in their body-heat warmed tents made Billick feel even colder.

He'd already determined that when he was capable, he'd be growing out his facial hair – just to keep his cheeks from freezing.

This was Dullot Pass – or so it was named. Billick didn't know which of the two passes was actually called Dullot – the one he and his division held, or the one across the small valley held by Lord Baron Depree's men. The thin valley had seemed destined to become the battlefield stage.

Then the early storms had hit. The snow had buried the two flanking passes in sheets of white, trapping the two opposing forces within the oval shaped valley between them. The frosty weather had caused an unspoken truce between the two camps as both sides labored to reinforce themselves against the elements. But there were always sentries. There were always men spying glances at the other side. The mountainous walls of the valley carried the echoes of sound well; sometimes Billick thought he could hear what was being said in the other camp.

And so both sides waited, and watched, and froze.

Billick jumped at a noise behind him.

"Easy, lad," said the man. "Thought you might have dozed off." The soldier was wearing the uniform of the Lancers, albeit frosted with snowflakes. Billick thought he recognized his face – one of the veterans of their division. The man trudged through the snow to the tree-line, and crouched down a few steps away.

"You're doing it wrong," the veteran said.

Billick answered between the chattering of his teeth. "What wrong?"

The other smiled. "Watching. Look, with your blanket draped over you, you look like you might just be some sort of rock that's planted itself next to that tree. In this snow, the enemy has little to no chance of spotting you."

"Isn't that the point?"

His answer amused the veteran. "Oy, that's what the commanders will tell you the point is, for sure. Stay hidden, right? Get the advantage over the dogs on the other side, right? Sure, that's tactically sound, I'll concede that." The veteran paused to blow a breath of hot air into his hands. "But you look like a smart lad, okay? So I'll ask you – if we were going to go attack the enemy camp – where would you make your point of entry? Where you saw a sentry standing, say? Or where you supposed it was clear?"

"Where it was clear," Billick answered.

The veteran nodded with great satisfaction. "Oy, I knew you were a smart lad. So see? If those dogs of Depree get a notion to start something, your little hill out here is going to look mighty inviting. And what with the tree cover, you aren't going to see them until they're coming out of those pines over there. So what? Fifty or sixty of them suddenly come out to crest your hill? What then?"

"I yell," Billick recited quickly. "I raise the alarm – so the camp can be prepared to meet them."

The other man chuckled to himself. "Oy, good lad! Right, proper, military answer! Very good – except for the fact that it's now you standing solo against those fifty or sixty while your camp is taking to preparing. Very good for the camp lad – very bad for you." He blew into his hands again and rubbed them together. "No, lad, the best thing is to move around a bit. Not too much, mind you, but enough that anybody watching from those trees down there can figure out you're up here. Oy, I even talk to myself sometimes – let 'em think there's more than one, right?" The veteran grinned. "Besides, stay in one place to long and your boots will freeze to the ground."

Billick nodded and allowed a grin. "I might be too late," he confessed.

The other man slung his pack from his shoulder, firmly entrenching it into the snow bank on the hill. "Oy, you got to be good to your feet, lad," he said as he rummaged through his belongs. "Feet are important to a fighting man. You see, you need your feet ready for when those trumpets call for a charge, right? And you need them even more when those boiling trumpets call for a retreat, see?"

Billick saw the veteran pull out a tobacco kit from the pack with triumph. He waggled it at Billick. "Only thing that beats keeping your feet moving is sucking on a little bit of fire, to be sure." He balanced the kit on the pack and opened the lid. Billick watched him work.

"You ever seen combat before?" the veteran asked.

"No."

"Ever killed a man, lad?"

"Not yet."

The veteran nodded as he spread out a small square of paper. "Oy, right. So, have you figured what you'll tell yourself after you've done it?" He dropped a few pinches from the tobacco pouch onto the paper. "You know how you're going to justify it?"

Billick fought the urge to shiver again. "We have to justify it?"

"Oh, certainly, sure we do." The veteran's fingers moved nimbly despite the numbing chill in the air to roll up the paper. "See – those poor dogs that are camped under Depree's banner are really just as boiling unlucky as you and I. They don't want to be here – up in the cold, right? They've got no stake in Depree breaking away from the Confederated Barons – just like it makes no difference to us if he's made to stay. Nope, it's Barons, in their estates, with their twenty fireplaces blazing tonight – it's them it matters to. And that's why they've got us freezing up here on either end of the valley." He proudly held aloft his roll of tobacco. "Trust me lad, you've got to be prepared with why it was right to end the life of some poor fellow – otherwise you're going to have a rough time doing it again tomorrow, for sure."

Billick nodded. In his training, they'd always talked about the enemy in such abstract terms. They weren't people. They weren't men. They were just things that needed to be killed. But how would it be to actually kill one? How would it be to watch the life drain from someone's eyes? What if there was a raw, freezing lad, just like him, waiting on the other side? "I'll think about that," he said at last.

"Oy, you should." There were sparks as a flint was struck against a knife, and the veteran masterfully caught one on his roll. Sticking the thing in his mouth, he took a long draw. The tip glowed an inviting orange. There was pleasure to his exhale. The veteran caught him watching and smiled again. "You smoke?"

Billick shook his head.

"Want to try it?" The veteran held the slow-burning roll out in his direction. "Will warm you from the inside, for sure."

Billick was tempted by the promise of warmth. His arms ached as he suddenly asked them to move. The weather was freezing more than just his toes.

The veteran stood to lean closer. "Now the taste is likely to ..."

There was a rushing whistle, then impact. The veteran slid backwards, down the hill. Billick, stunned, could only gape at the arrow protruding from the man's face. Turning back, he could see the shadows of men rushing from the pines below.

Tossing aside his blanket, Billick tore down the hill on numb feet, raising the alarm and praying he could outrun the horde on his heels. He ran right by the veteran, just as the orange glow of the tobacco roll winked out.

--- * --- * ---

Billick stared at the proffering from the soldier. "No," he said at last. "Never picked it up."

Bostitch took no offense at the statement. He took another draw. "Don't blame you. It's a miserable habit, that's for sure." He smiled around the thin roll in his mouth. "I swear, my mother will tell you that this gruff voice used to be clear enough to sing in a Deacon's choir!"

Billick nodded but kept his focus off of the burning tip of the smoke.

"I think you had the right idea, though – coming out here. Couldn't get a wink of sleep knowing there was a breathing Arcan no more than thirty paces away. Made my skin crawl." The barn door opened again, and Corporal Murphy, the man Northing had sent to guard the foreigner, stretched in the morning sunlight. He caught sight of the smoking Bostitch and sauntered over.

"Spare a pinch, friend?" the man begged.

Bostitch nodded his head toward his kit. "Just a pinch, mind you."

"Domus shower you with blessings!" the guardsman exhaled and he got to work on a roll. "My kit is back in Hollingston; was out on this excursion before I knew what was what. I've gone a full day without and I'll boil my own foot if I can keep my hands from shaking!"

They watched the guardsman prepare his roll, Bostitch monitoring the man's definition of a pinch very closely. "Didn't volunteer to watch over the dark-skinner then?" Reed's man asked.

Murphy lifted his attention from the roll long enough to answer with a very telling response. "First I hear about it, my commanding officer is calling for anyone that didn't serve in the Arcan war to step up immediately. There were seventeen of us stupid enough to report. Next, he sends away any that lost a father or brother in the war. Our number drops to five. If I could go back, I'd have thought to conjure up some fatal end for poor elder brother Tom, but how could I have known?" He lit his roll off the end of Bostitch's and took a heavy drag. His eyes closed in delight. "We drew lots – you fellows can see how that ended up."

Bostitch nodded. "No bad blood between you and the Arcans then?"

Murphy dithered. "Wouldn't say that. Tom came home, less a limb and less his full faculties." The smoking roll waggled in the guardsman's mouth. "But you two, you speak out against him more than the others have. You both fought?"

"I have crossbow bolts dying to taste that Arcan's blood," Bostitch answered. "But I was part of the reserve. Only Billick here actually saw Arca. Sixth Lancers."

Billick scowled. Boiling man was going to give everyone his life story now?

Murphy saluted once. "My commander had lots of compliments for the Lancers. More steel than flesh." He took another deep draw. "You ever need a moment alone with my blood-letting charge, you've just to ask." Billick watched the Corporal, wondering if the man was really promising all he suggested. The man, oblivious to the scrutiny he was under, turned to Bostitch. "For you and your bolts, though, it will cost another pinch of your tobacco!"

The two soldiers laughed. Billick decided he'd heard enough truth in the Corporal's trite jokes to be concerned. "You wouldn't draw the wrath of your Lord Baron should his Arcan meet with … an accident?" Billick made sure to emphasize the last word, suggesting to Murphy it would be nothing of the kind.

Murphy's lip curled in an assured smile around the roll. "You tell me, Lancer? If Lord Baron Northing truly cared for the life and safety of this Arcan, would have sent one lowly Corporal to attend him?" Murphy shrugged and leaned back against the tree. "Way I see it, the sooner it happens, the sooner I have to stop begging smokes, right?"

Billick stood and stretched his lips while the other two continued their smoke. "Reed would have my hide!" Bostitch complained, and Billick drifted away from the pair.

Despite his argument last night, Billick had left slightly unsettled. What if the creature couldn't be hacked apart? What if there was more to this? Could the Arcan and all of his science really be necessary?

You're going to need him.

The wizard's words rang through his memory. Murphy, the man charged with Kashif's protection, was as committed to his duty as a wall of sand in the face of a tide. Reed might act the deterrent for his soldiers, but nothing would stand in the way of the hundreds of bitter Tollians they'd undoubtedly face. Billick ground his teeth in frustration. Boiling wizard!

You'll have to keep him alive.

18.

When Sarah left the barn, she moved cautiously. Kashif had warned her that sometimes people got dizzy or lost consciousness after they had given blood. She, of course, felt the exact same way she always felt. She'd followed his instructions and sat on the bale of hay until she'd counted to a hundred. Or at least what she assumed was one-hundred. She usually fizzled out in the high-twenties. So she did it twice, just to be safe.

Although it didn't hurt to lose consciousness, Sarah still didn't want to do it. Especially not twice in two days. She was not over the embarrassment of keeling over on the road yesterday when her body had lost its battle to fatigue. While none of the others had said anything of the incident to her – she knew what they had to be thinking.

Wondering why they were being slowed down by such an inconvenient little girl.

Lady Greer stood in the shade the barn cast and walked as her soldiers prepared the horses. Sarah had still not found an opportunity to talk with the noblewoman – and she felt bad about that. She'd talked quite a bit with everyone else – but Lady Greer was always surrounded by her escorts. A thought struck Sarah, and she brightened. Maybe they'd stick her on a horse for fear of her fainting again! And with Sophie and Lady Greer in the midst of a fight, the noblewoman would need someone to talk to!

Sarah put the happy idea aside. She had another matter to attend to first.

She needed to find Dom.

She felt bad she'd not been able to go after him sooner. She'd meant to. She'd only thought to say hello to Kashif and see how his night had gone – he'd looked so busy that she'd not wanted to disturb him too much. But one thing had led to another – and he'd told her about blood and before she knew it she was watching crimson drops from her own arm fill the small glass tube.

She circled the barn without luck. Dom was nowhere to be seen. So she walked to the nearest of the farmhouses and began to ask around. The fifth person she asked finally gave her a clue – saying he thought he'd seen a boy in a big brown coat on the North Knob.

She followed the directions she was given – and sure enough, she spotted Dom sitting on the hill. But it wasn't just a hill. The gently sloping knoll was pocked with weathered stone markers.

It was a graveyard.

--- * --- * ---

Sarah looked forward to services. The twice monthly Holydays seemed like her reward for the long, lonely, repetitive hours that she spent by her upstairs window. She always woke up extra early to brush her hair out. She never had a new dress like some of the girls had, but sometimes her father would surprise her with a brand new ribbon for her hair. Sometimes she spent a week deliberating which ribbon from her collection she'd choose.

She didn't understand why more people didn't seem excited about services. Goodwidow Maybee always had some excuse for why she'd not be attending. Sometimes it was her feet, or her head, or her back ... but it was always something.

And the Goodwidow accused her of faking her illness!

Sarah thought the services wonderful. They sang together. They prayed together. The Deacons would orate to them, and exhort them to do better. Sarah found that she was one of the few people that would answer all the questions that the Deacons asked. One of the Deacons had even complimented her on her promptness in answering his rhetorical questions. Whatever that meant.

Today's service had been particularly wonderful, albeit not as rousing as others they had heard. It was only after the main oration was finished that Sarah realized her father had dozed off. His head was leaned forward, his arms folded, and Sarah would have guessed he was deep in prayer were it not for his soft snore. She watched him sleep for a moment, and felt loved. He'd worked late last night, trying to pull in a few extra coins. Certainly her father would have preferred sleeping in. But he'd awoken with enough time to get washed and walk her to the cathedral. He knew how much it meant to her.

She leaned over and kissed his shoulder, and slid down their bench. They'd started the meditative portion of the services now, and Sarah and her father usually walked the cathedral grounds during this part. Today, she decided she'd let him rest – she'd walk alone.

There was someone she wanted to visit.

Of all the Holydays, Sarah looked forward to All Remembrance Day the most. Her father would always pay the Goodwidow an extra penny to cut a few of the flowers from her garden. Every All Remembrance Day, before the service began, they'd first pay a visit to the cathedral cemetery. Her mother's grave was far towards the back – but it was beautiful. It was smooth granite, with the Embrace of Domus symbol etched above the name. Every year her father would say the same thing. He'd tell her how beautiful her mother had been. And then he'd say that she looked more and more like her mother each and every year. The flowers they left on the headstone only made the place more heavenly.

Sarah weaved between the headstones on the crooked path that she had long ago learned by heart. Her mother's headstone stood tall and proud in the sun. "Hello, mother," she said to the stone. "I've come to visit you today! Although I don't have flowers ..." She ran her finger along the deeply carved circles of the Embrace. "I am wearing a green ribbon today! Father says you always fancied green ..."

"Hello, little one," a deep, gentle voice spoke from behind. Sarah turned to see an elderly man wearing the vest and the flat-brimmed hat of a Deacon. "I did not mean to startle you."

"That's okay," Sarah answered.

"Admiring headstones today?"

She nodded, and let her finger trail down the emblem and into the letters on the stone. And a wonderful idea occurred to her. She turned to the Deacon. "Could you read these letters for me?" she asked.

"Off this stone?" he asked, and she nodded enthusiastically. He chuckled and slowly lowered himself to see the stone better. "My eyes aren't as good .... Ah, yes. Here we are." He cleared his throat. "In memory of Thom Barker, May he rest in Domus' eye forever."

Sarah crinkled her brow and crowded closer to the kneeling Deacon. "That's not right," she told him.

The Deacon looked at her with amusement. "It isn't?"

"No, see," she said, pointing to the letters that she'd traced many, many times. Traced, but never read. "Her name was Emiline. My mother's name was Emiline." She did not understand the look of sorrow that was growing on the Deacon's face – nor did she like it. "This ... this is my mother's grave ..." She looked back at the stone. "Isn't it?"

She felt the Deacon put a warm hand on her shoulder. "Oh, my child. Please forgive me."

"Sarah!" she heard her father call. "Sarah!" She saw him running the paths, and she ran to meet him. Her vision wavered through the tears in her eyes. "Sarah, are you alright?"

She ran into his arms and latched on. "That isn't mother's grave!" she cried into his shoulder. "Father, he read the words, and it isn't mother's grave!" Something caused her to stop – a sense that something was amiss. She's expected her father to ... to what? To cry with her? To be angry? She didn't know. But as she looked up at him, all she could see was shame.

"Father?"

"Sarah ..."

"Where is she?" she demanded. "She died when I was a baby. She got sick and died. And you buried her here. You buried her here and you picked out the most beautiful headstone." Her father could not look her in the eyes. "We come visit her every year! We come and we leave daffodils and woodroses at her grave." Sarah felt her heart breaking. "You tell me that I look like her. You tell me how proud she'd be of me."

"I'm so sorry, Sarah."

"Where is mother?" she pled. "Where is she?"

There was great sadness in his eyes. "I don't know. I honestly don't know."
He was crying. She'd never seen her father cry before. "I should have told you
... but I couldn't. The lie ... it was so much easier."

"Father?"

"Your mother left, Sarah."

"Left?"

"When you were a baby. When the Physicians first determined you were
Numb." He swallowed the lump in his throat. "She couldn't deal with it,
Sarah. I think she tried. She did. But it was too much. You crawled till you
were leaving bloody tracks on the floor. You had bruises ...." He looked sadly
into her eyes. "She tried."

Her father apologized, he cried and told her how sorry he was. Sarah did not
hear much of what he said. She could only wonder why he was apologizing.

After all, she was the reason her mother had left them.

--- * --- * ---

Dom was sitting between two headstones, idling picking at the long blades of
wildgrass. He didn't acknowledge her as she approached, but Sarah didn't
mind. Dom didn't talk much anyways.

"Hi," she said, and she plopped down in the grass as close as she could to him –
which still had them separated by a chipped headstone. "I saw you leave the
barn and I thought I better come out and see you."

Dom tied a knot into the long blade of grass in his fingers.

"You were pretty difficult to find, too! I thought for sure you'd just be outside
the barn, because really, by the time we got here last night, there was no time to
explore – and I didn't think you'd just wander around a place you didn't know –
I wouldn't, I think. I had to ask a lot of people if they'd seen you, and most of
them hadn't …"

With a flick of a thumb, Dom beheaded a goldenrod dandelion.

"And then finally, someone mentioned that they might have seen you pass this
way that I should come check this Knob … he didn't tell me that it was a
cemetery." She wiped a strand of hair from her eyes. "Did you know this was a

cemetery?" Dom responded by reaching for another long blade of grass. Sarah lowered her voice to a hush. "You do know that there are dead people underneath that grass, right?"

To her delight, the boy looked at her. "What are you doing here?" It was as many words as he'd ever spoken to her. Sarah decided to focus on the positive, rather than dwell on the tone it was delivered in.

"Talking," she said. "To you."

"Did it never occur to you that I wasn't talking back?"

She shrugged. "Father is quiet by nature ..."

Dom ripped the piece of grass in two. "Why won't you leave me alone?"

Sarah giggled. "Why would you want to be alone?"

He threw up his hands. "Why do you think I'm sitting in a graveyard? Because the dead people aren't going to bother me. They aren't going to talk to me. They aren't going ask me any questions. They aren't going to try to get me to do anything for them. They're leaving me alone!" He looked at her – and he looked upset. But she couldn't understand why. "Why won't you just go away?!"

He was angry at her – she'd done something! Sarah sought for answers among the headstones on the hill. She was only trying to be Dom's friend. That is what Ethiere had said. He'd said the three of them would be good friends. "I thought ... we could be friends."

Did Dom not want to be her friend? Perhaps, like her mother, Dom couldn't deal with being around her either.

"Friends?" he asked, incredulous. "Friends? Tell me, why would you want to be my friend?"

Sarah felt her eyes watering. "Tell me," she shot back, "why would you not want to be mine?" She lost it then – the tears. They fell like little raindrops, watering her dress. Sitting amid the headstones, she felt as if she were surrounded by strangers – not one of them caring the least bit about the sobbing girl.

It didn't come immediately, but it came. "I'm … I'm sorry." Through dampened eyes, Sarah saw that Dom's demeanor had changed. He didn't look angry. He didn't look like he was going to yell at her anymore. He looked … sad again. "There isn't anything wrong with you, Sarah. You seem like you'd make a great friend – a best friend, really. You're kind … and you're happy …"

"Then what is it?"

He bowed his head, back to the grass. "I've never had a friend. My father –" He stopped suddenly, his jaw tensing for a small second, before he relaxed. "I don't get to go out much … not even for Holydays. I don't know any boys or girls my age. I only see the people that come to our tavern, and none of them are the sort I'd like to be friends with." He turned to her. "I don't know how to be a friend."

To Sarah, it was an odd concept. You didn't have to *learn* how to be a friend – you just were one. Dandelions didn't need to learn how to be flowers, right? "You can start by not making your friends cry," she said softly.

"You still want to try to be my friend?"

She hoped he wouldn't spot the trepidation in her answer. "If you think you can deal with me."

He nodded. It was a small nod, little more than a jiggle of the neck – but it counted as a nod, Sarah was sure of it. She cracked a smile and – somewhat surprisingly – he did too. "You're genuine, if you're anything. The others in the Band all try and hide what they feel and think – but you don't." He sighed. "I guess we can be friends."

The decision made Sarah beam. Perhaps sensing that enthusiasm, Dom tempered his statement. "Just don't expect me to talk to you when the rest of them are around, okay?"

"Not a problem," she said. She plucked up a stalk of grass and began to rip in into littler bits. "It'll be just like regular. I'll do all the talking. You can just listen."

19.

The little bell attached to Physician Davies' door tittered as Martin pushed it open. No one else in Alben had a bell – it was definitely one of those curious customs Davies had brought with him from the Hollingston. Martin didn't often visit the Physician – Merciful Domus be praised. He'd always found himself in good enough health.

The bell bothered in – the levity in its tiny trill. It seemed very out of place at a physician's place of practice. Health and sickness weren't things to be taken lightly.

Despite his years in Alben, Davies was still very much an outsider. The bell was only one example. The man's clothing was another. His cuffs were always buttoned, the pleats on his slacks pressed, his vest fitted despite his girth. Davies looked the part of a physician – but not an Alben physician. Perhaps Martin would always be prejudiced. He'd grown up knowing only Physician Carroll and his habits. What Carroll had lacked in training he'd made up with decades of experience. Carroll had been the physician that would stitch the cut or set the bone – and then roll up his sleeves to tackle the work you no longer could.

"Martin!" the glad Physician called in salutations. He snapped the book shut he'd been reading as he spoke. "Is everything well?"

The bell fell quiet. "Well enough."

"And Elsa?"

"We're both fine," Martin assured the physician.

Davies wandered back to his bookcase – easily the largest personal collection of literature in Alben – and placed the book in its ordained spot. "Glad to hear it, of course," he said, but he shook his head. "I really should get out to the homesteads on the southern tracts more. I know I should. I have no excuse."

"The roadway isn't ..."

Davies raised an authoritative finger. "I lie – I have many excuses, but none that doesn't do my duty as a physician some degree of shame." Davies sat back against the corner of his desk and placed his hands in his lap. "Am I correct in assuming this is not a social visit?"

Martin nodded.

Davies shrugged. "I suppose my profession will always be burdened with the pall of the plague. No one willfully goes to the Physician. Who is more likely to catch sick than the man who seeks to visit them, hmm? No bother – what can I do for you, Martin?"

"Someone broke into our home last night."

Davies bushy eyebrows arched in surprise. "You don't say?" Whatever question the Physician intended to pose next caught on his tongue. Martin could almost see his curiosity shift from the story to why the story was being told. "Shouldn't you be talking to Constable Mercer about this?"

"There's no need," Martin answered. "Nothing was taken. And we caught the culprit." Martin paused. "She's a little girl."

Davies pursed his lips. "That's a new one." He rocked against his desk, testing the sturdiness of its construction. "A little girl? And Red didn't frighten her off?"

"Red's an old dog now," Martin reminded him. "He doesn't like her."

"Doesn't like her?"

"Won't come near the house."

Davies batted away the comment. "Stung pride!" he diagnosed. "Of course he doesn't like the girl that broke into the house he was supposed to be guarding! No mystery there!" As dismissive as Davies was, the old hound's behavior still ate at the back of the Martin's mind. Martin knew Red and he what he was seeing from his dog was fear. And he'd never seen fear like this from his steady hound. Still, Martin decided it was a debate not worth having. What would a city-man like Davies know about country dogs anyhow?

"The girl says her name is Pennie," Martin went on.

Davies muttered the name as if trying to conjure a reluctant memory. "No, can't say she is local. At least I've not met a Pennie during my tenure here. Did she say where she is from?"

Martin shook his head. "Doesn't say much, really."

"A runaway then?" Davies cocked his head. "You don't suppose she's come over from Hollingston? I wouldn't think many runaways would willingly cross those forested hills. Not that us country folks aren't generous of heart, but it would be far easier for your little Pennie to fend for herself in the city than out here in the open."

The farmer chose to ignore the physician's self-inclusive comments about country folk. "Elsa thinks she may have been mistreated."

"Poor thing," Davies said, pouting behind his trimmed beard. "Can't fault her trying to escape that sort of situation.   I'll certainly want to stop by and check up on her."

"Elsa was hoping you would."

"I should stop by to visit Bertrand Miller as well. Not that there is anything I can do for his leg at this point." The physician's smiled was self-deprecating. "But that's just another excuse, isn't it."

"Elsa will insist you join us for dinner."

The smile brightened. Martin left, wondering if that wasn't just the excuse Physician Davies was looking for.

*   *   *   *   *

Some people refused to be served.

They planted their feet against the personal storms of trial and misfortune, determined to show they were strong enough to persevere. It was something they had to prove. It was petty, how they'd prefer to suffer and starve rather than seek out assistance. Neck-deep in a riptide of trouble – and they'd still try to convince you they found the water refreshing.

It was a prevailing belief among the independent-minded farm-folk in the Alben valley – being in need was inherently wrong.

Young Bertrand subscribed to fully to the idea.

Elsa had hoped to get Judith alone – a faint hope at best. The injured leg kept Bertrand confined to the house. Limited as his mobility was, the man managed to skulk around whenever Elsa came to visit. She knew exactly what prompted

127

him to leave the pillow-padded chair in the parlor to buzz around Judith's kitchen like a horsefly. He had to monitor the guests.

After all, he couldn't trust them not to do something *nice*.

With a laborious, hobbled gait, Bertrand crossed the kitchen to investigate the basket Elsa had brought.

"It's only pies dear," Judith said, glancing behind her. Elsa noted the signs of weariness that marked the young housewife's visage. The lines of worry etched deeper into Judith's face with each visit. She bore the burden of being the only member of their household able to stand on two feet. Whereas Bertrand resolutely rejected all attempts at aid – Judith was to the point where humbling reality had deflated the hollow bubble of pride. "She brought us pies."

"I've been in a somewhat of a baking mood of late," Elsa said, trying to position the offering in as harmless a manner as she could. "The lamb pie is a new recipe – I'd appreciate your candid opinions on it."

The lame farmer dropped the checkered cloth that covered the basket, his disapproval over the goods evident. For the first time, he saw Pennie standing in the corner of the kitchen, but his focus shifted to Elsa. "You shouldn't have. We'll not be taking food from off your table."

Elsa waved aside the idea. "Nothing of the sort – Bertrand. You're doing me a favor – and Martin. He has no self-control when it comes to my cooking, I'm afraid. Never has. His mouth hasn't been doing any favors for his waistline." She smiled sweetly. "We've already got Red – we've simply no room for another old, over-stuffed belly by our hearth."

Which would be true – as soon as Red elected to come back to the house. The dog had remained outside the entire night, and had not ventured near the house all morning …

Bertrand pivoted stiffly on his wooden crutch. "You shouldn't have made the journey just for pies, Elsa, especially when you and Martin stopped in yesterday. We won't be taking you away from your house…"

"Actually, I came by to ask for a favor," Elsa interrupted. It effectively silenced Bertrand for the moment, who must have wondered if he'd heard correctly. Elsa widened her smile – genuinely pleased to have rattled the unhappy man. "Is that alright?"

It wasn't proper asking help of someone so obviously in need. It was like asking a drowning man if he couldn't spare a moment to fish while he was down there. But Elsa was counting on Bertrand's pride. He'd only ask whether he needed to provide his own hooks and line.

He was wary, but predictable. "Of course. We'd do anything for our friends."

Elsa turned back to Judith. "Well, you may recall last year at the Harvest Revelries, I told you how wonderful I thought your dress was? And you told me that you'd sewed it up yourself, and I was hard-pressed to believe that such craftsmanship didn't come straight from the shops at Wellsford Park. Marvelous work, Judith – especially when compared to the rag aprons I can barely cobble together – or even the stitchery done by Goodwidow Wensley."

"You'd like a dress?" Judith guessed.

Elsa held a demure hand up to her bosom. "Oh no, not me. No." She turned slightly and motioned Pennie forward – and was glad to see the young girl comply. "I'm hoping you'll make a dress – several, actually – for Pennie here. What my daughters left in the attic are all moth-worn and beyond repair – and she simply can't live the rest of her life in an old nightgown."

Judith's eyes darted around the young girl's figure, sizing her up.

"I'd, of course, provide the cloth ..."

Bertrand harrumphed, which startled Pennie into a slight cringe.

Elsa girded herself. "... and payment."

"I knew it," spat Bertrand. "This doesn't sound like a favor, Elsa!"

"The girl needs clothes ..." Elsa fought back, growing angry.

Bertrand hobbled over to stand between his wife and Pennie – as if blocking her view of the girl would prevent her from thinking it over. Pennie retracted a step, moving closer to Elsa. "You've got some older dresses in your wardrobe, yes?" he pressed his wife. Judith nodded, eyes lowering. "I know you do – some that you hardly wear anymore. That fabric could provide ..."

"Bertrand!" Elsa warned – and realized she'd adopted the disapproving tone she'd used with her own boys. But she was thoroughly disenchanted with his attitude.

He turned toward her. Bertrand, bent over his crutch as he was, stood tall nonetheless. "I know what you're trying to do," he said. "I know what you and Martin are trying to do. But they are our problems. We'll thank you to let us attend to them. And we'll leave you to attend to yours."

"Bertrand!" Now it was Judith, tears beginning to well up in her eyes …

And the visit was officially a disaster.

The farmer rounded back to his wife. "Do not challenge me on this, Judith!" he demanded. "We are strong enough to see through this – we'll come out okay." Elsa stopped listening. Her clever plan for furnishing Judith with a few well-needed coins was ruined. In the end, she only brought contention – and pies. She sought to collect Pennie and excuse herself … when she noticed the young girl making a silent approach on the unsuspecting farmer …

"Pennie...?" Elsa cautioned, just as the girl's small hand reached out to touch Bertrand on the back of his leg …

It was as if a thunderclap from a sea-squall exploded in the room. Bertrand loosed a terrifying scream of intense pain as he was simultaneously pitched forward. Judith had only enough time to raise her arms as her husband tumbled into her, his momentum taking the housewife and her chair to the floor with him.

Elsa found herself standing, her own chair teetering madly behind her. Bertrand wailed in horrid agony, Judith sobbed in shock, and Pennie …

The girl stood speechless – stunned. She looked up with wide, frightened eyes which connected for a moment with Elsa's. And then she fled for the door.

Elsa recovered her wits and ran after her. "Pennie! Pennie, wait!" Her wealth of years put her at a terrible athletic disadvantage, but every motherly instinct in her told Elsa she'd better make an attempt to catch the girl. Whatever had happened – whatever Pennie had done – her face had spoken clearly enough. She'd not meant to do it. She'd been as surprised as any of them. Whatever had happened – Pennie was not to be blamed.

Surprisingly quick with the door latch, Pennie slipping through the door at precisely the point it became wide enough for her svelte frame to squeeze through. By the time Elsa reached the porch, Pennie had a thirty pace lead.

Elsa's heart sank. Pennie would run ... although she had nowhere to go. She would run – and there was no guarantee those living at next house she broke into wouldn't try to do her harm. "Pennie!"

It was to no avail. The frightened girl ran like a startled hind and disappeared into the forest trees at the edge of Betrand's orchards. Elsa's pace slackened and she sank to her knees in the middle of the field. Pennie was gone, and Elsa knew that she would most likely never see the girl again.

From the direction of the house, Judith called out frantically. "Elsa! Elsa!" Reluctantly, she pulled her eyes away from the last spot she'd seen Pennie. Judith, tears streaked in wet lines down her red cheeks caught hold of the doorframe for support. Her eyes still spoke of shock – and Elsa realized then that she could no longer hear Bertrand's screams.

Her heart sank, and she instinctively stood to go to the young wife. "Oh ... oh, Judith ... I'm so sorry..."

In a moment that seemed to mock reality, the door began to open wider behind the stunned housewife. Bertrand pushed past his wife, on to the porch. He stood and wordlessly gazed down at Elsa. And then Elsa's grasped it!

Bertrand was standing! He was walking!

Elsa cast her eyes back towards the apple trees, to where the girl had disappeared. "Pennie ..." she whispered in awe, "... what did you do?"

20.

Ethiere had never ridden a horse before.

Most folk in Hollingston didn't own a horse, and those who did weren't the type to leave them out and available for the nicking. Master Hat had never fancied a scheme to steal a horse. What would you do with a horse? After you rode it around, then what? Ethiere was pretty sure you didn't eat horses – at least none of the Gang's Mothers had ever served horse stew.

Ethiere was familiar enough with the nature of horses without sitting astride one. He knew at least a dozen ways to get a horse to spook, and had three times as many stories of how a Gang member had used an agitated horse as a handy distraction.

They'd stuck Sarah up on a horse, which seemed like a good idea. No one wanted a repeat of yesterday – what with her falling due to the strain of fatigue. The little girl was dwarfed sitting atop the roan, and as a precaution, Reed's men had lashed her firmly to the saddle. If you didn't count the short ride to the barn yesterday, it was her first time on a horse. And Sarah, by her own admission, wasn't counting yesterday. She had been unconscious, after all.

The break they'd taken was over just as soon as it began as Reed called for them to continue. They marched ahead at the same urgency-lacking pace set by the soldier that was leading Lady Sophie's horse. Sometime in the morning, Sarah had managed to turn herself backwards in her saddle. The girl had worked her usual magic and had admirably managed to keep the noblewoman engaged in conversation for the better part of two hours. As the horses continued their slow canter forward, it appeared that Sarah had a fresh set of topics just waiting to jump from her tongue. Ethiere had found it very convenient to keep a few paces off to the side and just listen.

The horse was only semi-interesting. He found Lady Greer much more so. While she and her companion had ridden side saddle yesterday, the noblewoman had unequivocally told her bevy of soldiers that she was too sore to do so again today. She sat on the horse, her hiked-up dress displaying a generous portion of her leg, despite her attempt to keep a blanket over her lap.

Women intrigued him – and yet Ethiere found he had less experience with them than with horses. Sure, there were the Mothers that Master Hat found to cook and clean for his Gang. But they weren't women – not in that way. They were empty shells, hollow – dead in every sense except that their heart still insisted on beating. And there were the girls in the Children's Gang as well. Like Kari.

Kari. She was certainly becoming more and more like a woman – but … but what? He knew Kari favored him; she'd done nothing to hide it. And he enjoyed being with her, he wouldn't deny it. But he had never pursued it – a relationship. He was the leaf. The river eventually ripped everything he loved away from him. It was easier not to grow attached.

The women Ethiere had the most contact with were those that he stole from. He only knew women from what he could observe from his rooftop outposts.

What he observed was that women were far more interesting than men. The way they moved – their subtle bustle and bounce when they walked or the grace with which they carried themselves. The way they dressed – in bright colors or patterns, in various shapes and cuts. The way they openly expressed themselves

– a bashful flutter of eyelashes, an inviting smile, the animated manner in which they spoke with their hands.

Men were remarkably dull by comparison.

"I don't know what I'd do with all of that money," Sarah admitted. The innocent girl was still mesmerized by Greer's accounting of her family's wealth. It was not the first time the topic had come up today – and without fail, the Lady's companion made it a point to stare directly at Ethiere. He couldn't understand why? Did she think that the mere mention of gold was all it took to drive him into a thieving frenzy?

"You really don't do anything with it. It just sits there." Greer explained. "My father has advisors and agents that help him manage it."

Sarah kept shaking her head in disbelief. "My father says it's a happy week if we've got two spare coppers to rub together." Her admiration of the noblewoman was evident in her voice. "What stops you going to the market and just picking up anything that catches your eye?"

"What stops me?" The Lady smirked. "My father. According to him, the market is no place for a woman of my station and status. That's what we have servants for. " Greer paused and considered. "Or maybe he's frightened that I'd just go out and burn a hole in his coffers."

"My dad doesn't let me go into the market either," Sarah answered. "Says it's crowded. Says it's dangerous."

The assessments were correct on all accounts, but Ethiere noted a glaring omission.

Thieves.

--- * --- * ---

Ethiere had a talent for recognizing patterns.

The more he sat and watched from his vantage point on the rooftops, the more he realized how predictable life really was. Sure, there was chaos in living – and chaos generally took all the attention. Even in the Children's Gang, most of the conversations were about a board that groaned unexpectedly underfoot or a constable that had been a might too slow or a touch too fast on his route. The unanticipated got the notice – seeing past it to the commonplace took skill.

It was much like the streets themselves, he decided. At one single moment, you really couldn't tell who would be walking down 5th and Broad. Oh, someone familiar with the street would be able to count off a dozen or so merchants that regularly sold their wares on 5th. And if you were paying attention, you might know that the round faced woman with the bonnet always shops the markets on Twosdays, or that the butcher got his salted pork delivered on Thirdsday and Evensday mornings. But even if you watched that street for an age – you'd never get it all right. There would always be someone running some errand that only chanced to have happened that day.

But despite not being able to accurately account for the people – for the relative chaos in the world, Ethiere could readily predict the cobblestones of 5th and Broad. They were always there, steady and firm underneath the current of constantly moving men and women. There was always a sure foundation of predictability just below the chaos.

Predictability, Master Hat had taught them, was a thief's best friend.

The woman turned onto 5th, not a moment later than Ethiere would have guessed. He'd first noticed her several months back due to the small, tasseled parasol that she carried. Other women in the market carried parasols – Kari said it was a very fashionable thing to do. She knew better than him on such matters. But when other women carried their parasols, they carried them almost lazily over their shoulders, as if the spread of bright fabric was bought along to give a background to their faces. Not this woman. She carried her parasol in two hands and held straight up – as if she was bearing the royal colors in some military procession.

It was odd – and that oddness made her standout. And her continuation in that oddness, week after week, made her predictable. And it made her a game.

She came in to market every other Thirdsday. She hadn't missed in four months. Kari and he would usually race to see who could spot the woman and her grand parasol first – which led to them becoming more and more familiar with her routine. A routine, Ethiere guessed, the woman wasn't aware she even had.

The woman walked up the street. She tended to start left, veering towards a man with an open-stand cart of guavas and mangos from Taugaro. She veered and she looked – but she would never stop. Kari suggested that she liked the smells. Ethiere noted they'd never seen her purchase anything from an open-stand cart. After her short wander to the left, she'd always turn back to the right, weaving through the foot traffic, just in front of the long, crimson draped jeweler's booth.

The jewelers, three men, were also creatures of habit. They owned the building behind their booth, but only used it to finish striking a deal with a customer. Two men manned the street-side table, each brandishing the latest moonstone necklaces, gemstone laced rings and pendants, and jade figurines from Genault.

The woman stopped, without fail, every time.

The jewelers called out a greeting and eagerly held up their most recent acquisitions. Neither he nor Kari had ever seen her buy anything – and most likely she never had. But Ethiere knew merchants like he knew the insides of his leather slippers and he knew a merchant wouldn't suffer a woman every week unless he was seeing some coin come of it. She never bought – but Ethiere would have wagered his shirt the woman had a husband who did.

Ethiere watched as one of the jewelers held out a beautiful pendant. The chain was long, the individual links tiny, and at the end sat a ruby the size of a raspberry, encrusted around the edges with a golden framework. The merchants knew their customer – the woman's eyes always went wide when there were large stones in the proffered piece. They never bothered showing her anything with pearls.

The woman put her hand to the spot above her bosom – as if trying to feel where the pendant might lay if it ever graced her neck. Her hand stayed put, running a small, tight circle on the sea-foam green fabric of her dress as the jeweler highlighted his craftsmanship

The dresses. That was another interesting thing about the woman. He hadn't noticed this until several weeks of playing the game with Kari – but the woman wore her dresses in a pattern as well. It was always the pink one with the trim that looked like roses, or it was the yellow one that bunched at the hip. It alternated every week – or so he'd assumed until she showed up in the sea-foam green dress when she should have been decked in yellow. After careful observation and a few more weeks, Ethiere determined that on the Thirdsday after Holyday, the green dress was always worn.

Just like today.

The merchant held out the pendant, letting the woman fondle the ruby in her fingers. At his insistence, she took it, bouncing it in her palms as if assessing the weight. This was another of her routines. She inspected each piece of jewelry she was handed as if she expected to find out it was filled with sand. She'd tap on the gold, flick at it with a fingernail, spin the trinket in her hands looking for blemishes ... it was quite comical. The merchants bore the process with patience.

And then the hanky would come out. Each dress had a matching hanky, the sole purpose of which was to abolish the smudge of fingerprints. The colored cloth would give a thorough rubbing to each gem, before she set the hanky aside and held the piece up to see it catch the afternoon sunlight.

It was time.

Ethiere glanced across the street to see Kari already approaching the jeweler stand. She walked expertly behind a lumbering gentleman, keeping herself completely out of view of the ever-wary jewelers. Just as Kari got within striking distance, Ethiere kicked at the loosened panel of wood in front of him.

The nails, already worked loose the night before, popped free and the storefront sign made a wonderful, attention-grabbing groan as in slipped downward. Every eye on the street went to the sign, or to those below shrieking in panic as they tried to get away. No one saw the black-clad young man sink further into the recess between the building roofs.

And more importantly, no one saw the little girl that scampered away from the jeweler booth.

Ethiere raced back to the hideout, making it there just as Kari did. She smiled in triumph. She was a good little thief. Some of the other boys in the Gang gave him grief about spending so much time with a girl. Ethiere didn't see what the big deal was.

"I nearly jumped out of my slippers when that sign started down – and I knew it was coming! What a miserable groan it gave!"

"You did wonderful, Kari!" he told her. "They're probably just figuring out that it's missing!"

Ethiere was ecstatic the theft had gone so well. Usually Master Hat devised the targets and developed the plans, but today had been all Ethiere. And while Master Hat generally frowned on others running games he didn't devise, Ethiere had to believe their benefactor wouldn't mind this time.

Inside the hideout, he and Kari weaved through the other children into the room that served as the kitchen. The room was empty except for one of the Mothers. Most of the women that Master Hat found to tend for his little Gang were broken

– Ethiere didn't have a better word for it. There was something wrong about them – something in their vacant eyes and listless motions. There was never a drop of happiness in them. Never a smile.

They never seemed to live long. They only appeared half-alive as it was.

Kari slipped him their prize behind her back and ran forward after he took it. She bounded up to the sad woman and took her hands. Despite the bubble of excitement in front of her, the Mother seemed unaware of Kari's presence. "Mother! Mother!" Kari dropped the hands and took the woman by the face. "Mother Emiline!"

Slowly, recognition returned to the empty eyes. Ethiere snatched on the moment. You could never be sure of how long they would last.

With a flourish, he presented Mother Emiline with the sea-foam green hanky. "Kari tells me that you fancy green."

Their gift was accepted graciously albeit silently, but the unanticipated present seemed to fan the faint spark of life in the broken woman's eyes. She ran her fingers gently over the silk cloth and held it up to press it against her face. Kari beamed at the reaction – it was just what they'd hoped for. She began to relate the entire escapade ...

"How long did it take you to plan it?" said a voice behind them. Master Hat. Mother Emiline's face lost its luster as her brief flirtation with life collapsed in on itself. Kari, most of her tale concluded, managed to jump only slightly. Neither she nor Ethiere had heard Hat enter the room. Their teacher was an expert in everything he instructed on.

Ethiere turned to face his mentor and benefactor. "We've been watching the woman we stole it from for several months now, sir. But we didn't work up the plan until a week ago." Master Hat had a way of looking at everything and everyone in the room all at once, without letting up a gaze that could single you out. Ethiere felt very uncomfortable. He knew Hat didn't like them striking out on their own –but it was such a small take! "It was only a green silk handkerchief," Ethiere explained. "We just wanted to cheer up Mother Emiline."

Hat continued as the silent observer for a moment longer, before turning to the door. "Walk with me, Ethiere." It was only barely more an invitation than it was a command. The adolescent thief followed at Hat's heel, and waited for the benefactor to speak. "Was Kari's description of the heist accurate?"

Ethiere mind filtered through the details. "In the important details, yes."

"You really robbed a jewelry vendor for a silk hanky?"

Ethiere couldn't help a smile. "It would have been a mango vendor if she liked more than just the smell ..." They reached Hat's personal office – his carefully guarded corner of their hideout. The door had no less than five different locks on it – specialty locks, the Gang members had long ago observed. And not any from the litany that Master Hat had taught them to pick. The benefactor pulled out a set of keys securely fastened to a long chain and quickly worked the locks. After a moment, the door relaxed on its hinges and Hat pushed it open.

The office was one of the larger rooms in the building – but one without windows or other points of entry. It was cramped, however, between the large desk thrust against one wall and the stacked crates and boxes of stolen merchandise that huddled against the other. Ethiere quickly recognized several items from his more recent assignments – and saw several other trinkets that would have drawn his curiosity had he not been in Master Hat's company. Hat slipped behind the desk – a solid bureau with a scattering of papers atop it.

Hat reclined back into the office's lone chair and caught Ethiere staring. "This is your first time in my office, I see. It always brings a sense of relief to see that my brightest pupils have not yet found their way into my personal domain." The man leaned forward. "It is fascinating, is it not? The collection I have here – from past jobs? Not anything I'm set to hold onto, mind you, just things that are still awaiting the appropriate buyer with the appropriate willingness to pay."

"Fascinating indeed," Ethiere marveled.

"Have you given thought to it, lad?"

The question puzzled the young thief. "Thought to what?"

Hat smiled. "The future, of course. Your future, to be specific. Of course the option to cash out will always be available to you, Ethiere, but I don't foresee you ever taking it – am I wrong? No, I'm not, I can see it." Hat leaned back into the chair again, contemplating. "There is no denying your talent, Ethiere. This little action you ran today proves you've got the brain for it – not just the hands and feet. This was your first planned theft, correct?"

"Correct," Ethiere answered honestly – and afterwards wondered if there wasn't something more to the casual question than he immediately assumed.

The answer did seem to please Hat. "And a fine success for your first foray into the work of masterminding! A small take – to be sure – but success to a thief is measured by the objective and the escape, and those were executed marvelously. Did you find it thrilling?"

"The take, sir?"

Hat nodded. "Watching it unfold? It is why you took the post on the roof – am I wrong? Why Kari took the handkerchief. So that you could have the best vantage point – no?" Ethiere frowned. He'd not thought of that before. He'd taken the roof because he was the stronger of the two and they'd wanted the sign to teeter with a single kick. But he could not deny how wonderful it had been watching everything come together like he'd planned. "Admit it, you've tasted the thrill – how can you not hunger for more?"

Ethiere considered Hat's questions. Would he plan a second heist? Possibly. He'd not considered it. There wasn't a need for it – certainly not a 'hunger' like Hat was suggesting. Ethiere shrugged as his answer.

"Look around you, Ethiere. Look at this office. Can you see yourself here? Can you see yourself making the plans and sending children out to execute them perfectly?"

Again, Ethiere was forced to shrug. "I guess."

Hat caught the waver. "But?"

Caught it, but misinterpreted it. "It's not like I've got any control over it."

The man smirked. "But you can dream, no? You have ambitions, don't you Ethiere? What drives you?"

Ethiere thought about the question. What drove him? He considered the question and found it flawed. It assumed that he had control of his life. "I don't have ambitions," he answered plainly. "I just aim to survive what comes."

Hat eyed him curiously. "Like a leaf on the river ..." he commented – and Ethiere found the analogy fitting. He nodded. "No ambitions, really?" Hat commented. It was clear Master Hat had not expected the answer, but also clear that he did not doubt its validity. He shook off the awe and leaned forward *anew. "Ethiere, I find that I will soon be in need of a new deputy. I suspect Carl will soon be cashing out – perhaps setting up an operation similar to mine in another of Tollia's cities. His loss will leave me short of someone that can look after things while I'm out on business. You have my trust, Ethiere. What do you say?"*

The thief shrugged – more concerned over the revelation that Carl might be leaving than the idea of a promotion. "I guess. If that's what you want?"

Hat chortled another laugh and excused Ethiere from his presence. As the thief left, he heard Hat muttering under his breath. "Like a leaf on the river ..."

--- * --- * ---

Greer harrumphed and scratched at her wrist. "I wouldn't be able to say. We'd have to ask someone a little more familiar with that arena."

Suddenly, her head swung and she was looking at him. As surprised as Ethiere was, she seemed equally so. And he knew why. Greer had seen him staring at her. Her cheeks flushed red and her head snapped back to the horse's mane. At the same time, her free hand clawed at the blanket, trying to fix it back into position.

Her legs! She thought he'd been staring at her legs! It wasn't entirely untrue. He'd taken more glances at the curve of her calves than any gentlemen would have risked, but at that moment he'd been thinking about the market and ... Ethiere bit his lip in deep thought. He was at a loss for what to do. Should he try to explain what was ...

He stumbled forward, propelled by a well-aimed shove to his shoulder. Ethiere maintained his balance, if but barely. Trotting up beside him – getting right in between his line of sight to Greer – was the irate Captain Reed. There was nothing kind written on the man's face.

"You don't look at her," Reed warned. "Not ever again."

"But ..."

"I'm watching you, thief," the soldier rattled. "We all are. Don't talk to her. Don't go near her. Don't look at her. You might think you can try something. You might think you can get away with something." Reed put his hand to the hilt of his sword. "You try even once – I promise you'll never get an opportunity to try a second time. This is your only warning." Reed's warning was enough. Without a word of protest, Ethiere ran forward, distancing himself from the horses and their riders.

Ethiere slowed his pace as he neared Kashif and his single bodyguard. He rubbed his wrist as he tried to gauge if he'd positioned himself correctly in the company – away from any of Reed's men. What was he doing wrong? First Dom. Now Greer. It had only been two days! At this pace, he'd be out of people he was allowed to talk to by mid-week.

His eyes were drawn to his wrist – to the irritated skin that was chaffing under the scratching of his nails. He didn't even realize he was scratching it again – though he seemed to be catching himself doing it more and more today. Something was aggravating the skin – but what? A spider-bite while he had slept? Only Domus knew what kind of spiders and fleas were nesting in that barn …

Ethiere stopped … a pattern was beginning to emerge.

Lady Greer had been scratching at her wrists, just before she'd caught him looking, hadn't she? And now that he thought about it, he was certain she'd done it other times throughout their morning ride. He'd been too focused on … on other things to have paid it much attention. But he was certain. He was certain that whatever was ailing him was ailing her as well.

His ran ahead until his pace had put him on par with Billick, and Ethiere risked a quick glance to test his theory. Sure enough, the skin on Billick's wrist was red. The side-burned man coughed quietly – bringing Ethiere's eyes up. Billick was shaking his head slowly. "Whatever you're thinking looks interesting – I can guarantee it won't be worth it."

Ethiere looked away and slowed his pace again. Is that all anyone thought of him? A thief? Did they take any attention from him as nothing more than him working up a scheme to nick something from them? Yes, he was still very intrigued by Kashif's bag – but only to see what was in it. He had no attention of stealing something from it. What for? Where would he go with it? What would he do with it? He was just curious.

What did Billick have? Nothing. And sure, Dom had that necklace thing he kept hidden in his pocket – but Ethiere wasn't interested in that. It obviously was important to Dom, and that was good enough for Ethiere to leave it alone. Was he a thief? Yes … but he didn't just take things …

Dom. Wrists …

Could it be?

Ethiere looked back down the line, past the soldiers and the horses, to where the silent, brooding, Dom trudged forward, drowning in his coat. The long sleeves were together, hiding from view what was happening underneath. Ethiere shifted his attention back to the front. He was more or less back in step with the Arcan scientist. Kashif shifted the pack to the opposite shoulder, but didn't say anything.

"How are your wrists?" Ethiere asked.

The Arcan raised an eyebrow. He had his attention.

Ethiere smiled. "I have a theory for you."

21.

"This thing is hiding out in the Alben Valley?"

Captain Reed's question came with a large measure of skepticism. For the better part of the last hour, Greer had felt an urge to change directions – to angle further west. When they finally came upon the Alben River crossroads, she and the other Band members had unanimously agreed on the direction in which to change their course.

The soldiers were hard-pressed to believe that the evil creature they were pursuing wasn't in the highly populated city of Hollingston or the port and business districts of Wellsford that were a straight shot south. The sleepy homesteading valley of Alben seemed an odd location for a demon.

Greer waved a finger in a west by southwest direction. "It's somewhere that way," she said. "I can't tell you more than that. I can't even tell you how close it is."

Reed nodded to himself. The Captain had made it a point to stay by her side since the incident with the thief. Greer felt her face redden again just thinking about it. He'd been staring at her legs – openly staring at her legs! And as embarrassing as it was – Greer also felt the tiniest bit flattered. And that made her embarrassed as well. She – a nobleman's daughter – actually caring that a common criminal boy was caught gawking at her.

It was only the second time a man had ever looked at her in that way. Although … She frowned. She did not know what to make of Reed's reaction. Of course it was his duty to guard her honor – and the trouncing he'd given Ethiere was certainly within those bounds. So what then? Why did she wonder if there wasn't some other motive behind the vehemence in his voice? It was silly, especially for the daughter of a nobleman, to think …

"I do wonder what it's doing in Alben Valley," the Captain went on.

Greer felt like tossing something at him, but she didn't even have reins. "Merciful, merciful Domus, Reed! I don't know! Maybe it's helping them raise a barn! Does it really matter?"

Reed's lips went tight. "If we better knew its agenda ..."

"It's a monster! It doesn't have a face! Does it have to have an agenda?"

The Captain, discomfited, found something interesting on the opposite side of the road. "Just making conversation," he muttered apologetically.

She frowned, not so much at Reed but at knowing her words would be enough to keep him silent. She could have just order him to close his mouth – or better yet, switch out with one of his other men. But she hadn't – because that's not what she wanted. And it was more than just her dislike of having to use her title – or really, her father's title – to get results. She hadn't minded talking with Captain Reed. She had just grown tired of the entirety of their conversation centering on his doubts.

Greer turned her head to the front, making it a point to refocus on the still-backwards facing Sarah.

It surprised her – how much she'd enjoyed the talk they'd had. Oh, she'd overheard bits and pieces of the inquisitive interrogations she'd given Ethiere the other day and Kashif this morning. She'd known her time would come, and she would have to endure the limitless string of questions. But it hadn't been bothersome at all. Yes, the girl had been firing questions at her all morning – but she wasn't enduring them. She was enjoying them.

It was Sarah. She was so genuine. There was nothing fabricated in her voice, no careful check on her responses. She didn't play the stupid courtier games and praise Greer when she made a witty comment – didn't needlessly laugh at her jokes that were only borderline humorous. It was refreshing – especially after the hours with Sophie – to have someone communicating naturally, instead of rehearsing lines from a scripted friendship. Greer had actually forgotten several times already that miserable Sophie was riding just one more horse length ahead!

Greer didn't need all the fingers on one hand to count the people who had taken an interest in her. The real her. Not the Lady. Not the daughter of Lord Baron Cahill. Not the girl with the large dowry attached to her marriage. Just Greer.

It felt nice to be just Greer.

She hadn't felt that way since … well, since Bridgette left.

The slight-framed Sarah, lashed securely to the horse, was studying the engorged river that ran parallel with the road. The road drew near the banks as the water ponderously moved to where it would empty in the port. "Your first time seeing a river?" Greer called to her.

Sarah shook her head; her eyes remained locked on the water. "I saw the Alben in Hollingston once." Sarah peered up. "But it doesn't look the same. It looks a lot nicer here – out in the open – away from the city. It looks …"

"Inviting?" Greer guessed.

The small girl smiled and nodded. "I've never swam before."

Greer knew what was coming. "Your father says it isn't safe."

Sarah looked back towards the flow. "He might be right on this one. I'm more likely to sink like a stone than float like a duck, right?" The little girl brushed the hair from her eyes. "Have you ever swam before, Greer?"

Greer felt her own eyes drift to the lazy moving river.

"Once. Almost."

--- * --- * ---

Bridgette never lacked creative ideas.

She did lack a bit of inhibition – but Headmistress Packer claimed the two went hand in hand. Many of Bridgette's ideas – including all of her best ones –

landed them a scolding from the beleaguered woman. The Headmistress often told them that no woman should have to suffer the torment of raising two headstrong sixteen year old girls at the exact same time. "Surely," she'd told them once, "you've put me through enough to guarantee my eternity in Domus' Embrace – because heaven knows you're going to send me there early!"

It was on a humidly hot and unpleasant day that Bridgette gave her verdict. "We should go swimming." Greer, never having gone swimming, immediately bought into the idea. It was sure better than languishing within the walls of the estate. And it was certainly something her father wouldn't approve of.

Greer found herself doing that more and more of late. Purposefully aiming to cross one of the lines that her father had set. Was it a phase? Headmistress Packer spoke on and on about phases and about how they passed and on how – hopefully – Greer would one day enter the 'dignified' phase. But until then, Greer was finding the 'rebellious' phase very intriguing.

Under the excuse of 'picking flowers', the two young women escaped the confines of the estate and raced across the hills. Headmistress Packer hadn't believed their story – but what could she do? They hadn't technically done anything wrong – yet.

As they went, Bridgette told her of the place they were going – a bend on the Tizred River where the water was cool and deep, and the trees were overgrown and shaded the banks. What's more, Bridgette claimed the spot was well-known among the locals – and there was a chance there might be others there.

Maybe even some young men.

"Oh, Bridgette," Greer said, "let's not be ourselves! Let's not be a Lady and her companion! Let's just be normal – regular people – and not tell anyone."

Bridgette was game. "I won't be able to call you Greer, then. People might recognize your name."

Greer nodded. "Call me Anne. And what should I call you?"

"Jenna," Bridgette decided. "I shall be your best friend Jenna." The Tizred turned out to be quite the trek away, but they passed the time effortlessly as they expounded on their new identities. It was important, after all, what Anne's favorite color was or what Jenna would choose to do with her free time. Greer poured into her alias all of the secret desires her title was denying her.

Anne played the drums. Bridgette had laughed and applauded that one – and had added that Jenna always danced to the beat.

The Tizred opened up to them as they crested a gentle hill. The bend was pristine, the river stretching wider at the turn. The sun-shimmering water looked like it was barely even moving. The entire scene – the water, the trees, the birds lodged in the branches – it was like something she'd expect to see hanging on the wall of the estate. Indeed, vowed Greer, if she ever had the chance to commission a painting, she'd send the artist to this very spot on the hill.

"Look!" Bridgette whispered excitedly, her finger pointing toward the water. There was movement – and Greer wondered if it wasn't some kind of animal ... and saw it was something altogether better. Bridgette's grin blossomed. "Boys!"

There were two of them, neck-deep in the water, splashing and wrestling as only boys could do. It was silly, immature – and absolutely enthralling behavior. It was several long minutes before either noticed the two figures watching them from atop the hill.

The splashing stopped. Greer wondered if one of them hadn't just whispered "Look, girls!" to the other. One of the young men waded closer to the shore, his chest emerging from the water. He motioned an invitation and sank back into the water.

"What should we do?" Greer softly asked.

Bridgette had not stopped smiling, and her eyes were still firmly fixed on the heads bobbing in the Tizred. "I don't know about you," she said as she undid the bow at the back of her dress, "but I intend to go swimming." Bridgette turned her back to Greer. "Help me with the buttons."

Was she serious? Bridgette was bouncing on her toes. Yes, she was serious. Greer fumbled with the buttons, and her impatient companion waited not a second later to pull the dress over her head.

And just like that, Bridgette was standing out on an open hill in her undergarments.

"Are you coming?"

"Brid..."

The scandalously clothed girl held a finger to her lips. "Remember – it's Jenna!" she said, and giggled her way down the hill. The bank of the river didn't stop her, and Bridgette made a grand splashing entrance into the water – much to the delight of the two young men.

Who were now looking up at her - expectantly.

Greer felt her face redden.

Bridgette laughed. "Come on – Anne! The water feels marvelous!"

But Greer already knew she wouldn't be able to do it. She wouldn't be able to strip down – not out in the open – especially not in front of two boys! She would die from shame! But at the same moment, as she watched Bridgette glide through the water, Greer felt a pang of envy. Bridgette was free. Bridgette was fun. Those had always been the reasons they'd gotten along. Why they'd been such perfect friends. Bridgette discovered how to live life, and she was wonderful at pulling Greer along.

There was no one to stop her. No one to tell her what to do and what not to do. No one to remind her of her nobility and her father's name and the untarnished nature of his reputation. There was no one to stop her – but she couldn't do it. For all of her attempts at crossing her father's imposing rules, she could not find it in herself to cross this one.

Perhaps she was already lost – already too confined to the mold she was raised to conform to.

"I think I'll just dip my toes," she said weakly.

Bridgette shrugged. "It always starts as just toes ... "

Greer found a shallow embankment off to the side, removed her shoes, and stepped lightly into the water. It was crisper than she had expected. Her feet came alive with invigorating sensations – the bumps of the rocks under her heels, the course sand creeping between her toes. She sat and let her feet idly explore while she watched the others.

Bridgette fit right in. She splashed, and she shrieked when they splashed back. She would jump up on one boy's back, trying to topple him into the water and would beg for mercy when they moved to retaliate. Greer watched as Bridgette was caught again – and she smiled. Greer knew her friend was faster than that. But she didn't fault her companion for wanting to get caught.

Bridgette was forced closer to the bank by the darker-haired boy. She stood, taunting her pursuer, goading him to come after her. Her long hair clung together, a perfect drape over her shoulders, and her undergarments clung flatteringly to her figure. Greer felt the pang of envy again.

"How do your toes like the water?" Greer jumped. She hadn't seen the sandy-haired boy approach.

"Oh ..." She desperately tried to recover her wits – not the easiest thing to do in front of a young man that wasn't wearing a shirt. "Um, just ... fine."

He sloshed out of the river, his dripping hair arrayed in perfect chaos, and sat beside her. "You should see what the rest of your legs think." She smiled – and was mortified that it might look too girlish, so she stopped. "If you want to," he amended.

There was another big splash from the two in the river, which provided enough of a distraction to save Greer from responding. Where was her brain? The presence of the smiling young man with the taut muscled arms and the sun-bronzed back had nullified her ability to think. Or was it that he was wearing only his smallclothes? She felt her cheeks color – and resisted the urge to just stare at him.

"I think my friend likes your friend," the sandy-haired boy said conspiratorially. Bridgette and the dark-haired boy in the water weren't splashing anymore. Their heads, barely above the surface of the water, were close together. They looked as though they were trying to share a secret without talking.

"I'd say my friend likes yours as well," Greer managed, relieved that the words she spoke came out in the correct order. She risked speaking more. "I'm sorry we interrupted your fun."

"What?" the youth asked. "Interrupted?"

"You were having such a good time – in the water," Greer pointed out. "My friend seems to have taken your place."

The boy shrugged, and Greer watched the fluid play of the muscles in his shoulders and back. He looked at her – green eyes and a lopsided grin. "I think I like this place better." He leaned in closer to her – and it was as if all the air in the world vanished. She couldn't breathe. She couldn't care any less. "My name is Caleb."

Her throat was tight, but she managed an answer. "Anne."

Caleb lowered his eyes from hers, and his gaze swept down her dress to her toes. Her body tingled with nervous excitement, and she had to fight to keep from fidgeting. At that moment, she wished she looked more like Bridgette. Bridgette was the pretty one. Bridgette had the blonde hair and the ...

Caleb mussed his hair and interrupted her moment of self-agonizing dejection. "Has anyone ever told you that you have lovely calves?"

--- * --- * ---

"What did it feel like?" Sarah asked.

Greer laughed to herself. "It was certainly not what I expected," Greer said. "But it is one of my happiest memories."

"Well ... then why didn't you go back a second time?"

The innocent question swept the happy memories away like a rolling wave. Sarah had no idea that she'd said anything hurtful – the girl still thought they were talking about swimming. "Sometimes," Greer answered eventually, "regardless of what you want, the world works to make sure a second time never occurs."

The melancholy change in tone was not lost on Sarah. "Why – what happened?"

"My father happened," Greer answered. She would have launched into a diatribe against her father and the unfairness of life – except for her present company. Greer held her tongue, knowing the sulking words of a Baron's daughter would ring hollow over in the ears of the poor city girl.

Sarah's focus had returned to the river. Greer had an idea. "Stop the horses!" she called out. "Reed!"

"Neald!" the Captain relayed immediately and drew nearer. "Is something wrong?"

As the horse lumbered to a halt, Greer answered by slipping down from the saddle. Captain Reed was caught between assisting her down and just being in the way, and the result was an awkward arrangement that left them standing a bit too close together. She would have retreated a step had she not been right up against the horse's side – and Reed seemed momentarily paralyzed.

"My Lady," he apologized as he backed away. "What is the matter?"

"I'm tired of riding, Reed," she said – which was true. Hours of sitting in the saddle were not going unnoticed by buffeted muscles. And indeed, her legs didn't seem quite right underneath her now that she was back on the ground. So she was tired – and it was as good a reason as any. "I'd prefer to walk for a spell."

"Walk?"

"Is that a problem, Captain?"

She got the reaction she anticipated. "No, Lady Greer."

"Now we'll be forced to walk?" moaned Sophie.

Greer ignored her companion and gave another order to Reed. "Unlash Sarah – we'll walk together." The young girl beamed. "But first, we absolutely must dip our tired toes in that river!"

"Really?" Sarah asked, bouncing against her bonds in excitement. Greer laughed. They wouldn't 'swim', per se, but it would be ten toes closer than the girl had ever gotten before. As Neald lifted Sarah down, Sophie dismounted with a heavy harrumph. Greer wondered how she could disinvite her companion. Thankfully, Sophie all but did that on her own.

"If I'm going to be forced to *walk* to Alben," she said as if walking were akin to skinning babies, "then forgive me if I choose not to escort you down to the riverbank!"

Freed from Sophie, Greer took Sarah's hand as they picked a route down to the river's bank. Sarah, fully caught up in the moment, waded in to her knees, soaking the hems of her dress. With a mischievous grin, the little girl scooped up a handful of water and flung it towards Greer. Greer shrieked – decidedly unbecoming for a Lady – and splashed back. As she turned away from the next counterattack, Greer saw Reed watching from the top of the embankment.

He was watching – but in a very un-guardsman-like manner. He was even smiling.

And curiously, Greer found the nervous tingling had returned.

22.

"You tell me you don't think that's unnatural," dared Sergeant Bostitch as they stood on the lip of the road's embankment. "He was draining blood from his own arm – vial after vial of it like it's nothing to him."

Captain Reed couldn't argue against the unusualness of the Arcan's bloodletting, but he also knew that Bostitch wasn't looking for a counterpoint. He wanted to vent his disgust – and Reed was perfectly willing to let the soldier diffuse via words rather than via weapons. Reed was only listening with one ear. He was rather enjoying watching Lady Greer and Sarah play in the water below.

He'd not known it was possible. He'd never expected a Lady to know how to play.

"Neald and I spoke with Murphy," Bost continued, "and he says it's been going on since they left Hollingston! Least three or four times a day!"

Reed shook his head and muttered again how strange it was. He pulled his attention from the scene below – it wouldn't do for the Lady to catch him staring. The entire Band had halted with the swimming expedition, and Reed was given to once more assess the traveling company he was committed to protecting.

Their day's journey thus far had been uneventful. It had taken them the better part of the morning to get started – something Reed hadn't minded. Lady Greer's companion Sophie had demanded a bath after sleeping – as she put it – 'like some common swine'. The Lady, still in a cantankerous mood from their spat the previous evening, had ordered Reed to fill a pig trough with water so her companion – in her words – could "bathe like some common swine".

Then they'd had to search for the two children, who for some unknown and morbid reason had decided to entertain themselves in the graveyard. And then the Arcan had raised a fuss about 'jostling' the vials of his blood, insisting he be given time to record his observations. And then Sophie had started up again – contending that they should force Ethiere to empty his pockets, just to be certain he'd taken nothing in the night.

That was all just this morning. Reed was convinced this was no Band of Six. This was a Band of Lunatics.

He didn't blame Billick for wanting to strike out on his own.

Bostitch interjected the silence with a question. "What do you figure's going to happen if we do come across that thing we saw in the fountain?"

Despite his own reservations, Reed opted for the political answer. "Well, that's what the Band is for, right?"

"Sorry, slipped my mind there, Captain," the veteran offered a lopsided grin. "So should we hold the children's hands as they approach the monster, or do you think they can manage on their own? Maybe little Sarah can splash the thing into submission?"

"Bost …"

"Or perhaps I can teach that thieving fellow how to operate my crossbow?" he suggested.

Reed grinned dourly. "You getting to a point, Sergeant, or do you just like to listen to yourself talk?"

"I do have a fantastically sonorous voice, Cap …"

"I've already heard the bit about the Deacon's choir," reminded Reed.

"Could have mistaken me for an angel," Bostitch mused and stretched his arms. "Which reminds me, I shouldn't waste an opportunity like this. Smoked my last roll an hour ago."

"I've built fires that smoke less than you do."

"Don't get me started on your fire-building skills …" Bostitch mocked. "But back to our plan …" The Sergeant's mood was suddenly very serious. "Do we even have a plan?"

Reed frowned. He took two steps sideways and focused on the side-burned murderer at the head of the column. "Your thoughts on Master Billick's plan?"

"The 'run-a-sword-through-it' plan?" Bostitch's smile reappeared. "That's what you're going with?"

"You'd rather we let the Arcan out-think it?" Reed responded, knowing he was nettling the Sergeant's favorite topic.

Bost chortled. "Maybe he could bleed it dry?"

Reed shared the laugh, just as Neald called for him. The Corporal was still on horseback and was standing in the stirrups. "Incoming rider, Captain. It's Cox, if I don't miss my guess."

Reed pulled a small spyglass from his saddlebag and lifted it to his eyes. "It's Cox!" The rider slowed as he neared the waiting party, and as he got closer, his uniform in Cahill's colors became clearer and clearer. Cox was round-faced with thinning hair, something his bristly mustache was probably meant to compensate.

It was hard to tell who was more relieved as Cox dismounted – the horseman or the horse. "Captain," Cox acknowledged. His salute mirrored his obvious weariness. "This is, if you don't mind me saying, quite a long ways from that fountain, sir."

Reed shifted uncomfortably in his saddle. "Yes, sorry. I didn't think I could spare a man to send a message …"

Cox exhaled loudly. "Don't waste an apology on me, sir. Save them for the Lord Baron." Reed caught the implication.

"Lord Baron Cahill?" Reed asked. "He's coming behind you?"

"We'll have to send a rider on a fresh horse back to the crossroads." Cox stretched his legs – as if to point out that he was entirely too sore to be given the assignment. "We're close enough to Alben – the Baron can catch up to us there."

Reed nodded. "Faldrow – get started."

As Faldrow complied with the order, Billick voiced his disdain. "Why bother to come back? What does the high and noble Lord Baron possibly think he's going to do against that creature?"

The withering look came from Reed, but the retort came from Cox. "The Lord Baron? Nothing." The soldier smiled. "That's why he's bringing a wizard."

23.

Elsa was hovering.

She, of course, would deny it. For thirty-four years of marriage and five children she had denied it. Housewives, she frequently told him, were too busy to hover. Martin didn't believe it for a moment. In fact, the more he observed, the more he came to the conclusion that it was the busyness – the constant moving from one task to another – that allowed Elsa her freedom to hover.

From his usual seat next to the hearth, Martin smiled thinly. He simply could not accept actual chores had taken Elsa past the sitting room windows by chance yet again.

She caught him watching and shot him a knowing look. "Don't say it, Martin," she warned.

He held up his hands and pled innocent. "I didn't say anything, dear."

"Well, stop thinking it so loudly, then." She folded her arms across her bosom as her eyes strayed back to the still darkness beyond the glass. Thirty-four years of marriage had enlightened Martin as to when his wife was not of a mind to be teased, and he wisely opted for silence. He knew Elsa was worried about Pennie. The frequent stops at the window were each driven by the ragged hope that maybe, perhaps, the girl might be coming back.

It was a time to say something comforting – but Martin was at a loss for what he could offer. The girl had been with them for less than a full day, and yet Elsa was taking her absence so hard. Martin had seen it coming – he'd seen the look in his wife's eyes when she'd insisted Pennie would stay. But he'd also seen the look in Pennie's eyes. He'd seen that she was no more likely to stay in one place than a feral animal. This day had been destined. Elsa's motherly heart would have been broken eventually.

Red rolled as he napped on the hearth. Maybe it was for the better that it had happened so soon.

"Where do you think she'll go?" Elsa asked in a voice above a whisper, still unable to pull her gaze from the shadows lounging on their property.

"She's a resourceful girl," he offered. "She'll manage."

"She's a scared girl," Elsa countered. "You didn't see the look on her face … after she touched Bertrand. You didn't see how panicked she was."

Indeed he hadn't, but neither was Martin a stranger to the fantastic story. He'd just barely concluded his business in Alben when he'd heard the commotion – a crowd gathering to hear Bertrand, lively on his two feet, tell the story no one could discount. Healed. Completely healed. Bones askew in shards for months were mended whole. Pennie was as famous as you could get in sleepy town like Alben. The miracle girl.

Elsa mused aloud. "What I can't tell is if she knew what she was doing. The way she reached out for him – it almost had to have been on purpose. But then – that fear in her eyes. Perhaps it was his scream and his fall. Perhaps it had just shocked her. Or maybe she was just as surprised as the rest of us … And then she ran."

Martin closed his eyes momentarily, feeling the radiant warmth from the ember-laden coals. His eyes reopened as Elsa asked a question. "Do you suppose … it was a miracle?"

Martin ran a finger along the polished curve of the chair arm. He'd contemplated the same question on his walk home. What had happened could not be denied. His own wife was a first-hand witness. And yet … Martin hedged. "Bertrand certainly thinks so."

Elsa nodded. "Well I've certainly been praying for him and Judith," she said. "I like to think it was a miracle. I like to believe I witnessed a benign act bestowed by Merciful Domus himself." She peered over her shoulder, back towards the failing light in the window. "Perhaps it will always just be something I wonder about – a question."

Martin reclined back into the chair and closed his eyes shut again. Questions. His wife would not be the only one with questions. He sighed. "Then you can pray for Pennie now. She'll need it."

Elsa moved purposefully to the door. Martin rose from his chair – wondering if Pennie really had returned. He saw the approaching figure – Physician Davies. Elsa opened the door as the man of medicine crested their porch. "Good evening, Elsa. I hope you didn't wait on me for supper."

"We figured business at the Miller's had you occupied," she answered. "I set aside a plate for you. I'll have it warmed back up in a moment."

"That would be nice, thank you," Davies accepted. He lingered in the sitting room as Elsa disappeared into the kitchen. "You, of course … heard." Martin nodded; there was no wondering as to what the physician was referring to. Davies rubbed at his perfectly trimmed beard. "She hasn't, by chance, returned."

Martin shook his head. "I don't figure that she will."

"A pity," Davies whispered. "I would have loved to interview her – find out just what happened."

"She healed a broken leg," Martin answered for him.

The Physician waved dismissively at the obvious answer. "I'm aware of that," he chided. "What baffles me is how! That leg was fractured in two different places. The bones weren't aligning, despite my best attempts to set them, and at best Bertrand would walk with a cane for the remainder of his life. What Pennie is purported to have done – with a single touch, no less! – laughs in the face of modern science! It shouldn't be possible!"

"Would you say it is a miracle then?" asked Elsa, appearing in the doorway to kitchen.

Davies deliberated his response, first looking to Martin, then to his folded hands. "Miracles are more of Deacon Elsbury's forte, I suppose. Let them heal the soul – I say – and I'll take care of the body. My studies in the sciences trumpeted natural laws, theorems and proofs – that a logical explanation, however deeply obscured, lay at the heart of every question. Though I dare purport myself to be a religious man, I will admit that my profession has dampened my belief in what Merciful Domus is capable of doing." Neither Martin nor his wife answered immediately – perhaps in respect of the very personal feelings that Davies was sharing. The Physician looked at Elsa. "I dare say this might be a miracle."

His response satisfied Elsa, who ducked back into the kitchen. Martin closed his eyes and reached to scratch Red's belly. A miracle? To the old farmer, it really didn't matter. When Martin considered what Pennie would have faced had she stayed – inquiring Physicians like Davies, legions of sick and afflicted seeking their own respite, those that might seek to exploit her gift – Martin couldn't deny it. He would have chosen to run as well. "Run far," he whispered under his breath. "Keep running."

24.

Apparently all you needed to be considered a town were eight roads that ran perpendicular to the main thoroughfare. It had been growing dark as they'd entered Alben, but Dom was sure he'd seen open fields at the end of some of the street-ways. And cows. It seemed odd to a boy who had lived his entire life within the belly of Wellsford Park.

It went without saying – Alben had no inn.

Regardless, it looked like the party would receive better accommodations than the barn of the night before. While Alben lacked an inn, it did have a mayor. The short, energetic man had met them at the edge of town with a blue longcoat and a winsome smile. As soon as Captain Reed dropped the name of Cahill, the mayor was at their beck and call.

Currently he was rallying the villagers to convert the town hall into sleeping quarters suitable for nobility.

Dom knew he would probably end up on the floor with an old quilt or two. He'd consider it a blessing. After being tied to his bed two nights ago, and the horrible dreams of last night, Dom was certain he could fall asleep on a pile of chipped bricks if he needed to.

At the moment, Dom was following orders. Billick had snapped at him and Sarah to stay out of the way, and they'd tried to do just that. There was a grand oak tree just outside of the town hall, wide enough that he and Sarah could sit side by side without touching. True to her promise, his new friend had done almost all of the talking that evening – telling him about Ladies and their wealth, their training in the twenty-two Tenets, and about horses…

"Are you scared, Dom?"

The question came as a surprise, as he could not fathom how the girl had jumped from horses to fear. He looked at her, unsure how to answer. He was always scared. There was always something out there bigger or meaner than you were. "What do you mean?"

"This is all so new to me. The furthest I'd ever gone before yesterday was to the cathedral for Holyday services. Now I'm sleeping in barns, riding horses, talking to a genuine Lady! I'm so excited by all these new adventures I'm having, I've almost forgotten that we're chasing a demon. I should be frightened, shouldn't I?"

Dom shrugged. "I don't know. Between Lady Greer's soldiers and the others …"

"See, that's what I'm saying! We've got the soldiers, and Billick has assured us he'll be the one to kill it. And Kashif will think of some brilliant plan to beat it – and Ethiere said he'd look out for us … And now we're going to have a wizard, too. We'd be the last two to have to face the demon. Why should we be scared?"

She had a point. "They'll probably tell us to go hide somewhere when it comes time to face it," he added.

"Find some spot to sit that's out of the way," Sarah quoted Billick in as deep a voice as the girl could muster. She laughed at her own impression, but quieted quickly. "The problem is – if I'm out of the way – I don't know that I'm going to be much help."

Dom looked at her sideways. Help? How much help could either one of them really be?

"We were each Banded for a reason, right?" the girl pressed. Dom looked away. He already knew the reason he was here. This was a punishment. This was justice being doled by Merciful Domus for the sins his father had forced him to commit. Sarah leaned back against the tree with a sigh. "I guess I just want to know why it chose me."

The girl probably would have gone on – except for the sounds of the carriage and its accompanying horseman. Lord Baron Cahill was arriving, and the talkative girl knew to button her lips. One of the riders dismounted and ran to open the carriage door. The mayor rushed from the town hall and came to a standstill just as the Lord Baron emerged.

The mayor bowed and flipped the tails of his longcoat. "My Lord! Welcome to Alben!"

Lord Baron Cahill made a casual study of his surroundings. He didn't smile.

"Certainly you are tired from your long travels today! We are setting up the town hall to accommodate your men. I'll fetch some of the boys to tend to the horses. In the meantime, I've had my wife keep a kettle hot, if you'd care to join us for tea …"

"My men will take care of their own horses," Cahill amended, taking the steps down to the dirt road. "Find Reed," he told the horseman at his side, before turning back to the waiting mayor. "Where is my daughter? I need to speak with her."

"In my sitting room. She wanted to put her feet up." The mayor straightened to his full height. "I would be pleased to show you the way." Dom had to hand it to the mayor. The man was stone-set determined to be hospitable.

The Lord Baron had still yet to smile. "Show me the way," he said, at last. The look in his eyes, the way he said the words – the message was clear. The mayor was to be tolerated. For the moment. He looked back to his horsemen. "Find Reed," he commanded again.

As the nobleman moved off with the excitable mayor, another man stepped out of the carriage.

The wizard.

--- * --- * ---

Dom knew every good hiding place in the entire inn. There were only good ones left – not any great ones. You knew a great one when you stumbled upon it. Great hiding spots were never found when actively looked for. It made complete sense. Any place that looks like a great hiding spots is automatically disqualified, as other people will undoubtedly arrive at the very same opinion. The best hiding spots were those found by accident. By luck.

Or by mercy.

A great spot never lasted. Their father was no fool, and Dom and Joshua weren't expert at concealing their whereabouts. Young boys, even at their quietest, still made noise. Just as soon as the great spot was discovered by their father – it ceased to be great. It ceased to be a place of guaranteed safety, of rest. It became only a good place – a place of temporary refuge. A place where the raging storm would eventually find you.

There was a good spot underneath the keeper's bar. You could only get to it from the back, sliding in between two of the large braces that kept the bar firmly in its place. It was a tight squeeze – Dom had to turn his shoulders sideways to fit now; Joshua couldn't manage it at all. When he'd been littler, Dom had been able to contort his entire body into the dark wedge. Now, despite his best efforts, a foot and ankle always strayed out. It didn't matter. Their father knew about the spot under the bar. It was one of the first places he looked when he was angry.

The spot under the bar was wonderful because of its location. There was a seam between two boards that faced the tavern's common area, a seam wide enough for Dom to peek through. As long as there were no patrons sitting on the stool right in front of the seam, Dom had a perfect view of the entire room. A perfect spot to sit and watch, confident the people you watched weren't able to watch you back.

Even your own brother.

Joshua was at the far end of the room, sitting at the table with a white-haired old man. Their father expected them to help out around the tavern – mainly cleaning in the mornings before the guests arrived or late at night after most had retired home. Dom had never considered talking to any of the patrons. Most carried in their eyes deep-rooted vices the Deacons preached against. He and Joshua were supposed to be invisible – they weren't supposed to dally and gossip.

Dom shifted as well as he could within the cramped space of the hiding spot. He didn't know who the old man was – but he'd seen him here before. Recently. Maybe this wasn't the first time Joshua had stopped to talk to the stranger.

A debilitating headache rocked him suddenly – it felt as if someone had driven a nail into his forehead. Dom hit his head against one of the supporting beams as he writhed in pain. He knew what happened next. This wasn't the first time he'd experienced the headache. He almost wanted to keep his eyes closed and wait it out.

But he didn't. When his eyes opened next, he found the hollow shades of somber gray coating every surface and corner of the tavern. The patrons at their tables drank from tall, ash-colored mugs that left dull suds in their lifeless beards. No one knew anything was wrong – that anything was any different.

Dom looked across the room. Two men to the right were arguing – and not good-humoredly. It would come to blows or knives unless someone stepped in and intervened. The man seated idly next to the main door was bursting with nervousness so intense it was a wonder his heart wasn't exploding from his chest. And Joshua ...

Joshua was happy. Joshua was excited. It came as a shock to Dom – because Joshua was never happy or excited. No one in their family ever was. But there was an eagerness – one that burned in Joshua's core like an inextinguishable candle. It was so intense that Dom could not help but feel excited as well.

And that is when he noticed. Of all the people in the inn, only Joshua and the strange old man were glowing.

Something caught hold of Dom's ankle, and with a solid yank he was dragged from under the bar. He caught the fiery glow of fury that blazed within his father before the headache vanished and the world resolved into colors once more. "You lazy whelp ... where's your brother?"

Dom was unable to answer. His father frightened the words off of his tongue.

"Your brother, Dom! He never finished sweeping!"

He managed a feeble gesture back towards the common room, and it worked. His father scanned his patrons, and Dom recognized the exact instance Joshua was located. His eyes tightened, his jaw clenched. Dom didn't need to see his father's core to know his anger would be boiling over.

His father didn't just drop his ankle, he hurled it to the floor. "To your room, boy!" he snapped and stalked off in Joshua's direction. Dom didn't wait around to see how it played out. As soon as he could get on his feet, he was racing up the long flight of stairs. He ducked into the room he and Joshua shared and closed the door shut behind him.

Huddled on his bed, knees pulled tight to his chest, Dom shut his eyes tight. It did not stop his ears from hearing everything. The commotion downstairs was muddled, mostly muted by the thick floorboards. But Dom recognized the tenor of his father's voice – and he certainly recognized the hard bootfalls and rapid ascent that never ceased to induce a cringe.

His father was coming.

He heard them go into the next room – their parents' room. He heard Joshua pleading – begging his case. He heard the lighter, mercy-inspired steps of his mother taking the stairs. "Malcolm!" she cried. "Malcolm, wait ... "

"He was talking to that wizard again!" his father yelled. "Again!"

"Malcolm!"

"Dad, he says I'm special ... "

Joshua's voice cut out as he was struck. Dom heard his brother's body hit the floor.

"Malcolm, please!" his mother cried. "Please, no ... "

"You want to have business with wizards, boy?" His father struck again. "Do you?" A third time. Dom felt the tears race down his cheek; tears of empathy for his older brother's pain. "You pay attention, boy," his father commanded. "You pay attention good. I'll show you exactly what happens to people who get themselves involved with wizards!"

--- * --- * ---

The wizard exiting the carriage appeared extremely young. All of the wizards Dom had seen in the past were graying or bald – but not this one. He looked no older than any of Captain Reed's men. Wizards were always aged and ancient – carrying an aura of wisdom purchased by years of experience. Their power could be measured by the number of wrinkles on their face.

Judging solely on his appearance, Baron Cahill's wizard inspired little confidence.

As if able to hear Dom's thoughts, the wizard turned his attention to them.

"Children," he said, "I am looking for members of the Band of Six. Do you know where I might find any of them?"

"Are you really a wizard?" Sarah asked abruptly.

The man may have lacked white hair, but he had mastery of the unfaltering wizard stare. He employed it on Sarah, perhaps to impress how inappropriate he thought her question was. "The Band, please?"

If Dom had learned anything about his new friend, it was that she was not well-versed in picking up on subtleties. "Why aren't you wearing a purple stole?"

The wizard frowned. "Only wizards of the Sixth Circle wear the Amethyst Stole."

"Oh," said Sarah. Dom could see her digesting the information. The wizard took the silence to mean his explanation was satisfactory, but Dom new Sarah better. She spoke again just as the wizard was opening his mouth.

It was as guileless a question as any she'd ever asked. "What number circle are you in then?"

The wizard folded his arms across his chest, summoning his wizardly stare.

The light flashed across Dom's eyes, blinding him as to natural sight. The world went dark – inverting everything to shades of gray except for the colorful orbs in everyone's core. Dom felt his chest clench at the unbidden onset of his curse, disoriented by the sudden change in his surroundings.

His eyes were drawn to the wizard. His orb pulsed with a shining aura – the same shine that Dom had seen so intensely on the old wizard they'd taken to the fountain. Dom counted himself lucky to have avoided much contact with wizards, but every single one of them shared that same glowing aura. It wasn't something unique to wizard-folk – Dom had seen a handful of others that shared the glow. Like Joshua. And Kashif. But it was never as strong as with wizards.

Dom could easily make out the colors in the wizard's orb – a shallow pool of serenity that quivered under the sharp underpinnings of curdling fear. The wizard was scared? Maybe that was too strong – maybe he was just uncertain? Whatever the emotion was, it was the last Dom would have thought to see in a man who wielded magical power.

Definitely, not anything he would have suspected in the man the Lord Baron had hired to fix their demon problem.

"Dom?" Sarah asked.

"What's he staring at?" the wizard asked, growing increasingly irritated.

"Are you alright?" Sarah questioned.

It was time to leave. This was attention he didn't want. He staggered to his feet and ran towards the town hall without looking back. The only difference between the town hall before him and the sky above were the specific tones of bleak gray. He sidestepped two men as they hurried past him into the building, carrying stacks of blankets. Their orbs were nearly identical, irritation laced with fatigue …

Dom almost ran headlong into the figure standing in the door frame.

Billick.

Dom jumped at being so close to the murderer. He'd avoided Billick as much as possible – and he resolutely avoided looking at him when his curse was active. He hadn't seen the murderer – the man seemed to blend impossibly well in the bleak overtones of the gray world. Dom found his answer in Billick's orb. A ball of pulseless black, it occupied the core of the man's imposing silhouette. There were no swirls of emotion, no signs of movement in the ether of the orb – just rotting, lifeless black.

The man was without feeling.

Almost.

A sinister glow of pain that sung richly of remorse surfaced whenever Billick was approached by Sarah, of all people. Dom could not understand how his innocent friend could spawn such a violent reaction.

The searing light washed across his vision again. Dom blinked several times, his eyes trying to adjust after the blinding flash. It was over.

"I told you to stay out of the way," growled the side-burned man as he pushed by.

There were times when his father's beatings awoke Dom's ability. He'd cower under the drunken rage of his father, not only hearing the hateful words he spoke, but seeing the hateful emotions spawning in his heart. His father's violence was fueled by the emotions. He was an angry man, one who vent his frustrations on his family. Dom had learned to disconnect the man from the emotion. He considered the anger like a disease – something that burned in his father like a fever. Something his father couldn't control. Something he, his brother and his mother could only endure – and fear.

But here was a man – a self-professed killer – who felt nothing. There was no disease in him – no harsh emotion on which a life of blood and death could be consigned. There was nothing. Absolute hollowness.

The nothingness scared Dom even more than his father's rage did.

As Billick walked by, Dom realized he was still standing by the door – still within view of the wizard. He didn't dare a glance back. He slipped around the corner and looked around desperately for a place to disappear. Someplace quiet where no one would go looking for him. Someplace he wouldn't have to be scared of people with too much feeling – or people with not enough.

A hiding place. He would even settle for a poor one.

Alas, Dom was cornered before he could act.

The Arcan stood before him, with the thief hovering a safe distance behind. Dom sunk back into his coat as far as his shoulders would allow him.

"How are you feeling, Dom?" the dark-skinned man asked purposefully. Dom stared back at him distrustfully – he had no reason to talk to the Arcan. Kashif wanted to figure out how to use everyone to accomplish their task. If the Arcan ever learned of Dom's ability, he'd surely find some way to exploit it.

"I need to see your wrist," Kashif went on. His hands were safely buried in the coat pockets, his wrists protected by the bunching layers of sleeve. He intended on keeping them that way. "This is important," the Arcan said. "Are you experiencing any pain on your wrists?"

In truth, they stung. It had been worse in the afternoon. The weather had been too hot for the coat, but he'd kept it on. He'd sweat – and the sweat burned whenever it touched the welts on his wrists.

The Arcan must have seen the answer in his eyes. "May I see them?" It didn't sound like a request – and it only helped a little when Kashif added the labored "Please".

Cautiously, Dom withdrew his left hand from his pocket and extended his arm. The Arcan took it, and pushed back the folds of the sleeve. The inflamed skin of the welt stood out red against his pale skin. The area nearest the thumb looked and felt the worst, where the flesh was gashed and …

"Infected," the scientist diagnosed. Not dropping Dom's arm, he turned to Ethiere. "You were right."

"Right about what?" Dom said in a low voice.

The thief closed the distance and held his left arm out. The skin around his wrist was red as well, and Dom could see traces of where the thief had scratched with his nails. But only one area was so scratched up that the skin was beginning break – the area of the wrist closest to Ethiere's thumb.

Ethiere smiled. "Right about that."

25.

Greer wondered if her presence in the mayor's home was making the man's wife ill. While the mayor was an uncorked bottle of exuberance over the opportunity to host a Lord Baron and his daughter, his wife was unquestionably uncomfortable with the weighty arrangement. The mayor had left them in the parlor, rattling on about the business he needed to see to before the Lord Baron's carriage arrived. With a smile, he left them to, in his words, "get on as women like to do".

Apparently, women in Alben liked to have dreadfully silent tea parties. She, Sophie and the mayor's wife had made meager attempts at proper conversation – which only served to highlight the problems with proper conversation. The recited answers were just as trivial as the rote questions. They soon came to an unspoken understanding to just remain silent.

Her hostess' attention fluttered around the room – seeming to land on everything besides her guests. Following where the woman looked, Greer realize she was cataloging every thin veneer of dust on the furniture, every boot-scuff on the floor, every silky strand of spiders' webbing dangling from the ceiling.

The poor woman sat as if facing her Last Tribunal before Merciful Domus and the Jury of Those Wronged! As if Greer would banish her to boil in Oblivion because there were fingerprints on the silver platter!

Sophie, of course, wasn't helping matters. The companion was not-too-subtly playing with the frayed edge of the floor rug with the toe of her shoe.

Greer faked another sip of the tea. It was, unfortunately, awful tea. If she were forced to conjure an arbitrary reason for the mayor's wife to spend eternity boiling in Oblivion's depths, Greer voted for the tea. Merciful Domus, the tea tasted like it was boiled in the depths of Oblivion!

Greer held the cup to her firmly clenched lips once more, and smiled reassuringly to her hostess as she set the cup down. She hated it. She hated the way people acted in front of her and her family. She hated the timid, reverential fear of the wife just as much as she loathed the unabashed fawning and pomp of the mayor. She hated those people who looked on nobility as if they stood shoulder to shoulder with a deity.

And she hated the nobility for allowing – and expecting – them to do so.

When the door opened, both Greer and her hostess stood – both equally ready to be rescued from the socializing they'd been forced to endure together. Sophie hastily poured the remaining tea in her cup into a nearby flowering plant.

The Mayor rushed in, a pleased grin painted on his face, and stepped aside to present his home to …

The Lord Baron. His eyes found Greer immediately, and the look on his face caused her throat to catch. She knew that look. She'd seen it frequently growing up.

He was displeased. And Greer knew exactly why.

The mayor cleared his throat and spoke with large, expressive gestures. "Lord Baron Cahill, you do me a great honor by visiting my home. May I present to you my lovely wife …"

Lord Baron Cahill didn't let him finish. "I need to speak to my daughter."

The interruption nearly caused the mayor to bite down on his own tongue, but he recovered wonderfully. "Of course! You are anxious to catch up. My wife can reheat some tea …"

"Alone," the nobleman clarified. "Sophie, find somewhere else to be." He turned to the mayor, whose smile was waging a war with disappointment. "If you and your wife will step outside …"

The mayor was already nodding, but Greer could not hold back. "It's their home, father!" she said with open hostility – and instantly rued it. She needed to keep her emotions in check – like he did. As soon as she compromised her self-control, her father had already earned the victory.

"It's no trouble!" assured the mayor. He scooped up his wife's hand as she hurried towards the door. "No trouble!" The two most powerful people in Alben disappeared through the door, abandoning their home without another word. All because of her father's title. All because he let them. Sophie pouted as she left, but didn't have the courage to argue against her dismissal.

Her father wasted no time once they were alone. "Why did you leave the fountain?"

"The Band decided it was time to move …"

"The Band decided, did they?" her father countered. "Who decided, then? The children? Did they elect to move on? No … not them." He continued to probe her argument. "And please don't tell me it was the Arcan. He's smarter than that – too smart to go chasing after danger before he's worked out a plan."

He drew himself close to her, uncomfortably close. "The brute, then. I thought he would be trouble … I could see his open disdain towards rank and influence. He assumes himself the leader, am I right? Assumes that since he is the biggest and the strongest he gets to make the decisions?"

"You seem to have it all figured out," Greer sassed and turned away.

He caught her cheek and turned her head back towards his. "You disobeyed me."

She felt her face flush with indignation. "Didn't you just decide it was the brute …"

He sniggered – a mocking laugh. "Please, Greer. Please. Him? As the leader? He might think so. He might think his prowess earns him the right to walk at the forefront and command people around. He might think so – but we both know better." He paused, forcing her to contemplate in the small silence. "Who do you think your Band members looked to when the decision needed to be made? At the solitary, angry man with the thick arms? Or to the noblewoman with trained soldiers at her disposal? Who would you have looked at, Greer?"

She had no answer. It was exactly why he'd asked the question.

"You disappoint me, daughter." The rebuttal, delivered in his soft-spoken, emotionally-neutral voice stung as sharply as if it had been yelled in outrage.

She channeled the hurt into a cold retort. "I don't seek your approval."

"Nor do I seek for yours," he shot back as he walked to the tea serviette. He lifted one of the cups and examined the liquid inside. He returned the cup to the tray without sampling it. "I've spent the better part of the last two days in a carriage. I've not eaten a decent meal in just as long. Last night I threatened the life of the most powerful wizard I've ever acquainted – in his own study no less. The least you could do – daughter …" He paused, and amended the statement. "… the least I expect you to do – is to not make this any harder on me than it already is."

Greer crossed her arms over her breasts. "I didn't ask for your help. Don't trouble yourself on my account."

It struck a nerve in the Lord Baron. She saw a flash of irritation like a bolt of lightning against a dark sky. "Your account?" he repeated, and he began to nod. "Is that it – what this is about?" Though neither of them moved, he was backing her into a corner. She could feel it.

He harrumphed dismissively. "I would have thought you mature enough to not think solely about yourself." He waited long enough to let the barb sink in but not allow her a chance to fire back. "You think you are the only one affected by this? You honestly think my surrounding you with my best soldiers, my hiring of a wizard to fight this demon – do you honestly believe this is just about you, Greer?"

He stepped towards her – it was so unexpected she stepped back without thinking. "Do you even stop to consider your obligations to your family?" he continued. "To your house? Do you care your brother may never be allowed to hold the title of Lord Baron?"

He eyed her with an unrelenting stare. "What do you think will become of Cahill when Lord Baron Northing finally decides to end this charade of allied Barons and declares himself King? He's already consolidated power along the whole western coast through marriage or attrition. The generals that lead our confederated armies are all loyal to his house. Even if I and the other Lord Barons stood against him, we'd lose. Just like Depree did. This scenario is no longer an *if* – only a *when*."

Greer saw the opening. "If he can have the throne, then why doesn't he? What's stopping him?"

"He's stopped himself," her father answered, noting the irony. "He was moving soldiers into position two winters back. Setting the stage for a swift and succinct deposal of those who held no tie to the name Northing. It would have been over – and over quickly. But then?" He paused, reflective. "His wife got sick. She died. And though I can't say why – his ambitions to a king's throne died with her."

His eyes snapped back towards her. His brief moment of introspection was over. "We were granted a reprieve. I would praise the name of Merciful Domus if I believed he had any care for the mechanics of man's politics. We were given a second chance to tie the houses of Cahill and Northing together. To get

169

your brother a sympathetic voice – your voice – embedded in the Northing family lines."

She heard his subtle emphasis, the explicit reminder of what he must consider her most galling failure. He'd arranged the first chance – the ideal opportunity. In his mind, a second opportunity should never have been needed. The first should never have been allowed to slip away.

Greer felt her cheeks flush with anger. Her father didn't know half the details.

--- * --- * ---

They stayed at the river bend for another hour or so after the boys left. Neither Caleb or Owen had wanted to go – but Caleb had become increasingly antsy the later into the afternoon it got. It took several attempts for him to convince Owen they couldn't afford to stay any longer; his friend seemed loath to let Bridgette go. As they did finally wade their way to the opposite bank, the boys shouted their promises.

The boys would come back tomorrow night. They hoped they wouldn't be alone.

Bridgette and Greer laid side-by-side on the bank, letting Bridgette's underclothing dry out. The companion was surprisingly coy about her exciting afternoon. "You and Owen were awfully quiet." The blonde girl smiled knowingly, but stayed mum. "Not much to talk about?" Greer continued to pester.

"We ... found other things to do." Bridgette changed the subject. "You and Caleb?"

Greer could hardy lay still as she thought about Caleb. While they'd spent most of the time talking, the dear boy had still managed to steal a kiss or two on her cheek. She blushed at the memory. "We got to know each other quite well." Greer raised herself to her elbows and looked across to the opposite bank of the Tizred River. The sun was lowering, painting everything in golden perfection. Greer could almost picture Caleb smiling at her through the trees. "Bridgette?"

"Hmm?"

"We're coming back tomorrow night, aren't we?"

Bridgette bubbled with laughter. "What do you think?"

Greer sat up and hugged her knees. The water of the river shimmered. "I think tomorrow I might try swimming."

The walk home was filled with planning. Bridgette was already hatching up her scheme to get them outside her father's gates. A night escape would be difficult; Headmistress Packer watched them much more closely once the sun went down. They would have to find some excuse to leave dinner early – that would be the best time to elude the vigilant woman. Their plotting took them all the way up to the gates themselves – where a stern looking Headmistress Packer was waiting for them.

"Are there any flowers left in Tollia!?"

Greer swallowed hard and looked to Bridgette. They'd forgotten all about the pretense that had gotten them by the Headmistress in the first place!

Fortunately, Headmistress Packer didn't press the issue further. She swatted a hand to the side of Greer's dress. "But you're both absolutely filthy! Merciful Domus have pity – of all days for you two to roll around the countryside!" Taking Greer by the shoulders, she began to forcefully lead her in doors. "To your room! Strip down, I'll have the girls heat the bath."

It was not what Greer expected. "A bath?"

"With any luck," the headmistress said, "your father will never realize you've been out."

Headmistress Packer was a woman on a mission. She and two of the maids moved her from the bath, to her dressing room, to her powder room. Greer was trapped within the whirlwind of hands that pulled clothes down over her head, yanked her hair in various directions and painted her face with various glosses and creams. In record time, Greer emerged in her best silk dress with ringlets still warm from the hot-irons.

All they would tell her was the Lord Baron had company.

Flanked by the maids, Greer was ushered into the dining hall. As the porter pushed the large wooden door open for her, the first person that Greer saw was Bridgette. It looked as if someone – or multiple someones – had given Bridgette the same treatment she had experienced. Bridgette looked gorgeous – which wasn't hard for her – but her face spoke of gross discomfort. She stood against the far wall, her hands clutched together at her waist, refusing to make eye contact.

The second person Greer saw came as even more of a surprise. Caleb. She felt her heart leap in her chest – until she saw the same uncomfortable look etched on his face. He looked up briefly at her, and then ducked his eyes once more.

"Here she is," her father announced. "A little late, but that can be forgiven. I present, my daughter, Lady Greer of Cahill." As trained, Greer lowered her head and dipped her leg slightly. "Greer, I would like you meet our esteemed guest, Lord Owen of Northing."

She saw him then, standing next to her father, in a well-tailored black shirt with silver buttons. Owen. Lord Owen. He was a Northing. Greer felt the lump in her throat expand, she found herself unable to inhale. She swung her eyes to Bridgette, who was still locked in on the stones of the floor beneath her.

Greer had no idea of what to say. She didn't know what to do. She would have given her weight in gold to have a private conversation with Bridgette. Bridgette would know what to do – she'd know how to work this out.

Lord Baron Cahill cleared his throat. "I can see you've left her momentarily speechless," he said. Greer understood the underlying message.

"I'm ... certainly pleased to meet you, Lord Owen," she managed.

Owen advanced. "And I you," he said while taking her hand. He kissed it gently, and it was all Greer could do not to retract it. This was all wrong. This was backwards. Owen smiled. "I've heard so many good things about you; I couldn't resist asking your father to allow me a visit."

"He came all this way just to see you Greer," her father added. "Isn't that nice?"

Greer felt a chill in her veins – like she'd just been engulfed within the waters of the Tizred. All this way to see her? Hardly. He'd barely been able to pull himself away from Bridgette – who was what in his eyes? Some commoner girl he could take advantage of?

"Unfortunately," the Lord Baron continued, "Lord Owen will only be with us this evening. I believe you said that you have pressing engagements – "

"Tomorrow night," Owen confirmed. Greer felt sick. Looking at Bridgette, she could see the betrayal on her companion's face. She looked to Caleb – and realized she was looking at Owen's companion. And suddenly the events of the afternoon took on a slanted perspective.

172

Had Owen sent Caleb to occupy her, to keep her entertained, so he could have time to himself with Bridgette? She prayed for Caleb to look at her – she'd be able to see it in his face, she knew it. She'd be able to see in his face if those pretty words he used and the tentative touch of his lips were genuine – or if he'd simply fulfilled the assignment of his Lord.

One thing was obscenely clear. Owen had seen both her and Bridgette – he'd had his choice of either one of them. Caleb the companion would have deferred. Greer looked back to Bridgette – beautiful Bridgette. Boil him, he had deferred! Owen had his choice – and Greer knew with certainty he had not chosen her.

Owen turned slightly, speaking to her father. "I may be able to adjust my engagements, if ..."

"That's hardly necessary." Her words came out cold and biting – worthy reflections of everything that she was feeling inside.

Her father stepped forward. "I believe what my daughter is suggesting is we would not think to take you away from your responsibilities." He never looked away from Lord Owen, but Greer felt him warning her. This, like many other customs of the nobility, was a scripted scenario. This was the first introduction of two young nobles with hopes a betrothal might come of it. He was expected to be full of flowery compliments and well-mannered. She was expected to be enjoyable to look at and agreeable in conversation. They'd be introduced. They'd sit next to one another at the table for supper. There would be the arranged circumstances for them to spend time alone ...

Owen nodded. "You are both very understanding." He turned back to her. "We shall just have to make good with the time we have then." He held out his arm. "Shall we walk? Your father often brags to mine about these fabulous gardens he keeps."

She stared at his proffered arm. He intended to go through with it. He intended to keep pretending – what? That this afternoon never happened? That they both didn't know he'd been kissing her companion – who had been wearing not but her undergarments! Did he think he could speak to her – compliment her – and not have it sound like refuse coming from his lips? The arm hung in the air. He did intend to go through with the charade.

She did not.

"No thank you."

Her father's composure buckled, ever so briefly. "Greer ..."

"I don't believe I could manage a walk at the moment," she said. "I seem to have foolishly wasted all of my energy this afternoon. The sun must have sapped it from me." She smiled, and she didn't care how insincere it looked. "But you, Lord Owen, you look to have gotten even more sun this afternoon than I did." The Lord Baron would catch something insinuated in her words, but Greer knew he would not understand fully. But Owen would. And Owen would know she was choosing to slight him. In front of her father. In front of everyone. "You'll have to excuse me, Lord Owen, but I'm not feeling well."

"Of course," Owen said tightly.

He bowed. She curtsied. She left.

She was not half-way to her room before her father caught up with her. "Greer!" She did not stop for him. She didn't have an explanation for him. He latched onto her arm and turned her roughly to face him. "What was that?" She felt her face burn. She was humiliated. "You know who that is!"

"Lord Owen of Northing," she recited.

"You will return to the dining hall. You will apologize for your flippant behavior. You will invite the young Lord to walk with you in the gardens."

Greer felt the fury welling up inside of her. "No!" she shouted at him. "I won't!"

"Greer!"

She broke his hold on her. "I won't have anything to do with him." She stomped away, but turned after a few steps. "If you are so insistent he see our gardens father," she spat, "you should have Bridgette show him." She ran for her room, ran before he or anyone else could see the tears in her eyes. "He'd probably like that better."

--- * --- * ---

Her father continued. "The survival of the name of Cahill depends on your marriage to the Lord Baron's cousin. And we are lucky that he is amicable to the idea of marriage." The arrangement was nearly a year old now and seemed inevitable. She would yet don the name of Northing – marrying a cousin who was only slightly younger than her father. He would be gray – gray and withering. She would be the prized young blossom paired with the withering branch. He was amicable to the idea of marriage? The only thing he probably knew about her was that she was less than half his age.

"But how would he receive you if you're marred? If that creature takes a limb or damages your flesh? How do you suppose the prospect of marriage will look to him then?"

How would the old Northing feel? Her father talked of the demon ripping into her, and his concern was over how the old Northing would feel about their arrangement? Greer's jaw twisted. Her father didn't really care about her. Not about *her*. He didn't even know *her*. He only knew about the proper noblewoman – the one that followed his recipe. The one he and society's ideals had restricted her into becoming.

Her shell. Her façade.

That's what he really cared about. A marriage-ready daughter, one who met every expectation of a nobleman. That's all he needed – all the family really needed. It was that girl – that hollow, scripted mockery of an individual who he needed to survive! Who he intended to sell off to the first willing Northing!

"It must gall you that I'm not like Sophie. Wouldn't she be the perfect daughter for you?"

"It galls me even a dimwitted girl like that grasps something you refuse to. You don't like being a noble? You don't like what being a noble means? You don't like what is expected of you? I never heard you complain while you ate at my table! I never heard you complain while my servants attended you! I never heard you complain about the dresses and the shoes, the perfumes and the silks!" He grasped her by the wrist, his fingers constricting tightly over her flesh. She could not pull away. "It is time you earned all of that, Greer. It is time you earned the life of ease that has you so embittered. You will be kept safe – I will see to that. You will be married to a Northing – I will see to that as well. These two things are not open to debate!

"You disobeyed me. You may be inclined to do so again. Think carefully. You ruin your second chance – as you did your first – there won't be a third. There isn't another eligible Northing for you to turn your nose up at. And when the upheaval starts – when our house is swept away by the Northings – think of what you'll have then. You'll have no one expecting anything of you, Greer. You can take comfort in that thought while you starve for food on the streets."

He moved to the door. "You keep fighting against what is best for you, Greer – what I tell you is best for you – and you'll soon find you're left with nothing but the worst." He said nothing more as he exited the house, leaving Greer standing alone, and feeling shredded on the inside. In frustration, she took the little tea cup from the serviette and threw it at the door.

It exploded into an array of tiny fragments – just as a cautious mayor and his wife opened the door. The poor woman's eyes went wide, but the mayor, surveying the mess, never lost his smile. "Never you mind, we'll just get that cleaned up for you – won't we dear?"

26.

The one called Dominic was very distrustful. Kashif had expounded on the nature of the sores – how the infection would only fester and grow worse. He had then orated on the proper procedure to cleanse the area, kill the infection, and wrap it to keep the recovering wound clean. There was nothing in what he planned to do that should have been a mystery to the reclusive boy.

All the same, Dom withdrew his wrist from the table when Kashif neared it with his scoping tool.

"What is that?!"

Kashif frowned at the wasteful delay, but could see no alternative around it. He longed for an examination-table with sturdy leather binding-straps. He pinched the tool between his forefinger and thumb and held it out for his patient to examine.

If he were being honest, the scoping tool looked hardly benign. One end of the thin rod ended in a fine, sharpened point; the other fashioned in an equally honed hook. It was designed as an exploratory instrument, one that could reopen cuts and spread gashes to reveal what was beneath. The hooked end worked well in scraping splinters from an arrow or pus from an open wound. But it was hardly a weapon. No one had ever died by scoping tool before.

At least no one not already dying from something else.

"It is one of my tools," Kashif answered. "Place your arm back on the table."

"What are you going to do with it?"

He'd covered this – extensively – when he'd explained the concept of cleansing the wound. "There are most likely pockets of the infection underneath your skin. We have to lance all of them, or we might as well lance none." He waited. "Your arm?"

With great hesitancy, Dom slid his right arm back onto the table. His eyes didn't stray from the shiny silver instrument. The Arcan reached out with his left arm and placed it firmly on Dom's forearm. Slowly, Kashif lowered the sharpened point down towards the open sore.

"Is it going to hurt?" the boy asked tightly.

He could feel Dom flinching, trying to pull away. Kashif tightened his grip. He didn't want any more delays. "Yes," he admitted. His patient's eyes went wider, and Kashif felt the muscles in the thin arm straining. "But less so if I don't accidentally impale you! Hold still!"

Dom continued to squirm, despite the warning. Kashif brought the scoping tool in contact with the boy's skin anyway. "Can we just wait a moment?" Dom begged. Kashif paid him no mind – he was already probing the wound. With any luck, the boy would stay so focused on stopping the procedure that he wouldn't realize it had begun. "Can you just hold on for …"

There was a slight twitch in Dom's arm – which caused the scoping tool to press deeper than Kashif would have …

He dropped the instrument – the pain was so intense his entire hand froze in paralysis. Kashif stared at his wrist in disbelief. The skin was red and irritated – as was Ethiere's – but there was no physical evidence of injury. The Arcan looked at the thief – who was likewise examining his right wrist. Ethiere swallowed. "I felt it too."

Dom's right arm was already hidden within the safety of the coat sleeves. The wound still needed to be taken care of – especially seeing they were all feeling of its effects – but Kashif opted to postpone the battle. The scientist in him was demanding an experiment.

Kashif plucked up the scoping tool, flipped the pointed end downward, and thrust the tool into the open palm of his left hand. The eyes of both Dom and Ethiere went wide – but only from surprise. "Do you feel that? Do you feel of my pain as well?"

The two responded with horror-filled dumbfoundment. Ethiere had his right thumb pressed against the center of his left palm, as if trying to prevent bleeding from a wound existing on another person entirely. "What?"

"We share Dom's pain, we feel it together. Do you not feel mine?"

"No – no." With the answer, Kashif withdrew the tool from his skin. The tip of the instrument was red with blood, and a tiny drop of crimson welled up in the middle of his hand. He was intrigued. He'd specifically chosen the palm due to the nerves he'd be able to make contact with. In terms of actual pain, the Arcan knew his assault on his palm far out-weighed the tiny poke on the wrist – even if the swelling and inflammation were factored in.

Was this being caused by the Banding? If so, why was the sharing of pain not universal? Why was the pain of one not transmitted as equally as another?

He was very intrigued; he needed more evidence. Kashif turned once more to the thief. "Hurt yourself!" he ordered

"What?"

"Cause yourself physical pain!" the Arcan restated.

Ethiere looked sideways to Dom, before looking back to the Arcan. "No!"

The Arcan scowled. Both of the young men were obstacles to progress. It was no matter – Kashif could still instigate many experiments without their help. Under the table, he lifted his boot and brought the heel down squarely on Dom's toes –

His own toes burst into agony. Ethiere yelped and dropped to one knee, both hands reaching protectively for his ailing foot. Across the table, Dom revolved through layers of betrayal, pain and bewilderment. Kashif regulated his breathing, forcing the pain to subside. For some reason, the pain Dom experienced was more than just shared – it was magnified. Whatever he felt, Kashif and the other Band members appeared to feel five-fold.

Sarah ran into the room, a look of concern on her face. "I heard a yell."

Kashif's eyes were drawn to the girl's wrists – wrists bearing no signs of irritation. She'd run into the room, he noted; and had done so without any trace of a limp to her step.

"What's going on?" she asked.

The Arcan nodded. It made sense. It was the Numbness.

Sarah really didn't know.

27.

Captain Reed stood across from the sitting Lord Baron Cahill in the guest room of one of Alben's town councilmen – a room cleared of its owner under the direction of the mayor. The excitable man, eager to please, understood the Lord Baron's need for a room to conduct business from. The dour-faced, displaced councilman had looked less understanding.

The Lord Baron was a juxtaposition of composed intensity. He was like a wave of the sea – perfect in its motion, regal in its form – but ever ready to slam into the smaller ships in its course, ever able to dash them to pieces. There were benefits to working for such a man. Reed was never at a loss for what the Baron wanted done. His instructions were always extremely transparent as to the hows and the whats, the wheres and the whens. Such conditions were ideal to a meticulous man like Reed. He excelled at fulfilling the Baron's commands.

He also knew the consequences of disobedience. He'd foreseen this conversation as the consequence of allowing Greer to depart from the fountain with the others of the Band. Cahill was poised wrath. Reed felt like an unsteady ship facing a tidal wave on the horizon.

"I trusted you Captain – that you would be able to keep her safe."

Reed swallowed. While some men would choose to face their berating in silence, Reed knew better. The Lord Baron wanted answers. He wanted proof of thought – even if such thoughts went against his judgments. The Lord Baron didn't tolerate disobedience – but he tolerated thoughtless sycophants even less. "Lady Greer is in every way, my Lord, still safe."

"You allowed her to go after the demon, Reed. How close would you have allowed her to get? Can you even tell me how close we are to it now?"

The wizard, standing against the far wall like the Baron's shadow, frowned. Master Hartley had said nothing as yet, but looked on with the stern, disapproving look common among their ilk. Reed shook his head. "She refused to stay at the fountain. It may be the same force that propelled her to the fountain is pushing her and the other Banded to hunt the monster. They are driven to fulfill their obligation – at the expense of better judgment."

The Lord Baron weighed the response. "An excuse for the Banded, perhaps. But hardly an excuse for you, Reed." The nobleman sat back. "You could not keep them at the fountain? They refused to stay? I can concede that as probable. For the moment, we will assume you are correct. So the party advances forward." The Baron's eyes flashed with that unequaled intensity. "What did you do to slow the advance, Captain?"

Reed lowered his head, studying the weave of the rug at his feet. The full pressure of the wave was upon him.

"Could you not have found some excuse to delay? To make pauses? To rest the horses? To scout ahead – or scout behind? Boil you, Reed – you have the swords! You have the men! Are you meaning to tell me you couldn't have asserted authority by intimidation? Instead I have reports of my daughter sleeping in a barn, being gawked at by commoner, and making a fool of herself at a riverbank. Such behavior is completely inappropriate for a woman of noble birth! What can I assume from such utter disregard for my daughter and my good name? Have I misjudged you, Captain?"

Reed felt castigated. In truth, Sarah had done enough to slow their advance, he'd not thought to hinder them further. As for Lady Greer's actions – Reed elected to hold his tongue. The Lord Baron would not accept any reasoning on the matter. He would not understand what the wading at the riverbank had meant to Sarah. Yes, even in Reed's eyes, the actions had scraped away the mystique of Lady Greer's noble title. But he'd seen much more of nobility in her willingness to condescend than he would have expected.

Before this excursion, Captain Reed had assumed the Lady Greer to be merely an extension of her father – similar in attitude, beliefs, and expectations. He had been wrong. "My apologies, Lord Baron. I assure you, on my life and the life of my men, your daughter would not have come to any harm."

"Be that as it may," the Baron answered, "I intend to place a more substantial buffer between the demon and my only daughter." Cahill motioned the wizard forward. "Despite your recent utter lack of thought and creativity, I intend to allow you to continue as the personal protector of my daughter. You will pick three of your men to assist you in that capacity. Wizard Hartley will assume command of the rest."

The Captain and the Wizard exchanged a look. Wizardry and magic were foreign to Reed – those were talents he knew he'd never have. But Reed did have experience in battle, and he was a natural leader. Did Hartley possess either of those qualities? The Wizard's youthful face didn't reveal anything either way.

It was easy to feign leadership – until the moment of chaos arrived. In those moments, leaders led – or their followers died.

"I don't expect this to be a problem, Reed," Cahill stated into the silence. "For you – or your men." Reed looked to his employer, who wasn't naïve to the workings of his soldiers. The unit was tightly knit and the men were fiercely loyal to Reed. They wouldn't blindly follow a stranger – even a stranger with the title of Wizard.

Reed frowned. "They won't like it."

"I don't pay them to like it," the Baron rebuked. "I pay them to follow orders."

"I assure you, your men will be in capable hands." The wizard's voice rang rich and authoritative. It sounded practiced.

The Baron bore down with his eyes. "I'm not paying you to like it either, Captain. You make this work – you get your men behind it. Wizard Hartley leads the hunt for the demon – you keep Greer far from the action." Cahill nodded and stood, the matter done. "As for myself, I'm taking the carriage to Hollingston – tonight. Lord Baron Northing should know there is a demon loose in the heart of his barony. With any luck, he can be convinced to dispatch a regiment of his own men to bolster our forces. The more swords we can throw at this thing, the better."

Reed nodded. "Good luck, sire."

"You can go now," the nobleman told him. Reed managed a crisp salute and went for the exit. "One last thing, Captain," Cahill called as Reed neared the door.

"Sire?"

"The other Banded. They are not my concern, and they shouldn't be yours." The nobleman looked over his shoulder to the wizard. "Or yours. Greer is all that matters. If the rest die – they die. Do you understand, Reed? Have I made myself clear enough this time?"

Reed swallowed the sour taste in his mouth. "Yes, sir." He knew to the Lord Baron, he and his men counted as part of 'the rest'.

Cahill glowered, examining the trite response for any hint of dishonesty. He sat back, detecting none. "Good," he said, and dismissed the soldier with a wave. As he left, he could hear the Baron giving further instructions to Hartley. He pulled the door open – a bit more forcefully than entirely necessary – and walked through. Was he angry? For not getting to direct the assault? That the Baron thought him so easily replaceable?

Bostitch was waiting on the other side of the door, nursing the embers of his smoke. The crossbowman made no pretense of what he'd been doing. "Permission to be on your squad, sir."

It earned a smile. "You volunteering to stay back with the women and children?" Reed quipped as he moved on.

"I've always fancied women," Bost said as he fell in behind Reed. "You're going to have all eleven of us vying for those three spots, Captain. You've earned our trust – you've proven yourself. That wizard …" He trailed off – and flicked the smoldering end of the smoke into the dirt before him. "Did you know they hired wizards to fight in the Arcan War? Wizards just like that one – young looking, inexperienced, overly-confident in their magic."

Reed had. Magic on the battlefield was a tempting proposition. While none of the experienced wizards had participated, the Lord Barons had great success in recruiting out of the novice ranks. "I know it didn't go well."

Bostitch snorted a derisive laugh. "That – dear Captain – is an understatement. The mere presence of the wizards drove the Arcans into a mad, zealous frenzy. They targeted the regimens that had wizards embedded in them. Poured everything they had into massive offenses, not stopping for anything until they had the wizard's head. The dark-skins took heavy losses – but it didn't seem to matter. Those Arcans were driven to exterminate the wizards." Bost sighed. "Can't help but see similarities."

Reed nodded. "The Lord Baron thinks he's given us a leader …"

"…all I see is a target," Bostitch finished.

28.

Billick rubbed at his right wrist. He'd not understood why it had aggravated him all day. Then the Arcan had announced his discovery – as a Band, they would all share Dom's pain. When they'd started from the fountain yesterday, he'd known the young boy and girl would be burdens. He'd underestimated. In only two days, Sarah had slowed their advance considerably – and now Dom threatened to debilitate them all with any scratch he took. These children were more than burdens – they were true liabilities.

He did get some amusement in watching the Arcan chase the boy around, insistent the wrist be cleansed. The dark-skin had attempted to secure Ethiere's help in cornering the frightened boy – but the thief had voiced his unwillingness to help. The Arcan had looked to him next – and Billick had reveled in summarily rejecting the plea for assistance. He'd found a comfortable seat at the back of the council room, content to watch the frustration mount in the foreigner.

The fun ended when the Arcan managed to place a cloth over Dom's mouth and nose. The boy's eyes had rolled up into his head before he could blink twice. As soon as the boy succumbed, the pain in Billick's wrist had vanished. Billick didn't know what liquid the Arcan had splashed onto the cloth – but he was intrigued. Something so effective at rendering a man unconscious would prove helpful in his line of work.

Kashif had dragged the sleeping boy to the sturdy oak council room table, which had been pushed up against one of the walls to provide a greater sleeping area. One by one, the Arcan had set his tools out – foreign looking implements each appearing as if they'd been crafted to inflict pain. Billick had watched the dark-skin operate from his seat in the corner – Sarah had taken a more immediate vantage point. The inquisitive girl had kept her questions to a minimum, allowing the Arcan an atmosphere he could concentrate in. When the bandages were finally wrapped around the cleansed wrist, Billick thought the procedure over.

Then Kashif brought out the needle.

"That have anything to do with his wrist?" Billick challenged.

The Arcan, caught, shot a frown in his direction. He did not offer a response, instead plunging the needle into the unconscious boy's arm. Sarah spoke for him. "Kashif studies blood. He can learn a lot from your blood."

Billick's eyes remained on the cylinder filling with blood. "Does it bring back memories?" The question caught Kashif off-guard, his focus momentarily rattled. Billick probed the uncomfortable topic. "Having a helpless Tollian on your table and a tray full of tools at your fingertips." The murderer scoffed. "Tell me I'm wrong."

The Arcan stayed silent – a confession in itself.

Billick leaned in. "What happened to all the prisoners of war you took? So many never returned after the war ended. There were rumors – of experiments …"

The Arcan stood, still as stone. He addressed Sarah. "Can you fetch me some water. In a pitcher." The girl was listening to the exchange, and Billick wondered how much she understood. Kashif apparently didn't want her hearing more; the request for water an obvious excuse to clear her from the room. "Run to the mayor." The girl complied, albeit hesitantly.

Billick waited until she disappeared out the door. "Can't hardly imagine what you must have done with them …"

"Enough that we couldn't return them to you."

The retort from the Arcan was so chillingly cold, it caught Billick by surprise. He'd expected the scientist to remain quiet, ignore him – not respond with a smug confession. "No remorse? I would expect no less from those savage warriors I met on the battlefield – but you? You purported to be a man of learning, not blood."

"I did what had to be done."

"To helpless prisoners …"

"To invaders that came for a slaughter …"

"Did you find pleasure in it, Arcan? Watching them bleed out on your table?"

"The cost of progress." Kashif stated dispassionately, and then he smiled. "I should think you the last person to preach against blood."

Billick shrugged, unfazed by the comment. "I am what I am. I have no remorse for it. I'm a murderer. A cold-hearted murderer. I don't care who my victims are. I don't care what they've done. I don't care, because I don't have to. The blood washes off easy enough." He pointed a finger at Kashif. "Can you admit what you are, Arcan? Do you have the courage to admit you are as degenerate as I?"

The dark-skinned man would no longer meet his gaze.

Billick sensed a victory – but he had more barbs in his bag. "Perhaps I missed my calling in life," he said. "I should have been an Arcan scientist. No less blood on my hands – and one of the top castes to boot."

The last got to Kashif – Billick saw the hate briefly in the corner of his eyes. He savored the satisfaction in putting the Arcan in his place. There was nothing more he could gain by talking to the scientist, and so he stood to leave. Kashif spoke before he reached the door. "It must bother you – as much as you hate my people – that you see so much of yourself in me."

The murderer shook his head. "Far from it, Arcan. I find it fascinating that your perfect society didn't stamp out murder – it merely justifies it and calls it progress."

Despite the lateness of the hour, Alben's main thoroughfare was alive with pockets of conversing bystanders. Reed stood off to one side, musing with the smoking Bostitch. The crossbowman said something witty and the Captain chuckled lightly, the smile breaking the tense weariness on Reed's face. Billick sneered. The Captain had thought Billick was aiming to lead the Band? That's what leadership got you! Un-abating, tense weariness!

He spotted Sarah in the thickets of a small crowd – this one listening to a man orating from a top a small stool. Billick was just out of ear-shot – thankfully – as of the few words he could distinguish, one was "miracle". A Deacon, then? Preaching a late night, road-side sermon? The fellow wasn't dressed like a clergyman, and what he lacked in the usual Deacon decorum he made up for in pious zeal. Billick lost sight of the group just as the man held up a wooden crutch and waved it before the crowd.

Billick had no problem with the Deacons, their religion and their Merciful Domus. Though he'd not participated in services since Arca, he liked to believe that he and Domus had come to an understanding. The core tenet of their beliefs was exactly the same – no man was without fault. Those faults were ultimately what allowed Merciful Domus to exercise his mercy. Those faults justified Billick in sending folks to accept that mercy a bit earlier than they might have expected.

Just as he was reckoning he had found a spot to be alone, Billick noticed three men conversing in the shadows between buildings across the way. He only recognized one – Murphy. The Arcan's lone guardsman was speaking softly to the two others, who bore a decided family resemblance. One of the men extended his hand – and Billick spied the metallic flash of moonlight on silver.

The other man noticed Billick and hastily notified his co-conspirators. Murphy's alarm was evident – until he recognized Billick. He held out his hand in a calming gesture and spoke to the two men. Billick could almost guess the words. Fought on Arca. Hates the dark-skinned too. No need to worry. Whatever Murphy said, it did appease the brothers. After a few small exchanges, they left Murphy alone in the alley.

Northing's man palmed the coins he'd been given and stuck them into his pocket. Murphy left the alley, offering a knowing wink to Billick as he passed. Billick frowned as he watched the man depart. Murphy had something in the works.

He was forcing Billick to make a choice.

29.

The upper chamber of the town hall was one large room – intended to host Alben's town council and any other interested citizens as they debated the future progress of their small town. The room was warm, though Billick was far from the large stone fireplace set against the back wall. He'd spied several smaller fireplaces in the various rooms downstairs – the chimneys of which ran up through the walls. Cooler air seeped in through the glass-paned windows, four each on the two longer walls. These were crafted on a hinge – no doubt to be opened during the more humid months of summer.

The blend of temperatures was perfect for a fall slumber, and though the cots were makeshift, it would not have been hard to fall asleep. The others in the Band – at least the other four that were occupying the town hall – had not stirred in the last two hours. Billick was not even sure the quiet boy had ever regained consciousness since Kashif performed the operation.

The only person not sleeping, beside Billick, was Murphy. The Northing guardsman was doing his best to appear as if he slumbered. His eyes were closed, arms folded across his chest, head nodded forward as he sat against the wall. It was the best approximation of sleep that a conscious person can muster. The guardsman's breathing was off – the draws of air too irregular. His movements – a relaxing of the leg here, a roll of the shoulders there – were too calculated, too controlled to be attributed to a twitching muscle. And then there were the eyes, peering through barely cracked lids to survey the room.

Billick had chosen his place in the room to give him the clearest view of Murphy. Unfortunately, that also meant Murphy had the same unobstructed view of him. Billick was lying prone on the cot, body relaxed but mind fully alert. He wondered if Murphy didn't sense the falseness of his resting that Billick so clearly could identify in Murphy.

Billick kept his eyes closed, trusting in his other senses to alert him should Murphy make his move. It was clearly a plot against the Arcan, Billick just didn't know what the plot entailed. He'd have to watch Murphy, wait for the man to enact his part, and then move to stop it.

Billick grumbled in silence. He was committed then? To stopping whatever these men had conspired to do to Kashif? Was he really going to come to the defense of a boiling Arcan? A boiling black-skinned Arcan? Cursed wizards and their cursed, cryptic comments! Would he even be considering this had Wizard Algius not made his off-handed prediction?

Murphy stirred and Billick rejected the urge to open his eyes. Instead he concentrated on the sounds he heard. The guardsman was up, moving with soft, careful steps across the floor. Surely the man wouldn't be bold enough to commit the murder himself! Just as Billick prepared to leap from the cot, he heard a small, distinct metallic sound and Murphy's footsteps retreated back towards his station. They didn't stop, however. Billick kept his eyes closed until he was certain that Murphy had cleared the bottom of the stair landing and exited the town hall.

What had that metallic click been? The murderer did a quick calculation of how far Murphy could have advanced based on the number of steps he'd heard the man take. Finding the estimated range, he scanned the room for anything that could have made the unidentified sound.

He spied it. The lock on the hinge had been opened on the window closest to where the Arcan bedded down. Billick carefully crossed the room and refastened the locking bolt. The effort, while small, had most likely foiled the scheme, but he intended to do more than foil it. He angled towards the stairs and towards the door. He kept a look-out for Murphy – it would be no good to run into the guardsman now. He wanted the scheming Albeners first.

It did not take long to find them. Walking behind the building, Billick easily interpreted the scheme. The two Alben men were moving a tall ladder into place beneath the window Murphy had unlatched. Billick watched them from the deep shadows for only a moment, giving them a chance to secure the ladder's footing. As the slighter of the two men took to the rungs, Billick emerged from his hiding spot. Despite being a large and imposing man, the murderer moved well – displaying stealth that would have left even the Degan thief impressed.

The silent maneuvers were not entirely necessary – the two Alben men were completely focused on the task at hand. The one holding the ladder was intent on watching his partner, currently was two-thirds up the length and nearing the window. Billick's presence wasn't noted until he was standing next to the grounded man.

He turned, his eyes were wide at the sudden realization that he was not alone, and his mouth opened to express his shock. Billick jabbed him in the throat with a swift motion. The shout or scream died on the man's windpipe and escaped as a broken wheeze. Unable to breath, the man released the ladder to clutch at his throat. Billick directed a strong kick at the man's left knee cap, effectively eliminating him from the confrontation.

The second man had already reached Kashif's window and was prying unsuccessfully at the casing of the supposedly-unlatched pane of glass with his work-knife. His companion's collapse was loud enough to draw his attention to the stranger interfering with their plot. Billick and the ladder-bound man considered one another for a brief second before the murderer placed his hands to the ladder.

The intent was clear.

The second man started his mad scramble downward just as Billick pushed the ladder off balance. The entire span wobbled in the dim, cloud-screened moonlight. The panicked Alben clutched to the teetering ladder, as if there was some great difference between falling *off* a ladder and falling *with* a ladder. He landed in a heap twenty paces away, pinned beneath the ladder with the wind knocked clean from his lungs.

The second man efficiently dealt with, Billick rounded back on the first, grabbing him by his shirt collar and dragging him up to pin against the wall of the town hall. The man sagged, his left leg unable to bear weight without immense pain, and his eyes were wide.

"He said … you hated the black-skins!" the man rasped, his voice broken.

"I do," Billick told the man before belting him hard in the stomach. The man doubled-over and Billick pulled him up once more. "But he's under my protection while he's in the Band. Not you – not your friend there – not anyone touches the Arcan. Clear?"

The man sputtered, but managed a contrite, vigorous nod.

Billick threw him down in the direction of his supine collaborator. "Get your friend and get out of Alben. Find somewhere else to be. If I see either of you again – even a glimpse of your face – I will kill you." There was no need to expound the point further. Billick could see the man understood how serious the threat was. The Albener got to his feet, limped to his companion and helped him free of the ladder. Leaning on one another, the two hobbled away, not daring a glance back at their attacker.

Billick watched them until the night swallowed them up. He could have killed them. They'd come to stick that knife into Kashif; who couldn't justify sticking a knife in them? He didn't kill them, but only for one reason. The bodies. He didn't have time to be bothered with disposing of two bodies – not in an unfamiliar town, not without Hennessey making arrangements. He needed to focus on the demon – and not worry about the constables of Alben coming to see their own get justice.

Besides, there were more important matters at hand.

Billick went to find Murphy.

30.

Reclining against the wall, Ethiere remained lost in his own thoughts. He watched the sunlight streaming through the windows of the council room, each ray boldly announcing the new morning. He and the others of the Gang rarely saw a sunrise. The tasks Master Hat gave them were conducted deep into the night hours, most of the gang's children slept soundly until the mother's called for lunch.

It was so steady – the rising and setting of the sun. So predictable a pattern. It was chaos that went on in the interludes between those two predestined moments that Ethiere dreaded. It was the chaos that couldn't be planned against, couldn't be predicted, and couldn't be avoided. He still couldn't fully grasp how it was that he found himself here, in Alben, hunting a deadly, Oblivion-escaping demon.

But the sunrise was peaceful reassurance – in that small moment of dawn. Lowering his head, the Degan youth regretted not being awake to witness more sunrises.

Nearby, Sarah's eyes began to flutter open and the young girl sat up with a start. She blinked madly at the fog of morning and reacquainted herself with the room and its strange assortment of inhabitants. The girl bore deep markings on her left cheek, a design etched by the tassels of the quilt she'd slept on. Sarah, of course, would have remained blissfully unaware of the discomfort.

"Good morning," he said softly. "Sleep well?"

"I think so," she answered, an unusually succinct answer from the talkative girl. Her mind had not yet fully risen to the prospects of the new day. Sarah stretched out her legs, freeing them from the quilts. "When did I fall asleep?"

Ethiere offered a crooked smile. "It was late. Do you remember me coming back?"

"Yes," she answered. That conversation had begun with her questioning him about why he'd not stayed to watch Dom's operation. He'd mostly avoided her questions, changing the subject to something he knew she could chatter on about for hours. Truthfully, Ethiere felt guilty. It had been clear – Dom had not wanted the Arcan's procedure performed on his wrist, infected or not. But Ethiere had noticed the itching, had pointed out the apparent connection between the silent boy and the pain sensations the Band shared. Dom already didn't trust him – he'd surely view this as an unforgivable betrayal.

"Do you remember telling me all about Kashif patching up Dom?"

"I do." And she had. Ethiere had been amazed at the details that Sarah had been able to recite. The names of the various chemical compounds, surgical instruments, infection terminology and stitching techniques. Sarah's retelling had been only a shade behind witnessing the whole procedure personally. Either Kashif had narrated the entire time – or Sarah had peppered the scientist with her usual inquisitive questions. The thief would have laid favorable odds on the later. "Did I finish telling you about it?"

"Not quite," Ethiere responded. He looked her in the eyes. "You fell asleep mid-sentence!"

"I did?"

"You did," the thief confirmed. "I'm shocked that you didn't pick up where you left off when you awoke!"

She laughed at his teasing. "I was trying to stay awake for Dom. I wanted to be awake when he woke up."

Ethiere motioned to the prone, blanket-covered lump between them. "It looks like you'll still have that chance. I don't think he moved all night."

"I would be surprised if he were still asleep," said Kashif. Ethiere had seen the Arcan up and stirring when he'd awoke – already busy playing with the mysterious objects in his pack. He hadn't been aware that the scientist was listening in to the quiet conversation he and Sarah were having across the room. "The tincture that rendered him unconscious will have lost its potency some two hours ago. The sedative I administered will still be in effect – but only for another hour at most. I would suspect he is alert."

Ethiere looked back towards the lump. He'd seen cobblestones with more animation than Dom displayed. Sarah leaned over and lifted the corner of the blanket covering Dom. Her face broke out into a surprised grin. "He is awake! He's just not moving or talking!" She threw the blanket back, revealing the prone boy in the oversized coat. His eyes were indeed open – albeit glassy and distant. He blinked at the sudden intrusion of light. "Good morning Dom!"

The boy did not respond verbally. The only indication he'd heard Sarah's salutation was the leisurely roll his eyes took to look in her direction.

"Is he okay?" Sarah asked the Arcan. "He doesn't look right."

"It is the sedative," Kashif explained. The Arcan stood and crossed the room toward them, a vial in his hands. "It numbs the pain of the recovery – thereby sparing the rest of us from enduring it as well. As you've noted, Sarah, it does have the added repercussion of dulling the subject's faculties. While Dom is still in full use of his senses, his ability to interpret that data has been drastically diminished. He will not be able to speak – as the formulation of distinct words will be far too demanding in his current condition."

Ethiere looked with pity on the injured boy. Sarah gave voice to what they were both thinking. "That sounds terrible!"

Kashif shrugged. "The recovery process is what it is. Would you both please help Dom into a sitting position? I will administer the next dosing." Ethiere and the young girl reluctantly compiled. It was what it was. Sunrises, Banding and Arcan medicines. "Tip his head back slightly," Kashif instructed. "Open his mouth."

"How long will he have to be like this?" Sarah asked.

"For the rest of today and tonight." The Arcan removed the stopper from the vial and tapped a small sampling of the white powder within onto the pad of his forefinger. "I would anticipate a decreased dosage tomorrow, but we will analyze that when we've reached that point." Gripping Dom by the chin with his other hand, the Arcan stroked the white powder across the gums above the molars. The dazed boy lurched in Ethiere's arms and made a half-hearted attempt to gag before sinking back into his semi-oblivious, unburdened state. "He should not be left unattended."

Sarah brightened. "No worries! I'll stay with him!" Ethiere wondered at the wisdom of leaving the unresponsive Dom in Sarah's hands. But it wasn't as if the lad was going to wander off into trouble. She would probably talk at him and he would probably not respond – which was how their relationship regularly functioned. Sarah's volunteering seemed satisfactory to the Arcan, who nodded and went to return the vial to his pack. "Can I take him outside?"

The Arcan raised his head slightly. He was already busy examining his vials of blood. "Do not go too far. He will tire easily."

With Ethiere's assistance, Sarah helped Dom to his feet. He wobbled only slightly, nothing that holding Sarah's hand couldn't fix. She towed him to the stairs and talked him down each of the steps. Just before they disappeared from view, Ethiere saw something drop from the boy's hand.

The other occupants in the room hadn't noticed. Ethiere waited a few moments before rising. He saw Sarah and Dom out of the large window and moved towards the stairs. It took him only a moment to locate it – the token on the thin silver chain. Ethiere picked it up, watching the Circle of Domus dangle in front of his eyes.

He had a choice to make.

31.

Reed rolled his shoulders, trying to alleviate the knots that had formed during the fitful sleep of the night before. He and the three men Lord Cahill had allocated him – Bostitch, Neald and Sperry – kept watch over Greer and Sophie in the master bedroom. The soldiers had attempted to rest on the mayor's parlor furniture in between their watch rotations. Whoever had designed the couches and chairs had not done so with a soldier's frame in mind.

Young Sperry, just finishing off the last of the night watch rotations, rocked on his heels. Reed recognized the motion – he'd utilized it to stay awake many long nights. Sperry saw Reed watching and saluted. The youngest man in their unit was probably still uncertain as to why he was selected to Reed's small detachment – but he knew how coveted the spot had been among the unselected men.

"You alright?" Reed asked.

"Yes, Captain. Who doesn't like to see the entirety of a sunrise?" His assured response was ruined by a sudden, unstoppable yawn.

"If you liked that," Neald told him, "you should see how the stars twinkle in the dead of night sky!"

"We'll take it from here, Sperry. Go shut your eyes – I can't guarantee how long it will be before we start moving again." The young guardsman nodded and abandoned his post for the blanket he'd laid out by the sitting room hearth. Reed looked to Neald. "You awake enough to go scrounge up some breakfast?"

"I figure the Mayor should be by any time with a full spread, don't you?" the balding soldier joked. The Mayor had found several reasons to check in on his esteemed guests during the waning hours of the evening – hoping to see that every need of the Cahills was met. His diligent hospitality had not – at least thus far – afforded any of the same benefits to Reed and his men.

"I figure you're right," Reed agreed. "But I doubt any of it will be for us."

Bostitch shifted on the couch where he slept. "Maybe," the crossbowman muttered, "they'll deign to offer us the rinds and crumbs?"

Neald coughed into his hand – a warning sign. Reed turned to see Lady Greer standing at the bottom of the stairs. Bostitch lifted his head to see the trouble, frowned, and sank back down to the pillow sheepishly. Before Reed could offer an apology for the inconsiderate statement, Greer added her opinion.

"I should think, by now, you would all know the delicate nature of Sophie's stomach." The companion girl had found something to complain about with each of the meals the Band had taken together. Reed had been quite impressed at the sheer amount of variety she'd managed in her complaints. "Besides, she's still resting off such an unpleasant journey and I wouldn't dream of waking my dear friend after such an inconvenience. As such, you'll be forced to eat her share, should anything be brought around."

Neald sent a questioning look in Reed's direction. The man was unsure how he should be interpreting the Lady's statements. Reed, likewise, was baffled at what he could only assume was bald sarcasm. "Are you certain, my Lady?" the Captain asked.

Greer's smile was weighed by self-depreciating spite as she took an open seat in the sitting room. "Of course, Captain Reed. I myself wouldn't condescend to eat the local-variety fare if I wasn't so hungry. What would my father say if he knew I was eating food not prepared in a proper manor kitchen?"

No one knew how to respond to the Baron's daughter. Even the superbly witty Bostitch seemed discomfited by the situation. As such, Reed did not blame his men in the slightest when they opted to retreat. Bost waggled his smoking kit. "With your permission, Captain."

Reed nodded and Neald stood to follow the crossbowman. "I'll go see about the food as you asked." The exodus left Reed alone with his charge, aside from Sperry. Reed did not doubt that the young guardsman was feigning sleep in the corner just to avoid being part of the conversation.

"Did you sleep well, Lady Greer?" Reed tried.

"What did my father tell you last night?" the noblewoman overrode him. Reed clenched his jaw, suddenly wishing he had a reason to excuse himself as well. It was his recent inescapable reality – caught in the unenviable position between the Lord Baron and his daughter.

What should he say? Had the Lord Baron intended his instructions to be private?

Lady Greer glared at him. "Do I have to order you tell me, Captain?" she asked. "Apparently, I under-appreciate my role in society that gives me the ability to make your life as pleasant as a picnic in Oblivion. My father would be so pleased if I were to practice brow-beating my inferiors."

She spoke the words with such venom, but Reed knew he was not the target of her wrath. This wasn't about anything except her father. With this realization, Reed considered how to frame his response. "Expectations," he chose. "The Lord Baron expressed his disappointment in my recent inability to meet his expectations." The Lady's stern expression faltered in a moment of empathy.

"You can't give him the pleasure," she told him coldly. "You can't let him assume complete control."

Reed shrugged helplessly. "He is a Lord Baron. I am merely the Captain of his Guard."

The explanation ruffled Lady Greer. "He is just a man!" she scolded him. She lowered her eyes, perhaps realizing that both of their statements were true. "What did he tell you to do?" she repeated, but without the previous edge.

"He told me to keep you safe. At all costs." Her expression told Reed that his simplified summary wasn't sufficient. "Your father has given the wizard he brought the task of destroying the demon. He'll have the support of most of the guard in doing so. I've been given a small detachment of my own men to serve as your personal shield. We have no other charge but to keep you from harm's way."

"You'll keep me from the demon," she clarified.

"That is my order."

"And what about my role in the Band?"

Reed stayed silent.

"What about the children? Sarah?"

Reed looked at Lady Greer, hoping she would see his personal feelings despite the words he was forced to say. "They aren't my concern."

The noblewoman slumped back in her chair, her posture definitely not befitting her station. The questioning in her eyes stung more deeply than he would have suspected. It was as if she were calling his integrity – perhaps even his very soul – into question.

The silence stretched; at last lifted by a thought from the Lady. "Perhaps duty isn't as noble as we've been taught to believe." Reed considered the statement. On the surface it seemed like a barb aimed to bite deeply into his pride. He was a soldier – a soldier was defined by his exactness to his duty. But Lady Greer had said it with a subtle undercurrent of self-reflection. This, too, was her burden. And suddenly Reed understood his charge better. This was not a rebellious daughter striking out against an overbearing father. This was not a spoiled child blinded to the luxury fate had afforded her. This was a soul emerging in awareness that duty was often at odds with doing what was right.

Neald flashed by the parlor window, knocked lightly and opened the door. "Sorry to disturb," he said – and his face showed he meant it. "Captain Reed, the local Constable would like a word with you."

Reed stood and nodded. He cast a glance back at Lady Greer. Neald took the cue. "I'll take over, sir."

"Did the Constable say what it was about?"

Neald shook his head.

"What about breakfast, Corporal Neald?" the Baron's daughter asked. "I should so like to provide you and the dear Sergeant with your daily allotment of rinds and crumbs!"

Reed patted Neald as he passed him by the door. "Just don't say anything," he counseled the soldier. Exiting the Mayor's home, he spotted Sergeant Bostitch chatting up an older gentleman while he finished his smoke.

As Reed neared, Bost stamped the end of his roll out with his heel. "This is Constable Mercer," the crossbowman said by way of introduction. Reed extended a hand which the Alben lawman shook firmly. Mercer had the quiet steadiness of a moss-covered boulder. Still, the tenseness in his eyes suggested this boulder was close to rolling downhill with unrelenting force.

"Captain Reed," the Constable said. "Welcome to Alben. If rumor serves, you are in charge of the Band of Six?"

Reed guffawed aloud; Bost turned to hide a smile. "If there is a man foolish enough to think he's actually leading that disjointed lot, I pity him. I command the Lord Baron's personal guard ..." He stopped, realizing that was no longer accurate. "Or at least I did up until last night. What is the problem, Constable?"

"Do you know what the Band is hunting?"

"A demon," Reed said simply. If the wizard Algius hadn't thought to contrive a better name, who was Reed to attempt to?

"Does it have claws?"

It seemed like an oddly specific follow-up question. "I can't say. Our brief view of the monster wasn't particularly clear on that point. Why do you ask?"

Mercer licked his lips. "Murders. Three last night."

Reed nodded. "Interesting timing."

"Never been a man to believe in coincidence," Mercer admitted. "These murders aren't ... typical." He'd struggled choosing the last word. Before Reed could ask for clarification, Mercer continued. "It would be best if I just showed you the bodies."

"Where?"

"Lamond's Field. Thirty minutes or so on horseback."

Reed had the orders for Bostitch on his tongue, but swallowed them. His place wasn't on the frontline anymore. "We'll send the bulk of my men under the authority of Wizard Hartley to accompany you, Constable. And I'm sure a few of the Band members will demand to go as well. Come with me." Reed walked towards the town hall, Mercer in tow.

"Why not the entire Band?" the Constable asked.

"There's hardly a need for the entire Band to go trekking out when a portion will suffice."

"I should think that if the demon is out there ..."

Reed looked over his shoulder at the old lawman. "No one has told you about our Band, have they?"

Mercer shook his head. "Why?"

"Good morning, Captain Reed!" Sarah waved, the frail girl perched atop the rail of a nearby fence. Dom, vacant-eyed in his drug-induced daze, sat with his back against the post. He swung his head lazily in Reed's direction and squinted against the rising sun.

"That's why," Reed mumbled. He cleared his throat. "Is the wizard around, Sarah?"

The girl nodded and pointed back towards the town hall. "One of the small rooms on the ground floor. He wanted a place to do his morning meditation."

"Billick? The Arcan?"

"Kashif is still upstairs, working with his vials. Billick was gone when we woke up, but I've seen him around this morning." Reed nodded a thank you and continued up the road. "Come to think of it," the little girl added, "the only person I haven't seen – besides those of you that went with Lady Greer – is Corporal Murphy."

Reed frowned at her observation, but tucked it away. He caught Cox loitering by the town hall entrance. "Cox – fetch the wizard and the Arcan. We need them now." The ruddy-faced man saluted and ducked back into the hall. Reed turned to address Mercer, but found that the man was wandering around the side of the building.

Reed noticed what was drawing the man's attention.

A long ladder was lying in the grass. A small section of it appeared to be dotted with blood. In unison, Mercer and Reed looked up to the second story windows of the town hall.

"Someone lose a ladder?" The question came from Billick. Reed hadn't seen him watching from the morning shadows.

"The Jervis boys have a ladder like this," Mercer commented, eyes scrutinizing Billick. Reed wondered what the Constable's discerning eye would see on a stained soul like Billick's.

Reed made the introduction. "This is Billick. He's one of the Banded. He has a – questionable past." The meaning was not lost on the Constable. "You know anything about this?" Reed asked the murderer.

The side-burned brute shrugged. "I found it like this this morning."

Mercer turned back to Reed. "You said there was an Arcan? The Jervis boys have a strong disliking of Arcans. Lost two older brothers in the war." Reed was still watching Billick. The murderer's smile looked anything but innocent. "What am I going to find if I stop by their place?"

"Two men in no condition to come fetch their ladder," Billick answered. "If you're stopping by, it wouldn't hurt to return it to them."

Constable Mercer was slowly losing his easy-going persona. The man had seen enough misery come upon his citizens to have to deal with a devil like Billick. Reed patted Mercer's shoulder, but the Constable shrugged him off. "I watch after my own," he warned Billick.

"Relax, Constable," Billick offered. "No Albeners died by my hand last night. I swear it."

Strangely, Reed found him believing the murderer's vow. As the Wizard Hartley and Kashif joined the gathering, Mercer began to tell them about Lamond's Field and his suspicions. It was during his review that Reed remembered an off-hand observation by young Sarah. The Captain's eyes flashed to Billick, and his mind replayed the exact wording of the murderer's assurance.

Corporal Murphy wasn't an Albener.

As the group broke to prepare for departure, Reed stopped Billick by placing a hand on his shoulder. "Should I ask? About Murphy?"

"Do you want an answer?"

Reed wasn't sure. What would he do with a confession? While having the smug murderer arrested would be satisfying, an incarcerated Billick would greatly diminish the capacities of the Band. Letting him free – making him available to face the demon – was the logical choice in fulfilling his charge to keep Greer safe. It was the choice the Lord Baron Cahill would want him to make. But what about Northing's guardsman? What if the murderer had taken out one of Reed's men instead? Would that change how Reed chose to justify his choice? Should it?

Reed let his hand fall.

Billick nodded and stepped forward. "I thought not."

32.

The bulk of the expedition going to Lamond's Field left on horseback – which posed a problem for Kashif. Horses were not native to Arca – and no Arcan that valued his dignity would even consider straddling an animal! The closest indigenous species to the equine on Arca were small, stout burros – but these were only ever used as pack animals by the lower castes.

Gratefully, none of the Tollians offered the distrusted, dark-skinned foreigner one of their beasts to ride. He was relegated to the horse-drawn wagon being driven by Alben's lone physician – a bearded man by the name of Davies. Kashif imagined that the wagon served to transport those of Physician Davies' patients whose illnesses and injuries mandated they be brought back to town for care. As the wheels of the wagon continued to jar against the unkempt countryside roads, Kashif allowed himself a small pang of pity for the ailing souls that had to endure such a bone-cracking ride.

Kashif was able to push aside the discomfort of the trip using the focusing techniques Marooke had taught him. The rocks and rivets in the road could do nothing to shatter his meditative calm. Indeed, the only emotion that gnawed at Kashif's serenity was the small measure of joy he felt in watching Billick – also relegated to the back of wagon – curse as the uneven road threw him around like a willow branch in a spring gale. None of the Albeners had offered the cruel-eyed, side-burned stranger a horse either. So while Wizard Hartley, the Constable and the balance of Reed's men rode up ahead, Kashif was left with one of the men he despised most in all of the Architect's grand creation.

Strangely, the worse the road grew, the more talkative Billick became. Due to boredom or want of distraction, Kashif could not say what prompted the usually brooding murderer to open a dialogue. When it began, Kashif had worried. Most of the conversations he and Billick had held had not been pleasant. The Arcan war veteran had a litany of topics he could needle Kashif with – and Kashif was as captive an audience as they came. But thus far, the brute had avoided all things Arcan. They'd discussed Reed's apparent demotion, and the subsequent promotion of the man who headed the horsemen out front.

"What's your assessment of Wizard Hartley?"

Kashif did not know much about the man. He hadn't spoken to the wizard – nor did he plan to. The wizard was not part of the Band – and therefore was not part of the puzzle Kashif had been Banded to solve. Kashif offered a simple answer from his brief observations. "Young."

"A liability?"

He remained non-committal. "It remains to be seen."

The wagon lurched again; Billick narrowly avoided smacking his head against one of the side beams. "What if he starts using magic?"

The Arcan shrugged. "Isn't that the point? Isn't that why Lord Baron Cahill hired him?"

Billick sniggered. "Not going to be honest then? I know what your kind thinks about wizards."

Kashif allowed the jostling of the wagon to mask his irritation. "And what is it that you assume to know about my kind?"

The murderer stretched his legs. "I saw what happened to the wizards we brought to Arca," he said, completely nonchalant. "Seemed to drive your warriors berserk whenever we took one into the field. Fastest way to death on Arca was to wear a knotted cord around your shoulders – but we never knew why."

"I am not a warrior," Kashif said carefully. "We are not at war." The wagon hit a rut that inflicted a sudden blow against his tailbone. He quickly whisked the pain away. "I don't go berserk."

"But you don't care for him," Billick answered. "You can't stand him, unless I'm misreading you. Is it the magic? That was the only theory that ever made sense to me. It's always struck me as odd – all my time on Arca and I never saw an Arcan wizard. With as many as we brought over, it surprised me that there was never an Arcan wizard brought in to retaliate. Do you not have wizards on Arca?"

"We do not refer to them as such …"

"What do you call them then?"

Kashif looked at the side-burned man. Billick was an absolute troll when it came to anything regarding Arcan culture – and Kashif wasn't sure if educating the man more on the topic was wise. Nothing he said would change the murderer's hatred for the dark-skinned foreigners. But then, Kashif saw nothing to be ashamed of in the superiority of his race. "They are the Magistad. They are our ruling class."

The revelation was unexpected; Kashif could see it in the murderer's eyes. "You are governed by wizards?"

"We do not call them that," he reminded the man as the wagon forced them to sway in unison. "It would be quite insulting to assume our Magistad are anything like these wizards of your homeland. They share the same ability – yes. But the similarities end there."

"How so?"

"Your wizards are shameful in the way they administer their ability. Most hide away in their Wizard's College. They separate themselves – secret themselves away – and by so doing waste what they could accomplish among the masses. The Architect – or Domus, as you so call Him – does not fashion a man with power unless he expects him to harness that power for the good of the race."

"And yet," interjected Billick, "nothing angered your warriors more than seeing our wizards use their power to swing the momentum of the war."

Kashif nodded. "Even more criminal than those who vanish away in their reclusive college is the behavior of this Wizard Hartley and those that sailed to fight in Arca. They sold their talent – willing to work magic for lucre. That is beyond despicable. No Magistad would ever dream of doing something so debasing. This Wizard Hartley seeks to use the very power of the Architect – to *destroy*."

"To destroy the demon," Billick clarified. "Isn't that a noble thing?"

Kashif frowned. It was not hard to understand. "This power they wield – this magic – we have found the root of it. It is in their blood – a particle which we have called Essen. We believe the Architect to be a being of Essen – the incarnate form of the power which was used to shape the world and mold all things thereon. This Essen has a divine purpose – one that spans the eternities. To create." Kashif looked on the murderer, willing him to see. "What shall we think of one that uses the creative power of the Architect to destroy? What can we call such an act if not blasphemy?"

Surprisingly, the Tollian murderer nodded in agreement. "Worthy of death."

Kashif felt it the appropriate time to bring up another topic. "Speaking of death, how is Corporal Murphy?"

Billick's lips thinned to a knowing smile. "Everyone makes such assumptions about me …"

Kashif nodded. "I certainly did. I would never have suspected you'd allow the two men with the ladder to live." The comment left Billick momentarily stupefied. He quickly checked to see if the physician in the driver's seat was listening before rounding back on Kashif. The Arcan felt a thrill at having shocked the murderer.

"You saw what happened?"

"From the window," Kashif confirmed. "Not the quietest melee." He let out a breath. "You were not the only one concerned about the behavior of Corporal Murphy. I sleep with my eyes open in case my supposed guardian turns into my opportunistic killer." The conversation paused as the wagon bounced over a series of rocks. "I suppose I should thank you."

The grimness returned to the brute. "I don't want your thanks."

"I said I *should*. It doesn't mean I *will*." Kashif offered a conciliatory smile. "Don't fear, I won't tell a soul that you saved the life of an Arcan."

Billick grinned wickedly. "I do have a reputation to maintain."

The wagon rolled to a halt as Davies reined in the horses. Before the motion subsided, Billick was already out on the ground, a hound after his prized prey. Kashif gathered his pack of supplies and thought on the journey. What had just happened? Had he really just shared a smile with a man he reviled – a man who most assuredly detested him back?

Physician Davies rounded the back of the wagon. "Sorry about the ride," the bearded man apologized. Davies was the picture of rural civility. He wore the pressed slacks and matching vest befitting a man of his profession, but lacked the neck-cravat and dour expression that his compatriots in the city adopted. He was a heavy-set man, but wore his weight well. Kashif frowned. A student of health sciences such as Davies should know to take better care of his physique. "The driver's seat has springs – lessens the jostling."

"I'm sure it does." Kashif disembarked from the wagon bed, landing in the tall meadow grasses of Lamond's Field. He angled towards where the other men had gathered, Davies in tow.

"I must say, I'm honored to have a chance to work with you," the Physician said. "I was never personally instructed by an Arcan in the medical arts – but the man who instructed me was and he spoke very highly of the scientific prowess of your people."

"Your opinion of Arcans is not widely shared among Tollians."

Davies waved off the observation. "What? Should I blame you for beating us in a war we started?" The bearded man's voice descended into a hush. "Between you and me, there couldn't have been a better outcome. The Lord Barons trifling in your affairs – well I'm sure the research of your scholars would have been dampened in the very least. What a backward nation Tollia would be if it lacked the advances the Arcans have brought to light!"

Kashif hid a smile. The gushing physician was maybe the first person on Tollia to truly appreciate what Arca represented. Perhaps he could see to forgive the man his excessive girth.

"Oh, Merciful Domus," Davies whispered as they finally reached the corpses. The hunting party formed a semicircle at the bottom of the hill. The shepherd that had acted as their guide was already retreating back to the flock and his still living fellows. There was nothing more that the shepherd had not already seen of the remains of his three fallen friends.

There were three of them – the spread between them not more than fifteen or sixteen paces. None of the bodies appeared to have been touched – each lay in unnatural positions in their own gore. While Kashif was grateful that the scene of the attack had been left relatively unaltered, he knew the shepherds had not done so out of scientific respect. Even now, the Tollians hung back from the bodies, as if they marked unhallowed ground. What, did they think death could be contracted like a disease? Had the Arcan-sent plague scarred them so deeply? Kashif pitied their ignorant, superstitious fear.

"No one touches anything unless I direct them to," Kashif announced to the men. Reed's soldiers looked unappreciative of his tone, but they were men equivalent in standing to the Arcan Ballistad. Kashif was accustomed to giving orders to those of the lower castes. Wizard Hartley, whose authority was being usurped, watched with a frown but said nothing. What could he say? Could any of them dispute Kashif's unmatched expertise on the subject of the human physiology?

"Whatever did this might still be in the vicinity," Constable Mercer reminded.

The Wizard latched onto the idea. "Let's search the area," he ordered. "In pairs. Spread out. Call out anything you find amiss." Billick, in his usual manner, marched off alone through the meadow grass before the wizard finished giving his instructions. Reed's men divided into twosomes and went in separate directions. In short order, only the constable, the wizard and Physician Davies remained as an audience.

Kashif toured the murder site, stopping at each of the bodies in sequence. Davies remained at his heel – an eager acolyte despite the gruesome scene before them. The first body – identified as Shad Kestell by the Physician – bore the worst wounds. He lay on his side, his unpinned arm nearly rent from his body by a series of deep lacerations. Kashif was unable to tell by initial observation whether the man's torso bore the same mauling – though the sheer amount of body draining below the corpse suggested some major arterial line had been severed. The second body in the row bore similar deep gashes, but fewer. The cause of death was evident – one of the cuts extended straight across the man's throat. Hugh Kestell had died painfully and quietly.

The last corpse presented a completely different picture than the first two. "Denny Boyd," Physician Davies announced. "He was a cousin of the other two." While the Kestell's had been ripped open by their attacker, their cousin Denny bore no visible evidence of an assault. He was ashen faced, skin pallid in the morning sun, but otherwise appeared unmolested.

"We'll examine him first," Kashif determined, unslinging his pack from his shoulder. "Physician Davies, can you keep a ledger?"

The simple question startled the physician. The way the man fumbled for his response made Kashif consider rescinding the offer. Davies took the ledger as if he was being gifted the secret to Perfection and perused a sampling of the content. "My shorthand is – quite rusty," he admitted. "I've not kept up on my notation symbology."

Kashif retrieved his autopsy toolkit from the pack. "Just mind the details," he instructed. Marooke would be appalled at the intellectual compromise he was making. He could already envision Djemal mocking his ledger full of longhand notes and irregular Alben-inspired symbols. He flushed the thoughts from his mind and focused on the body of Denny Boyd that lay peacefully before him.

Kneeling before the corpse, he first called out the positioning of the limbs – noting the angle and rotation of the various joints. He went slowly, giving the Physician behind him ample time to record each figure. The positioning measurements were critical should they need to recreate the exact arrangement of the body in the lab. Next, Kashif took temperature measurements, placing the mercury-filled disks over various locations on Denny's body. As he did so, Kashif noted the first indication of cause of death.

"I note a small puncture wound, through the clothing covering the right shoulder." Using the thin scoping tool, he pulled at the woolen shirt until the hole aligned with a similarly shaped hole in the shepherds flesh. He called out the diameter of the wound to Davies and plunged the tool into the waiting hollow. The depth he announced surprised him, but revealed a fact Kashif suspected was important. "The placement and depth of the wound would suggest a puncturing of the auxiliary artery."

Lab sheers made quick work of the remainder of Denny's garb. The Arcan quickly located similar puncture marks, the symmetry of their locations painting a clear picture. "Six punctures in all," he told Davies. "Diameter is consistent. Three pairs – one each over the aortic, auxiliary and iliac lines."

"Each of the major arteries," Davies commented.

Kashif stood. While there were other measurements that could be documented, those could wait until they were back in Alben. "Load all of the bodies into the wagon," he instructed Mercer.

"Shouldn't we assess the other two?" Davies queried.

The scientist threw a last look towards the fallen Kestell brothers. "It will not be important. They were slaughtered without forethought; their wounds will show no pattern worth analyzing. Only Boyd was subjected to the methodical death we have observed. We will study the differences between these three men. We must learn what set Denny Boyd apart from his cousins that earned him such a carefully implemented death."

"Is it the demon?" the Constable asked. "Is the creature you're hunting responsible?"

Kashif nodded. "Most certainly." He could see on the Wizard's face that an explanation for such a definitive statement would be sought. Kashif thought it rather obvious. "The six wounds – perfectly placed over the body's main arteries. I would suggest that since your Physician would have missed that connection, your common Tollian shepherd would probably not possess such amazing insight into the human body. Secondly, there is the matter of the blood."

"What blood?" asked Hartley.

"Precisely," Kashif answered. "A man is punctured on each of his major arteries. His loss of blood should be staggering, should it not? So where is it? The ground beneath him is clean – unlike the reddened soil beneath his cousins. On his clothing? Yes, there was a spattering of drops around each of the punctures – but not anywhere remotely close to the amount that we would have expected to spray from his ailing frame." The Arcan licked his lips, his mind still steeped in the mystery. "There is only one explanation. The blood was taken."

Davies looked aghast. "Taken? Why?"

"Why indeed," Kashif replied. The blood was the key. He could only hope that enough remained in the shepherd's body to do a complete series of tests. "When we can answer that question, Physician Davies, we very well may uncover the secret to defeating the demon we hunt!"

33.

She intended to watch over Dom the entire day. It was something a good friend would do, and Sarah was seeking for ways to demonstrate just how seriously she was taking their new friendship. So far, the duty had been as simple as smiling. Dom didn't do much. He sat there, eyes glassy and vacant. She talked with him anyway – telling him about the operation. She thought it only right – he'd been unconscious for the entire fascinating procedure. As it turned out, a drugged Dom was only slightly less responsive than a fully alert one.

Still, Sarah didn't like it. She didn't like seeing her friend in such an impaired state. And the reassurances she'd gotten from Kashif and Ethiere did little to ease her mind on the subject. Before he'd left in the wagon, the Arcan had authoritatively told her that Dom would be much happier not knowing the pain he should be feeling at the moment."

Sarah understood what the foreign scientist had meant – but she couldn't accept it. She knew a lot of people thought the same thing about her – that she was lucky not to know what pain she might be experiencing. Maybe that's what bothered her most about the way Dom acted – they both were less than whole because of what they couldn't sense.

Ethiere brought them some bread around midday; and Sarah delighted in the Degan thief's company. It was strange – she would have never picked such a nice young man to be a thief. Stealing, she knew, was inherently wrong. All the Deacons agree on that. Thieves and burglars were supposed to be untrustworthy ilk, but Ethiere was as genuine and truthful a person as she'd ever met. She was left to wonder if Ethiere was knowingly committing acts that offended Merciful Domus, or if, perhaps, he'd never had the chance to attend a Holyday service.

Sarah broke a piece of bread into little bites and placed them in Dom's lap. Vacant as he was, he could still manage getting the bread bits to his mouth if he worked at it enough. As she finished, she decided it was time to push the conversation to a spiritual topic – and one that had been on her all night.

"Ethiere, what do you think about miracles?"

He cast her a curious look as he finished chewing. "Miracles?"

"You know," she prompted. "Those wonderful things that happen that can only be attributed to the love of Merciful Domus."

Ethiere brooded on the definition before answering. "I'm afraid I don't have much experience with miracles. Perhaps you should tell me what you think instead."

His answer pretty much confirmed her suspicions – he was not a regular at the services. But she'd work on that. She'd be sure to invite him once their demon hunting was done. "Last night, when Kashif sent me to fetch some water for Dom, I saw a man out here on the street, standing on a box. He was holding a crutch and he was telling a story about how he'd been healed."

The thief was nodding. "I saw him."

"Do you think what he was saying was true?"

Ethiere smiled. "The man is no stranger in Alben – many people I spoke with last night verified his story. He was lame – the physicians had been unable to mend his leg. There was speculation that he'd never walk again. And suddenly – he's running into town – announcing his miraculous healing. No one really knows what to think – they can't dispute his story. They know he should still be leaning on the crutch."

"So it was a miracle."

He shrugged. "Everyone wants to believe it."

His tone made his meaning very clear. "But you don't?"

"Sometimes," Ethiere said, "people desperately need something to believe in."

--- * --- * ---

He poised the upturned bottle over the pewter spoon they'd borrowed from Goodwidow Maybee, letting every last droplet of green eke its way through the opening. It was the last night – the last dose. Sarah tried to calm her stomach; not an easy task given the stress of the situation. Every last one of their hopes was pooled into the bowl of the tiny pewter spoon.

Her father forced a smile – a brave one. "Gilley said it might take the whole bottle," he told her again, and she had to refrain from not speaking the next part in unison with him. "Told me that with a special case, like yours, it might take the whole bottle – bottom to cork – to see it work." Finally convinced nothing else would be emerging from the bottle, he set it aside. His eyes, however lingered on the drained decanter of glass. "But he told me – looked me square in the eye – and he told me he's never seen a case that his Cure-All hasn't been up to beating!" He swallowed hard, and looked over to her. "He looked me straight in the eye."

"Then tonight's the night then," she told him, willing a smile of her own.

Her father had never told her how much he'd paid the traveling apothecist – he most certainly never intended for her to know. He couldn't have known that years ago she'd discovered where he stashed their savings. The modest upstairs room they shared couldn't hide something away from a home-confined girl forever. Counting up and stacking the coins; dreaming about what would be done with them was one of her secret hobbies. Sarah knew precisely how many went missing the day her father returned with the bottle. She knew what each coin represented – the number of days and weeks of toil it took her father to eke out one coin to put aside in their savings. The vial's cost could be measured in money, in time, and in sweat.

By any estimation, it had not come cheaply.

"Tonight's the night" he echoed. Sarah wanted so badly to tell to him it would be okay – that no matter what happened, it would be okay – but she couldn't. She realized she didn't know if it would be okay or not. She didn't know if failure would break her father's heart. She didn't know if the dam of hope would crumble and let the longsuffering despair flood back into his eyes. "Are you ready?"

She nodded and he advanced, carefully balancing the spoon. She opened her mouth, although she fought her instincts in doing so. The Cure-All was tongue-curlingly bitter – it was all she could do to not gag on the stuff as it went down her throat. The acrid taste stayed with her for hours. She heard the metal make contact with her teeth and she closed her mouth around the spoon.

The bitterness brought tears to her eyes as she tried not to choke. She forced herself to swallow – and it was over. The last dose. Her final taste of the remedy that never failed. She laid back into her bed, and wondered what she was supposed to be feeling at that moment. Happy? They'd had so much hope after the first dose – so much hope at the promise it held. Now?

Her father swallowed hard, his jaw set. He was determined to carry out their little ritual. Determined to see it out through the end. Gently, he pulled the stocking from her left foot. Without instruction, Sarah turned her head to the right and closed her eyes. There was nothing – and then she felt his touch – five distinct brushes by his fingers to various parts of her foot.

She felt the pressure of his touch – but nothing more. She kept her eyes shut, if only to keep herself from crying.

"Nothing then?" he father guessed in a stoic whisper. She turned to him, her vision swimming with un-cried tears. He sat on the edge of her bed, contemplating the blood-tipped point of the tack, nodding but not saying a word. She wanted to apologize. She didn't know why – it couldn't be her fault the remedy hadn't worked. She was not to blame, was she?

"I'd ..." he paused to catch his voice. "I'd better go return the Goodwidow her spoon." He patted her absently on the knee, stood, and took a slow walk down the stairs.

Sarah shut her eyes, and the tears squeezed out. She wasn't to blame – and yet she wanted her father to blame her. She wanted him to yell, and to curse, and to cry – she wanted him to release everything he was feeling – everything he was silently bearing alone. This would be one more burden – the load of one more dead hope – that would ride on his shoulders and would weigh on the corners of his weary eyes.

One more burden courtesy of having a daughter like her.

--- * --- * ---

It was an odd combination of words, but they resonated deeply within the young girl. *Desperate belief.* It succinctly described what she and her father had experienced with each new medicine, with every new physician. Hope was a bitter blessing, promising temporary respite with deeper grief coming fast on its heels.

"Don't get me wrong," the thief corrected. "I would love to live in a world of miracles. I would love a world where all the wrongs could be righted by some supernatural force. But I can't."

"Why not?"

"My belief in miracles died with my family," the thief admitted. "My father was a dockworker – probably among the first to make contact with the ships that brought the plague. First my father got sick, then my sister and brother, finally my mother – one by one they succumbed, suffered and died. I prayed – I pled with Merciful Domus to save them. I begged for a miracle. It never came."

"You survived," Sarah pointed out. "Isn't that a miracle?"

Sarah couldn't quite decipher the look she saw on Ethiere's face. "Alone. Abandoned. Hungry and hopeless. The plague so ravished the dock communities that the needy severely dwarfed what compassion could be mustered. If you knew what those first few weeks as a forgotten orphan were like ... it might have been a greater blessing had I just died too."

No one could deny that terrible things happened in the world. That is why Sarah took so much comfort from the Holydays and the faith-building sermons preached. "The Deacons say all things happen for a reason ..."

"Like the Banding?"

"Sure," Sarah answered, trying to be optimistic. "I would never have met you, or Dom, or Lady Greer ..."

"And your numbness?" Ethiere cut in. "Did that happen for a reason too?"

The young girl knew how the Deacons would answer that question. All trials, afflictions and sicknesses were part of the farseeing plan of Merciful Domus. They were meant to build divine attributes like patience and humility. They allowed others to exercise charity through service. Sarah had heard these explanations orated on the Holydays for as long as she could remember the sermons.

But did she believe it? Could she honestly look at the sacrifices her father had made because of her condition and say he was better for it? Was Ethiere's life better because of the adversity he'd faced? Was her numbness the will of Merciful Domus or just an unfortunate draw of fate?

Why heal a farmer's leg but not fix her condition? What crucible of faith could the farmer have gone through that she and her father hadn't experience one hundred times more?

Sarah frowned. It was a miracle – it should raise her spirits. But Ethiere was right. Why were miracles so selectively distributed?

"I'm sorry, that's not fair," Ethiere apologized, interrupting her thoughts. "It was wrong of me to bring up your condition." Sarah nodded weakly, happy to be relieved of making a response. "You know, your attitude, despite how unfair life has been to you, is heartening. You're an example, Sarah. You really are."

She'd thanked Ethiere for his kind words, but Sarah didn't feel like an example of anything to anyone.

Down the road, the sleepy afternoon Alben main thoroughfare was stirring to life. The crowd had been gathering as she and Ethiere had talked, and now it had swelled to a considerable size. Something had the citizens of the small town excited. "You should go see what is happening," the thief told her. Sarah was intrigued and immediately stood up – but then she thought about Dom. Her drugged friend didn't seem to be aware that anything was going on, but Sarah still felt obliged to stay with him. "I'll watch Dom," Ethiere assured her. "Go – I'm curious, too."

Sarah ran as fast as her legs could take her down the roadway. Everyone seemed to be congregating around the small but beautiful building that served as

Alben's cathedral. People clustered into small groups, whispering excitedly, though Sarah could not see anything which would have them so animated. A youthful Deacon, wearing the robes of the clergy, stood in front of the door, barring entry though no one attempted to gain access. But they were waiting, whispering – and Sarah heard the word 'miracles' more than once.

The large door of the cathedral opened and the young Deacon stepped aside. Another Deacon stepped out into the afternoon sun, followed by the man Sarah had heard speaking last night – the farmer whose leg had been miraculously healed. The farmer had a wide grin on his face – and it was he who first addressed the anxious crowd. "It's her!" he announced. "Thank Merciful Domus, it's her! She is well and sleeping!"

The crowd broke into cheering and applause, repeating the favorable news from the farmer. "They've found her!" Sarah heard one woman say. "They've found the girl that works miracles!"

34.

"Lord Baron William Cahill," the steward announced into the cavernous space of the courtroom. Lord Northing sat on a raised dais in a chair that was a throne in all but title. The frame was made of polished mahogany, inlaid with burnished brass decorations; the cushioning wine-colored velvet, sewn with lattice-stitching of gold thread. It was as fine a seat as existed in Tollia – much finer than the throne of the King whom Northing and the other Lord Barons had risen up against to depose.

But Tollia had no King, and hence, it had no thrones and throne-rooms. While Northing had been the most powerful of the baronies in the new political order, it had not been prudent then to assume a throne. The other barons, fresh from a successful coup, would have quickly pooled their strength and taken him down.

Such was no longer the case. Tollia had no King only because Lord Northing hadn't taken a crown.

Cahill crossed the courtroom, completely unattended by guardsmen in his own colors. It was strange, seeing him so defenseless in light of the unspoken tension between their houses. Tollia had been a breath away from having a new King two winters back. Northing had set the stage with puppet-leaders in other baronies and loyalists in the armies to strike a death blow to all those that might have risen against him. Lord Baron William Cahill was chief among those numbers.

Lord Baron Cahill knew the game. He could survey the board just as astutely as Northing could; he knew the outcome was already decided. Northing would be King, when he elected to be King. The only thing that was still in question was what part Cahill would play in the new kingdom. As an ally, Cahill could be left to govern his barony, a steward in Northing's service. In desperation to capitalize on this option, Cahill had tried to tie his house with Northing's through marriage – attempts that had come up lacking.

Lord Northing was unsure whether he could trust Cahill as an ally. Cahill was shrewd, one of the master strategists that had architected the secret rebellion against the old King. Could the crafter of one coup be trusted not to plan a second? It was almost assured that any resistance to a Northing as King would have Cahill at its head. No, it made sense to strip Cahill of his title and power.

"Thank you for your hospitality," Cahill said. His head dipped ever so slightly – was it a bow? Northing realized it was as close a bow as he was likely to see Cahill willingly give. "And for allowing me to interrupt your days' affairs."

"William, my old friend and partner," Northing deigned. "You should have sent word of your coming – I could have been better prepared to entertain you. I am not used to having such prestigious guests arrive unannounced in the middle of the night. Especially so – unattended."

"Circumstances dictated I bring certain matters to your attention as soon as possible," Cahill answered. "You have a demon in your barony, Lord Northing."

The surprise that Northing allowed his face to show was genuine. "A demon? Are you sure?"

"I am. A Band of Six hunts it and their hunt has led them to Alben. But of course, you already knew there was a Band formed; you have an Arcan who is part of the Band. I, too, have a vested interest in the success of this Band. My daughter Greer is also numbered in the six."

The news of the noblewoman in the Band was so unexpected and at the same time so unfortunately awful for Lord Cahill that Northing could barely suppress a delighted grin. Lady Greer – the girl who her father had tried in vain to betroth to a Northing – was now a demon-hunter! "How terrible!" Northing professed, though he felt nothing of the sentiment he expressed. "Your daughter hardly seems like a valuable asset to such a Band!"

Cahill nodded. "She has no place traipsing along the country-side with the company she is being forced to keep. It's the reason I come unattended – I left my entire regimen of guards to watch over her. Still, I fear it is not enough."

Northing frowned. "No? You've spoken so highly of your personal guard in the past. Surely one demon …"

"The wizards fear it," Cahill stated, blue eyes cold. "The one who gave the Band their charge hides away in their College even now. I have laid twelve swords between my daughter and the demon – I would rather it be twelve-hundred. I would request you send in a battalion or two."

"Would that not be an overreaction to the threat?"

Cahill stood as poised as if he were carved from marble. Northing knew that his composure was superficial at best. "Surely, for the sake of your Arcan, we can send in additional soldiers. Surely you want your Arcan to return safely to you?" The ploy was not unexpected. Cahill needed to make this personal to Northing.

It wouldn't be. Northing already considered Marooke's Banded apprentice a loss. His fate was in his own black-skinned hands. But this was an opportunity to pacify Cahill. "Of course. You're right, of course. We must act – and we will. We'll gather in some of the units stationed in Hollingston and send them to Alben."

Cahill nodded deeply – almost again approaching a bow. "Thank you, Lord Northing."

"Of course, we will need to send word to the other Lord Barons," Northing continued, and he saw the words slice into Cahill.

"A vote will waste precious time," Cahill answered tightly.

Northing shook his head, trying to look disinclined but resolute. "We must abide by the rules we agreed to, William." He left the statement hanging in the air, daring Cahill to make the next logical plea. Inviting him to say something he would loathe saying.

The old Lord Baron struggled in silence before his pride wilted to his concern for his daughter. "Surely you could just give the command," he said softly. "Surely none of them will oppose the action." Cahill looked up, defeated. "Surely none of them would dare oppose you."

Northing looked down from his throne that was not a throne on the complex man before him. Once an ally in a deadly coup, then a rival in game for power, now? Northing saw little of the dynamic man he'd associated with over the past decades. His adversary's soul had died in his invitation for Northing to take power. What remained was only a husk – in the form of a sad, worried, graying man.

"I'm sorry, William," he answered. "I would, but I am not the King."

They both let the unstated truth remain unsaid. *Not yet.*

Once Cahill was clear of the room, Marooke emerged from where he had hid and listened.

"What we seek is in Alben," the foreign scientist said.

"The demon?"

"And the girl," Marooke added. "We will find them together."

Northing nodded. "I'll gather a regiment – in secret. It wouldn't do to have Cahill find out about it now. They'll be ready to leave by nightfall."

"I will send Djemal with them. He will be able to identify the girl – and perhaps neutralize the demon."

Northing nodded in agreement, but could see that Marooke was not finished. "What is it?"

"The Band of Six," the Arcan said, voice subdued. "They may try to interfere. They will certainly try to kill what they have been sent to kill." The scientist straightened, reason ruling his thoughts. "You will instruct your men accordingly?"

Northing nodded. "They will be given explicit orders. If the Band is present, they will be eliminated."

35.

Elsa sat next to Judith Miller on a short wooden bench that was scarcely big enough for two adult women. Still, Elsa would not complain. Sitting was far better than standing – which is exactly what the rest of Alben was doing that very moment. The Revelries at planting and harvest time were not this well attended – and if this type of throng showed up for the Holyday services, Alben would need a second – if not a third – cathedral. Deacon Elsbury, as gentle of a man as Merciful Domus could have placed on the earth, looked both overjoyed and overwhelmed at the sheer number of people that congregated before the cathedral.

Such was the reaction a miracle brought.

Martin had been correct. He'd predicted this when they'd learned Pennie had been found. "You spill a drop of molasses," Martin had said, "and every ant on the homestead fancies he ought to go check it out."

Bertrand Miller, he of the once-broken-now-healed leg, stood before the crowd, recounting his experience yet another time. Elsa had heard the retelling three times now. Each accounting was a little different than its predecessor: the lame man more humble, his wife more prayerful, the little girl more angelic. Elsa was not one to fault a man for little embellishments in his stories – stories, like properly prepared dinners, needed garnishes and dressings – but Bertrand was taking it to excess. Elsa had to remind herself that she was an eye-witness, though she hardly recognized her character in the retelling.

She would suffer it, for it was Bertrand's fame that had granted her a prime location on the cathedral grounds. The wooden bench was just off to the side of the main cathedral door. Pennie was just inside that door – so close. Every motherly instinct she possessed demanded that she push aside the youthful Deacon guarding the door and find the girl. Surely Merciful Domus would forgive the mishandling of one of his clergy in the name of comforting a poor runaway girl!

Elsa understood why Deacon Elsbury was sequestering the girl. The entirety of Alben wanted to see Pennie – Elsbury was keeping her safe while he tried to figure out what to do next. What does one do with a girl who worked a miracle? Whether he deemed it the prudent course of action or just a way to stall while he figured out what to do next, Deacon Elsbury had made it known that Physician Davies would be the next one to allowed access to Pennie.

Elsa was determined to follow in on his heels.

Unfortunately, the Physician was out afield with a Band of Six. A Band of Six! What business would a Band of Six have in little Alben? Now there was a story that the entire town would be embellishing for years to come – Elsa was sure of it.

Bertrand was getting to the crux of his tale – he'd found ways to drag the actual moment that Pennie touched him into several narrative minutes. At the climax, he began waving his crutch around in grand spectacle. The crutch seemed to accompany Bertrand at every telling – as if it was destined to become a new relic! The people erupted into cheers and applause – praising the miracle and the mercies of Domus.

Front and center on the milling throng were the invalids of Alben, those whose condition was deemed incurable by the physicians. Farmer Weeks' boy, Percy, had never had more than the barest amount of control over his limbs. He sat in a wheelbarrow next to his father, arms and legs arching unbidden in the excitement of the moment. Elsa saw blind Lucinda Coombs, blank eyes hopeful, surrounded by supportive townsfolk.

A single question sated the atmosphere. Pennie had healed one. Could she do it again?

Elsa soured on the thought. Such manifestations of the Mercy of Domus could not be called forth on a whim … could they? And the healing had to be attributed to Domus. Elsa had seen it in Pennie's face when she'd touched Bertrand and he fell screaming. She hadn't known what she was doing. It was a miracle, yes, but it was also an accident, and accidents are seldom so easily repeated.

The crowd stirred and Physician Davies bubbled to the forefront. Alben's physician looked worn from his day with the Band – smears of dirt and flecks of crimson marred his ordinarily well-kept clothing. On seeing Davies approach, the young Deacon blocking the door began to move aside and Elsa knew it was time to act. She sprang from the bench and reached the cathedral door a footpace behind Davies.

The youth grimaced at the pending confrontation. "Many apologies, but Deacon Elsbury has instructed that only Physician Davies be allowed in."

Elsa chose instead to state her case to Davies. "She's scared. She's alone. You can go to her – but wouldn't it be better for Pennie is she saw a familiar face? The face of someone who had showed her kindness?"

The Physician pursed his lips behind his well-trimmed beard, reviewing the request. "I think you are right," he said at last and turned to the young Deacon. "Elsa will accompany me. I am sure Deacon Elsbury will understand and agree with this allowance."

There was no further resistance from the Deacon, who opened the door for them and saw that it was firmly shut behind them. The cathedral, small and unassuming when compared to the great edifices of Hollingston, was inviting under the reverent glow of candles. Deacon Elsbury, sitting in the first row of pews, saw them enter and looked relieved. He hurried down the aisle, robes swishing.

"Thank you for coming, Physician Davies," he said, and turned slightly to Elsa.

"She is here at my request," Davies answered, anticipating the question.

Elsbury nodded. "The girl – Pennie – was unconscious when she was brought in. Though I do not have your training, Physician, I could find nothing wrong with the girl. It appeared nothing more than an incredibly deep sleep. She has only awoke within the last two hours …" Elsbury frowned. "Perhaps it is best you are here, Elsa. The girl is quite distraught and nothing I say seems to comfort her. Come, I have her in my personal study."

Deacon Elsbury led them up the cathedral's narrow staircase to the simple rooms on the floor above. He produced a ring of keys from his robe and began to turn the lock.

"You locked her in?" Elsa asked, and immediately regretted that it sounded so accusatory.

The gentle Deacon nodded humbly. "She is quite persistent in her attempts to escape," he acknowledged. "I am not certain what exactly should be done with her. I fear the enthusiasm of the crowd …" He trailed off, having said enough. The lock clicked and the door cracked open. Elsbury stepped back and Davies motioned to Elsa, inviting her to enter first.

Elsa peered within. The study was small and dark and she could not see Pennie.

"We lit the candles for her," Elsbury clarified. "She snuffs them out as soon as we leave."

"Pennie?" Elsa called as she entered the room. "Pennie, dear?" As her eyes adjusted to the lack of lighting, she took note of the Deacon's study chair, which was pushed up against the far wall. Stacked atop the seat were three large tomes of sermons. Elsa raised her eyes, to the small window set close to the room's ceiling. Pennie sat in the sill staring out into Alben. "Pennie, won't you come down?"

"I need to leave," the girl whispered back. "I need to run."

"Pennie, the Deacons have only kept you here to keep you safe," Elsa explained. "They've not meant you any harm."

"It's not safe," she replied. "I can't stay."

Elsa's heart ached for the terrified girl. "We just want to help you, dear. That's all. Will you come down? Come down so we can talk it through." The runaway slid from the sill, nimbly catching the back of the chair and the stack of tomes as she alit on her feet. The act was so gracefully performed that it seemed almost commonplace. Elsa took the girl in her arms and kissed her on the forehead.

"Will you tell them to let me go?" the girl asked.

Elsa lowered to one knee so she could look at Pennie in the eye. "Why do you need to go, Pennie? What can be so urgent?" The girl dropped the gaze and stared shamefully at her feet. "Wouldn't you consider coming back to the homestead with me? The bed is still made up for you. We'll keep you safe, you must believe me."

The runaway's eyes rose up and they were so filled with a yearning sadness that they nearly brought Elsa to tears. "I'd always wished to find a mother …"

The door creaked open under a gentle interrupting knock from the physician. "I do not wish to intrude …" Davies offered in prelude. He stood back and looked the young girl up and down. "So you are the very special girl that has the entire countryside in a stir?"

He said it with a smile and meant it to be good-natured, but Pennie flinched – as though his words were an accusation. Elsa interceded. "Pennie, this is my very good friend, Physician Davies. He's a nice man and he's here to help you as well."

"Indeed," agreed Davies. "I understand from the Deacons that you were unconscious for a spell. I'd like to give you a quick look-over if you don't mind …" Davies set his black physicians satchel on the corner of the Deacon's desk. In that same moment, Pennie flinched so hard that she tore herself from Elsa's tender hold. Elsa reached out a hand, but grasped only air. The nimble girl, panic in her eyes, leapt for the tomes stacked on the chair.

"No!" she screamed. "Don't let him hurt me!"

Davies' singular reaction was to stand with mouth agape at the girl's absolute terror. Elsa stood immediately, trying to comfort the child. Pennie continued to yell. "Leave me alone! Leave …" As she reached for the window sill, the chair teetered off-balance. The tomes slid from the seat, yanking Pennie's feet away from underneath her. She fell, her body in a diagonal slant. Her legs collided with the up-ended feet of the chair, her head …

Her head clipped the corner of clothing trunk. The impact rolled her back towards Elsa – and gave the farmer's wife a perfect view of the bloody gash that ran from temple to ear. Pennie didn't make a sound. The rapid succession of events left both Elsa and Davies petrified. The physician recovered his wits first.

"Move aside," he pled as he grabbed his satchel. Elsa rocked backwards, allowing the wide-frame of the doctor a better angle from which to attend the fallen girl. Davies placed one hand on the girl's chest and studied the wound with the other. "She's still breathing," he declared. "The wound's a deep one – I'll have to stitch it! If she's cracked her skull …"

"Merciful Domus!" gasped Deacon Elsbury from his doorframe.

"Clean towels!" demanded the physician. "As many as you can find!" The words were forceful enough to chase the gentle clergyman from the room. Davies turned toward Elsa. "I'll need your help, if you're up to it. I can do the stitching, but it'll be terrible if she were to come alert in the middle of it. You need to hold her head still as …"

He stopped. Elsa could see why.

The gash on Pennies head was closing itself. Already it was only half its original length.

"It can't be …" Davies muttered as he sank back onto his haunches. "It shouldn't …"

The wound continued to mend itself as they watched, the skin coming together as if pulled by invisible threads. As it closed completely, Elsa could only marvel. Aside from the blood running down the poor girl's face, there was no sign of the injury. Not a scar, not a scab, not a single mark.

Elsa felt her toes go numb and she leaned against the back wall. As she looked at the mysterious girl, her mind could only frame one question. "Pennie dear, who are you?"

36.

Ethiere would never have expected Alben capable of producing so fine a throng of people. Truly what he was witnessing on the villages sole road was comparable to the high customer traffic hours of the Wellsford Park shops. The only difference, as far as Ethiere could observe, was that the citizens of quaint Alben were less accustomed to dealing with thieves than their Hollingston kin. No one thought to secure their bags, ripe coin-purses teased him from belt loops, and the shops! Given, Alben's variety of shops in no way compared to the menagerie that was Hollingston, but at least the store owners there had a mind to lock their doors when they stepped away!

Ethiere was very tempted to explore the wares of the unattended shops. Tempted, but he resisted. He wouldn't have stolen anything – he was sure of that. And it wasn't just because he lacked a convenient way of carrying anything he acquired with him on the journey – though it was a factor.

No, tempting as it was, it wasn't worth the damage it would do to his already scrutinized reputation. That was the heart of it. Besides innocent Sarah, no one trusted him in the slightest. Not Billick. Not Kashif. Not Captain Reed. Not even Dom. The others he was fine giving up on – but he'd really tried hard with the silent boy. His actions, no matter how well-intended, only served to create additional obstacles in befriending Dom.

Ethiere felt the caress of the silver chain in his pocket. The necklace – Dom's prized personal possession – was destined to be the next well-intention-laden disaster. Of course Dom would accuse him of stealing it. Of course everyone in the Band would come to that same lazy conclusion. No one would believe that he was keeping it safe for Dom. No one would understand that as much as Dom absently played with the necklace that he would lose it given his current state of mind. No, it would be too much for anyone to give a thief the benefit of a doubt.

So Ethiere kept his hands in his pockets, tried to ignore the bags that begged to be rummaged and the purses that jostled with calling coins, and attempted to just be one of the crowd.

The mass had reached a fever-pitch for miracles. As Ethiere snaked through the throng, he caught small bits and pieces of the various conversations taking place. Though the discussions were distinct, the thread of their conversations carried on in near uniformity.

Miracles.

While the topic spread a contagious feeling of hope, Ethiere resisted joining in. What good did the hope do for these people? For the lame and the sick, for the blind and the deaf? What good did the hope do for Sarah? Though the girl remained true to her charge to stay with Dom, it was impossible not to see how enthralled she was with the happenings at the cathedral. What good does the story of a miracle do for Sarah? Should she believe she's due to receive such a bounty? That there was an end in sight from the daily trial of her affliction?

Why were people inclined to ignore the reality of life? Existence was hard, it wasn't fair and there was nothing that could be done to change that. You took what fate dealt you and did the best you could with it. There was no bright horizon, no happy tomorrow. There was only the river, keeping your head above water, seeing where the currents took you until you could swim no longer.

So why did he linger? It was true – he had nowhere better to go. He didn't have the heart to talk Sarah out of her optimism. Kashif had three corpses in the back of wagon down the road, and Ethiere didn't have the stomach for watching what he was doing with them. The soldiers and Billick were lounging by the town hall. Weary and short-tempered from a long and unsuccessful search for the demon, they would be miserable company.

As much as he hated to admit it, Ethiere waited and watched the cathedral for one reason.

The thinnest thread of hope – a wish so impossibly slim that he was embarrassed to have conceived it.

He'd not been able to help himself once he'd learned of the miracle-working girl's name.

--- * --- * ---

There wasn't a member in the Children's Gang who didn't know what it was like to lose someone. Most were like Ethiere, orphaned and alone. Left to the mercies of the streets. Others were abandoned – given up by parents short of bread and love. Yet others were runaways – desperate to escape one nightmare; only to find themselves locked in a new one. But even they would speak reverentially about someone from their past life who had shown them kindness.

Ethiere had vague recollections of his family. His dockworker father with his bulging forearms and crushing hugs. His gentle mother with her knowing smile, ever ready with a just-baked slice of hearth-bread. His elder brother, David – rough on his kid brother; but also never failing to come to his rescue. And Marin. He remembered the day she made him watch her practice winking – just so she could be sure she was doing it correctly.

That was all he had left of them – these fractions of memories, these fragmented vignettes of the happy life he used to have. The life they'd had together – before the fever robbed him of everything. First their father. Then Marin. David succumbed only hours later. His mother – she was the last. The fire in their hearth died out the same moment she did.

Ethiere didn't know why he survived – why he never caught the sickness that killed everyone else in his home and completely ravaged the dockyards. He'd survived – but he was a causality of the plague just as much as any of them were. A loved boy had died the instant his mother had. An orphan had taken his place.

It was easy to understand the bonds which developed between the children in the Gang. This was a new family – with dozens of brothers and sisters, each as lonely and as anxious to belong again as you were. This was a new life full of exciting games and daring-do and laughter ...

Most of the time.

Loss always crept its way into the new life as well.

He could see it on Kari's face the moment he entered the large kitchen in their underground hideout. She'd protest otherwise, but Kari could out-eat most of the boys when she had a mind to. She was staring into her bowl of soup – a fish chowder by the lingering smell in the kitchen – as if comfort could be found in the creamy base.

"Does no good to mourn the fish at this point," he said lightly – more to announce his presence than anything else. The tease earned him a brief look coupled with a fleeting crack of a smile as she pushed the bowl toward him. He straddled the bench beside her. "Did we lose someone?"

Kari's non-response was answer enough. They knew what they did was risky. Master Hat called them games – but they weren't ignorant to the dangers. A slippery roof could mean a broken neck. An unaccounted for dog or a fleet-footed constable could mean capture. People didn't consider getting robbed a game. And some people would rather flick their knife then stand a child-thief before the Justices.

Carl had waved goodbye five years ago. Waved, smiled – and never came back.

Ethiere took hold of the spoon in the bowl and trolled for chunks. He never knew what to say, exactly. Boil him, but he'd sure had plenty of chances of late. He opened his mouth ...

"Just don't say anything," Kari murmured.

He swallowed his sentence. "Really?"

"It didn't help the first time – four months ago. And it hasn't helped any of the three times since." She shook her head, and he could tell she was blockading her tears by keeping her anger in the way. "Just don't say anything, not if you don't have anything better to say."

"What would be better?"

"Maybe that you know what happened to them? To any of them!? Depths of Oblivion, we don't hear anything? No rumors? No bragging from the constables?"

Kari was right. If there was anything worse than losing eight of their brothers and sisters in the last fourteen weeks, it was that there was no accounting for what had happened to them. Usually there was word – they'd be spotted at the Justice trials or they'd see a body riding in the back of the gravedigger's wagon. Some – like Carl – remained a mystery – but most ... at least there was closure. But not recently.

"Are the rules of the games changing, Ethiere?" she demanded of him. "Is this what we've got to expect now? We're going to lose someone each week? One less of us coming home each night?" A tear escaped. She whisked it away, but

another followed in its tread. She was breaking. She swallowed hard. Her next question was soft, and heavy with fear. "What if – one night – it's you who doesn't come home?"

He let the smile slowly spread to his lips. "You know anyone quick enough to catch me?"

He got her – Kari reciprocated his grin, but banished it not a moment later. "I'm serious!" she snapped at him as she snatched the spoon away. She shook it at him – scolding him – but words failed her. As she gently set the spoon back on the table, she finally broke. Kari almost never cried – members of the Gang rarely did. It was part of the unspoken code to pretend sadness had no place in their new lives together.

"What can I do?"

"You can talk with Master Hat," she sniveled.

"I did."

"Then talk to him again!" Her face flushed in the frustration she was feeling.

"He doesn't know what to do, Kari! He doesn't know what's happening to us out there! What are we supposed to do, just stop thieving? How long could that possibly last, before we're out of food?" He left off there, knowing that Kari didn't need more questions. "Sometimes," he said softly, "life just takes bad turns ..."

Kari bristled. "If you even mention your boiling 'leaf on a river', I'll ..."

He grinned. "You'll what?"

Ethiere put his arm around her and pulled her close. He caressed her hair while she wept on his shoulder. He wished he had answers – but there were none to be had. There was only tomorrow, and it would bring whatever it intended to bring. As Kari sobbed, Ethiere was confronted with a most unhappy thought.

What if Kari disappeared into the night? What if she were the ninth ...

But no, there was already a ninth – already another missing. "Kari?" he whispered into her ear. "Kari, who didn't make it home last night? Who was it this time?"

226

"Pennie!" Kari said between racking sobs. "We've lost Pennie!"

--- * --- * ---

It was a silly notion. How many Pennie's were there in Tollia? One hundred? One thousand? Whoever it was they were hiding away in the cathedral, it wouldn't be *his* Pennie. It wouldn't be the girl that disappeared from their gang nearly seven weeks ago.

But it frustrated Ethiere – that thin thread of hope that he couldn't annihilate with a snap. There was just not enough people who actually knew anything in the crowd. Yes, Pennie was a girl – but how old? Ethiere had heard everything from six to sixteen. What did she look like? Brown hair? Some said yes, but others said she was blond, or dark, or ginger. It was excruciating to be among people so uniformly focused on a single person – and for them to be so ignorant of the person at the center of their attention.

He considered alternative ways of getting the information he needed to silence the hope. His tutelage under Hat had given him many options for gaining access to the inside of a building. But a cathedral – Ethiere had never broken into a cathedral before. It just seemed wrong. The thief didn't know if there was such a being as Merciful Domus, but in the off chance he did exist, Ethiere didn't think he'd take kindly to anyone picking locks on his property. And Ethiere didn't need anyone else working against him.

The cathedral door opened and the crowd fell into an anticipatory hush. Ethiere had wend his way to near the back and was at a severe disadvantage for seeing anything through the masses. Pushing forward would be to little avail – the press of people and their sharp elbows indicated success would be minimal. So, Ethiere swam his way to the very back and angled towards the closest of the Alben shops.

He made a quick study of the window sills, door frames and eaves of the roof before taking his approach. A quick sprint, one foot to the sill, a hand on the eaves, foot on the top of the door frame for leverage – and Ethiere was on the roof with a clear view of the proceedings below.

The bearded physician that had accompanied the demon-hunting party was on the cathedrals landing, addressing a worried crowd. Ethiere had to strain to hear him over the anxious buzz from the throng.

"She's fine," the physician was assuring them. "She sustained an injury to her head, but the mercies of Domus are with her. I was witness to a miracle – she healed before my eyes!" These words energized the crowd – a second miracle. It was impossible not to reach the conclusion that if there were two, there could be three. And four. And so on.

The physician carried on above the excitement on the street. "It is my belief that she has a gift from Domus – a gift of healing. I believe that while this gift may be new to her, it appears to be one that can be repeated. When she awakens, we will ask her if she would be willing to try."

"We have much to be grateful for," said a man in Deacon robes, coming forward to stand aside the physician. "We do not know why Alben has been graced with the presence of this miracle-bringing girl. Perhaps we will never know the reason why. As you return to your homes, reflect on Domus – the truly Merciful One. As you gather your families, please take a moment to bow your head in reverence."

Ethiere smirked. They expected the crowd to disperse? After telling them a second miracle had just occurred? It came as no surprise that the Albeners stayed put – though several looked to be obediently bowing their heads.

Ethiere reclined on the roof and looked longingly at the warm glow from the cathedrals glass-paned windows. He let out a wistful sigh. "Who are you?" he asked to the girl hidden from his view. "Are you our Pennie?"

Because that – getting one of their missing number back – would be the greatest miracle Ethiere could imagine.

37.

The revelry of the crowd outside the cathedral eventually simmered down. Sitting far enough down the road, Sarah was able to watch them without really being a part of them. It was a very familiar feeling. It was almost like she was back in her room again, watching the people on the street from behind the glass of the window. Almost a part of the world – but not quite.

As the hours had dragged on towards the full of night, the mood of the miracle-seekers had changed. Though no one was inclined to go home – especially those that had come in from the homesteads – they were inclined to find a bit of space to claim as their own. Blankets were spread on porches – tents sprang up like wildflowers in an empty field one lot over from the cathedral. Someone constructed a circle of stones in the middle of the street and built up a large fire where folks could congregate and warm their hands. The anticipation of miracles had not diminished in the Albeners – it had merely changed forms. It was still there, fermented into their waking dreams, awaiting the promise of morning.

Sarah turned to her companion. "All this has made me think," she told Dom.

His head swiveled slowly towards her, lost momentum, and rocked back. Kashif had stopped by only long enough to give Dom another dose of the sedative, and the effects appeared to be at full potency.

"All this about miracles and healing," she tacked on as she spoke to the back of Dom's head. "I have to wonder if it's just a coincidence that I'm here. That I'm this close." She resisted the urge to stare back at the cathedral. "Maybe it was supposed to happen this way."

She shook her head and stared at her hands in her lap. "I know what Kashif said to us back in the barn two nights back got everyone upset – about there being a reason for us being the ones Banded. That it wasn't just bad luck or fate or the like, but that there was something unique about us. That there was a reason." She fought the lump in her throat. "And I've been trying to figure out why I'm here. What makes me unique? Besides – you know, the Numbness. What can I do to help?" She shook her head. "And I don't know. I'm still trying to figure it out, Dom. Still trying to make sense of it."

A roll of laughter from down the road interrupted her thoughts. Down by the town hall, Lady Greer's men were joking with one another. Sarah could see Lady Greer and her companion, seated on the steps of a nearby store, listening in to the guardsmen's jests. Sarah had not spoken with Lady Greer since her father, the Lord Baron, had ridden into Alben.

"That's the other thing," she told Dom as she refocused on her hands. "I know it's stupid, but sometimes I think about Greer and Lord Baron Cahill. I know she's mad at him – I know they don't get along very well. I know that she wishes he'd just leave her alone and stop trying to intercede on her behalf. And I think I get why she feels that way – about what he's doing. I think so ... and yet it makes me wonder." She swallowed hard again as her emotions began to win the battle. "I think about my father – and it makes me wonder why he's not here – why he's not trying to intercede ..." She hastily brushed the tear from her cheek. "Who knows, maybe I'd be mad at him, too."

She glanced up, and was surprised to see Dom looking at her. It was vacant – but even so she couldn't hold eye contact. She was forced to look away and swipe at another tear.

"I guess I would be mad at him. I've always thought him too protective of me. He's always trying to save me from myself – from even the smallest of dangers – and I've always wished he wouldn't. Wished he wouldn't care so much ..." She shook her head. "It might have made things easier – for both of us."

The large fire by the cathedral popped, showering sparks. People sang hymns from the colony of tents in the field. Sergeant Bostitch finished a story and Lady Greer's laughter rose above the rest. Even so, even with Dom sitting right beside her, Sarah felt completely alone in the world.

"You know I did come up with one reason – for me being here," she admitted. "The only one that I could come up with. And it's sad, and it's stupid, and I know I shouldn't give it any more thought." The tears were coming freely now. There was no use trying to catch them. "But I can't. I can't help but wonder. What if I'm not here because I was needed? What if I'm here because someone needed to be freed from me?"

She let herself cry for a moment. It was a different sort of cry – as not a single other part of her body seemed open to participate in it besides her eyes. There was no sobbing, no grief. It was just a simple, honest cry.

"I know he loves me," she said. "I've never doubted that for a second, and I never will. But all the same, I wouldn't blame him – not in the slightest – if he had ever prayed for respite. From his burdens. From me." She turned back to Dom. "I can only imagine he's sad. But I can't help but wonder if with that sadness came a sense of relief."

She rubbed at her eyes, clearing them. "I have to hope," she said finally, "that maybe he's happier now."

The fence creaked behind them as someone leaned against it and Sarah jumped. Dom's reaction was much more gradual, but his head eventually completed its rotation towards the unexpected noise. The robed wizard Hartley loomed over them.

"Not interrupting, I hope?" he asked.

Sarah wiped her hands on her dress and opted to shake her head rather than voice her answer. The feelings were hers to keep forever – she'd be able to shed tears on them again tomorrow should she choose. But wizards – it was an opportunity to talk with wizards. Hartley walked around the fence and settled in on her other side.

"An interesting place you've chosen here," Hartley commented. "Neither by the fire," he pointed with one hand, "nor with the Band," he indicated with the other."

Sarah shrugged. "I think Dom likes it here best."

Hartley raised a bemused eyebrow, and Sarah turned to see Dom momentarily occupied by the glow of the fire. She hung her head sheepishly.

"It seems that Dom has found a true friend," the wizard observed – then stopped. "You are his friend, are you not?"

Sarah nodded. "Of course I'm his friend." She thought to say she was the best friend Dom had ever had, but didn't. It was probably true – but it sounded quite boastful. "That's why it's important for me to look out for him. Especially when he's like this. He shouldn't be alone."

The wizard came and took a seat next to her on the log. "He's very lucky to have you, then. Most of the others don't seem to hold a high opinion of him."

Sarah thought the comment – regardless of how true it might be – quite rude considering Dom was sitting only an arm's length away. She glanced over at him. He blinked absently. "They haven't taken the time to get to know him," she said in his defense.

"I'm sure they haven't," Hartley readily concurred. "Although – I must say – he doesn't appear to be giving them much of a chance, as I've heard it."

"He just takes time to warm up to you, that's all." Of the Band, Sarah knew only Ethiere was making an effort – and was meeting with discouraging results as Hartley suggested.

"But he talks to you, does he?"

Sarah frowned. She'd hoped to be able to talk about the wizard – but all they seemed to be talking about was Dom. "Yes – but he doesn't say much."

Hartley nodded. "Has he confided in you?"

"About what?"

The wizard shrugged, but did so woodenly. Sarah didn't like it. "I don't know. About dreams."

"Dreams?"

"Dreams. Or headaches? Has he ever told you about headaches?"

Sarah shook her head.

"Hasn't told you his secret then?"

She was starting to get frustrated. The wizard was pressing for something; he wasn't even pretending anymore. But Sarah hadn't a clue what confidential secret the wizard was after. But even if Dom had confided such an important secret to her, she surely wouldn't go sharing it with the first person to ask about it – wizard or not!

So she decided to change the subject. "Let's not talk about Dom anymore. I'd like to hear more about wizards."

The wizard smiled, knowingly. "Ah, my dear girl. Of course. But then, wizardry is exactly why we're talking about Dom."

38.

Dom would have wished himself awake, if he thought himself still asleep. The world was too real to be a conjecture of his imagination. There were too many sensations on the periphery – the play of sunlight and shadows, background noises, the smell of people – small, unimportant things that would have been omitted in a dream. It was real – it was really happening – which was what made it even more terrifying.

He was not in control. There was nothing his alert and active mind could do to snap his body out of the passive trance it was in. The world was happening around him, and Dom felt incapable of reacting to it. It was all moving too quickly – even for his frantic mind – to sift through the distortions flooding his senses.

Sound seemed to come intermittently – likes waves rolling on the ocean. One would crest, bursting, vibrant with echoes of voices both near and distant. And then there would be the lull, the silence, where he would be left alone to the whispers of the things in his head.

"I wouldn't blame him – not in the slightest …"

It was Sarah. He could hear her – he thought he could hear every word. But he couldn't follow along. He knew every word, but his mind failed to string them together. It was like trying to catch the waves – they broke around him at the very moment he tried to take hold of them. It was like trying to capture a fistful of sand; and seeing it slip through the cracks in your fingers despite your futile attempts to grasp it.

All Dom knew was she was talking about her father – and it was awakening things he'd repressed in his own mind. It had awakened the familiar voice in his head – one all too willing to fill the silence-laden gaps.

Tell me what you see.

The shade of his father seeped from Dom's unconscious, staining the distorted world with his greatest fears. His father found shape in the shadows, found voice in the shaking of tree branches. Perhaps it was the feeling of being trapped – a prisoner inside of his body – that summoned the essence of his father. Dom could almost imagine an invisible, heavy-corded rope impairing his ability to act.

"Not interrupting, I hope?"

It was the wizard – Hartley. The wizard's words were lost to Dom – scattered like sand in a gust of wind – but the man himself elicited a reaction. Dom felt his insides freeze at knowing the wizard was close at hand, and he willed his body to find Hartley. He'd be unable to react to the wizard, unable to run as he would have liked – but not being able to see the wizard – to watch him …

I'll show you exactly what happens to people who get themselves involved with wizards.

Dom wanted no part of Hartley. He was already unnerved by the attention the young wizard had given him when he'd first arrived in Alben. Hartley had stared at him – summing him up. It was if the man was turning over the rocks in the recesses of his soul; seeing what skittered away out of the exposing light.

What if Hartley were to find out? What if he already knew?

His eyes momentarily focused on the fire in the distance, the heap of dancing flames, the smoke pluming upwards like steam off a kitchen pot. The firelight flickered, casting a warm burnish onto the faces of those who stood by for warmth. The Deacons spoke descriptively of Oblivion – that miry lake of pure evilness that boiled and hissed like a hot cauldron. It had frightened Dom, as a child, hearing them speak so candidly of the fate of those who disappointed Domus. An eternity sinking into the filthy depths, howling at the blistering, inescapable pain.

You'll tell me what you see!

Dom couldn't deny what he had done – what his father had made him do. Perhaps he and his father were destined to boil in the mire together.

"Of course I'm his friend."

It was Sarah again. His friend. He still wasn't sure he wanted a friend. Maybe he didn't believe he deserved one. But the girl was insistent – she was going to make this a friendship with or without his support. Frankly, it was reassuring to have her next to him. The crippling fear hadn't left when she'd returned, but at least … at least there was someone close by that would look after him.
Someone to react for him should he not be able to do so on his own. Dom knew he'd done nothing to merit Sarah's friendship; luckily, she seemed as forgiving as Merciful Domus.

"Has he confided in you?"

The wizard's voice rolled back into his conscience, and it reignited the worries he had over Hartley. What had Sarah told him? What did Sarah really know that she could tell Hartley? She'd been closest to him at the onset of his cursed ability back by the town hall, but she couldn't have known what was happening.

"Hasn't told you his secret then?"

Dom felt his insides clench up. The wizard did know! He wanted to run, but his legs were dead weight, oblivious to the pleas coming from his mind. It was over then – the moment that Hartley let the group in on his secret – it would be over. The Arcan would add his ability to his list – and he and the others would plot on how to exploit his unwanted talent.

Once I learn your secret, I'm sure we'll find a way to put it to fantastic use!

Ethiere, and everyone else in Dom's life.

Do you see joy in his heart? Disappointment? You tell me what you see!

"Don't be silly," Sarah said, "Dom isn't a wizard!"

You want to have business with wizards, boy?

Dom didn't. The thought had intrigued Joshua – the idea of being special, having a natural talent in the magical arts. To Joshua, it had meant a chance at a better life. But Dom, he didn't want to stand out – be special – be noticed. He wanted the perfect hiding spot – the spot that no one in the entire world could ever find him. The only spot in the entire world that could deliver true freedom from his fears.

"I can sense it in him," Hartley said. "We wizards can sense the potential in others. We see what can't be seen."

When the card turned - was he happy with what he saw? Tell me!

Dom wanted to close his eyes – close them and just disappear. He wished he could drown in the waves of sound crashing in all around him. But he couldn't even get his eyes to close. Not even that.

We see what can't be seen.

Hartley was right; and he was wrong. Dom saw what shouldn't be seen. The reading of men's hearts – the glimpse into their souls – it should be reserved for Merciful Domus only. It should never have been given to a boy unable to keep others from denigrating and corrupting it.

Look!

The shout from his father blasted through his mind – and it triggered his ability. As if the dream-like state he was in wasn't twisted enough, his vision skewed, painting his distorted and shifting surroundings in the familiar bleak hues. His mind throbbed as the ability fought against the stupor – neither side finding victory.

"Dom?" Sarah called out. He felt her gripping his shoulder.

Hartley sounded pleased. "I think … yes, he's working magic …"

He could not run. He could not close his eyes. He could do nothing but sit on the log and stare up the open road before them. His chest felt tight – like his lungs were not working – like he'd forgotten how to breathe. He had no outlet for his panic – no way to fight it. He was trapped.

Look!

It was all he could do.

Look!

And pray it would end.

Look!

It shown like a beacon, shimmered like diamonds in the dismal gray world. He couldn't make out the shape, obscured as it was on the cathedral's pitched roof, but the parts that he could see simply gleamed. It was the same sheen that he saw on wizards, in their orbs, that made them sparkle like star-dust. But this – this was so much richer, so much denser. Hartley looked dull by comparison. And it didn't seem confined to a sphere – the dazzling stuff seemed to be shifting free-form. Paralyzed as he was, Dom momentarily forgot to be afraid, so beautiful was the aura in atop the cathedral.

And then it moved, rising to its full height, giving Dom its silhouette in the bleakness.

He recognized it.

It was exactly what he'd seen in the fountain. Same bent body, same long, thick arms. It was the demon – it was here! It was watching!

Dom felt the fear spread to every corner of his body – to the tips of his fingers to the soles of his feet to the hairs on the back of his neck. The fear filled him – consumed him – as he watched the creature pounce from the cathedral onto the grounds below. Dom felt himself suddenly staggering upward – surprising himself as much as those near him. He felt Sarah grab onto him – attempting to steady him. He stretched his jaw – trying to voice a warning that came out as a tongue-rich moan.

"What's gotten into …" Hartley began.

At that moment, the people nearest the cathedral began to scream.

39.

Sarah stood just in time to see one of the men by the fire fall like a limp doll to the ground. Instinctively, she screamed – joining her voice to the dozens that were raising the alarm. The glow of the flame was just bright enough to catch the gossamer sheen of the demon's pitch black skin – and then it was gone! It vanished into the darkness of the night, blending into shadows.

Wizard Hartley placed himself between Sarah and where she'd last seen the creature. "Run, girl!" he commanded her as the air around his palms began to percolate with magical energy.

Sarah was paralyzed – mesmerized by everything happening around her. Hartley conjured a flame in his left hand that he held out into the darkness, while his right held another readied spell in reserve. All around them, Albeners fled, though their varied paths suggested they did not see what they were fleeing from. Constable Mercer appeared near the wounded, sword at the ready but lacking a target. Dom, eyes wide, stared out into the night, his mouth working in vain to form words.

She knew what she had to do. She had to get Dom to safety – he wasn't lucid enough to save himself. Perhaps that was the entire reason why she was Banded – to befriend Dom and to save him. She looped Dom's left arm around her shoulder and wrapped her right around his waist. He was taller by several finger widths and heavier as well, and she met against both of those factors as she tried to compel the boy back down the road.

Back to where the soldiers where. Back to Billick and Greer. Back to Ethiere and Kashif. Sarah didn't have much of a plan formulated, but she knew that they needed to be with the rest of the Band.

Out of the corner of her eye, she saw Mercer fall and the demon lunge. "Watch out!" she yelled. Her alert gave Hartley just enough time to turn and lose the pent up spell into the chest of the oncoming monster. With a crack that sounded like thunder, the creature was propelled backwards, crashing through the storefront windows of one of the little shops.

Sarah did not wait to see what happened next. She dug her heels into the Alben road and urged Dom forward. The tears sprang forth in her eyes again, but they were not tears of sadness any longer.

These were born of fear.

*   *   *   *   *

Billick knew what was happening the moment the screaming started; he'd been waiting on it. In his heart, he'd known that the afternoon search of Lamond's Field would be fruitless. The creature that he'd seen in the mists of the fountain was a predator built for darkness. It came as no surprise that the demon had waited until nightfall to attack again.

Axe in hand, Billick charged towards the action, Reed's regulars on his heels. It was strangely familiar – a charge, surrounded by comrades, running to meet the enemy, courting your own death. Billick had assailed beach fortifications. He had rallied against an Arcan war machine. Racing towards an Oblivion-escaped demon seemed unexceptional in comparison.

It was right that he was leading the charge. This was his place. This was the very reason the Banding had chosen him. Billick knew he was a killer – and now it was time to kill! Up ahead, the demon materialized out of nowhere. The young wizard only barely caught it with his spell – rocketing the creature through the front of a store. The force might have killed a man, but Billick knew the demon survived. He could feel it. The kill would be his.

Sarah loomed before him, struggling under the weight of the boy she was supporting. Dom was still drugged – which was fortunate. Should the boy meet with an injury, he'd pose no threat to Billick's fighting ability.

"Billick, help!" the girl cried to him. "Please!"

He ran past without hesitation. He'd told her father he wouldn't make any promises, she was not his concern. The vivid fear in her eyes haunted him – why had the Band included a young girl? – and he fought to shove the thought aside. He needed to focus on the battle. He had a demon to slay. Boil Sarah!

Hartley was already sweating. It was hard for Billick to not think of the wizard as a battlefield target after the Arcan War. The murderer just hoped that the stress of the fight wouldn't cause Hartley to panic. "You can hardly see it!" the wizard spat.

"Don't need to see it," Billick muttered as he hoisted the axe. "Just cut off its boiling head." Bravado aside, Billick approached the shop with caution. The window pane was shattered, the wooden boards that framed the upper sill hung askew. Two of Reed's men came alongside him – Cox and another that Billick couldn't name. Billick motioned towards the door and the two soldiers nodded. A third man, wielding a crossbow, took position five paces back. Taking a breath, Billick kicked his booted foot into the door, which popped like a cork.

Weapons raised, Billick charged into the shop – a butcher shop of all types. Knives and cleavers hung from the ceiling and reflected ominously in the moonlight. The murderer's eyes strained against the darkness, seeking for movement within the deep night shadows. Reed's men fanned out behind him, each watching a different corner of the unlit shop. "Where are you?" Billick whispered under his breath.

The creature lunged; cutting down the man to Billick's left in a heartbeat, and leapt through the open window. The crossbow sang, Billick heard the dart whistle into the shop, and the crossbow man screamed. Billick dashed to the window and dove through, narrowly missing the jagged shards of glass that hung from the broken sill like teeth.

Outside, two more of Reed's soldiers fell upon the demon in a coordinated assault. Several sword-blows connected with the demon's dark skin, but the creature responded violently, shredding leather armor and severing limbs. Billick charged from behind, eager to end the engagement. He raised his axe – but the creature evaded him, ducking under his blow. As it rose, the demon's fingers extended. Billick stumbled backwards, but not quickly enough. He screamed as the icy fingers scraped across his chest like knives.

*　*　*　*　*

"My Lady, we need to leave."

Captain Reed didn't wait for a response, not that Greer would have been able to offer one at the moment. Everything was happening so quickly. Reed's men drawing their weapons and charging towards the fray. Sophie stood quivering to her side, equally dumbfounded. Within a few heartbeats, only Reed and the men assigned as her personal shield remained. Shouts and screams continued to sound from up the street – already there were wounded and dying …

Reed took her by the forearm, dragging her towards the horses. "Your men …"

"... are doing their duty," he interrupted. "Just as I intend to do mine!"

It took Greer a moment to recover – none of the soldiers had ever spoken to her like that. She felt her cheeks flush, but before she could voice a complaint, he was pulling her back towards the horses. Greer pushed him away, but made a quick showing of going towards the mounts of her own volition. She would not bear the indignity of Reed manhandling her onto the animal!

Sophie, pale-faced, hurried past and frantically tried to climb into a saddle. Greer lifted her skirts and put a foot into one of the stirrups and crested the saddle.

"Billick, help! Please!"

It was Sarah. From high on the horse's back, Greer saw the poor girl, Dom leaning against her, struggling towards them. The murderer didn't even pause as he ran by.

Greer looked down at Captain Reed. He kept his eyes fastened to her horse, but she could see the turmoil raging inside him. "Reed!" she snapped, and he raised his eyes. There was no need to explain what she meant.

"Your father ordered ..."

"Get them or I will!" she shouted as she swung a fist at him. She missed, but the effect was enough. "Get them to safety, Reed! On your life, you get those children to safety!"

Whatever indecision the Captain had been experiencing fled. Reed snapped quick orders to the other men in her personal shield. They mounted their horses and began to lead her and Sophie away at a gallop. As Greer turned in her saddle, she saw the tall soldier rushing towards the chaos to fulfill her last command.

*   *   *   *   *

Ethiere sat on the eaves of the Physician's roof, trying not to think about the conversation going on inside the building. He knew there were bodies inside and he knew that Kashif was examining them. He heard the Arcan call for tools

Ethiere was unfamiliar with – but the mere names sounded sharp. Listening to the dissection of bodies was only a shade less sickening than witnessing it.

While he'd rather find somewhere else to wait the night, he was anxious to talk with the Physician. Of all the people in Alben, Davies was one of the few that Ethiere new had closely interacted with the miracle-working girl. He would be able to provide Ethiere the description he so desperately sought.

As the thief tried to work up the courage, the screaming began from nearby the cathedral. He stood on the roof, peering into the night to try to find the source of the disturbance, even though, in his heart, he already knew.

The demon had come.

Ethiere jumped from the roof, bounding to the wagon buckboard before landing on the ground. He steeled his nerves as he pushed into the Physician's shop, a little bell happily announcing his presence. Both men were facing him, blood on their hands and clothing. Ethiere blanched and diverted his focus. "It's the demon," he told Kashif. "We need to help!"

"We need to withdraw," the Arcan argued and began to hastily gather various vials of blood into his large pack.

Ethiere was stunned. "Withdraw? We're the Band of Six!"

The efficiency at which the pack was collected and secured was amazing. "We aren't ready," the foreigner stated. "We can't face it now." Resolute, the Arcan shouldered, past Ethiere. "Davies! The wagon!"

Ethiere turned, still not believing what he was hearing. Kashif was running? Just abandoning the others? "We're supposed to help!" he yelled.

As the Arcan climbed into the back of the wagon his eyes met Ethiere's. They were calm and passive and devoid of remorse for the decision he was making. "Then go help," he said, and he disappeared behind the canvas. "Davies! Get us away from here!"

The bearded Physician had been wavering, but the last urgent commands from the Arcan stirred his feet. He bustled through the door and up onto the buckboard.

As the wagon lurched forward, Ethiere ran after it. "You're a coward!" he yelled. "A boiling coward!"

"Perhaps," Kashif answered as the distance increased. "But I intend to survive!"

*   *   *   *   *

Battlefields were always chaotic – shouts and screams, the twang of bowstrings, whistling of arrows and the metallic ring of swords. The Alben streetway was no different. The fleeing citizens heightened the level of pandemonium, and the suffocating darkness amplified the confusion. Already his men were engaging the demon – which Reed found nearly impossible to detect. The Captain had confidence in the skill of his men – he'd assumed any two or three could cut the creature down with ease; but under these adverse conditions?

Reed reached the children speedily but kept an eye on the action before him. As he relieved Sarah of supporting Dom, a shadow burst from one of the shops and cut down Granger has he fired his crossbow. Immediately the demon was assaulted by others of his squad – Falding and Baites, Monroe and Simms. Swords swung in the intense melee – and one by one his men went down.

And then, their party took another blow. Billick went down. The wizard reacted – blasting the demon away with another wave of magic, but how much time would that buy them? Reed hesitated. He'd not anticipated losing Billick so early. As much as Reed didn't care for the man – he recognized a veteran when he saw one. Of everyone in the Band, Billick had seemed best suited for accomplishing the task they'd been given. He'd been a key piece in Reed's plan to keep Lady Greer safe.

You could end this.

The thought crept to the forefront of Reed's mind. Only a handful of his men were still standing, rallying around Cox to make another assault. Another sword – it could make a difference. Another sword might sway the outcome.

You should end this.

Sarah whimpered. The girl could feel no pain, but she was not immune to panic. Chaos was no stranger to a battlefield, but children were. They didn't belong here.

On your life, you get those children to safety!

Lady Greer's words rang in his memory, out-shouting the sounds of the conflict. Reed sheathed his sword and took one of the children in each arm. Turning, he raced towards the horses – away from the battle. The battle continued behind him. Men shouted and died – voices he recognized – but he didn't waver. While Lady Greer's order had killed the temptation to join the fray, Reed found himself spurred on by a new motivation.

He'd seen Billick fall. One of the Band down. Reed didn't see why Sarah and Dom were vital to defeating the demon, but he was certain he could not afford to let the ranks of the Band shrink any further.

*   *   *   *   *

Billick writhed on the ground, his left hand pressed against the gashes to his chest. His fingers were slick with his own blood, the pain was severe, but he was still breathing. He rose up on his right elbow just in time to see another cadre of Reed's men engage with the demon. The black creature emerged from the pocket of soldiers, cutting them down as it rose, and just that quickly it was rushing for the wizard again.

With mere paces to spare, Hartley loosed a fireball directly into the demon's glossy black chest, leveling it to the ground. Almost instantly, the creature rose again; crimson flames dripping away from the demon's unmarred chest like water off a rock. Billick sunk back to the ground, stunned. A fireball of that magnitude should have opened a gaping hole in the creature's chest – yet it did nothing!

The young wizard began to focus on another spell, but it was too late. The faceless monstrosity was too close. Hartley stumbled backwards as the creature reached out – fingers extending into long, fine points. He screamed as the creature's fingers punctured through his robes and into his chest.

The wizard's collapse momentarily broke Billick out of his own agony. Craning his neck, he saw the demon hunched over the hapless Hartley. The creature obscured most of the wizard's body – only Hartley's weakly flailing limbs were visible. Was the wizard still alive? The creature had killed Reed's men with unnatural speed …

The realization came. *The demon is feeding.*

243

This first insight was followed quickly by a second.

The demon is distracted.

Billick pushed aside the pain in his chest and rose as silently as he could to a knee. The creature was oblivious to him – it hardly moved as it fed on the wizard. Its back, hunched in its crouching pose, offered an ideal target. Billick clenched the axe in his fist, and propelled himself forward.

The sound of bootfalls alerted the creature to oncoming danger. Its head lifted, the feature-less face turning. With all of the malice-born strength Billick could muster, he planted the head of the axe directly between the creature's shoulder blades. The sharp wedge sunk deep, biting into the inky flesh … before slipping free and diving into the ground at the demon's feet.

He'd sliced right through it! And yet … the creature's back was already mending the rift, the oily blackness reforming to its original shape. In mere seconds, there was no indication the demon had suffered the killing blow Billick had just landed.

Billick, on his knees, hands still clasped around the hilt of the axe, could only stare into the smooth, black face of the demon that could not be killed.

Soundlessly, the creature brought its right arm around, crashing a massive back-handed fist into Billick's face.

*   *   *   *   *

The Alben night lit up briefly with the burst of the wizard's fireball. The fleeting flames served to highlight the shapes of the unmoving soldiers scattered across the street. The scene gave Ethiere pause. He'd been so focused on getting to where the action was, he'd unwittingly run himself directly into the ghastly scene. There was no longer any action here – only death.

At the center of it was the demon and Billick. The proud killer was on his knees, without hope – like a thief before the Justices. Awaiting his sentence. Awaiting …

The black thing swung a long sinewy arm back towards Billick; the fist whipping directly into the man's unprotected face. Ethiere winced as Billick was lifted from the ground by the blow; landing unceremoniously in a heap two bounds way.

Billick lay still.

"No ..." Ethiere cried in disbelief.

The creature's head swiveled on its sinewy neck towards the sound. Ethiere's blood froze. The monster was lording over the ruined body of the wizard – one hand of long fingers still digging into Hartley's chest. The demon just crouched there, waiting, watching with its featureless face.

In that moment, Ethiere realized how terribly unprepared he truly was. He'd run into the battle, without a weapon in hand or a thought in his head, to do what? Beat the monster? How? With what? Ethiere swallowed, his breathing constricted by the lump of dread in his throat. He was one of the Band, one chosen for this moment, and yet ....

The creature had bested the wizard. The creature had beaten their trained killer. A half-dozen professional soldiers lay sprawled on the road. What was he – a nobody thief – supposed to do? How could he possibly succeed when all these others had failed?

He could almost hear Carl. *Rocks in your stomach – and candle-wax for brains.*

They stared at each other, the thief and the demon. Ethiere's mind cataloged the various weapons scattered around him. None were close enough to do any good. His legs tensed – his insides begging for his brain to turn and run. Ethiere knew he was fast, but he knew the creature would outpace him for sure. Instead, Ethiere froze. He watched, and he waited. He understood completely what he'd seen on Billick's face the moment before .... before ....

The glossy black head ducked back down, refocusing on the body of the wizard. The fingers on the demons other hand lengthened and thinned and plunged into the wizard's chest as well. As soundlessly as he could manage, using all of the skill Master Hat had taught him – Ethiere crept backwards, towards the safety of the buildings. His leather pads moved silently over the hard-packed street.

He knew Domus didn't care about him, but he prayed anyway.

He prayed he'd live to see the light of dawn.

*　　*　　*　　*　　*

While most people had fled from the vicinity of the cathedral, Martin was one of the only people who urgently moved towards it. With the blessing of deacons, Elsa had opted to stay at Pennie's bed-side. When the screaming began, Martin had no other object then to find and protect his wife.

He was not alone in trying to gain access to the cathedral. The edifice was one of the most solid in Alben and many of the miracle-revelers were at the door, pleading to be allowed in. The young Deacon finally relented, letting a dozen people besides Martin rush within the safety of the sanctuary. While they took refuge among the pews, Martin went directly for the stairs in search of Elsa.

The upper floor, which provided study and sleeping quarters for the deacons, was disturbingly quiet. Up the hallway, Martin saw a downed man – Deacon Elsbury slumped against the wall and bleeding. Martin ran past the man, no longer able to contain his anxiety. "Elsa!" he called into the stillness. "Elsa!"

A door up the hallway hung open, and Martin knew it held the answers he sought. He rushed to the room and surveyed the inside. The study was a mess, furniture in shambles, bedding torn. Martin found his wife lying on her side on the floor near the high-placed window. He knelt beside her, fearing the worst, and took her hand. Her skin was still warm to the touch – she was still alive. A large bruise was already coloring a large area of her forehead, but she was still alive.

Martin wept openly. Taking his wife in his work-weathered arms, he leaned back against the wall and whispered prayers of gratitude to Merciful Domus.

He did not know how long he sat there, holding Elsa as if she were a child, overcome by relief just as strongly as the worry that had preceded it. It was long enough that the entire world went silent – the sounds of agony outside the cathedral walls quieting to match the stillness within. Martin kept his eyes closed and focused on the rise and fall of Elsa's chest.

It was some time later that he realized Pennie was not in the room. His eyes were accustomed to the darkness, he'd long become familiar with the layout of the small space. There was nowhere she could be hiding; nowhere that he wouldn't have become aware of her presence. As he pondered these thoughts,

Martin became aware of a new sound, coming from above. He focused his ears on the sound, the soft creaking of wood in distress. It moved across the roof; Martin tracing its location as it passed over top him.

Someone was one the cathedral roof.

They were heading towards the spire with the bell.

Out in the hall, the ladder to the spire stuttered against the floor as it was mounted. Moments later, feet landed on the hallway floor. Martin held Elsa tighter as the footfalls drew closer.

The figure that came through the study door wasn't human. The shoulders were broader, the arms longer, the face devoid of features. This was a thing of nightmares – a creature of Oblivion. Martin tensed and held still. His prayers to Domus fell silent on his lips but continued to pour from his heart.

Whether the creature did not see them or just lacked interest in the farmer and his wife, Martin could not say. The creature plodded forward, its motions heavy and lethargic ... and it began to melt. The monster's shape became nebulous, imploding on itself, its mass diminishing. As the oily blackness of the creature ebbed, human limbs appeared. Martin could not look away. The monster was no more than a cowl now, hovering over the quivering form of a little girl.

It was Pennie.

As the nightmare finished its collapse, collecting into the thin run-away's body, Pennie wobbled and fell to the floor.

Martin did not move.

He did not dare.

40.

Try as he might, Kashif could not prevent the slight tremor in his hand as it hung over the glass vial. He steeled his breathing, willed control over the limb, but it would not obey. He'd battled it the entire night – the compelling discomfort of the Banding. The infernal magic knew he'd run – it knew he was not where it thought he should be.

Kashif clenched his fist in tired frustration. One unsteady touch to the vial would ruin the night's efforts.

"Come. Take this."

The words – the first spoken in several hours – woke the physician from his comatose watch of the barren country road. They were an hour at the most away from Alben. The aching pain in Kashif's shoulder had prevented them from going farther. Kashif believed them to be far enough away to be safe – far enough away the demon wouldn't come after them.

Davies was less concerned about their individual safety. The Physician was experiencing a crisis of conscience for having abandoned those in his stewardship. They both knew any battle with the demon would result in injuries. By running, they had effectively deprived Alben of medical expertise – even if it was the crude standard that Davies provided.

"What?"

"I need you to take the measurements. It's light enough out."

They'd worked through the night – the pain-laden Arcan and the morose physician – under the dim gleam of Davies' lone oil lamp. They'd only been able to extract a small sample of blood from Denny Boyd earlier that afternoon. The creature, a probing finger in each of the shepherd's main arteries, had drained most everything from the man's body. The lamp had lasted just long enough into the dark night for them to mix in the powders to decompound the blood and finish the experiments they'd started in Davies' office.

After that, there had been nothing to do but sit and stare into the darkness. Sit, and wait for the chemicals to do their work, and for light to come on the horizon. Though exhausted, sleep was the farthest thing from their minds.

Davies rubbed ponderously at his face while he watched the growing light. The morning sky was overcast, somber in its threat of rain. "I thought the sun might never rise." He slid himself off woodenly from his seat in his wagon and walked around to where Kashif sat with the vials. Davies took a moment, reacquainted himself with the samples they'd taken, and looked up. "It's worse now, isn't it?"

Kashif dropped his fist from view and summoned all of his willpower to hide the shaking in his hands. "Just take the measurements." His training had taught him to tune out the yearning cries of his physical body – but not something like this. Not for so long. It was constantly there, probing the cracks of the mental barricades, searching for weaknesses to exploit. His willpower was waning – he'd have to succumb. Eventually.

Davies didn't press the issue further. The bearded man took up the first vial. Davies' shirt and vest bore traces of the work they'd performed last night. Though not trained to the exacting standards of an Arcan scientist, Davies was not a complete loss as a physician. He listened well and didn't ask ignorant questions. It was more than Kashif had expected.

"The strata should be clearly defined by now," Kashif continued. "The heavier red matter will have sunk to the bottom – and the lightest of the fluidic matter will have risen to the top. The powder we mixed with the blood will have dyed other elements … it is those that should be most telling …"

"I'll say …" Davies murmured, and he held up the twin vials for the Arcan's appraisal. The difference was pronounced. Amid the various hues both vials contained, only one had a thick, silvery-gray band through the center. "What is it?"

"Essen." The familiar thrill of discovery was blanketed by reality of what it meant. "That vial is from the shepherd that was drained, yes?"

Davies nodded. "Essen …, as in … well, wizard Essen?"

Kashif's initial hypothesis had proved correct. The creature had specifically hunted down the shepherd, drained his blood – because it had been feeding. He now knew what the creature fed on. "It's after Essen. That's what sustains it …"

The bearded physician still grappled over the insight. "But if Denny … if he were … if he had Essen in his blood … shouldn't he have …?"

"Manifest?" Kashif finished. "Not always."

Davies rubbed at his beard – and came away with a hardened fleck of human matter which he promptly shook to the ground. He eyed it, pursed his lips, and returned to his thoughts. "It feeds … on Essen. Well, that isn't terrible. Bad news for the wizards, alright, but I don't have any Essen. It'd have no reason to come after my blood. The only people with need to worry …"

"Are those with Essen-rich blood."

--- * --- * ---

The chair was hard. It was flat – unlike most of the chairs in the laboratory, which were shaped with a more natural sitting contour. Kashif could feel his tailbone against the unforgiving wood. A thin and gangly fourteen years of age, there was not much fat anywhere on his body to cushion his bones. He'd chosen the chair on purpose. It was the best chair of the lot when Marooke was instructing on his favorite topic.

Pain.

"Focus, Kashif," he heard his mentor murmur as a reminder. "Ready your mind ... it lords over your body ... it controls the reaction ..."

The lance of agony touched off near the small of his back. The jolt twisted his insides. Kashif steadied his hands on his knees – attempting the tricks of concentration Marooke had taught him to block the pain. He focused on the chair – on the singular spot where his tailbone ground into the wood, and he funneled all of the pain there. He sent all emotion there, and tried to contain it with all of his might.

As quickly as it had come on, the pain subsided.

"Very good," Marooke lauded. "You hardly flinched."

He swallowed down the acrid taste of bile before answering. "Thank you, Master."

"You still have much to learn. Your breathing went irregular. And you've perspired."

"Yes, Master."

He felt Marooke lean in. "It takes years of practice." The pain erupted again, this time near his left shoulder blade. The location had not been chosen randomly – the unexpected distress shocked the air from his lungs. "Breathe," he heard the stern command in his ear. "Breathe normally! Focus!"

Kashif wrapped his mind around the pain – bundling and banishing it to the sore spot on his tailbone. His breath came short – he could feel it. It was as if his mind feared the barrier to the pain would explode should he inhale too deeply. "Do it! Breathe!"

*Obediently, he drew in a breath. The throbbing ball of pain quivered to life –
but his focus held. He exhaled, and drew a second breath more confidently than
the first.*

*"Good." Marooke stayed behind him, but leaned in closer. "I should like to
tell you a story. You shall continue to breathe as you listen." Kashif prayed
that the man didn't expect an answer and gratefully he continued. "You
remember the day of your Sifting? Of course, it is not a day that any boy can
forget. I wish you to know, Kashif – you were the subject of much debate.*

*"Most boys sired by your father were taken by the Ballistad. The three officers
representing their caste in the Procession were keen on having you as well.
Apparently your bloodstock lends itself well to tactical leadership. But I saw in
you the makings of a scientist – a fine Scholastad after my own image. You had
a mind capable of achieving great things for Arca, and I fought for you to join
our caste.*

"I almost didn't succeed."

*The comment caught Kashif by surprise – but Marooke veered the conversation
along a different path.*

*"Do you know why I subject you to this pain? You have never asked me why –
and the respect in not doing so is not unnoticed. None of the other apprenticed
boys in our caste endure what I make you endure. Their training revolves solely
on the mind – in the learning and experimentations of their masters."*

Marooke laughed merrily, quite unexpectedly.

*"Should the Ballistad have known how much pain you could endure, my student,
their clamoring to have you would have been even more urgent. But if the truth
had been known then – you would never have been theirs – or mine – to claim."*

*His teacher was prodding at some secret – getting just close enough to excite
curiosity without exposing the whole matter. If not the Ballistad or the
Scholastad ... the only caste to exceed either in rank ...*

*"As the primary biochemist in our ranks, it falls to me to work the blood
samples from each boy. We lay out clearly just what amount of perfection runs
through your veins, well before your body matures to exhibit it. I saw in you,
Kashif, a reflection of myself. In intellect, in physique, and in your blood. And I
knew I had to have you."*

Marooke wheeled around, standing before the chair now. He crouched, bringing himself near eye level. "I falsified your results. I returned an inaccurate accounting of your blood."

Kashif's mind raced, attacking the veil hanging over his Master's words, trying to shred it to pieces.

"You would have discovered it eventually. See, even now – your breathing, your focus – you have eliminated the pain, have you not? You have exercised control, have you not? It is not by mere meditation you or I can do these things, my student. It is a secret we share together."

His mind hit upon it, just at that moment. The notion left him in disbelief. "Master?"

Marooke smiled. "Our secret, Kashif. We would be executed swiftly should it be discovered. No one can ever know the magnitude of Essen we carry in our blood."

--- * --- * ---

They rode back to Alben in silence, two men consumed by their thoughts. The pain in Kashif's shoulder ebbed the closer they neared to the Tollian town. Davies broke the spell with a question. "Do you think they will blame us for leaving? If there were lives that we might have saved?"

Coward!

Kashif silenced the accusatory voice in his head. "Of course, some will. It is to be expected. People will be frightened, they will feel unnerved. They will seek to place blame in an irrational effort to navigate emotions that they are unable to deal with in their current state." As he said the words, Kashif eyed the man driving the wagon, and realized he'd diagnosed Davies' turmoil.

Few people stirred on the streets of Alben – it was a stark contrast to the compressed crowd of the night before. Davies stopped the wagon outside of his door, perhaps out of habit – or perhaps in respect for the scene before him. The Alben roadway was strewn with the dead, sheets and coats hiding them from the rising sun.

Kashif exited the wagon. "Gather your medical supplies," he instructed Davies. "They will have gathered the wounded somewhere. We will locate them and do our best to alleviate their suffering." As Davies disappeared into his office,

Kashif ventured into the street-turned-memorial. He let his eyes drift to each corpse, judging the size, searching for identifiers in their clothing.

Though he was loathe to admit it, he was searching the dead for members of the Band. He came across the remains of Wizard Hartley first.

"It fed on him."

The voice came from above. Kashif would have startled had Marooke's intense trainings not cured him of that human weakness. Looking to the roof, the Arcan saw Ethiere spying down on him. The young thief's face was passive – gone was the vitriol of his parting words. Kashif had last seen Ethiere charging towards where the demon fought. While surprised the thief was not numbered among the dead, Kashif observed a despair in the thief's eyes that leached life from the living.

"Did you see how?" the Arcan asked.

"Fingers. They dug into his chest." The answer was given without feeling, without emotion.

Kashif nodded. "Is the demon still here? Did you see where it went?"

"You'll want to talk with the man at the cathedral."

Kashif waited to see if the thief would elaborate on who the man waiting at the cathedral was or why he would be vital to speak to. When nothing came immediately, the foreigner scientist decided to go seek the answers himself. Ethiere did not move from his perch as Kashif pressed forward.

The Tollian cathedral looked forlorn in the growing morning light. The door was closed but not locked, and the Arcan let himself inside. A lone weathered workman sat in the polished benches, facing the raised lectern at the far end of the structure. As Kashif walked the long aisle, he saw that the man was armed.

It appeared to be Billick's axe.

The Arcan also realized that the man was not here to worship. Lying near the base of the lectern, arms and legs cuffed in heavy chains, lay a small, sleeping girl.

"The girl who works the miracles?" Kashif asked.

"I suppose," the man answered, his eyes never leaving the girl. "But also a girl who carries in her a monster." The man licked his lips, the words unsavory. "I saw it draw itself back into her. It's in her – right now."

The Arcan stared at the slumbering girl. This was their demon? This was their tormentor?

A chill went through his spine, knowing what the monster inside this girl would do to him. He'd end up like the wizard, drained of his blood.

Kashif's eyes went to the axe. The weathered workman somehow knew what he was thinking, though he did not lift his steady watch over the girl. "I've been sitting here, wondering if I should … wondering if I even could …" The man trailed off, his throat catching. "How are you supposed to take an axe to that? To a sleeping child? To a poor, frightened little girl?"

The Arcan shook his head. He was trained in science, not compassion. But still, he knew the weapon would do no good. He was quite certain that swords and axes and arrows would do nothing to harm the girl. The stories of her healing – both others and herself – suggested as much. But Kashif had even stronger proof.

His own witness.

For not too long ago, he'd witnessed this very girl's death.

41.

Greer wasn't a religious person. Yes, the Cahill's attended the Holyday services without fail – it was expected of them. They had their own row near the front of the cathedral – the prime spot for such prime people as everyone assumed they were. Greer could recite the key passages from the holy tomes – those any girl of high station would be expected to be able to recite. She sang the hymns – though her voice was far from beautiful. And she bowed her head whenever the Deacons called for a prayer.

Yet it wasn't until last night that Greer had truly prayed. The observances she and her family made – they were all by rote. They were a learned behavior – a façade, much like everything else she was composed of. Greer had always been outwardly religious – but last night … fleeing on a galloping horse into the darkness … knowing of the carnage being wrought behind them …

She'd echoed prayers to Merciful Domus all of her life. Last night, for the first time, she desperately hoped against hope he truly existed.

"At the first sign of trouble ..." Captain Reed reminded her as Alben grew nearer. He was on edge – and rightly so. None of them had slept last night – but Reed ... Greer actually felt bad for the man. He looked to have aged a decade overnight. As the grey-clouded morning dawned, he had adamantly resisted returning to Alben – to where the demon had attacked. But Reed and his remaining men couldn't comprehend the urgent discomfort that drove her and Dom – and to a lesser extent Sarah – towards the evil creature they were obligated to kill. He couldn't comprehend it, but he'd eventually relented when the pain had become more than Greer could bear.

It was something she had not expected in the soldier – the compassion. Reed was all polish and procedure around her father, but the events of the previous night... He'd caught up to them, leading his horse with Dom and Sarah safely atop the stallions back. His eyes had spoken volumes as they'd met with hers. He'd done more than just fulfill the order; he'd done it for her.

Greer wondered what Reed expected to find back at the homestead. He'd left his men there – and Greer was just beginning to understand how much Reed considered them *his*.

" ... We turn the horses," she recited mechanically. "Neald and Sperry ride with us. You and Bostitch will stand ground and allot us what time you can." Reed nodded vacantly in approval. It was a simple plan –on the surface it fulfilled the mandate of the Lord Baron. Greer thought it best not to remind the troubled Captain that should they be forced to flee again – it would only be a matter of time before the pain would drive them to return once more.

They'd have to face the demon eventually. They'd run out of soldiers before too long.

Sophie must have seen that coming. Perhaps that is why the companion girl never stopped her galloping horse. She was running not only from the creature, but from the company of those that would be forced to reencounter it.

Greer could not help but wonder if this was all that remained of the Band of Six? It was a thought that Greer banished. What could she, two children and four soldiers do against a demon from Oblivion?

With a quick command to his horse, Reed pulled ahead of the group. Greer leaned forward on her mount – wanting to take in all there was to be seen the first moment it appeared. She found herself holding her breath as Alben's main thoroughfare swung into view.

The quaint town was ghostly still. There was no sound – even the whispering of the wind through the trees seemed to have gone silent – a respectful reverence to the motionless bodies of men lying scattered on the road. Greer felt her jaw tremble. Someone had seen to the dead. Someone had carefully laid a covering – a blanket here, a coat there – over the fallen.

Reed dismounted, his sword hanging limply at his side, his suspicions and greatest fears confirmed.

She heard Bostitch counting to her side. "Two …. Four … five … six …"

"Some may have survived then?" Neald cautiously suggested.

"Ethiere!"

Sarah jumped from the horse and ran past Reed. It took Greer a moment to spot the thief – sitting motionless atop the roof of one of Alben's shops. The girl's approach seemed to wake him from his personal fugue. His eyes went from Sarah, to Greer and to Dom. Slowly he stood and with a controlled grace, dismounted from the roof.

Sarah ran to him and flung her arms around his neck. "Oh, Ethiere! I hoped you would be alive! I hoped it! I didn't know where you were, and I was so worried!" The thief hardly moved, as if in a trance. As Greer urged her horse forward, she recognized the robes under the sheet near where the boy stood.

She gasped.

Reed saw it too. "The wizard's dead."

It woke Ethiere from his silence. The thief raised resign-filled eyes towards Reed. "Swords couldn't stop it. Magic couldn't stop it. Nothing they did – nothing they tried … they couldn't even slow it down." His head sunk down, his voice low. "We're all doomed."

42.

There had been eighty-six of them when they'd started. Eighty-six captured officers with a pact to rush their guards rather than continue learning what horrors an Arcan prisoner camp held. There were enough stories – about living dissections and twisted mutilations. There were stories – although most of them were told second or third hand. They were passed down, like lore, from one prisoner to another. They had to be – the average life expectancy in an Arcan camp was a mere one hundred days.

No one lived long enough to be an eye-witness to the horrors the stories detailed.

There were only three of them now. To their knowledge, none of the others had escaped. They'd run in mass at armed guards – and even unsuspecting the uprising, the black-skinned soldiers' swords were ready. Billick had received a thumb-long gash, high on his right side, but was unscathed besides that.

Eighty-three others hadn't fared as well.

They had no bearings on the foreign island – no knowledge of where the two engaging armies were encamped. Too much of the Arcan island was open plains with grass yellowing in the summer sun. So when they came upon the river, they decided to follow it. Second Lieutenant Coltaire had voiced opposition to the idea. Rivers, he pressed, meant cities. Cities meant people. But Billick and the other man, Major Adams, overruled him. Yes, rivers meant people – but people meant food, as well. And eventually, the river would lead to the shore.

And somewhere along the shore, the armies flying Tollia's colors would be waiting.

They moved at night, keeping hidden in the river's undergrowth by day. They passed several compounds – small clusters of buildings enclosed by a wall only shoulder high – surrounded by farms or small orchards. They scavenged what food they could find, devouring the produce though it wasn't yet in season. They found tools – Coltaire found an implement shaped like a grain-scythe and Adams a ground pick. Not ideal weapons – but better than fists.

Billick's wood-axe, swiped two nights earlier, was their prize by far.

He looked at the sky through the slits of the fronds masking him from view. The sun would sink below the horizon in another two hours, he estimated. Another two after that, and it would be dark enough to travel. The river they followed was growing wider – and it was getting slower. Both excellent signs they might be nearing the coastline they sought after.

Perhaps tonight they'd make a run for it? Or maybe one more night following the river ...

A splash upriver drew his attention – an Arcan girl of nine or ten years was in the water to her knees, a small basket of clothing sitting on the bank beside her. Their venture through the heart of Arcan territory had showed Billick another side of the enemy. The farmers and the planters, those that toiled and labored – they were very different from those Billick and his company had faced on the front. The soldiers were tall, sculpted and powerful – as if each had been cast and cut out of same pristine mold. But the laborers? They looked thin, ragged and ill-begotten by comparison.

More splashing – as the girl lost the shirt she was rinsing to the slow, steady current. It should have been quickly retrieved, but she moved awkwardly in the water, mistimed her reach, and the shirt drifted further and further downstream. From their hiding place across the river, Billick could barely make out the looks of concern on his two companion's faces.

The shirt was plotting a lazy course, directly for the thick bushy growth where Billick was hiding.

Wading downriver, she drew closer and her features became more distinct. Her hair – like that of most of the women they'd seen – was cropped close to the scalp. It gave her a very boyish appearance – but her long curved eyelashes lent her face a definite feminine quality.

Billick looked back to Coltaire and Adams – hoping to read some advice in their expressions. Both were in no position to assist him – not without giving up their own hiding spots. Billick lifted the axe, readying it, and saw Adam's face fall. The Major was shaking his head silently. No. No, you can't.

The shirt – as if directed by the cruel winds of Oblivion – caught on one of the bush's water-born roots, and its progress stopped. It was close enough Billick could have reached out from under the bush and touched it.

He tightened his grip on the hilt. The Major said no? Was there really a choice? The girl would see him – any second now, she would spy him out.

What then? Would she simply collect her shirt and pretend she did not see the white-faced foreigner hiding in the underbrush?

Wasn't she an Arcan? Wasn't she the enemy?

You know how you're going to justify it?

He'd killed plenty of men now, in his time with the Lancers. He'd lost count – although there were some nights where nameless faces who had found death at his sword point haunted his dreams. He'd never given a second thought as to why he'd killed them. They'd stood at the opposite end of the battlefield. They'd lifted their swords, had raised their battle-cry. They were soldiers. Death was part of the game.

But a child ... even a boiling black-skinned Arcan child? This wasn't a soldier; she wasn't part of the game. She didn't have a weapon ...

Unarmed or not, she represented a danger. If he let her live, what would stop her from raising the alarm the minute she could? She could bring the whole village on alert – which would assuredly give away their position to the Arcan forces. What would stop her? What would possibly cause her to return the gift of compassion should he extend it to her?

She reached out, touched the shirt – and her hand stopped. Her eyes focused on him.

She would run, she would tell. He knew she would.

It was an act she had not yet committed. Billick condemned her for it anyway.

No compassion.

--- * --- * ---

He tried to sit up, straining against bonds he hadn't known existed. They were taut at his elbows and knees, and severely limited his movement. The exertion of the movement sent a rush of pain into his chest, and a wave of nausea to his stomach as his vision swam. He tried to regain his bearings, but his eyes refused to focus – his surroundings gyrating in slow, tight circles.

Like a specter sent from Oblivion, a dark form loomed over him, a contrast to the blinding starkness of the sky. His vision continued to dance, but he saw with enough clarity to recognize his captor as a dark-skinned Arcan.

Billick fought against restraints on his limbs, full of rage.

No compassion.

He was a prisoner! The Arcan's had him! He was back on their boiling tables!

"Let me go!" Billick attempted to shout. His tongue felt thick and lazy in his mouth, and the words ran together in a hoarse bellow.

"Hold him still!" he heard the Arcan command. There were others, grabbing ahold of him, pinning him down. Billick tried to fight. He needed a weapon. Domus's boiling shadow, where was his sword?

I'm meat. The thought paralyzed him. *I'm meat – and I've seen the face of my butcher.*

In one last moment of desperation, he tried to rise once more. Yet again, it proved to be in vain. In exhaustion, he collapsed down against the hard surface he was tied to. His head rolled to one side … and he saw the tiny girl with the worry-filled expression … the Arcan girl with the long eye-lashes … the ghost from his past.

She was always there, always depriving him of peace!

She reached out for him.

Everything went dark.

43.

Dom couldn't say why he'd opted to stay with Sarah once they reached Alben. He wasn't reliant on her anymore – not like he had been while the Arcan had kept him sedated. While Dom would have normally preferred being alone, he wasn't sure he wanted solitude in Alben. The entire town was infected by an aura of dread – a concoction of the sadness over loss and death blended with the fear that it could again. The emotion hung – it hummed – over the entirety of Alben, the heart of each citizen picking it up and propagating it like a series of tuning forks.

The boy had only ever known one other place where the very walls seemed lined with such crippling emotions – his father's tavern, where he'd grown up.

Perhaps, he thought, as he sank deeper behind the lapels of his oversized coat, it explained why he didn't want to be left alone. There was nowhere in the town he could go and escape that resonating, familiar fear.

When Sarah had decided to find Kashif, Dom just about reconsidered. The boy knew he was a distrusting person. Growing up the way he had – with the father he'd had – it wasn't unexpected. But the Arcan had done something to him that his father had never been able to. The Arcan, with his drugs, had taken away Dom's ability to think, to act, and to choose. The Arcan's medication had crippled Dom more so than any beating he'd taken at his father's hands.

Merciful Domus taught forgiveness. It was one of the most divine of virtues. Perhaps in his infinite mercy, Domus would be able to forgive him for not being able to forgive the Arcan.

Billick suddenly came to as Kashif and Physician Davies were working on his chest wound. They'd taken a portion of fence down and had used the slats to construct a frame, tying the murderer's arms and legs to the wood with rope. It was a good they had, watching the delirious murderer thrash against the framework.

Unbidden, Dom's curse awoke and painted everything around him gray. He fought against the pressure in his head and opened his eyes.

The ever composed Kashif was surprisingly tense beneath his poised veneer. "He needs another dose!" the Arcan ordered Davies, who was rummaging through the supplies littered on the ground before him. "Quickly – he'll rip the stitching!"

Billick's head swung towards Sarah, and his demeanor instantly changed. The rage that had fueled the colorful ball of his emotions at his core was extinguished by an overwhelming wave of terror.

"Is he okay?" asked Sarah, painted with concern.

Together, Davies and Kashif managed to pin the frenzied murderer's shoulders long enough for Davies to empty another measure of powder into Billick's mouth. Billick coughed and sputtered, exhaling some of the powder in a chalky puff of white, but the numbing effects set in quickly. The murderer's muscles relaxed, his breathing slowed, and he sank back against the construction.

Dom didn't believe for a moment that Billick would appreciate being sedated any more than he had.

"He will be okay, right?" Sarah asked again as Kashif went back to work on the stitching. A slight tremor of irritation washed through his calm – and the world resolved into full color again. Dom blinked rapidly and turned away.

The Arcan didn't answer the girl's question. Dom knew Sarah didn't mean to pester. He knew how worried she had been through the night. Worrying about the Band. Worrying whether or not the others were still alive. For Ethiere and Kashif. Even for Billick. Yes, Sarah had humbly pled to Merciful Domus for the lives of a thief, an Arcan and a murderer.

Dom reached out and touched Sarah's shoulder. "Kashif will fix him up. Let's go."

Their course took them past Captain Reed, Guardsman Sperry and Lady Greer. They were interviewing a Guardsman named Phelps – the only man in Reed's unit to have survived the direct confrontation with the demon. Phelps had survived, but not without loss. The man's right leg was missing below the knee. Phelps was ashen-faced and in pain despite what the Arcan had given him, but he was still alive.

"I don't know what more we could have done, Captain," Phelps said in apology. "That thing is nearly impossible to see in the darkness – it just blends in with the shadows. Ryans and I didn't even see it until we were a few paces away." The soldier shook his head at the memory. "It's vicious, sir. It was boiling efficient at taking us down – hamstrings, throats, slashes across the gut. That said, we must have scored a dozen killing strikes against it – I know I gashed it at least twice with blows that would have disabled a man. It didn't even flinch. It didn't even slow down. I'm sorry."

Captain Reed listened with real pathos. Dom knew he truly cared for his men. "You couldn't have done more, Phelps. You bravely faced a demon spawned from Oblivion."

"You've nothing to be ashamed of," Lady Greer added. "You have my gratitude for the service you have given me and my family."

Dom and Sarah continued past, not wanting to disturb the scene. But it was hard not to dwell on what they were learning. Though the Band had survived intact, they'd lost nearly everyone who'd faced the demon without inflicting any damage to the creature. There was no one left to shield the Band from facing the monster that couldn't be hurt and couldn't be seen.

Dom lowered his head. The last wasn't true. He'd been able to see the demon last night – he'd seen it long before any of the others had, long before the demon had begun its assault. It had been impossible not to see the demon – lit up like a million stars against the gray hues of his cursed vision.

Dom fully realized why he had been Banded. He would have to be the eyes of the Band. He would have to see for them what they wouldn't be able to see.

But that introduced an entirely new problem. How could he see for them without telling them his secret? Was there a way that would not force him to tell the Band about his curse? He knew he should tell somehow, but Dom dithered.

He knew telling came with a slew of consequences.

--- * --- * ---

Any gambler will admit their profession is based in no small measure on luck. So much of a game was beyond their control, decided by whatever gods of chance inserted their will in the shuffling of the deck. But those gamblers with considerable time in their trade – they could utilize their skill to offset a rash of bad luck. Reading a 'tell' here – feigning a bluff there – folding a certain hand if only to throw your opponents off-guard. Gamblers became magicians with a dealt hand of cards, making tens seem like twos, and vice versa. They could manufacture any expression – but more often than not it wasn't anything close to what they were truly feeling.

Dom's father had a penchant for gambling. It was a consuming vice - just like the bottle. What skill his father did possess was usually subjected to the whim of his passion – the more heated and involved he got in a game, the less control he kept of his emotions. His opponents – those with any credibility at the table – became privy to exactly what they were up against, and used the information to their advantage.

No one minded playing a stack with Malcolm. With patience, you'd walk away a richer man. No one ever gave mind to the seething, drunken man they left at the table when the game was through, or what he might do to his poor wife and children cringing in the rooms upstairs.

Dom didn't like to watch the games; preferring the safety of hiding in his upstairs room. He hated when his father gambled, because he knew what that meant. His father generally lost – and when he lost, he made sure each one of them shared in it. Joshua's absence meant more of a beating for Dom and his mother to endure.

Lucky Joshua. Even being with a wizard had to be better than this.

But tonight there would be no hiding. His father had collected him by the shirt collar and pulled him down the stairs. "A glass broke," he said sternly, as if the accident where somehow Dom's fault. "You get it swept up and get yourself back upstairs and you don't call attention to yourself, you hear?" He released Dom near the kitchen door, drawn back to his game. Dom fetched the broom from the behind the bar, and timidly ventured towards the table in the far corner as the game restarted.

They played Three Tens – the game of choice at the gatherings his father put together. The two other men seated with his father were regulars to the tavern and to the gambling table. Dom often wondered if the drinks the two men bought during the day were purchased with coins his father had lost the night before.

"Cards are out, gentlemen," said the red-headed man – a local constable named Lange. "Pray to Domus and cast your bids." Dom knew the workings of the game. Four cards to each man, each bidding on his hand by placing coins under their cup. The two men with the highest bids would play the hand; the lowest bidder's coins forfeited to the pot in the middle. The brief pause came with the diminutive sound of coins rattling in the cups. No one spoke until the bids were revealed.

"Just one thin copper, Dickory?" chortled Lange. "Don't think much of your hand, then?"

"Not as much as Malcolm must think of his," Dickory answered as he held the pipe he smoked between his teeth. "Two silvers is quite a bold bid, my friend."

"My table is no place for timid men," his father answered with bravado supplied by the bottle he'd generously nursed since the game began. He turned to see Dom hesitating ... and waved him forward. Dom complied, keeping his head down for the hurried assault on the glass fragments.

"Think this is your hand, Mal?" Lange asked. "I should be cautious with this one then?"

"Deal the cards," his father said sourly.

Two more cards, face up to each of the remaining players. Lange narrated as he passed out the cards. "An eight, in Suns for you. Four of Stars for me. A five of Stars for you – and look, the seven of Stars for me." It was a chance for each of the men to get a glimpse at what their opponent held – but it was only the beginning of the round. A dice bounced on the table, Dickory the roller.

"Suns are out," the smoker declared.

"Stars still in play," Lange noted – a comment directed towards the deal. With two of Lange's cards revealed as Stars, this hand was already stacked in his favor. His father would see it too well, but Dom knew it wouldn't make a difference. With two silvers invested, he'd not back out now. Glass fragments in a single, neat pile, Dom began to push them away from the table.

"Mal, your play," directed Dickory.

There was silence, and then the sound of another coin joining the pot. Of what size, Dom couldn't tell, but the reaction of the other two men was telling. Lange beat his hand against the wooden table. "Well played! I'll match."

Another card would be dealt to each man, face down – the last of the cards they'd receive for the hand. Next, three cards would be turned for the pot. Owned by no one, they provided the last bit of information on what cards the opponent might hold. Dickory scooped up the die, and Dom found himself drawn to the game. If it landed Stars, maybe his father would have the sense to get out. Or if it landed Moons, maybe there would still be a chance ...

Dom's vision flashed, and he held onto the broom as his head spun with the disorientation. He reached out for one of the nearest barstools – now just a grayish silhouette in his vision – and toppled into it.

"Boil me, Dom! Are you that clumsy?!" his father yelled, above the faint rattle of the dice.

As it came to a halt, Dickory called out the power suit. "Stars it is, gentlemen. Boil me, Lange, but the dice loves you tonight."

Dom looked up towards his father, fearful of angering him further, and stopped. While his father rippled waves of irritation, it was Lange who drew Dom's attention. Dickory had called Stars – and yet, the lucky Lange wasn't radiating confidence or joy or anything like it.

His aura shown with disappointment – and a tint of cold panic.

"Bless the Stars, I say," the constable quipped. "At least when they're powerful, am I right?"

His father latched onto his shirt collar, assuredly displeased with his son's lack of response or movement. "I thought I made myself clear," he said, hauling Dom up by the shirt, "No interrupting my concentration." His father brought his face down close to Dom's, so close Dom could smell the gin on his breath. In that moment, his vision popped, and color flooded the world again. "Got it?"

Dom glanced around his father's looming face towards Lange. The red-haired constable was sitting back in his chair, arms folded contently, watching the proceedings with amusement.

Feigned amusement, Dom reminded himself. Lange wasn't content at all.

Dom spoke before he realized what he was saying. "He's not got the hand, Dad," Dom whispered as lowly as he could.

It brought a pause. "What?"

"It's Stars – but he didn't want Stars," Dom confided. "He's not got the hand. I saw it."

The irritation burned off his father's face, replaced by contemplation mingled with confusion. Finally, he released Dom's shirt with a small shove and wagged a finger. "You better be right," he hissed, and returned to the table.

Dom waited on baited breath as his father sat down and collected his cards.

"Came up Stars, Mal," Dickory advised.

"Heard you the first time," his father bit. "I'll hold, Lange."

The constable laughed. "You'll forgive me if I choose to dig into your pockets a bit more?" he asked as he threw a handful of coins to the pot. A bluff! It was a bluff! Dom watched his father's head turn, just enough for Dom to see his expression. The look said everything. It told him what awaited him if he was wrong.

"I'll play in," his father said, to the bemusement of Dickory – but not to Lange. Dom watched his face carefully. The smile never cracked, it didn't waver, but it ceased for a second to be genuine. The hand unfolded, each man trying to best

the other's proffered card. When it ended, it was Dom's father that was raking in the pot.

"Boiling bold move," Dickory opined. "This table isn't for timid folk, indeed!" Lange glowered moodily across the table, fingering the diminished stacks of coins in front of him. Dom saw his father turn towards him once more. The expression Dom saw was not appreciation. It was not love. What he saw scared him more than the thought of the retribution he'd escaped.

His father's eyes shown with unmistakable greed.

An hour later, his father's frame loomed over his bed. "You saw something, didn't you?" His eyes were glassy from the bottle, but his words were focused and clear. His mouth was curved in a knowing smile. "Oh, yes, you did. Yes, my boy, you did. And Dom – you are going to tell me exactly how you called that hand. You and I – we are going to figure out how to do that again, and again, and again ...." His father sat down on the bed, and laid a firm, unforgiving hand on Dom's shoulder. "Tell me boy, what did you see?"

--- * --- * ---

Telling was to concede his secret. To concede his secret was to open himself up to be used. His father had pushed him tirelessly to cheat for him. He became the ultimate antithesis to everything that kept gambling a true game of chance. His father's greed had known no bounds. Through his curse, Dom had filled his father's coffers – selling his soul in the process.

He was cheat. He was lie. He used his gift, as his mother called it, to rob people. No doubt Merciful Domus was angered. No doubt the Banding was Dom's punishment.

The faceless demon was his first taste of Oblivion before he was doomed there for eternity.

But he couldn't just sit on the information, he couldn't just keep quiet. Someone had to know. For once his cursed gift might serve a greater purpose.

Perhaps this was his chance to atone for his wrongs.

Dom reached into the pocket of his coat, seeking to draw comfort from his mother's necklace. His fingers dug into the deep pocket, searching through the folds for the priceless token, but came up lacking. Trying to ignore the worry growing in the pit of his stomach, Dom rifled through the other pockets on the coat, hoping he'd just misplaced it. What if he'd lost it during the day he'd spent sedated? What if he'd lost it on the frantic ride out of Alben with Reed? It could be anywhere! He didn't even know where to begin looking!

"Are you feeling any better, Ethiere?" Sarah asked. Dom's focus went from his pockets to the thief leaning against the fence, lost in his own thoughts. Unbidden, Dom felt his fists clench inside of the oversized sleeves of the brown coat. The thief! Of course, it was the thief! He knew about the necklace – he'd seen Dom holding it! There was no mystery as to where his prized token was.

Ethiere had taken it.

With a cry of fury, Dom charged towards the thief.

The normally nimble Ethiere, still deep within his melancholy mood, could not react quickly enough. The timid boy rammed into him with all of his weight, taking both of them to the dirt of the Alben street.

"You took it!" Dom bellowed. "You stole it!" Dom was able to free himself enough from the scrum to begin assaulting the thief with his fists. Dom had never considered himself to be a violent person. He'd never picked a fight – never acted aggressively. But there was something instinctive about sending his fists towards Ethiere's face – something intoxicating about the release of built-up frustration.

Ethiere was on the defensive. He raised his hands and arms, effectively managing to deflect a majority of the blows to which he was subjected. The ease at which his attack was deflected only enraged Dom more.

"Dom!" Sarah screamed. "Dom, stop!"

Her words bit into his conscience, but he didn't relent. He wanted to see Ethiere hurt. He wanted Ethiere to feel as much pain as he'd caused Dom to feel. "It was my mother's!" he yelled at the thief. "She gave it to me!" A picture of his mother flooded his mind and brought tears to his eyes. Suddenly, Dom became repulsed by his actions.

This is what his father did – inflict pain, release rage. This was the behavior he hated his father for.

Dom's arms went limp as he began to sob. He saw it clearly, his hypocrisy. He was no better than his father; he was no different.

"Stop it!" Sarah shouted, demanding his attention. The girl was red in the face, alarmed at the fighting … and she was holding the necklace. Dom blinked, his mind trying to make sense of it. Sarah? Sarah had the necklace? "Ethiere saw it fall out of your pockets – you were playing with it while you were drugged! He was worried that you might misplace it – he knew how important it was to you!" The girl's volume dropped as the tension of the situation deflated. "He didn't steal it. He gave it to me – for safekeeping."

Dom, his self-righteous anger shriveling to self-loathing, looked at the thief he knelt upon. Ethiere's eyes shone brightly with accusatory vindication. In one motion, Ethiere shoved Dom from atop him. While the oversized coat shielded him from the ground, it also caused some degree of difficulty in righting himself. "I'm … I'm sorry," he tried, knowing the words were not enough. "I … I didn't …"

Ethiere stalked off. It was obvious that he did not want, nor did he accept, the lacking apology. Dom next turned to Sarah, and cringed at what he saw written on her face. His friend – his one true friend – looked upon him as if she no longer knew who he was. "I'm sorry," he repeated. It was all he could think to say.

For while Dom had grown-up with an ever-present example of violence, his father had never given him an example of remorse.

44.

The Mayor of Alben bristled. "You mean to tell me that the demon is in the cathedral – sleeping – and you're not going to go in and finish it off?" Captain Reed completely understood the Mayor's frustrations. His own men were raising similar objectives. Their complaints were being voiced from a well of loss – seven of their closest comrades dead at the demon's hands.

"It isn't that simple," cautioned Kashif. The Arcan was only cursorily involved in the conversation, still busy attending to those that had been injured in last night's debacle of a battle. While the heaviest losses had understandably been inflicted on those that rose to fight the monster, the demon had managed to kill Constable Mercer and three other Albeners as well as maim a half-dozen more in the chaos. These had not been soldiers – merely common people caught in the wrong place at the wrong time. The creature hadn't cared to make a distinction.

The Mayor looked back to Reed for support. Before Reed could voice his opinion, the Arcan gave his explanation. "The demon is not flesh like I and you are flesh. It doesn't have parts – organs, bones, skin. I suspect that the form we have seen it take – both in the fountain and in the battle – is merely a product of the host it inhabits. The girl has a head, two arms, two legs – and such is the physical form that the demon takes. As such, you will find no success in trying to severe a limb from the creature – it has no limbs. You will not be able to bleed it to death – it has no blood. Short of destroying it in its entirety – you cannot kill it."

"You should at least try," the Mayor pressed.

Kashif continued to shake his head. "Whatever wounds you think you could inflict on the demon would merely be inflicted on the girl acting as host. Severe her limbs, make her bleed, chop off of her head – yes?" Reed felt uncomfortable having such a topic discussed around Lady Greer, but what choice did he have? He needed to know what the Arcan had discovered and he was not willing to let the Lady leave his side.

The Mayor frowned. While they all knew it was the demon in the cathedral – it still looked like a small girl. The idea of torturing that poor girl wasn't palatable, not even to Reed's battle-hardened veterans. Despite the obvious hesitancy, the Albener pushed forward. "You are the Band of Six. You're charged with destroying the demon. What harm can come from trying?"

Kashif sighed. "The demon has shown a proficiency at healing the host. Physician Davies witnessed it mend a severe head wound." The Arcan held up a glass vial filled with crimson. "Her arm immediately cleared away the puncture from where I drew blood. The demon's prowess at healing may be so great, that these healing powers can actually be conducted to other people."

"The man who was lame," Reed provided.

"Precisely." Kashif set the one vial down and picked up an empty one in its place. "Wounding the host will not hurt the demon – but it may arouse it. It would heal the damage you have caused – and might seek for retribution. If the creature graces us by remaining dormant for a time, I say we allow it to remain dormant."

"That's it then?" Lady Greer asked. "That's your grand conclusion – that our task is impossible?"

"I didn't say that," Kashif muttered. He'd moved back down the line to Billick. The murderer was awake but heavy-lidded, sedated by the scientist's chemicals. He was still fastened securely to the wooden braces made of fence slats – a precaution against any repeated outbursts.

"No, his plan is to let it slumber!" the Mayor grumbled. "Never mind that it will ravage my town when it wakes! What shall I tell my citizens? Should we all abandon our homes – flee into the hills?"

The Arcan had made it clear that he would not be interrupted from his work by the conversation. His answer also made it clear that the homesteads of Alben were not his primary concern. "That may be advisable."

Kashif's tone finally frustrated the Mayor enough to get the man to stalk off. As he left, Lady Greer whispered covertly into Reed's ear. "I would wager my father's entire estate that the dear Mayor is nowhere to be found in Alben after sunset."

"He's not wrong, though," Bostitch growled around his smoking roll. It was a foregone conclusion for the Sergeant to smoke a roll when he got aggravated like this. Bost had gone through most of his box last night, the tiny spark at the end of the paper winking between dim and bright as if it had had a life of its own. Reed stayed focus on Kashif, watching as the foreigner began to draw blood from Billick. The murderer protested under the treatment, but remained powerless to stop it.

"So what is the solution, Kashif?" Lady Greer asked, her patience waning. "What of the Banding's riddle you were so keen to solve?"

Finished with his work, the Arcan finally raised his eyes to theirs. "The answer is in the blood, Lady Greer. I am sure of it. Any hope we are to have of defeating the creature will come from an understanding of what it truly is. Give me time to analyze the blood – I will give you the answer to the riddle."

Captain Reed was not a learned man. He knew that Kashif and Davies could talk circles around him when it came to things like science. But Reed was an excellent strategist, and he clearly saw the strategy in Kashif's claim. His simple assertion had provided the Band a single option for survival – and had made him the single most crucial asset to protect.

"I would like to also analyze the blood of each of the Band members. I have samples from myself, Sarah, Dom and now Billick. All I need ..."

"No," Reed interrupted. "You'll not be taking your needle to the Lady."

"It may help ..."

"He said no," barked Bostitch.

"Find a different way," Reed instructed. He could feel Greer's eyes on him, but he didn't look at her. He didn't know if he'd find approval or disapproval waiting for him. The Arcan shifted his eyes quickly to Greer, but quickly returned to meet Reed's decided stare. He shrugged, obviously unhappy with the outcome. As he went to his bag, Reed could imagine the Arcan muttering all sorts of things about Tollian ignorance.

So be it. Reed wasn't about to let a noblewoman be bled by a foreigner!

"Captain?" Bost motioned towards the horizon, where a horseman was riding in. "Looks like Neald has news."

Since their return to Alben, Reed had elected to keep one of his men watching the country road that served as the most direct route from Hollingston. As bleak as their situation currently appeared, Reed was holding out hope that Lord Baron Cahill would be able to muster additional support from Lord Northing. In any reinforcements were to arrive, they'd march in along that road.

It didn't take long for the balding Neald to close the distance. Sperry took the reins as Neald dismounted to report. "We've got at least eighty soldiers marching in on the Hollingston road. Surprised they aren't kicking up more dust than they are. About thirty minutes out. They're marching under Northing's banner – but no sign of Lord Baron Cahill among them. He might just be bringing up the tail ..."

"Is there an Arcan with them?"

The question from Kashif caught them all by surprise. Reed turned to offer a quizzical look, but found that the Arcan was disturbingly engaged in Neald's report. Kashif's composure was laced by tension; Reed could see the mental calculations being run behind his eyes.

He knows something that he's not telling us.

"Actually, there is," Neald answered, the acme of his report spoiled. "How did you know?"

The Arcan immediately went to work. "It doesn't matter," he stated. "Davies, pack everything up – now!" Kashif fetched his bag and went to work on his equipment. "Captain Reed, find the children, prepare your horses. We must vacate Alben immediately!"

Bostitch guffawed at the suggestion. "Must we?"

Lady Greer balked as well. "Surely the promise of additional soldiers …"

"Davies, we'll need your wagon!" Kashif ordered. "Billick will have to go in the back!" The Arcan looked up from his pack only briefly enough to see that no one else in Reed's contingent was acting with any sense of urgency. "Captain Reed!"

"How did you know there would be an Arcan," Reed demanded. "What does that mean?"

"It means they are coming for the demon," Kashif shot back.

"Boiling shadows, of course they're coming for the demon!" Bostitch balked.

"And when they find it," the Arcan retorted, raising his voice above the detractors, "they will have the Arcan – one of my fellows – verify that the girl is indeed the girl they believe her to be. And we need to be gone before that happens!" Kashif looked deeply into Reed's eyes, imploring for support. "You must trust me! This force is not coming to slay the demon, Captain. It is coming to slay the Band."

45.

Ethiere stalked away from Dom and Sarah, livid at life. The pain caused by the timid boy's flailing fists was already starting to fade, but the false accusation – an accusation Ethiere had known would come and had planned ahead to allay – still stung sharply. This was his fate – his inescapable fate. A Banded thief, responsible for killing an unbeatable foe that no sword or magic could touch. Wizard Algius had been clear – failure meant death. Sometime during the long night spent on the roof, listening to the moaning of the injured and dying below, Ethiere had resigned himself to failure. He was going to die. His tragic ride on the currents of life would come to a fitting end.

While his first impression was only to escape the situation with Dom, Ethiere found himself purposefully heading towards the Alben cathedral. He'd not set foot it in yet – knowing that the demon lay waiting inside. He'd heard all of the rumors – every scrap of speculation by the Albeners from his vantage point on the roof. He knew that the creature resided inside of the miracle-girl.

But he still didn't know if the miracle-girl was the Gang's Pennie.

Spurred by his frustration at having no choice in any other matter – Ethiere resolved on one last act. Regardless of whether it hastened his impending demise, he would see the girl. He would discover Pennie's fate, if he could.

As Ethiere stepped onto the cathedral grounds, he felt like a stranger. The beautiful buildings with the well-kept gardens were common in Hollingston. It seemed that each parish was keen to outdo the others in their monument to Merciful Domus. Ethiere had never seen the inside of a cathedral. While he may have once found refuge their as an orphan, he'd not find welcoming arms now that he wore the leather pads of a thief. Merciful Domus sorrowed for the sinner – and stealing was a sin.

But Merciful Domus had stolen his family. In a way, Ethiere was just repaying the debt.

On entering the door, Ethiere was presented with a long walkway, with small, tightly bunched benches to either side. He approached the stage at the far end of the cathedral, each step solemn. At twenty paces he could see her face clearly enough. He knew he recognized her.

It was his Pennie.

For all of the hope of the previous night that he might have answers to the fate of the missing Gang members, Ethiere had hoped equally hard that he would not find his Pennie here. He could imagine several terrible fates for his brother and sister thieves, but none worse than this. None worse that being possessed by a demon.

He stopped at five paces and bowed his head. "I'm sorry, Pennie. I'm so sorry."

"Did you know her?" Ethiere turned to see a woman sitting at the far end of the first row of benches. She wore a bandage around her head, the wrapping partially obscuring one eye. A man lay with her, sleeping fitfully, his head resting in her lap. Billick's axe lay near his feet.

Ethiere responded to the question with a quick nod. "She was my friend."

"Would you tell me about her?" the woman pled. "Would you tell me who she is, the poor dear? Can you tell me how ..." the woman paused, her eyes going to the sleeping girl. "How did she end up like this?"

The story Ethiere told was not a long one. He supposed that he could have lengthened it, talking about Pennie's life before joining the Children's Gang. But it didn't seem important. Ethiere told the woman about the Pennie he knew – the girl that was his sister and fellow-thief. He spoke of Kari teaching Pennie how to braid hair, her balking at any meal that had fish, of Pennie once stealing a basket of peaches and eating them all before getting back to the lair, of how she'd lost a tooth working one of Master Hat's jobs and had gone back to the same shop the next night to try and find it.

As he spoke, he could not interpret the woman's reaction. Perhaps it was the bandage which masked her expressions, or perhaps she remained unexpressive and still to allow the tired man to rest. Ethiere's stories told of a thief – but he didn't even think to hide it. Pennie was a thief. It was not *all* that Pennie was – but it was a part of what made her Pennie. Leaving it out, he would not have been able to do his friend's story justice.

"She disappeared a few weeks ago," he concluded. "We lose brothers and sisters from time to time – things happen. But we didn't know what happened to Pennie. She just never came home." Ethiere cleared a tear from his cheek. "I don't know how she got like this. I don't know what happened to her. I just know that she doesn't deserve it."

"Of course she doesn't," the woman agreed. "I've only spent a few hours with Pennie, but I spent enough to know that she is a kind and loving girl. I know she isn't in control of what the demon is doing."

Through his tears, Ethiere allowed his focus to drift to the axe. The woman fell quiet, but Ethiere knew she was watching him.

"I know what you are considering," she whispered into the void. Ethiere looked away from the sharp edge of the axe to the gentle face of the woman. "It would relieve her of the burden she carries. It would be a kindness."

Ethiere rubbed the back of his hand against his eyes, trying to clear the haze of moisture. She was right – about him thinking about it, about him justifying it. Pennie wouldn't want this – she wouldn't want to live knowing she was sowing death. But could he? Could he really pick up the axe and do that to a friend? However pure his motivation, would he ever be able to forgive himself?

"I know you consider it because it is all I have been able to consider as I've watched her." Ethiere watched the turmoil of indecision enfold on the woman's face. "I try to tell myself that Merciful Domus wouldn't judge me poorly for doing it. I try to tell myself that I would be able to forgive myself should her blood stain my hands." The woman shook her head. "I try – but cannot sell myself on any of the lies my mind conceives."

The quiet of the cathedral for the two unacquainted but unitedly solemn mourners was interrupted by harried voices outside the walls. The thief recognized the tenor of the commotion – something was happening. By his best guess, it sounded like this something wasn't a turn for the positive.

His instincts taking over, Ethiere sought higher ground. He bound up the narrow staircase until he had sufficient height to catch the base of the row of high-set, stained glass windows. The beams that supported the ceiling were easily attained, providing him with a hidden outpost from which to spy on the cathedral floor below. The woman on the bench looked up at him, wonder exuding from her bandaged face.

The cathedral door was pushed open and a soldier took a few steps inside. It was one of Reed's men, though Ethiere couldn't place the name. The fellow turned back towards the door. "He's not here!"

A muted voice replied – it sounded like Sarah but Ethiere couldn't decipher the words. More voices – arguing – before Kashif's distinctive accent became clear.

"We can't wait any longer!"

More arguing and the soldier in the cathedral's entryway trotted back out. Moments later, a wagon rolled away, and things were quiet. Ethiere could see nothing of the outside through the stained glass to confirm his suspicions, but he was all but certain the Band had just abandoned him. Again.

Not that he had a mind to go with them. Where did they think to go? How far would they get before the pain of the Banding drew them right back here – right back to the cathedral. Right back to Pennie and her demon. Ethiere leaned back against the sturdy ceiling brace – as comfortable a place as any. The view, with the sun streaming through the shards of colored glass was amazing.

If he was going to die today – he'd at least enjoy what hours he had left.

His peaceful meditation did not last through the hour. As the cathedral bell tolled the time, the din of a crowd of men returned once more. He could count out the measure of their march – the steady beat of their boots against the ground. Calls – issuing orders, relaying reports – this was a military body.

Only a short time later, five men entered the cathedral, led by Alben's mayor. The newcomers were uniformed in the colors of Lord Baron Northing; the epaulets on the shoulder of one marked him as an officer. Their swords were drawn as they surveyed the cathedral – their focus quickly going to the chained girl and the quiet Alben couple watching her. They didn't spy Ethiere – no one ever thought to look up.

"There she is," pointed the mayor – as if any of the soldiers he was directed hadn't seen Pennie as they'd walked in. "That's the girl possessed by the demon."

The officer was eyeing the Alben couple. "Get them out," the officer ordered to one of his men. "Go fetch the Arcan," he told another. Despite their protests, Northing's men made quick work of clearing the kindly woman and her newly roused husband from the building. The woman begged to stay, though her pleas were not aimed at protecting Pennie. Ethiere offered a tight-lipped smile. The woman knew that Pennie didn't need protecting.

Northing's soldiers were on alert. Ethiere counted three swords below – three thousand would still not have made a difference. If the demon awoke, these men would not last a minute.

One of the soldiers returned with another man in tow – and Ethiere received his first surprise. It was an Arcan – but not Kashif as Ethiere had expected. A second Arcan? The dark-skinned man moved quickly to the front of the cathedral and stopped in front of Pennie. He relieved himself of his large pack – nearly identical to the one that Kashif carried – and opened it up.

"Well?" the officer asked. His impatient tone was consistent with the rest of body language; he wasn't bothering to hide his disdain of the foreigner.

"I must compare her to the notes ..." the Arcan stated. His native tongue lent his words an accent that was thicker than Kashif's.

"You studied that little book of yours the entire way here," the officer pointed out.

The Arcan didn't respond. "I was brought to be thorough." He brought forth a little book from his bag and began to turn the pages. The script was too small. Even if he knew how to read, Ethiere would not have been able to make out the words. Still, why did the Arcan have a book about Pennie?

"I'll need to see the back of her neck," he told the soldiers. They complied begrudgingly. "Lift the hair away, please – yes, there!"

"What is that?" asked the mayor.

The Arcan closed his little book. "Success. But I am not at liberty to say more." He motioned to the officer. "You will remove the chains and prepare her to return with us back to Hollingston."

The mayor nodded vigorously. "Yes, thank you. Take her far away. As far from Alben as you can ..."

Ethiere could not see what was wrong with Pennie's neck, but he watched as one of the men holding the girl brushed his fingers against ...

The girl jolted to life, her movements so quick the soldiers lost their footing as she strained against her restraints. She whipped her head around, eyes wide and wild ... and she saw them. "No!" Pennie screamed. "No! Not you! Leave me alone! No!" She thrashed, chains quivering.

Ethiere saw it. She recognized the Arcan.

The connection came naturally – the Arcan had done this to her.

The soldiers reestablished their holds on the girl, and the Arcan advanced with a new implement from his pack. "Keep her still!" he commanded as he brought the thin tip of the instrument to bare against Pennie's exposed upper arm. The effect was near immediate; the girl's energy rapidly leaching from her. The terrified look did not leave her eyes until the sedative forced them shut. The Arcan lifted an eyelid in assessment and nodded in satisfaction. "Continue on. With the dosing I just gave her, she'll pose no further problem until Hollingston." As the soldiers hesitated, he harrumphed. "Or you may chain her to the coach, if you feel it best."

The Arcan took a seat on the first row of benches, almost directly beneath Ethiere's beam. Ethiere was certain the man had assaulted Pennie – that he was the source of the demon. It was all the thief could do not to drop from the ceiling, down on top of the boiling foreigner. Ethiere knew he was already dead – why not avenge Pennie with his final breaths?

"What of the Band?" the Arcan asked the mayor, still unsettled from Pennie's outburst.

"They fled," he reported. "Heading east. They left just before you arrived."

"A pity," the dark-skinned man replied. "Such a pity. I had hoped to share this moment with Kashif. My brother deserves as much credit in this as I do."

The revelation bit into Ethiere's soul, and rent his heart. Kashif? Kashif was a part of this? Of course he would be! He was responsible for the fear in Pennie's eyes! He was responsible for the demon – for the entire reason they were Banded! Ethiere leaned back quietly against the support beam, trying to steady himself despite the rage he felt. The Arcan below him was no longer a concern and the thief paid him no mind.

Ethiere still wanted revenge, but he would be patient.

He would exact it on Kashif.

46.

What had started as a light sprinkle just minutes before quickly gained in intensity. The rain was nothing compared to some of the downpours Kashif had experienced in Hollingston – and even those were trifling when compared to the monsoon season on Arca. But this constituted the first storm he'd experienced without a roof over his head. The drizzle had made quick work of his clothing. His pack – by far the most important thing to keep dry, was under Davies wagon with Dom and Sarah. Kashif disliked the discomfort of the storm, but he bore it.

He pondered as he kept his eyes on the road they'd just traveled – the way back to Alben. Reed had two men watching the way should Northing's soldiers pursue them. Kashif was not sure he'd convinced Captain Reed of the danger, but to his credit, the soldier wasn't questioning the advice. With hope, the storm would discourage any pursuit – though it might not matter.

Already the pain was returning, ever so gently making its presence known. They'd hold while they could, but they'd be drawn back to the demon eventually.

I need more time!

He whispered the words to the pain being birthed in his shoulder. He had the girl's blood; he had several tests in process. The answers would be in the blood – they had to be! But finding them – being able to read the results correctly and discern what secrets they would divulge … Would he need hours? Days? Weeks?

He watched Physician Davies, a man of mediocre skill but tremendous heart, try to keep the rain off Billick's bandaged dressings. It was foolish to think they'd be able to survive the demon for weeks when a single encounter had stripped them of a majority of their fighting force.

It was foolish to think that the creature wouldn't come seeking him out.

The demon would be drawn to the Essen-rich blood in his veins.

To the side, Captain Reed, Neald and Lady Greer took refuge beneath a tree too meager to shield them fully from the rain. Lady Greer looked miserable – even more so than the unhappy noblewoman generally looked. Perhaps this was her first unsheltered storm as well? At least her blonde companion had departed. At least the Band was spared her incessant complaining.

Reed saw him watching, uttered something to Neald, and ventured out into the open field. A distant rumble of thunder sounded as he came. The Captain came to a halt at Kashif's shoulder, joining him in his appraisal of the empty road before them. The rain continued to tap at them, prodding the conversation to start.

"You've figured it out," Reed stated.

Kashif frowned. "Not all of it."

"But enough of it?"

He nodded. Kashif now knew enough to comprehend how difficult the task that lay before them really was. While it was not hopeless, there was no way to speak about what was to come with any sort of optimism.

"I need you to tell me what I need to know."

Kashif considered the specific wording of the Captain's request and found it was an admirable one. It was almost Arcan-like in its desire for efficiency. Kashif was not blind to reason – he knew he needed Reed. The Captain commanded what remained of their limited fighting force. Should the pain drive them to face Northing's men in Alben, Reed needed to be informed as to what he might face.

The problem the scientist faced was common to those of his caste – historical events of any magnitude hardly even had a clearly defined starting point. Kashif opted to convey as much of the story as he could; he would leave it to Reed to sort out the valuable details.

"This began when my Master received an urgent and wholly unexpected letter."

--- * --- * ---

He could almost see it – some thirteen years prior, an armada of ships tying onto their berthings in the port of Hollingston. The passengers disembarking, scattering amid the thick-shouldered dockworkers, the deadly fever they unwittingly carried propagating to a second round of hosts.

Standing on the gangplank, Kashif had been able to visualize the plague sweeping through the city. He'd been able to imagine the bodies, too many to be attended to, lining the streets, rotting where they lay. He'd stood there, taking in his first glance of Tollia, knowing he had once ushered death to untold thousands. The dockworkers attending to the ship were not willing to meet his eyes. It was almost as if they knew.

They knew he was responsible. They knew what he'd done – his grand accomplishment in the name of Arca.

They were ushered off the ship into a waiting carriage, and from there were taken to the manor. No one spoke to them – not a single word. Maybe it was the color of their skin and the history with the war. Maybe it was the lateness of the hour, the darkness in the deepened sky.

Or maybe the people of the Northing barony were mourning with their Lord.

They were led to the Lord Baron's courtroom by a bevy of guards, a ceremonial escort into the heart of the manor. "Master Marooke and his two apprentices," a heavy-lidded steward announced in a calm and careful voice before stepping aside. Marooke walked forward, Kashif and Djemal flanking him to either side, and approached the most powerful man in all of Tollia. As a youth, Kashif had marveled at how his master could remain so calm. He knew now – through the experience of the pain lessons – how a man could exhibit unwavering control over his body. What worked with pain worked even better on nerves.

The accompanying guardsmen took up posts around the room. A bit excessive in numbers, in Kashif's estimation. But then again, Arcans were not regular guests – and many of the soldiers in the Lord Baron's employ had probably personally fought in the abandoned conflict.

"Lord Baron Northing," Marooke said, his head lowering slightly in respect.

Lord Northing sat motionless on his dais, brooding, chin leaning against his intertwined fingers. He had a hard face, the lines etched and well-defined, and his statuesque pose only amplified his craggy features. At the salutation, the Lord Baron's eyes lifted up, but he did nothing else to acknowledge them.

"We have come ... as you requested."

His chin lifted off of his fingers, his eyes declared a challenge. "My wife is dead – lying in a wooden box. You have been purported to be the foremost expert on the human body. So tell me, Master Scientist, what can you do?"

Marooke tilted his head thoughtfully. "I can offer condolences for your loss."

"And nothing more?"

"I work with the living, Lord Baron. Perhaps if circumstance had brought us here sooner ..."

"You could have saved her?"

Marooke smiled humbly. "I would not be able to say. The Sleeping Sickness, as your physicians call it, is an aggressive disease. In its later stages, little can be done to prevent death. Could I have staved the illness off for another few days? Maybe. But in all honesty, the fate of your Baronessa was already decided before you sent your envoy to fetch me from Arca."

Northing retracted inward into his thoughts again. "Yet you came ..."

Marooke smiled. "Your letter implied things, Lord Baron ... about what your true purpose in enlisting my services may be. I was led to believe ..."

The Lord Baron sprang from his chair, a sudden fire ignited in him. "Huellard!"

The sleepy-eyed chief steward stepped forward. "Lord?"

"Clear the room. I will speak to this Arcan in private."

The steward and the soldiers exchanged a wary glance. "Surely a guard or two should be allowed to ... ensure my Lord's safety." Kashif doubted there was a man in Tollia willing to trust an Arcan.

"Do it – now," came the order, this time with a little extra bite. With reluctance, the mass of swordsmen and servants began to file out. The steward sighed silently, and motioned for Kashif and Djemal. Before either of them could take a step, Marooke spoke.

"My apprentices stay."

The steward looked to the Baron, who frowned. "I would prefer to discuss this ..."

"These are my right hand, and my left," Marooke indicated. "They assist me in all things. If I am to have part in this – they will have part in this as well." It was another indication Marooke had an inclination towards what their purpose in coming to Tollia was. Kashif glanced to Djemal, and it was clear the other man had not been privy to their master's secrets either.

After a moment, the Baron lifted his hand and waved the steward off. As the double-doors to the courtroom came together, the sound echoed through the now emptied room. As the sound faded, the Baron returned to his throne-like chair, and resumed his scrutiny of his guests.

"Can it be done?"

"Lord Baron?"

The man's mouth twisted. "My wife lies in a box. The most powerful woman on this island – a vision of perfect health and well-being not five weeks prior – and she rots in a box." He stood again, but only to pace in agitation on the dais. "You said my letter made clear my wishes?"

"It did."

"And?"

Marooke nodded thoughtfully. "I had to be sure I was not mistaken ... of whose life we've truly come here to save." He looked behind him, towards the closed doors. *"No doubt your courtiers believe our business pertains, in some fashion, to the Baronessa. But, as you have so eloquently stated ...she is 'lying in a box'..."*

The pacing stopped, and the Baron's voice was low. "And I ... do not wish to join her."

Kashif fought the urges to jump to a conclusion and instead tried to focus on the conversation.

"All who live – die, Lord Baron," Marooke observed.

"I have never been one to fixate on my own mortality," Northing began. "I have seen the legacy of my line – of my father and grandfather. I knew one day it would be me passing the sum of my achievements into the hands of my son. But my wife, when she died ..." Northing's jaw clenched as his emotions crept to the surface. "The most powerful woman in all of Tollia!. She wanted for nothing – she feared nothing. And yet – in that final moment – in that last instance before the disease consumed her – I saw the fear. I saw her eyes an animalistic panic as she faced the unknown. In her fear, there was no title to hide behind, no sum of treasure to placate the dread ..." His eyes swung back and forth, reliving the memory. When Northing's focus returned, his countenance burned with the intensity of the position he held.

"I will not face what she faced. I do not wish to die."

Kashif could hardly believe he was hearing correctly. It almost seemed like the Lord Baron was petitioning for a cure ...

A cure, for death.

Marooke's answer was the one Kashif expected to hear. "Death is not a disease, Lord Baron. It is a natural occurrence. The Architect of Man designed the human frame to age, to decay and to die. Death is not some flaw in his over-arching scheme. Such a thought would be blaspheme."

Marooke's summation of the doctrine was correct. While there were men of the Scholastad caste pursuing every avenue of natural sciences, the Magistad strictly prohibited certain topics from study. One did not experiment with Essen – the spark of the Architect. And one did not experiment on death.

"And yet," the master scientist continued, "I have often found it curious. Our people, from the highest of the Magistad to the lowest of the Dynad, are unified

in our singular goal – we seek to create the perfect man. It is our mandate from the Architect – to build our race in his perfect image. I make no claims of knowing the mind of the Architect, I am no theologian. But I have never been able to resolve: how can we be expected to pattern ourselves after the image of the Architect of Man – one who reigns immortal – without breaking the shackles of death."

Northing pressed. "Can it be done then? Can death be broken?"

Marooke's nod of the head was barely perceptible, but it was there. "Of course, I cannot say for certain ..."

"But you believe it can be done?"

The master scientist smiled. "I would not have come if I hadn't." That sealed it, in Kashif's mind. Marooke's intentions – from the outset – were clear. He intended to blaspheme. He intended to toss aside the strictest of commands given by the Magistad. What's more – he clearly intended for both of his apprentices to participate in such actions with him. "I have thought on this matter long, Lord Baron. Perhaps it is because I feel my own death stealing closer. If there were no way to overcome the specter of death, there would be no reason for the Magistad to prevent such a study. Provide me with what I require, Lord Baron, and I will uncover the secret of the grave."

For the first time in their interview, Lord Baron Northing smiled. "Whatever you need. Name it."

"A lab. Here, in your manor. Someplace isolated from those of your estate. There will be supplies – some scarce, some expensive, most both. Above all, Lord Baron, I will need time. There is no precedent to exploring this avenue of study. Progress will not come at a rate consistent with our efforts. You will need to have patience, Lord Baron. I need your word, if we proceed, you will see this to the end."

There was no hesitation. "Done."

Kashif felt conflicted. He felt trapped. If anyone on Arca found out what they intended to attempt, they would all face execution. But all the same, Kashif could not deny the bubble of excitement in his stomach. The mechanisms of thought were already turning in his brain.

He'd brought death to this place years ago. Now, he had come to tame it.

"One last thing I require ... something you may find distasteful."

"Anything."

"I will need people to experiment on."

There was no pause at all. "It will be arranged. Criminals and debtors serve me no use rotting in my prison houses. You may have ..."

Marooke shook his head. "No, Lord Baron. Those having grown weak and feeble in your prisons do me no good. You will need to find me subjects who are healthy, who are fit. It would be preferable if they were younger – their bodies still resilient enough to withstand the stresses of experimentation."

The Lord Baron smiled. "You shall have your subjects to experiment on. Young and whole." The smile widened. "I have a source – and they will not even be missed."

--- * --- * ---

"We worked under a simple hypothesis. Death was the breakdown of the human organism. To prevent death, we hypothesized, meant making the body immune to the tolls of life and aging. Such a body, one that perfectly warded diseases, one that rejuvenated itself – that was the solution."

"The girl possessed by the demon – she was experiment number twenty-two. Marooke insisted that we retry several promising methods that had none the less resulted in the deaths of numbers seventeen and eighteen. As such, I was not surprised when this girl likewise died. What I did not know then but know now, is that my Master ventured further into the morally forbidden areas of our craft. He began to experiment with Essen."

Even speaking the words aloud, Kashif could hardly believe them. Marooke? Would he really betray all their caste held sacred? Would he really think to tinker with the very spark of the Architect? And Djemal! The man was the epitome of careful ledgers and exact details. He would have known – he would have had to have known what was happening in those experiments! He must be complicit. But how could they agree on such an objectionable course?

Kashif already knew the answer. Morality was easier to push aside when it blocked a vision of promised progress.

"Essen?" Reed queried.

"The biological component that allows men to perform acts of magic. Your wizards. Our Magistad. The creature feeds on Essen. While it has shown no restraint in killing whoever crosses its path, only those with Essen-rich blood are in danger to be fed upon. Hearing your surviving man describe the events of last night, it is logical to assume that the demon was hunting the wizard – that it has some method of sensing those with Essen. Anyone with a high degree of Essen in their blood – whether their abilities are latent or have manifest – will be in grave danger."

Reed nodded. Kashif was not sure how much of this was actually making sense to the soldier. He would have never tried to go this in depth with a warrior of the Ballistad caste.

"That's why you are taking samples of blood." The conclusion the Captain drew came as a surprise to the scientist. "To gauge which of us may be targeted."

"Correct."

"And what have you found?"

Kashif frowned. "Sarah's blood is clean. I have not had sufficient time to test Billick's blood." He paused. To say what he would say next, if heard by an Arcan, would lead to his execution. "My blood is very Essen-rich. I will no doubt be a target should we face the creature again. But I will not be the primary target."

Reed's eyebrow rose. "Dom?"

The Arcan nodded. "His levels of Essen exceed even my own." Kashif gave Reed ample time to process the information before proceeding. "As for the others …"

"I'll see that you get samples."

The definitive response drew skepticism. "Your men do not trust me."

"My men will obey a direct order."

Kashif smiled. The crossbowman, he was sure, would sooner volunteer to be eaten by the demon than have his blood drawn by the dark-skinned foreigner he so hated. "And what of Lady Greer?"

"I will talk to her." Reed looked back to the noblewoman waiting under the tree. "I will try to help her understand." The rain continued to beat against them, the gray clouds overhead seeming to offer a glum forecast for the task ahead of them. "It heals itself. It is immune to magic and the blade. Can we actually beat it, Kashif? How are we supposed to kill what cannot be killed?"

"I do not know," he answered. "But I will not stop in my pursuit of that answer." The Arcan lowered his head. "It is fitting, is it not? It is just that I should have to face her now – one who I had a hand in creating."

Before Reed could answer, Kashif became aware that the pain in his shoulder had intensified. He had been shielding it, burying it in his mind without realizing he was doing so. A quick look to Lady Greer and the children under the wagon confirmed they were feeling it too. Even Billick, heavily sedated, was stirring in the wagon-bed.

The pain had come quicker than expected – much more so than what he'd experienced last night. There was only one conclusion that could be reached.

"The demon – it is moving." He quickly found his bearings, orienting himself to where the Banding magic was directing him to go. "Northing's men are taking it to Hollingston."

47.

Billick's subconscious shuffled through a series of memories, creating perfect images of the landscape, fleshing out the scenes with the subtle textures and smells and voices. There was the frigid air of the snowy mountain valley tucked away on Dullot Pass. There was the rhythmic rush of the tide and the gritty sand of the Chalase beaches. There was the metallic clicking scream of the steam-belching Arcan war machine, and the taste of blood-mingled sweat. Each memory, each fragmented scene from his past was a sliver of his own personal purgatory.

He was bound for Oblivion. He knew that. But Oblivion could not hold any more horror than what he'd already witnessed. He'd seen the full extent of human depravity; no description any Deacon could give of Oblivion put a shred of fear in Billick's heart.

He was bound for Oblivion – and he was certain he'd fit in fine.

As his mind resolved onto the next scene in the sequence, he found himself looking into the studious eyes of a small girl. His throat caught.

Of all the haunting images of his past, she was the worst.

--- * --- * ---

He stared out into the lapping waves, watching as they desperately clawed at the Arcan sands. The sprawl of a thousand tents spread behind him on the beach – the last stronghold of the Tollian force. The full fisher's moon hung low, illuminating the third-watch sky.

He didn't understand why he came to the water's edge when he couldn't sleep. After so many days wading in the river, Coltaire and Adams avoided the ocean. Coltaire and Adams avoided him as well. They'd not spoken to him since the day ... since the girl ...

Close-cropped hair, long lashes. Skin the color of charcoal. She'd flailed as he'd held her beneath the water's surface. She'd pulled desperately at his iron grip. She'd thrashed – and then she was still; the life draining out of unseeing, wide eyes. When he was certain she was dead, he'd pushed her body out away from the bushes, chasing the shirt that had sealed her fate.

No mercy.

"Are you Billick?"

He turned and saw the man standing ten paces up the beach. His uniform named him an officer, but Billick could not place his name. "Who wants to know?"

"A lot of people," the man replied, boots pocking the sand as he strode down the incline. "You've earned quite the reputation what with the incident ..." He smiled, prodding. "...with the girl ..."

Billick turned back to the ocean. He had nothing to say to the rumor-monger. He'd done what needed to be done. That was the whole of it. The officer came to a stop at his elbow, the two of them surveying the expanse of the ocean before them. "It's true then?" the other continued. "With your bare hands?" Billick fixed his gaze forward; he'd not give the man the satisfaction of an answer. "I hear you watched the entire time while she drowned." He shrugged. "My men would never do that."

"I'm not one of your men."

"I know". To his surprise, the officer laughed. "I find that unfortunate, too. Domus knows we need ten thousand men like you if we're going to beat the dark-skins. Men who understand how things really are – who see the bigger picture. Who don't feel remorse over an unlucky, unimportant Arcan girl." He paused; Billick could feel the man's eyes studying him. "You don't feel remorse, do you?"

He'd had no other choice. "No."

"You'd do it again if you had to?"

Billick finally gave in and turned to look the other man in the eyes. "Without hesitation."

The officer's eyes glowed sinister in the full moon, an odd accompaniment to his open grin. Malevolent thoughts worked behind the eyes; Billick could see them twisting like maggots. "I knew I liked you," the man repeated, and held out a gloved hand. "My name is Hennessey."

--- * --- * ---

There was a girl. But it wasn't *the* girl. The canvas behind her– infrequent patches of gray sky through the thick layers of branches and leaves - whisked by at a steady pace. Billick became aware of the gentle jostle he was receiving and heard the clopping hooves of horses. He was in a wagon bed – and he was on the move. The girl leaned in a tad closer as if to appraise him better, and then smiled. "Oh good, you woke up!"

Sarah was a sharp contrast to the horrors his mind replayed. She didn't fit. There was nothing in his life – nothing in his past experiences – that held any similarity to what he saw in her. Simplicity. Trust. Openness. These were foreign to him.

More than just foreign – they were in conflict. What she was – what she represented – it stood boldly against what he was and believed. It was a cosmic joke, them being Banded together. The punchline? She kept trying to pull him up, out of his personal purgatory; when really, he was dragging her down …

The demon was invincible – he knew that. They were charged with killing it – an impossible task. Billick knew what he was – he was a fighter. He was a survivor. But Sarah?

Would he watch the life drain from her eyes as well? Would she be nothing more than another horrific vignette for his mind to replay?

"Kashif said you'd probably wake up on the way, so I stayed awake the whole time. Even though I'm really tired. Dom didn't last much past Alben."

"Where are we?"

"On the road to Hollingston," Sarah answered.

Billick fought the fog from his mind, trying to catch his thoughts up with his current situation. He tried to move his arms, but found them securely tied to the boards he felt beneath him. "Why I am restrained? What happened?"

"You fought against the demon," she reminded him. "You lost."

He remembered – kneeling before the creature, helpless. He remembered the head of the axe, deeply planted in the soil before him, having gone completely though the glossy black skin with no effect. He should be dead. The demon should have killed him. It had no reason not to.

"We came back to the camp and Kashif and Physician Davies were already back and attending to …you probably should lay still …" He didn't heed her advice as he again tested his bonds. He paid for it in pain. His chest burned fiercely, to the point he hardly dared breathe. Slowly, he sank back into the wagon. "Your face looks pretty bad with the bruises. The cuts on your chest are really deep … but Kashif stitched you up good."

That ignited his ire. The Arcan had laid fingers on him? He'd been on the black-skinned butcher's table? It so infuriated him he would have considered ripping out the stitches in spite.

"Then the Lord Baron Northing's men showed up and we had to run away and they took the miracle-girl from the homestead … except she's really the demon, which doesn't make a whole lot of sense but everyone else says it's true. We went out on some country road and hid while it rained, but it wasn't but a few hours later that Lady Greer and Dom felt the pain returning. And I started to feel like we should get moving as well. There's only ten of us now …"

The girl paused. She'd said it so simply, but it was clear she was aware of the loss. "Lady Greer, Captain Reed and three other soldiers. Physician Davies and Kashif. Me, you and Dom. We don't know where Ethiere is. We couldn't find him when we needed to flee Alben, and he wasn't there when we returned.

Kashif says the Banding will drive him to Hollingston, just like it is driving us. He'll show up sooner than later, if …"

She stopped again. Billick knew how the sentence ended. *If he is still alive.*

"But I'm glad you're awake. Kashif says everything should heal up fine, but that you should conserve your strength.   He wanted me to watch you so he'd know when you woke up – I think he wants to keep you sedated.   But I'm not planning on saying anything.   I don't think Dom like being drugged, and I don't think you liked it either.   You've been muttering in your sleep … I don't think you've had pleasant dreams."

Billick was certain she only stopped because her lungs forced her to breathe. He jumped on the silence. "What do you want?" he said coldly.

He'd made it sound accusatory, and she seemed to take it that way. "I … I don't want anything," she said, fumbling over her words. "I just … you were hurt … I wanted you to know I was looking out for you."

"I don't need anyone to look out for me." He thought about adding 'least of all you' to the end, but held his tongue. The girl was trying to be nice – but that was exactly the problem. There wasn't room for *nice* in his life. He didn't associate with *nice* people; he didn't do *nice* things.   Why couldn't she see that? Sadly, he couldn't walk away this time. Aside from the sleeping Dom, they were the lone passengers in the back of the rambling cart. He was stuck – and he knew she wouldn't stop trying.

Sure enough, Sarah was only momentarily quailed by his abrasive attitude. She pouted, and Billick wondered if it was the closest Sarah ever got to true anger. "Why do you feel like you need to make everyone afraid of you?"

"They should be afraid of me."

"Because you do 'bad things to people'?" she quoted.

Billick considered the girl. What did she know of bad things? What did she really think he did? A homebound girl would have no idea of the degenerate acts happening just beyond the view of her windows? "You have no idea what the world is really like, do you? What people are really like? I tell you I do bad things – and you think, what? That I don't pay attention to the Deacons on holidays? You want me to be clearer? You want to know who I am? I am a murderer, Sarah. I kill people. People tell me who should die, and I hunt them down, and I kill them."

The bout of brutal honesty set the girl back again, and she lowered her eyes away from his. Billick felt a bit of satisfaction. She would see him for what he was now; she'd realize that they shared nothing in common. Surprisingly, she lifted her eyes again. He was not expecting her next question.

"Do you enjoy killing people?"

"What?"

She cast her eyes aside again, but managed the question again. "Do you like doing it?"

The question made him angry. Angry, because it made him uncomfortable. He sputtered his response. "It isn't … it's not like that. It isn't something you like to do or don't like to do. It's just something that you do." He scowled at her. "You wouldn't understand."

The girl pressed on. "Why do it, if you don't like doing it?"

"Because they pay me to."

"They?"

"The rich … the powerful. People like Greer's father, or Lord Baron Northing. Them, their relatives, their cronies, and anyone else who's bought an estate and a title. They have the money – that gets them the power – and that lets them create all of the rules. If they don't like something – they can change the rules to get rid of it. If they don't like someone – they can pay me to have them removed – no questions asked."

"So … you do it for money?"

"Yes."

The girl sat back, evidently disappointed. "That doesn't seem like a very good reason."

Billick thought of Hennessey, the man that worked the contracts, the man that had connections interwoven into every category of sin and vice in Hollingston. "Depending on who you ask, it's the only reason."

Again, the silence was only short lived.

"What if they're wrong?"

"Wrong?"

"What if the person they want killed didn't do anything? What if they don't deserve to die?"

It wasn't a difficult question. "Everyone deserves to die."

"Everyone?"

"Everyone."

Sarah shook her head. "What if they're innocent?"

"Innocent?"

"What if they didn't do what the rich person says they did?" the girl argued. "What if the rich person is lying? What if the person they accuse is innocent?"

Billick shrugged, and instantly regretted it. His chest felt like it was about to pop open. Despite the deep grimace, he managed to mutter his rebuttal. "It doesn't matter."

"Why?"

"Because everyone deserves to die," he repeated. "Innocent, are they? Of that one thing they are accused of – sure. Maybe. Do the rich lie? Are they corrupt? Absolutely. But even if they're innocent of that one thing; they've done something else. It really doesn't matter why someone wants someone else dead. I don't need to justify it. They've done something wrong –" The Arcan girl flashed back into his mind. "– or at least they would have, at some point." He cast her specter aside. "Nobody is innocent."

The girl swallowed, and Billick knew he had her. "Nobody," he hammered. "Isn't that what those pious Deacon's preach? Isn't that what they proclaim to everyone – how nobody except for perfect Merciful Domus is without fault? How the reason we call him 'Merciful' is because he'll reach out to save a wretched lot of sinners like us?"

As the first tear-drop slid down her cheek, Billick grew uncomfortable again. He'd gone too far – and for what? Why had he felt the need to convince this little girl? Why had he needed to explain himself to Sarah? She didn't matter! He tried to convince himself her crying was a good thing – it would be another wedge to keep her away from him – but ...

Boil him, he didn't care about her. He didn't. She was worthless. She was a liability. She didn't matter – at all.

"I think you're right," she said at last, wiping her eyes with the back of her hand. "We all deserve to die, don't we? We've all done things – we've all caused people pain they shouldn't have had to experience." She smiled – but it was a sad, resigned smile.

"What?" he demanded.

Another tear slid from the corner of her eye. "Everyone is thinking it – even if they won't say it. Everyone thinks I'm going to die. I couldn't understand why I was chosen for this – why I'd be Banded to this group – if I was only going to die. I couldn't see why Merciful Domus would have it be that way. But now – now I know. I deserved it to be this way. I'm part of this group because I deserve to die."

She turned to look out the back of the wagon, and surprisingly didn't say anything more. Billick lay as still as possible in the rolling cart; mired in the company of his own thoughts. He'd won. He'd chased the girl off emotionally. He'd convinced her he was right – that his way was right. He'd convinced her she deserved to die – and that was the extent of her usefulness to the group. Boil him, he could hardly look at her now.

He knew what he should tell her – that she was wrong. That – that what? She didn't deserve to die?

Billick felt the discomfort again – but it wasn't in his chest. It was in his heart. He understood now why it had been so important, so vital he justify himself to Sarah. To get her to accept the way he'd lived for the past two decades. She represented something. Billick saw in her the purest, most guileless soul he'd ever seen.

She was innocence.

He didn't believe in innocence though. He'd never found a heart that wasn't corrupt by greed or hate or worse. Sarah's purity flew in the face of everything he'd convinced himself of – no wonder he felt compelled to push her away; to tear her view of the world apart.

She was innocence – and her innocence was threatening.

He'd won. She was converted to his way of thinking – but as Billick continued to ruminate in the wagon, he couldn't help but wonder if he hadn't lost as well.

Somehow, in some way, Sarah had done something no one had ever done before.

She'd convinced him – she deserved to live.

48.

Turning on her horse, Greer watched Physician Davies' head bob as his wagon trailed the advance group of horsemen. Luckily, the deep-forest road was thin enough for the horses to navigate themselves without coaching from the drowsy man. Kashif sat to the side of Davies. The seat they shared was intended for a sole occupant, yet they somehow managed being wedged in there together.

Perhaps the Arcan found the cramped seat better than sharing the back of the wagon with Billick, Sarah and Dom. While more spacious, it probably didn't offer any greater level of comfort – especially considering all of the odds and ends of the fence-works Billick was strapped to.

Remarkably, given the death that had come to Alben last night, their Band was only missing one.

It was hard to say if Ethiere was being missed or not. Sarah was taking his absence the hardest. She'd put up the greatest fuss when they'd fled Alben that morning – adamant that they had to find Ethiere and stay together. Though overruled and quieted, Greer knew enough of the guileless girl to know that she was still praying for the thief boy to return.

But the rest of them? Was it wrong that she felt a little more at ease knowing the thief wasn't plotting in the corners? Sophie had certainly been forthcoming of her distrust of Ethiere. But Sophie had been forthcoming in her misgivings about the murderer and her anxiety over the Arcan. She'd even voiced concern over Dom being too quiet and Sarah too talkative – all in the same breath. There were probably not five people in all the expanse of creation that Sophie wouldn't have found some fault with.

That was the world that she and Sophie came from – a world of expectations to which everyone and everything would always fall well short. It was a world that locked people into inescapable, prison-like roles.

Greer knew she was a fool. Born into privilege – what complaint could she possibly have? Did she envy those like Ethiere who knew the pangs of starvation? Did she wish to join the ranks of the working – find employ next to Sarah's downtrodden father and toil away her life and health? No, nothing of the sort. She understood how easy she had it – it was not the ease she chaffed at.

It was the expectation. It was the role. That the cell was of silver and the bars leafed with pure gold made no difference. A beautiful cage was a cage nonetheless.

She didn't expect anyone to understand; she didn't need anyone else to understand. If the thought was truly unique to her, she would embrace it. There was so little about her that was unique as it was.

She knew now how impossible it was to change the roles. The grand play of existence could continue marching on. You met your expectation – you played your part …

Or you risked being written out of the charade entirely.

--- * --- * ---

Greer's room in the manor was marvelous in every way, except for one. One end of the room was flush with glass windows and a balcony. Greer could not deny the terrific view of the gardens below – but the windows faced east. Thanks to those windows, her entire room lit up like noonday with the rising sun. She'd complained loudly enough Headmistress Packer had installed heavy draperies on the windows – which did the trick. Until someone wanted her awake.

She heard the draperies running along their track as they were pulled, and saw the extra infuse of light through her closed eyelids. Greer turned unhappily in her bed, hiding her face in the dark crevice of her elbow, and entertained murderous thoughts. Bridgette knew better than to awaken her so rudely … she knew …

"What a beautiful morning it is!"

Greer sat up in bed. The voice was dripping with happiness; the words had hovered between being spoken and sung. But more concerning - it was not Bridgette who'd spoken them.

297

With effort, Greer opened her eyes. The girl in the room was backlit by the glowing windows, as if she was surrounded by some blessed heavenly aura. "Oh, good morning, Lady Greer!"

"Who ..." she swallowed an un-ladylike swear ... "are you?"

The stranger walked forward, her image becoming clearer as she did so. She was short, but not petite; not thin, but neither was she curved. Her blonde hair hung like a wave, and her features were pleasant enough ... but only just enough to be pleasant.

She curtsied. "I'm Sophie!"

It didn't help.

The girl – Sophie – kept on smiling, then added, "I'm your companion!"

Greer knew that wasn't right. "No, you're not," she said flatly and tried to free her legs from the tangle of sheets. Boil Bridgette, if this was another one of her pranks! She was probably doubling over with laughter – watching this all from behind the dressing room curtain!

Sophie giggled nervously. "Well ..."

Greer slid feet into waiting slippers and pulled a loose summer robe over her nightgown. "I have a companion, Sophie," she interrupted. "And I am very certain you are not her." She veered towards the dressing area and threw back the curtain to expose ... an empty room.

Sophie was trailing behind. "Who are you ..."

"Bridgette," Greer said in annoyance to the girl, and then thought better. "Bridgette!" she yelled. "This isn't funny in the slightest ... come on!" She rounded on Sophie. "Where is she?"

The blonde intruder blinked. "Bridgette?"

Fed up, Greer marched to the door. She'd get answers, from someone, and when she did ...

"... She's not here anymore."

Greer stopped, and slowly turned.

Sophie withered uncomfortably under the gaze. "Perhaps you should go talk to your father."

Greer found him at his table, eating his breakfast while a steward collected signatures on a variety of documents. Both of them looked up as she stormed in – and she realized she was hardly dressed for appearing out in the open as she was. But she was boiling mad and she wanted answers. It only fueled her anger when both men refocused on the stack of papers.

"Father!" she stamped a foot.

"What is it?" he asked without looking up.

"Who is that Sophie girl in my room? Where is Bridgette?"

Her tone earned her a warning glance from her father. "I can only surmise, Greer, this Sophie is the new companion I asked Headmistress Packer to seek out for you. I wasn't informed she'd found a replacement so rapidly."

A replacement? "Where is Bridgette?"

She waited as her father scrawled his signature onto another form. "Bridgette requested a release from her obligations." He looked up again, almost accusingly. "I would have thought you two would have discussed such a matter."

Greer's mind swam through the past few days. It was true; Bridgette had hardly seemed herself this last week – ever since the unfortunate incident with the young Lord Northing. Greer had just attributed it to her friend pining over a love that could never be. But released? Why would Bridgette ask to be released? It didn't make sense.

"Why wasn't I told?"

Her father smiled dismissively. "If Bridgette chose not to tell you, should you not be asking that question of yourself?" He motioned for the steward, who dropped another paper down for his signature. "I would suggest you forget the matter, daughter. It is only a companion, after all. It is a position – a highly coveted one, true – but it isn't as if some other girl isn't going to be able to fulfill the role ..."

Greer swallowed the hurt. The role? "Yes, father," she said meekly, and fled from the room. A role? Bridgette had not been playing a role! Everyone else in

*this Oblivion-filled manor was playing a stupid role, but not Bridgette.
Bridgette had been her friend – her only friend! She ran all the way back to her
chambers, managing to work herself into a determined rage by the time she did.*

Sophie saw it. "My Lady?"

*"Get me dressed," she snapped at the girl, who immediately traipsed to the
dressing room. Greer shucked the robe and attacked the ties on her nightgown.
"I'll be wanting a riding skirt!" she ordered the girl rummaging through her
wardrobe.*

"Riding?" the girl asked with faux-curiosity. "Where are we going to go?"

Greer looked back into the mocking sun. "You'll find out when we get there."

--- * --- * ---

To her side, Sergeant Bostitch rubbed the lit end of his paper-roll out on the horn
of his saddle. "I don't know – we could treat recent developments as a
positive."

"You found a bright-side," asked an incredulous Neald. The two rode on
opposite sides of her – and long ago had ceased to realize they were conversing
through her. "We're on the tail of a demon-girl that just tore through half our
rank and a wizard ... and there is a bright-side?"

Bostitch shrugged. "If we're lucky, the Arcans take it home to Lord Northing
... and the creature goes to work. Two less of those dark-skins in the world, and
it solves Lord Baron Cahill's problems with Northing rather well in the
meantime." The soldier laughed to himself. "Domus forgive me, but I've got
another half-dozen people I'd like to hole up in Northing's manor, just in hopes
..."

"Yeah, but you've got half-a-hundred who'd vote to save you a room!" Neald
pointed out with a smirk.

Greer couldn't help herself. "You've got fifty people who wish you dead,
Sergeant?"

The stubbly-chinned man lowered his head in a cryptic grin – and it was Neald
who offered the answer.

"That, my Lady, is just the men. We could add half-a-thousand in spited women-folk."

She turned back to Bostitch, not knowing whether she should be shocked or smiling.

He shrugged. "It's not as bad as it sounds. You snub one barmaid ..."

"... she tells her friends ..." Neald added.

" ... and her family – sisters, ...

" ...they tell their friends ..."

" .... – cousins, various aunts ..."

Neald stopped. "Aunts? Really?"

Bostitch shrugged again and offered her an aside. "His estimate might be low." As if finally realizing their topic of conversation, the smoking man became discomfited. "If we've offended in any way, my Lady ..."

She shook a hand in their direction. "It's nothing you've said," she tried to assuage them. "In fact, I've a few people I'd wish to see visiting Northing's manor tonight."

Neald raised an eyebrow. "You, my Lady?"

Sergeant Bostitch eyed her knowingly. "I recall a certain young woman with a gratingly cheerful demeanor who was recently released from your service ..."

Greer let a smile creep onto her lips. Yes, Sophie. Dear, wretched Sophie. "Not so much released from my service as fled from it," she clarified. "If only I'd have known, I would have sent her to the Northings instead of making her sleep in barns. She'd have jumped at the chance, I know it."

All jesting aside, there were some at Lord Northing's manor she was concerned for. Her father. Bostitch and Neald weren't mentioning him; but they knew he was there too. She wondered if the two soldiers didn't assume she wished death on her father as well. Yes, they didn't ever see eye to eye. Yes, she was a disappointment to him – and there was much in him she loathed. But he was her father. She did want him safe ...

And Caleb. Sweet Caleb, companion to Lord Northing's son. She'd not seen nor spoken to him since the fateful night they'd learned each other's true identities. The night they'd learned they could have no future together. But that was all silly, really. Had Caleb really cared about her? Hadn't he just been instructed to distract her while his Master had his fun with beautiful Bridgette? Everything about that afternoon had been one perpetual fraud – it wasn't a leap to believe Caleb's interest was a lie as well.

Or was it? The afternoon at the river – despite the cascade of horrible events it had led to – was one of her most wonderful memories. Despite the evidence, despite the doubt – Greer chose to believe that Caleb had seen *her*. Not her title. Not her station. Not the wealth attached to her name. Just her, for who she was. Just her – and he'd smiled nonetheless.

If there was a demon heading for Hollingston – she hoped Caleb was safely far away.

49.

The entry into Hollingston was officially marked by a gated archway and a shoulder height wall. They were designed to be decorative instead of defensive; neither the gate nor the wall would give an invading force more than a second thought. But they did give a clear definition of what was city and what was country. The buildings of Hollingston seemed covetous of every hand-span of space, crowding one another and the ornamental wall.

Ethiere watched from atop one of the buildings, well concealed in the evening shadows. He'd arrived at Hollingston no less than two hours earlier, nearly arriving at the same time Northing's men did. Ethiere blamed the horse. The animal – one that had once belonged to one of Reed's men – had been anxious to be untethered and had been quite willing to give the country road a spirited sprint. It had been all Ethiere could do to stay in the saddle and not drop Billick's axe.

The thief twisted the axe's helve in his hands. It was an unnatural marriage – him and the axe. Though Master Hat was proficient with knives, he'd never made weapons part of the games the Gang played. It made sense. What good would it be to teach a skinny, ten-year-old lad combat, when those he'd face up against were constables and angry shop owners. Those that didn't have three-times his skill with a blade would at least be twice his weight and a head or two taller. No, it was better to teach the Gang to hide and climb and run.

The moment a thief needed to pull a weapon, it was probably too late for him anyway.

So why had he taken the axe? It wasn't for the demon – that was sure. The sharp, curved blade had already been given a chance to vanquish the monster. It was not up for such a lofty task.

Was it for Kashif, then? This was the question that Ethiere had wrestled with while clutching to the horse. By all appearances, the dark-skinned foreigner was at least partly responsible for the disappearances of his friends. He was to be credited with the achievement of burdening poor Pennie with the demon that inhabited her. Ethiere's blood boiled just thinking about the Arcan.

But did he have the audacity to believe he'd use the axe against Kashif? Was he really waiting on the rooftop, watching for the spiteful Arcan, preparing to let the weapon bite into the foreigner's black skin? Ethiere knew he was guilty of a lot of things – he'd been thieving for the majority of his life. But he'd never intentionally harmed anyone. Not in any of his jobs had he ever tried to hurt or maim.

Could he really work up the resolve to take Kashif's life?

What of the others that deserved to pay?

--- * --- * ---

Master Hat was waiting at the head of the alley, standing over a box full of glass bottles that represented the latest of the Gang's successful heists. He was a lean man, sinewy and surprisingly strong. The moonlight stretched and distorted Hat's shadow, casting him as a lanky spider awaiting prey. Ethiere did not recognize the man who had met Hat here the two previous weeks – the man who apparently fancied exotic bottles.

Ethiere's vantage points on the rooftops had not provided him a close enough proximity to overhear any of the muted conversation. Though each of the previous meetings had ended in an exchange of money for the box of pilfered goods, there had been plenty of discussion and debate preceding it. So tonight, he hid in the recesses of the alley, hoping that he would be near enough to listen in on the two men.

As the time for the meeting grew nigh, Ethiere found himself longing for the roof. The building tops just felt safer – more open. The alleyway was narrow, crowded and confining. While he was confident in his hiding spot among a series of discarded crates, the pressing walls taunted and tested his resolve.

Ethiere wasn't sure what he hoped to find on this late night tailing of his employer. He knew it was Kari's incessant urgings that had gotten him this far. Kari had never held much trust in Master Hat, though Ethiere could not say why. When the members of the Gang had begun to disappear, she'd immediately resolved that Hat was the guilty party. Ethiere was following Hat to put an end to Kari's haranguing.

Ethiere intended to find proof. He just did not know if the proof would speak to Hat's innocence or his guilt.

It didn't make sense for Hat to be behind the disappearances. The ranks of experienced, able-bodied thieves in the Gang were diminishing. Master Hat invested hours training each of the children he employed on the street – would he really be complicit in a scheme that deprived him of a resource he'd worked so hard to nurture? Each missing thief was one less set of hands to do a job, to bring in a rich score. Ethiere was confident that nothing in this world was more important to Hat than filling his personal coffers.

Maybe that was what gave him pause. Hat bartered in jewels and trinkets and bottles with strange labels. Would he barter with the lives of the children? Who would possibly find value in an orphaned thief?

Maybe it was the history that fed Ethiere's doubts. People that worked for Master Hat had disappeared in the past. Carl, who had been a surrogate big brother to Ethiere, had been at the supper's table one evening and had disappeared the next. Hat said Carl had cashed out – had opted to seek his fortune abroad. But Carl had never said anything to Ethiere. Wouldn't he have? Wouldn't he have at least said goodbye?

Hat shifted his weight to his left foot as he waited. The other man was running late, which was odd. He'd been the first to arrive on the previous nights. Did this mean something had happened? A thief learns to despise the unexpected. This new factor only seemed to embolden the voice in the back of Ethiere's head that was telling him to abort. But he couldn't quit now! He couldn't just stand up and leave the alley – not without Hat seeing! No he was stuck – he'd have to see this through.

He was stuck. The constricting walls of the alley rejoiced in echoing the thought.

Ethiere wasn't sure how long Master Hat might choose to wait ...

Like a viper, a strong hand caught hold of Ethiere's neck from behind and threw him out towards the head of the alley. The thief's legs and feet, intertwined as they were with the wooden crates, brought a shower of splintering wood as he landed on the Hollingston pavers. Shocked as he was, Ethiere was quickly to his hands and knees, his eyes seeking for handholds ...

The strong hand clamped down around his shoulder and Ethiere was dragged towards the watching Master Hat. The young thief looked up at his captor. It was the other man – the man Master Hat had been meeting with. Ethiere's mind puzzled over that. Perhaps the man had not been late ... perhaps he had been extremely early ...

Ethiere was deposited, with a forceful push, at Hat's feet. "I take it he's one of yours?"

Hat was looking down upon him, disappointment evident in his frown. "Should I ask what you were doing here, Ethiere?"

The thief swallowed. "I wanted to see where you went." Ethiere saw a silent exchange happen between the two men that stood over him. He couldn't read the expression of either, but disturbingly, the bottle-buying stranger had his hand on the hilt of his weapon. Ethiere wondered if he should say more. Certainly it wouldn't be wise to bring up Kari's suspicions – not when they might be unfounded. Should he concoct a lie? What was the answer the men wanted to hear?

Ethiere's ears picked up on the sound of steel sliding from a sheath and his heart quickened – until Master Hat raised a hand in pardon. "It's alright," he told the other man. "I'm sure he meant no harm in it. Master Rice – this is Ethiere. He is my deputy and one of the finest thieves in my employ. Ethiere, I would like you to meet Master Rice. Master Rice is one of our important contacts, so it is good that you two be introduced. Master Rice is an unofficial representative of the House of Northing."

Ethiere wasn't certain that Rice had abandoned his design of skewering him with the sword. He was Northing's man? What interest could wealthy nobles like the Northings have in simple street thieves?

"Those Master Rice represent have a keen need for alchemy solutions – hence all of our recent raids on the city's apothecists." Hat nudged the box towards Rice with his foot.

"Is it all there?" asked Rice.

"Everything but the full order of verisene oxide – I promise you Rice, we've stripped Hollingston of every drop of it. Your employer may have to consider placing a legitimate order for the chemical with the shippers as it seems your demand far outstrips our apothecaries' standard supply."

Rice frowned through the news. Finally taking his hand fully away from his sword's hilt, he reached into his coat and brought forth a large bag that bulged with coins. *"Payment as promised. You'll find a new list of requests with their associated reward in the bag."*

Hat nodded as he untied the drawstring to admire the money. He paused his revelry with a revelation. *"But this is too much – what with the unfilled order for the verisene."* Hat began to draw golden coins from the bag, counting under his breath.

"Hat," Rice said, calling for attention. Master Hat looked up. *"We'll put what's extra towards something ... else."* There was something again exchanged in the glance that completely escaped Ethiere. It was clear, however, that Hat understood the request. He looked to Ethiere, his glee over the money suddenly subdued.

"I see."

"The standard rate ... "

"I'll arrange it," Hat said quickly, cutting Rice off. Northing's man wasn't bothered by the interruption. He nodded and bent to pick up the box of bottles. As he lowered, his eyes drew level with Ethiere's. The young thief was distinctly impressed that Rice still would have preferred to see him dead. Ethiere didn't exhale until Rice disappeared into the Hollingston shadows.

As he picked himself off the ground, Ethiere was left under the disapproving gaze of Master Hat. *"Did you learn anything tonight?"*

Ethiere had. He would have died on Rice's sword had Master Hat not intervened. He should have realized what little good could have come from spying on Hat. This was Fate sending him a warning. This was the *consequence for trying to turn an outcome rather than just accept what life doled out. This was the punishment that could be expected for any little leaf bold enough to think he could turn the course of the great River.*

"I've learned that asking questions is dangerous," he replied – an answer which seemed to satisfy Hat.

Despite the earnestness of his answer, Ethiere couldn't help himself. As he and Hat walked back to the lair, dangerous questions continued to roll around in the thief's mind. Ethiere tried to chase them from his mind. He was better off not knowing what Rice was having Hat arrange.

--- * --- * ---

He should have been able to fit the pieces together. He should have been able to divine the clues. The Arcans had needed people to experiment on for Northing. Northing had gone to Rice for the unscrupulous task. Rice had gone to Hat. And the children of the Gang had been taken, one by one.

The Arcans had carried out an atrocity.

Hat had sold children for gold.

But Ethiere had committed the greatest travesty of all of them. He'd simply done nothing.

Ethiere knew he'd led a hard life. Circumstances always seemed to be aligned against him. But as he sat and he waited, he grew more and more appalled at his malaise, of his inactivity, of his unwillingness to struggle. Accepting that bad things happen is one thing – allowing that acceptance to wear down your resolve to seek for better things, was an entirely different matter.

Life might be a river. Drowning might be in the cards. But Ethiere was no leaf. He was not some lifeless object, unable to think, unable to choose. The current might carry him in a direction, but that current would not keep him from navigating a course of his choosing.

It was irony. The Banding had plucked him from his life and forcibly compelled him into peril – and in so doing had opened his eyes to his freedom. And his responsibility.

At the gates below, a wagon rolled into Hollingston, the bearded driver coaxing the horses through the heavier foot traffic. Ethiere recognized Physician Davies

– and felt comfortable guessing the identities of the three men riding in the back. The first was the only one of the three to have his head uncovered – he was the youngest of Reed's men. The second stayed huddled in a large blanket – that would be Kashif, unwilling to expose his dark skin to the prejudices it would no doubt arise. The last, lying prone, would be the injured Billick.

Two accounted for.

A few minutes later, two men entered, leading a line of horses. On the back of the first sat a woman. Despite the efforts Reed and his blunt crossbowman made at blending into the crowd, Lady Greer stood out. The woman apparently was not capable of sitting on a horse without looking the part of nobility.

That made three.

Finally, following a ten-count behind, was the last of Reed's men, the balding one. His right hand was joined with Sarah's, his left gently guiding the shoulders of the boy in the large brown coat.

Four and five.

The Band was all present. Everyone was accounted for. But Ethiere let them pass, let them continue down the street. He'd need to rejoin them. The magic of the Banding would force him to eventually. But the thief sat, and waited. This was a time for patience.

After Sarah and Dom disappeared into the city, a shadowy figure emerged from the alleyway across the street. There was nothing remarkable about the way the man dressed, there was nothing the man did to draw attention to himself. The man mingled into the flow of citizens on the walks and began an unhurried stroll in the Band's wake. To a casual observer, it would have looked like coincidence.

But it was exactly what Ethiere had expected to see.

As the thief began to trail the man, Ethiere smiled at his small victory. Tonight, he'd arrived even earlier than Master Rice had anticipated.

50.

The inn was called the Crescent Head; it appeared the innkeeper intended no one to forget it. The waning moon insignia swinging from the street-placard was carved into the tables and the chair-backs – Reed even saw it on the bottoms of the wooden mugs when the patrons took a draught. It actually surprised him not to see the moon tattooed onto the innkeeper's broad forehead.

At the moment, the man was happily tabulating figures. "Five rooms, you said?"

"Five rooms, meals, and privacy," Reed directed. The last brought up a curious eyebrow from the keeper. "No questions, no trouble," the Captain restated. Reed could almost see the keeper's imagination rolling as it wrestled the cryptic statement. The soldier had no intention of making it less cryptic.

The innkeeper would get no clues from how Reed was currently dressed. Though Northing's men had not lain in wait in Alben, Kashif still mulishly clung to his claim that the Lord Baron would attempt to destroy the Band. As a precaution, Reed had sent Davies to purchase workman's garb from the small communities they passed as they neared Hollingston. It was strange, being out of uniform. Captain Reed hardly felt like himself.

Lady Greer had smiled at his discomfort. She'd made it a game of pointing out each time he tugged at the collar of his shirt. It had taken all of Reed's professional resolve to not call to attention every piece of lint she plucked from the well-worn cotton blouse Davies' had bartered for her.

As strange as it was for Reed to be out of uniform, it was even stranger for him seeing Lady Greer out of hers. No fine dress, no visible jewelry. She'd pulled her hair up and tied it off with a ribbon – something so simple yet so far beneath her class. Lady Greer's disguise made Reed's job more difficult. The Lady looked like a commoner. She looked approachable like a commoner. Reed had to focus to remind himself who she really was, and how she really should be treated.

"You make me wonder just who it is I'm letting these rooms too …" At Reed's frown, the innkeeper threw up his hands in defense. "Wasn't a question, sir. Just an observation." He slid the keys towards the soldier. "All five rooms are on the third floor. Welcome to the Crescent Head."

Reed scooped the thin bronze keys from the counter and headed back towards the entrance. He opened the door to signal Sergeant Bostitch, and turned to survey the common room once more. There was a slow moving game of Tens at one of the tables, a trio drinking at another and two men carrying on a friendly, yet animated, debate at a third. As he expected, everyone's eyes went to the door as the party began to filter through.

Bost came first, leading Lady Greer. Reed felt a sudden pang of embarrassment subjecting the Lady to the ogling of the men in common room. What would he do if one of them were to leer? To make an inappropriate remark? Didn't he have an obligation to defend her honor? Would she want him to defend her honor?

Surely there were better inns than the Crescent Head – something more befitting those of Lady Greer's station. Traditionally, the Cahills wouldn't have deigned to sleep anywhere but in the guest rooms of Lord Northing's manor. Thankfully, Lady Greer hadn't voiced a word of complaint at his choice.

The Crescent Head might not be extravagant, but it had good sightlines out the windows and from the stair-landings. The doors to each of the rooms came with a distinct key-lock, and if worse came to worse, there was only a single entryway he'd have to defend. With his force whittled down to him and his three remaining men, Captain Reed was willing to take every advantage he could get.

Reed slipped the keys to Bostitch. "Find the best room," he instructed, knowing the soldier would understand what he meant. Reed didn't care if Lady Greer got the smallest room – so long as Bost thought it the easiest to defend.

The children came next – a distrustful Dom in his baggy brown coat and an unsettlingly quiet Sarah – followed by Neald and Sperry supporting a still-wobbly Billick. On spying a table, the murderer pushed away from the soldiers and landed heavily into one of the chairs. Sperry looked to Reed for direction, and Reed just shrugged. He returned to watching the innkeeper, who swallowed the question waiting to spring from his tongue. Reed folded his arms. Now came the test.

Kashif, heavy pack slung over one shoulder, entered with the Physician Davies. There was an immediate flood of disgust coming from those in the common room; one of the drunks offered a slur. The innkeeper voiced the concerns they all shared. "You didn't say anything about *his* kind staying here!"

Reed nodded as he followed the Arcan to the stairs. "Another good observation."

51.

Sarah was certain the small room would have quickly lost its charm anyway. It was boxy, dominated by a double-bed against one of the walls. A small circular mirror hung across from the bed, tacked a head higher than would allow Sarah to see her reflection. The only other piece of furniture was a short bureau of drawers with a tarnished brass vase – devoid of flowers – sitting atop it.

Nothing in the room would have kept her entertained for long, and Neald's words as he shut the door sealed their fate. "Stay up here," he warned sternly. Three words – and the room became unbearably confining.

It was as if she'd never left home. After the hurricane of events of the last few days, Sarah was right back in Hollingston, right back in an upstairs room with a single window out to the world. Everything was different; nothing had changed.

Sarah walked over to the darkened sill and stared out. She knew it was incredibly unlikely, but she still watched the shadows just in case a stealthy thief darted by. She missed Ethiere. She felt so bad for him – to have Dom accuse him for a crime he'd never even thought of committing. Sarah hoped he was okay. She hoped that he'd survived Alben. She hoped that he'd come back.

She worked the thin rod from the window lock and raised the window a finger's width. It was a small, silly gesture, but Sarah thought it appropriate for a small, silly girl. She'd leave it open for Ethiere. It would be just one additional means by which he could return to her life, if he so chose.

Behind her, she heard Dom move towards the door. She watched as he cracked it open enough to peer out into the hallway. Satisfied, he opened it wider and stepped out.

"Where are you going?" she whispered anxiously. Ethiere leaving was one thing. He was a street-thief – he wasn't likely to stay put. But Dom? Quiet Dom? Sarah suddenly felt very alone. She'd spent far too many days of solitude in an upstairs room to want any more of them. "We were told to stay here!"

"He said to stay *up here*," Dom clarified, "not *in here*. I'm going to go sit at the top of the landing." Sarah wasn't sure that the landing would offer anything better than the room did – but then she remembered! Dom grew up in a tavern – which was close enough to an inn, right? If anyone knew where to go, he would.

As she followed him out, she wondered if Dom was enjoying his almost-homecoming more than she was hers.

The landing proved to be far more exciting than the room. There were a few railings at the top, perfect for covertly peeking through. Below them, displayed in lively lamplight, was the common room. Sarah smiled – this was much better than a glass-paned window! From the landing, she could hear the buzz of the conversation, the jingle of coins, the hollow thud of emptied wooden steins. If she concentrated, she could even make out individual sentences.

She sat and listened, smiled at the jokes and was swayed by the arguments … and could not help thinking of her father. The men with their mugs, and their careful stacks of coins; their cards and the serious way that they studied them – her father had never sat at one of those tables. He'd never been able to squander an evening swapping stories and chasing down exaggerations with foam-headed drinks. He'd never been among people like these – because he was always with her. He was always at home.

She'd always chaffed at being confined to the house – how many times had he chaffed at being chained to her?

The questions revived her sadness. Her father was a great man, a wonderful man. What had he done to deserve a broken, imperfect daughter? How could he continue to come home to her, after the heartaches she'd subjected him to? Her illness had driven her mother away. Her illness had caused him to spend his money on worthless cure-alls. Her illness had put the worry in his eyes and the grief in his tired smile.

It wasn't right; it wasn't fair. Not any of it. He was a good, good man – too good to have had to face a burden like her. How much should he have to sacrifice? What more could Merciful Domus ask of him?

But then – isn't that why she'd been Banded? Isn't that why she was an ill-fitting part in this group? So she could die. Wasn't it all just Merciful Domus finally granting peace to a man who deserved it?

Sarah didn't realize she was crying until she noticed the tiny pools forming on the landing below her. She wiped at her eyes, which drew Dom's attention away from the games he had been watching. She ducked her eyes, as to not to have to meet his gaze.

"Want to go back to the room?" he asked her.

She shook her head.

"Want to talk about what's making you so sad?"

She waited until she was sure of her voice before responding. She'd tried to make it sound jesting. "I talked to you all about this already, Dom."

"Back in Alben?"

"Yes. When you were drugged."

"I think I remember." Sarah looked at the boy, wondering if it could be true. Dom had been so vacant – he'd not responded to a single thing she'd said that evening. Was it possible that he'd still been listening? Was it possible that he'd been able to understand?

"I'm sad for my father," she told him. "I'm sad he ever had to have me as part of his life."

His response was disappointingly short.

"Oh."

She waited for more, before remembering it was Dom she was talking to. Was she really expecting Dom to give a long, comforting speech? The boy made it a point to not talk. She remembered the first time they'd met, riding in the back of her father's wagon on the way to the fountain. How she'd blathered on! How had she not seen how annoying she must be to other people? No sooner out of the presence of her father than she was already making life more miserable for her fellow Banded.

"Can I tell you a secret?"

Sarah's eyes raised to meet Dom's. She found herself without a response. The offer was so completely unlike anything she would have expected Dom to ever say. Wizard Hartley had mentioned a secret – something Dom would have surely shared with his best friend. Dom's offer alone meant more to Sarah than anything that he could have said afterward. She nodded.

He started slow, his mind working to gain footing on the topic it was trying to tackle. Sarah stayed silent, giving him the time he needed. "A few years back … I started being able to see how other people felt inside." The boy sunk into his coat, almost as if he intended to hide from his own admissions. "Wizard Hartley thought it was magic. My mother thought it was a gift. My father thought it was the windfall Fate owed him. I've always thought of it as a curse."

"You see how people feel?" Sarah prodded.

Dom smiled behind his lapels. "You'd be surprised at how practiced people are at smiling and laughing on the outside despite the terrible sadness they feel on the inside. The whole world feels so much, Sarah, and everyone is determined not to let any of it show to anybody else."

"What does it look like?"

"Colors." It was another decidedly brief and altogether disappointing answer. Dom shrugged. "I can't explain it better than that – I'm sorry. I just can look at the colors and I understand what they mean. I actually can almost feel exactly what that person is feeling."

Sarah tried to picture it. What would it be like to see into people's hearts? It certainly would have made all of her days watching out the upstairs window more entertaining! Not only could she have made up stories about who people were and where they were going – she could have layered her stories with how they were feeling.

"I saw your father's emotions once."

Dom's words jarred Sarah from her imaginative world.

"It's why I'm telling you this – why I'm trusting you with my secret. Back when we'd just arrived at the fountain – when you were getting out of the wagon, I saw what he was feeling."

Sarah felt her hands shake as she nodded. She knew what she expected to hear, but knew she had to hear it.

"He was really worried about you – but I expect you already knew that."

"He's always worried about me."

"There was love too," Dom added. "He really loves you, Sarah. There was no mistaking it." She stayed silent, wondering if he wasn't just trying to tell her what he thought she wanted to hear. She didn't doubt her father's love, she just hated the burden it had to bear. "You know what I didn't see?"

She swallowed. "What?"

"Regret."

Sarah ran the back of her arm across her teary cheeks once more. "You're sure?"

"Not a trace," Dom assured her. "You might be sorry you are a part of his life – but he wasn't." Dom went back to watching the card games below. Sarah leaned her head against the railing in front of her, pondering the boy's words. Could they be true? Surely Dom wouldn't lie to her about this!

"Really, no regret? You're not just saying it to make me feel better?"

"You lucked out, having a father like that," Dom answered. "I distinctly remember what I saw in his heart as he helped you down from the wagon. Distinctly. I remember it because the emotions I saw in your father's heart aren't something I've ever seen in mine."

52.

The bed groaned when she sat on it – and Reed apologized.

Again.

It seemed to be the twentieth time the soldier had apologized for the nature of her accommodations – which Greer found odd. In sequence, she'd spent the last few nights upright in a carriage, sleeping in a barn, in a bed commandeered from an Alben councilman, and awake roadside after fleeing the monster's attack. The room the Crescent Head offered was better than that entire lot – and yet the stalwart Captain hadn't apologized as profusely for any of those.

Perhaps – Greer reasoned – every time previous, Reed had managed to provide the absolute best accommodations given their circumstances. Now, for the first time in their journey Reed was knowingly holding her below what her station demanded. There were nobles in Hollingston – not just the Northings – with manors with hallways full of guest rooms held in-the-ready just in case someone like a Lord Baron's daughter was in the vicinity.

"Sounds like slack in the ropes," Reed said. "I'll see if the innkeeper can send someone up to …"

"Its fine, Reed," she said wearily. She was tired, which was a bit strange. The Banding had taken the edge off of hunger and had diminished her need for sleep – but with the last few nights, the strain was building. She was tired, and ready for a night of peace. Reed shifted uncomfortably – she could see he was still stewing on it. "Let it go."

"As you wish, Lady Greer," he said.   Would the creaking ropes bother her? Perhaps they would. Would the beds in the noblemen's guest rooms creak? Most definitely not! But to stay with them would mean being Lady Greer again and having to act within the rigid guidelines of her formal role. She'd much rather have a creaky bed and one more night of freedom.

A light knock sounded on the door. "That would be supper, I suppose," he said as he unlocked the door and opened it a crack. His assumptions confirmed, he stepped aside to let the serving girl in. "You can set it on the bureau," Reed instructed her – albeit there was simply nowhere else she could have set the tray. The food, steaming on the plate, smelled delicious, but Greer's attention was drawn to the girl.

Greer felt compelled to study her hands.

The serving girl couldn't help but note the scrutiny she was under, and blushed humbly. She set the tray down, and stole a brief glance into Greer's eyes. "Will there be anything else?" she asked.

--- * --- * ---

Putting the plan together took longer than she anticipated. Bridgette had always been the schemer – she'd had the connections among the manor staff. But with persistence, Greer had done it. And today, as the plan fell into place, it felt wonderful. Tobias, the stablemaster's son, had accepted her lucrative bribe to alter the route of their ride today, and Sophie, as new as she was to the routines of her lady, was only barely catching on.

"Have we ridden here before, my Lady?" Sophie asked with a discordant mix of blissful concern.

"We have a guide," Greer answered her.

Sophie tried again. "But ... yes ... but ..."

By the time they reached the village, Sophie had to know her suspicions to be correct – and also that Greer wasn't going to listen to them. It was time to enact the second phase of the plot. "Oh dear," Greer muttered.

"My lady?" Tobias answered on queue. "Is something the matter?"

"It's my bracelet – it's gone missing!" Indeed, the bracelet was no longer on her wrist – and truthfully it hadn't been all morning. It was safely tucked away in Tobias' saddle bag – ready for him to 'find' when the time arrived. Sophie looked leery. *"It's my favorite bracelet – the pearl one I admire so much ..."*

"We should look for it then," suggested Tobias.

"Yes, you two should go ..." Greer suggested.

"Just us two?" Sophie questioned. "What about you, my Lady?"

Greer had anticipated such a concern. *"I'm feeling sun-weary from the riding. I would prefer to stay here, in the shade."* She continued before Sophie could volunteer to stay. *"You should go with Tobias, though. He doesn't know what he's looking for."*

Tobias shook his head dutifully. "Not a jewelry man, I'm afraid."

"I shouldn't leave your side ..." Sophie argued.

"Sophie ..."

"Your father would be upset ..."

Greer stomped her foot, which got the girl's attention. *"I'll be upset!"* she declared.

And that was all it took to get freedom from the companion girl. She couldn't imagine doing this with Sophie in tow. No, there were things that she was glad to keep from the spying eyes and ears of the companion. The village wasn't large; the small tavern it boasted was it's one and only. Greer felt a tingle of excitement well up in her stomach. Her father would erupt if he knew she was visiting such a place ...

The air inside the tavern was stale, the lighting poor despite the full sun outside. The place was near deserted – and yet, with it not being a dining hour that could only be expected. The only other person in the room with her was a tall girl that was clearing off the dirty tables. Greer moved forward, intending to ask the girl a question, before she realized ...

It was Bridgette.

Yes, it was Bridgette – but not exactly. The golden blonde hair that had shone with vibrant radiance fell limply and lifeless around Bridgette's shoulders. The companion had always carried herself with a royal air, but now? She moved as one weighed down, as one defeated. The simple linen blouse and skirt she wore was of lower quality than those worn by the servants in the manor.

It was Bridgette – but with all exuberance sapped out of her.

Her former companion saw her and stood frozen three paces away.

Greer was struck speechless. For all of her planning – for all the thought she'd invested in finding Bridgette – Greer hadn't considered what she was going to say. Which wasn't odd, she'd never had to work to know what to say to her friend. They'd always just ... talked.

But now?

"I came to find you ..." she tried.

The words seemed to wake Bridgette from her trance. She quickly moved to the cluttered table and began clearing away the dishes. "You shouldn't have." The terse, almost angry response put Greer on edge, and she didn't know how to respond. Bridgette looked up from the table. "You should leave."

Leave? She'd just arrived. She'd just spent weeks tracking her down and she was just supposed to leave? "No," she whispered to herself, and then repeated more forcefully. "No! You leave without a word – without a goodbye – and ..." The anger in her voice surprised her. "I demand you tell me what happened!"

Bridgette's lip curled into a belligerent smile. "Demand?" She stacked the last plate atop the others. "I don't take orders from you anymore."

"Orders? I never gave you orders! You were my friend ..." She was. Bridgette was her friend.

Wasn't she?

Greer swallowed her emotions with the lump in her throat. "Why did you leave?"

Bridgette braced both hands on the table and shook her head. "You don't get it, do you? You think this was my choice?" She grabbed a fork, slammed it into the stack of plates, and then held up her hands as if putting them on display. What Greer saw both saddened and horrified her. Bridgette's hands were calloused and cracked – they were near bleeding. "Do you honestly – honestly! – think I chose this!"

Greer shook her head. "Then why?"

"Your father sent me away."

"Why would he do that? You're my companion?"

Bridgette tossed her hands in the air in disbelief. "Don't be stupid, Greer! Owen Northing! Owen Northing is the reason I've been banished to a kitchen in this speck of a town!" Bridgette's mouth twisted with bitterness. "What did you say to him? You must have said something! He knew! He knew something that happened – something between me and Owen – he knew it! What did you tell him? When you ran out – what did you say?!"

Greer's mind dug into the memory – the shock at seeing the boys in the manor, discovering Caleb wasn't some fascinating country boy, but the companion to the heir of the Northing estates. She remembered her disgust as Owen had continued with his feigned interest – and how she'd slighted him. How she'd run from the room, her father trailing behind her, demanding she return and walk the gardens with the Lordling.

Her words welled up in her ears, a ringing echo: If you are so insistent he see our gardens, Father – you should have Bridgette show him.

Greer felt her insides grow cold; the guilt rushing like ice water through her veins. She was responsible. The dried and cracked hands – she was responsible. "I'm ... sorry ... I ... "

"Sorry!" Bridgette screamed at her. "You're sorry? What good does sorry do me, Greer? Does sorry get me my old life back? Does sorry get me away from here – out of this kitchen? Does it free me from the tired feet, and the sore back, and the endless stack of dishes!?" The blonde woman paused, daring her to

319

answer. When she didn't, Bridgette scowled in frustration and with single sweep of her arm knocked the utensils to the floor in a clattering cacophony. "How is this fair?" she demanded. "Tell me – how is this fair?!"

"Bridgette ..."

"Why do you get to be the nobleman's daughter? What did you do to deserve your status? How is it fair? You've always despised it – the life, the expectations. You've always bucked against what your station requires of you. Admit it, Greer – you are completely ill-suited to be nobility."

Greer felt the cold inside intensify – but no longer with guilt. Bridgette's tirade was shocking – no one spoke to her like that. No one. Greer was awash with icy indignation. "Stop talking ..."

But Bridgette wasn't done. "Do you know what I think, Greer? Do you want to know?"

"Stop it!"

"The day when your father banished me from the manor – when he told me my services were no longer needed ... do you know what I saw?"

"Stop!"

Bridgette was crying, but her face was a mask of hatred. "I know he looked at me, and I know that when he looked at me, he wondering why, oh why, couldn't I have been his daughter!"

Her hand acted of its own accord, violently swinging upward as her open palm crashed into Bridgette's cheek. The former companion cringed at the sting of the blow, but defiantly stood her ground. There was a singular moment of silence, before Greer, not knowing what else there was to do, what else there was to say, turned and hastily moved towards the tavern door.

Bridgette was her friend – but not anymore. She didn't know exactly what she'd expected to find – but she saw there was nothing to be salvaged.

"It should have been me, Greer!" Bridgette yelled at her retreat. "He wishes you were me!"

The door closed, providing a barrier that effectively cut off Bridgette's biting words. Greer didn't doubt the vicious verbal assault was continuing on, that

Bridgette still screamed at her. They were hurtful words – but only because Greer believed they were completely true.

How much easier would her father's political maneuverings have been if he had a beauty like Bridgette to barter with? How many Owen Northings would be lining up at the manor gate? How many times had he supped with her and Bridgette at his table and wondered why fate hadn't blessed him with a better daughter.

Sophie and Tobias were milling around by the bridge, still engaged in the futile efforts of finding the bracelet. The guide must have seen the storm in her eyes, and wordlessly went to checking the saddle straps. Sophie saw it too. "Lady Greer?"

And it dawned on her. Her father's act was two-fold – not only banishing Bridgette, but employing Sophie. He'd removed the glamorous girl his daughter could not compete with, and replaced her with a girl Greer couldn't help but outshine. And seeing Sophie – and seeing how much she detested in her new companion – Greer felt her heart break anew.

If this was indeed the girl her father thought her better than, his opinion of her was lower than she'd ever imagined.

--- * --- * ---

"My lady?" the serving girl attempted, and looked to Reed for further direction.

"No, that will be all," Greer managed. The serving girl bobbed a curtsey and made a hasty exit from the room. After locking the door behind her, the Captain moved to examine what had been brought on the tray. He scooted the vegetables around on the plate with the fork, before looking up to her.

She felt the ire rising, and cut Reed off the moment she saw his mouth open. "Don't do it, Reed. Don't make an apology for it, do you hear me!"

He was taken aback by her sudden outburst. "I'm … sorry, Lady Greer … it's just …"

"No, Reed! I don't want to hear it! I don't want to know if the pork is undercooked or the vegetables mushy or the bread stale … I don't want to hear

about it! And I don't want to hear about how beneath me it all is – the food, the room, anything! Alright!?"

"Yes, my Lady," Reed hurried to agree.

His attempts to appease her were only making it worse. "And stop calling me that! Stop being so boiling deferential! Stop coddling me! Stop with the formality and cordiality! It's just me and you in this room, Reed. Me and you. Stop talking to my station, Reed! Boil you, talk to me – not my title!"

Wisely, Reed kept his mouth closed.

Greer steadied herself, calmed herself. "If you are going to stay here while I eat, Reed, then I want you talk to me like you would anyone else. Any of your soldiers. Any of the other Banded. I want you to call me by my name! Just my name!"

The soldier lowered his eyes. "I … I can't …

"Reed!" Greer was surprised at the tinge of desperation she heard in her own demand. She was surprised that Captain Reed's compliance held so much importance. Why should it? He was, after all, just a soldier. But her heart betrayed her, even in the midst of that thought. The events of the past few days – she'd seen a different side of the Captain. She'd seen his sacrifice, his compassion, his kindness and determination. Even more so, Greer realized she'd seen past the *Captain*. She'd seen *Reed*. It was not the title that impressed her, but the man that held it.

She yearned for him to see her in the same light.

He flinched. "I'm sorry, my Lady … but, you are the daughter of my Lord Baron …"

Greer bowed her head – and looked at her hands. Her soft, perfect hands. "Maybe I shouldn't have been."

53.

Marooke focused on the work at hand, ignoring the door to the laboratory as it opened. Djemal had returned with the girl four hours ago and the scientist had wasted no time in running his experiments. Several samples of the girl's blood were spread before him, each being worked on by a specific chemical compound. The Lord Baron hovered over his shoulder, but Marooke continued to work. He assumed Northing would speak to him when he was inclined to.

The assumption was correct. "Your conclusions?"

"Are still very raw," Marooke answered. He cast a wide glance over the spread before him. "But all in all, the preliminary results are encouraging."

"A cure?"

Marooke lifted a vial to take a measurement. "Not exactly," he clarified. "The demon – it is bonded to the girl's blood. The two have entered a symbiotic relationship. The demon is keeping her alive, using her as a host during its periods of inactivity." He gave Northing a moment to digest the summary before asking his question. "Do you accept this finding as a success, Lord Baron? Does the rejuvenation provided by the demon qualify as the cure you commissioned me to seek?"

The most powerful man in Tollia considered his answer in silence. He wondered if Northing wasn't thinking about his wife stuck in her wooden box. Marooke filled the time transcribing new notes into the ledger. "When can a treatment be prepared?"

Marooke quelled the bubble of excitement in his stomach. There were still tests to run – still facts to check – but everything pointed to success. "By tomorrow afternoon."

Northing did not offer commentary on the forecast. He instead changed the subject. "I just received word that the Band of Six just entered the city limits," Lord Northing said.

The news was not surprising. They'd both known the Banding magic would draw the pitiable party back to Hollingston. It was why the Lord Baron had felt no urgency in hunting the Band down in the Alben valley. Why go to such an effort when the Band would inevitably be forced to your front gate?

"Have you given the order to have them eliminated?" Marooke asked.

Lord Northing found humor in the statement. "Do they really worry you?" he asked. "All accounts say that this demon tore through a rank of Lord Baron Cahill's men and shredded the wizard they'd brought along. If steel and magic are so ineffective against the creature, what really do we have to fear?" The nobleman lifted one of the samples that fizzed within its vial, fingering it curiously before setting it down again. "Eliminate them? I see no reason to hurry. If we destroy this Band, another will be assembled to take its place. And another, and another ..."

"I do not fear the next incarnation of this Band," Marooke answered. "I fear this one." He lifted his eyes from his compounds and vials to address the Lord Baron directly. "If steel and magic have no effect against the demon – it would appear it can only be beaten by one thing …"

"And that is?"

"Intelligence." Lord Northing's reaction showed it was not an answer he agreed with. "These Bands – as it has been explained to me – are formulated with the design to complete their mission. My apprentice, Kashif, has more than likely faced this creature once. He may have already had an opportunity to study the girl. He may already have a sample of her blood. I have no doubt that he will subject it to the same methodical tests that I am. He is brilliant; I trained him to be. If anyone can find a weakness – a way to destroy what we've created – it will be him."

Northing spread his arms. "Without a lab? Without your fine instruments? Without the vast amount of resources I've lent you in your study?"

The Lord Baron's incredulity didn't sway Marooke in the slightest. "As I said, he is *my* apprentice." The statement said everything that needed to be said on Kashif's qualifications. "He needs to be dealt with."

"Then I will have it arranged," the nobleman answered."

54.

Two steins sat before Billick on the table. The first was merely water; a request the serving girl had found odd. Nobody ordered water – not with all of the other brews and draughts on tap. But he could still feel trace effects of whatever the Arcan was drugging him with lingering in his system, and he was doing his best to flush it out. The other stein held hard ale. As much as he wished to be rid of the Arcan's serum, the more it ebbed, the more the pain returned. Ale was a secret from his battlefield days – and he drank just enough to keep the edge off.

He had the table to himself – just as he preferred it. Bostitch and Neald had come down awhile back, had eyed the open seats at his table, and had taken a different one to eat their meal. Billick downed what remained of the water in a single swallow. Catching the eye of the serving girl, he waggled the stein. She was promptly at his side.

"Another, good sir?" she asked.

A familiar voice sounded in his ear. "Make it two." Hennessey slipped into the chair at his side, smiling widely. "Hello, Billick." The serving girl, sensing the dynamic in the air, hovered at the table only a moment more before escaping to the kitchen.

Billick waited for her to disappear behind the swinging door. "What do you want?"

Hennessey feigned disappointment. "No hello for an old friend? Especially after all this effort to track you down!" Billick doubted the contractor had gone to any great lengths; the comment was more Hennessey patting his own back for having such a widespread network of informants. Hennessey's eyes narrowed. "What happened to your face?"

"I asked – what do you want?"

The other man would not stop smiling his disarming, disingenuous smile. "I've been worried about you. Ever since that night – you running out of the room – right in the middle of a negotiation, of all things! Hardly a word, no explanation … Our esteemed client was rather put off by that little display." The smile slipped. "People don't walk out on Northings, Billick. If you had to choose a family to walk out on …"

"It wasn't by choice."

Hennessey raised his hands in calming reassurance. "Of course, of course … and I know that now. Rumors started day before last about the forming of a new Band of Six, and it became apparent what had happened to you. Have to admit – did get a laugh of it though! You – Banded? A man of many lethal skills, to be certain, but not my first choice to help save the world!"

The serving girl returned from the kitchen bearing a stein in each hand. She slipped alongside the table, depositing one in front of each man. Hennessey saluted her with his, and she blushed as she scurried away. "Janns needs new serving girls. Those at the Eight have been there long enough that they won't look me in the eyes anymore." He shook off the thought. "But that's a different matter. You look awful, Billick."

His chest throbbed at the reminder. "I'm fine," he said tersely.

"Of course you are!" Hennessey chirped. "What's this compared to Arca, right? Nothing stops Billick – it's a quality I've always appreciated about you,. Your resilience – your grit. It's your tenacity that makes you so dangerous." The contractor laughed and took a sip from the stein – and frowned. "What is this? Water?" He looked suspiciously to the other man. "You're drinking water now?" He slid the mug away and wiped at his chin. "Where was I?"

"Tenacity …"

"Ah, yes. One of your better qualities. You commit to something … you aren't letting up until you've met it. Makes you reliable to do business with." Hennessey leaned in closer. "You're still reliable, aren't you Billick? Still just as resilient?"

"Why?"

The contractor shrugged. "Have to ask the questions, you know. I've always felt I've had a decent read on you, Billick. Ever since Arca, I've known the measure of your character – and look how that's served us. You and I have done very well together in our joint ventures … am I right?" His eyes were fiercely alert. "But sometimes people change. They get changed by unusual circumstances. I wanted to check in on you, as a courtesy …"

"To protect your business interests," Billick deciphered.

Hennessey conceded the point. "You are very good at what you do," he pointed out. "But if I'm being honest – I don't like what I'm hearing or seeing. Is it true you've got an Arcan with you? A dark-skinned, Oblivion-begotten Arcan?" Billick glowered to his stein of ale, and Hennessey clicked his tongue. "It's true then! Couldn't believe it – not the Billick I knew! He'd never share a camp with a filthy Arcan, not a chance." The man forced his easy smile again. "He'd never be sitting here drinking water!"

"You're questioning – what? My ability to do a job?"

"No, not ability," Hennessey assured. "Never ability. Only … motivation. Because if you're not up to keeping your commitments …"

"I've never missed on a job," Billick felt to remind him.

"I know."

Billick lifted the ale. There was something different – something that had changed. Was it facing his demise against the faceless creature? His triumph in breaking a little girl? There was something new; he could feel it inside of him. It was vulnerability; and he hated it.

And he hated Hennessey could sense it as well. "Then that should answer your question. A question you should have never asked in the first place."

The conniving man sat back happily. "Good. It's what I wanted to hear. You never missing – it's what I like about you. It's a very good selling point to new clients! And that's where our teamwork comes into play – you and me. I've got it all worked out for you."

Billick downed the ale in a series of gulps. "What do you mean?"

"You remember you're on a job right now, right? The whole matter of young Northing's cheating tavern man?"

Billick froze. "You took the job?"

"I didn't know where you'd gone, you left so quickly," Hennessey offered in defense. "You'd already accepted the contract – the only thing left to work out was the payment details – and you leave those to me anyway. I didn't think you'd be detained by this Banding ..." Hennessey leaned in again. "The delay in fulfillment hasn't gone unnoticed by the Lordling – and it hasn't gone unnoticed by those in our circles, trust me. But don't worry, I've made arrangements."

"How?"

"He'll be coming to you. Here."

"The target?"

"Yes. Tomorrow morning." Billick sat back, soaking in the news, as Hennessey prattled on. "It's actually quite the bit of luck, my friend. Turns out that our cheater has been in quite a heated mood since his boy went missing. No one but his wife to beat on, now that the boy is gone. But he didn't just run – as

it turns out –he was Banded. Oh, how about that? You've been running around with the son of the man you've got an appointment with!"

Dom. It was Dom's father. The welts on the boy's wrists. His nervous nature –
the way he shied away from people. The way he never talked. Dom's father
was responsible for the every horror living in the boy's eyes. Billick rubbed at
his chin. Hennessey enjoyed a laugh with himself. "So I'm having someone
slip to him that his boy was spotted here ... I'm sure if he wasn't tethered to his
tavern he'd come for him tonight ..." The laughter quieted. "You're good for it,
right?" His voice grew serious. "I can count on you, right?"

Billick willed himself to nod. "I'm good for it."

It did nothing to convince either man, but Hennessey stood and smiled anyway.
His words spoke of confidence his voice did not convey. "I'm sure that you
are."

55.

Ethiere surveyed the entrance to the Gang's lair, the apprehension in the pit of
his stomach gaining strength. It was well past the time that Master Hat should
have sent the children out on their assignments. Ethiere had planned to catch
one of the thieves, preferably Kari, and strategize what to do next. She'd been
right all along – Hat was dangerous. Every night with the man was a night that
Ethiere's brothers and sisters were at risk.

But there was no activity. No Kari or anyone else. He didn't know what that
meant.

Had the rest of the Gang already discovered Hat's treachery? Or was Ethiere
too late? What if there was no one left to save from the villain?

When he could bear waiting no longer, Ethiere crept towards the hideout
entrance. He still had Billick's axe, though he had still not worked out if he had
the stomach to do what he knew he needed to. All he could think about was
Billick – and the deadness in the murderer's eyes. Was Ethiere being shown a
specter of his future?

He tightened his grip on the helve. Could the Gang afford him not to act?

Could Ethiere live with himself if he didn't? Would he lose his soul if he did?

He opened the doorway and descended the flight of stairs. The lair was dark and
silent. Despite having grown up in this place, despite knowing the floor boards

and the walls by memory, despite the happy memories with loving friends, the lair felt cold and foreign. With practiced stealth he snuck down the hallway, heading towards the hall where the children slept.

He passed the kitchen along the way and almost didn't see her.

Mother Emiline sat alone on one of the long benches, eyes vacant, skin pale. She kneaded her hands together in her lap, the only visible clue to the woman's inner turmoil. Though she looked at him, her eyes didn't register his presence. She was a ghost, haunted by her memories, broken by the pain of her past life.

"Mother?" Ethiere whispered when he'd neared. "Mother Emiline?" He tried to keep his voice low. If Hat were somewhere in the lair, Ethiere did not want to give up his sole advantage of surprise. "Mother, have you seen any of the other children?"

Mother Emiline blinked rapidly, cognition flashing like lightening in her eyes. She looked at Ethiere, her lips parted as her tongue began to frame a thought. "I had ... a daughter ..." Just that quickly the emptiness returned, her eyes locked on something in the distance, the dialogue dead before any additional words were able to take flight. Ethiere decided there was no use in pressing the poor woman.

He slipped around the corner into the wide hall. The walls of the room were lined with bunks, stacked up to the ceiling three high. The beds were all empty – still no sign of the Gang. Could Master Hat have relocated the group? Moved everyone to a new location? Ethiere could not think of any reason the man would do so. He had no reason to believe he had been discovered. He had no reason to suspect a thief with an axe was coming to seek justice.

Ethiere took the next corner slowly, peering around the edge to assess the small room in the back corner. It was Hat's personal office, where he stored the pilfered items and hoarded the money he collected. Ethiere's stomach jumped to his throat.

Lamplight spilled out of the door that hung slightly ajar. It was the only light to be found in the entire lair.

The axe seemed to soak in the illumination. *Act!* He clenched his teeth against the bitterness of the fear he tasted in his mouth. *Act!* Carl would have acted. Carl had passed the mantle to Ethiere. He was the oldest now. He needed to protect his brothers and sisters. *Act!*

Ethiere swallowed, wishing that he indeed had the stomach full of rocks as Carl had claimed so many nights ago. Indecision still raging, the thief sprang into action, crossing the expanse to the office in quick, soundless steps. Taking one last breath, Ethiere ducked through the opening and into the brightened room …

There was no Master Hat sitting behind his desk, inspecting merchandise or counting out stacks of coins. The flame in the lamp that glowed on the corner of the desk wavered, laughing at the trick it had played on the thief. Ethiere lowered the axe, the surge of intensity fleeing his veins.

He saw the leather pads sticking out from the darkened area behind the desk. As Ethiere moved around the corner, he saw legs, the body – and a second individual. Hannah and Rissa! Two of his sisters in the Gang! Ethiere threw the axe on the desk and knelt beside them. Neither moved – their legs and hands bound by knots, their mouths gagged. They didn't stir at his touch, but there were still alive. He began to work the knots at Hannah's ankles, determined to free her. He'd need them to wake up if they were …

He felt the cord tighten around his neck before his fingers could reach it. He clawed at the cord, knowing it would do little good. Ethiere looked up.

Master Hat was crouched amid the beams in the ceiling, looking down at him. "Isn't it true, what I taught you?" he observed. "No one ever thinks to look up?" Hat jumped from the rafters, the other end of the long garrote wrapped around his wrist. Ethiere's eyes shot towards the axe – a mere lunge away – but he knew he'd not make it. One more firm tug on the rope and Ethiere would be strangled.

"I wondered what had become of you, Ethiere!" Master Hat said. "You just disappeared one night – and I finally could understand how unsettling the other disappearances must have been for you children!" The statement came as a surprise; Ethiere had not expected Hat to admit to what he'd done. Hat smiled. "Oh, I know that doesn't come as any shock. You rushed into my study with a wicked looking axe, Ethiere. You'd have no reason to do so – unless you already knew."

"You sold us to Rice," Ethiere accused against the restriction of the cord at his throat.

"I did. I would have never suspected my little thieves would fetch such a price, nor did I expect that he would demand so many of you!" Hat leaned up against his desk. "Sure, it was nowhere near the price I could fetch for you all later –

once you'd grown. Once you were of age to cash out." Master Hat laughed. "The boys get sold to bondsman on merchant ships, the girls … especially the pretty ones …"

Faces and names ran through Ethiere's memory. Carl! He and the others that had practically raised him under this very roof never got the happy ending all of the children thought awaited them. They never got their piece of Hat's accumulated wealth. They saw servitude, chains … or worse.

Kari!

"But now it is my turn to cash out," Hat said wistfully. "It had to end someday, I guess."

"Where's Kari?"

Master Hat nodded. "Quite the temper on her. She had some choice words for me on the night you vanished – accused me of being behind all of the disappearances. Naturally, I couldn't have that. And Master Rice needed a few new bodies …"

Ethiere's heart sank to his heels. The Arcans! The Arcans had Kari!

"I wish you the best, Ethiere. I really do. I'll be dropping off the girls for Master Rice – I'm sure he'll find a buyer for you as well. It will be an adventure, won't it? What is it you're always talking about – with your river? It's a new current, Ethiere. Isn't that exciting?" Hat's visage fell. "Or would you rather I just kill you now?" The tension of the rope lifted Ethiere to the tips of his toes. "Would you rather just give up and drown?"

Flecks of blackness began to dance in Ethiere's vision; the cord was pulled so tight he could do nothing be sputter. He could hear his heart pulse frantically in his eardrums as his vision began to fail …

The rope went slack and Ethiere collapsed onto the floor. His fingers fought against the cord, desperately seeking to loosen it. It shifted, the ropes relaxing their complex hold, and the loop came free. He coughed, his lungs seeking to satiate his need for air.

Ethiere raised his head.

Master Hat lay dead on the floor before him.

Mother Emiline stood behind him, a bloodied kitchen knife in her limp arms. The woman was pondering the man who she'd stabbed in the back. Her eyes came up and found Ethiere's. There was understanding – a purpose – lost within the emptiness of the void. "He took my children," she murmured. A tear fell from her eyes as she whispered. "I had a daughter once …"

The broken woman dropped the knife and wept. Ethiere, not knowing what else to do, wept with her.

56.

"Whatever was happening appears to be over now," Davies said. He'd spent the last several minutes standing at the doorway, peering curiously out into the hall, as if it would give him any clue to the revelry they'd heard coming from the common room. The noise had been enough of a distraction for Kashif to suggest Davies go have a look, if only to get the unfocused man away from his desk. The physician was useful when he stayed on task, but Kashif wasn't willing to work around him when not.

As strongly as he'd tried to impress the urgency of the situation on the Tollian Physician's mind, it had taken only the slightest bit of shouting to divert his attention.

"Can we close the door then?" Kashif asked. The question discomfited Davies, who offered a tight-lipped smile as an apology as he shut the door. "Come examine this." He removed the magnifiers and held them out. The advanced spectacles had awed the Physician – such technology was unfound among the Tollian men of science.

Davies accepted the magnifiers with delicate reverence, and took a moment to turn them over in his hands before giving his attention back to Kashif. "Start at the lowest magnification and work up to the fifth lens. Lean directly over the sample and focus on the center of what you are examining before switching lenses or risk losing it."

Davies took the instructions, rotating the next lens in sequence as soon as he got his bearing with the last. The Physician took a thoughtful moment to examine the slide before asking. "This is her blood?"

"Yes," Kashif confirmed.

Davies examined the sample again. "What is it you want me to confirm?"

"You should be able to see individual cells ..."

"Yes. I've never seen them with my own eyes before – only depictions during my studies. This is incredible, being able to view them like this!" Davies raised his head and pulled the magnifiers from his eyes. "It has been years since I've seen the diagrams, but those cells appear to be exactly as they should be."

Kashif nodded. "My conclusion as well." He picked up his ledger. "But they shouldn't be."

"No?"

"That specimen has been sitting out since we arrived. It should have oxidized fully by now – yet there is no sign of discoloration. The cells should be dried out and deteriorating, but they continue to thrive." Kashif put the ledger aside. "The demon has altered the Essen to sustain them – there is no other explanation. The Essen is healing the cells – regenerating them. Now look at this."

Davies repositioned the magnifiers and bent over the new sample.

"This sample was mixed with two drops of bosoric acid. Note the break-down of the cells? The Essen fought against the acid, it preserved the cells even as the acid tried to burn them away. In the end, the acid prevailed, but only because the Essen in the sample was exhausted as a resource." The facts were connecting faster now, his mind illuminating. "The girl was dead – I watched her die in Northing's laboratories! This altered Essen must have reanimated her. It explains why the creature feeds. Essen is expended just to keep the host body alive, so the demon is forced to draw additional Essen into the bloodstream."

The Physician paled. "... Merciful Domus ..."

"It's why we can't attack it like flesh and bone. We could hack away at it all we want – the demon would apply the Essen to heal the damage. It could die then – if we could inflict enough injury without it getting an opportunity to replenish its reserves ... but that would never work. Almost everyone has Essen in their bloodstream in some small quantity. Should we attempt to starve the creature, we'd only be forcing it to kill a greater number of people."

"So what then?" Davies pressed. "What can be done against it?"

"The demon heals itself and heals the host. As long as there is Essen …" The Arcan pulled the ledger closer and angrily flipped pages. The answer … he could feel it. It was so close. He couldn't help but wonder if Marooke wouldn't have found it already. He could hear his mentor chiding him for missing the obvious. He shoved the book aside, pushed away from the bureau and paced towards the window. He gripped the frame with both hands and leaned his forehead against the cool glass.

It was right there! He should see it!

The street below was dark with night, the only light coming from sentinel streetlamps at the corners and a few oil burners in windows. A slithering fog crept up the streets, making its nightly venture from the harbor. The streets were still. There wouldn't be people out, not at this late hour …

I sent death to this harbor. I lined these streets with bodies.

The memory – one that Marooke said he should be proud of – returned to haunt him. Looking down from the third story window – it was like standing on the compound wall, looking down on the captive Tollian men. They'd been like rats in a cage, ignorant of the horrible disease being injected into their bodies. The disease he created …

The skin at the base of his neck tingled.

"Infection," he whispered to the window.

"What?"

Kashif's mind raced. "An infection of the body would be healed – but an infection targeting the Essen? One that renders the Essen useless? It would strip the creature of vitality – it would kill it! Even were it to try and draw additional Essen in – the new reserves would be polluted and contaminated by the old." Kashif looked at the Band marking the flesh of his arm. "I know how to beat it."

Davies clapped his hands. "Wonderful! How? How do we create this infection?"

Quickly he was back at the bureau. To corrupt the Essen, what would he need? Grabbing the ledger, he took up the ink-pen and immediately began to construct the disease. It flowed freely – his experiences under Marooke's guiding eye giving him all the knowledge he needed. The left-side of the ledger filled with names of required chemicals and elements. Davies watched in silent amazement as it came together. He spoke only after Kashif dropped the pen.

"Nitro-sulfate? Powdered antium? I can't say I've heard of half the rest ..."

Kashif, fresh off of his success, was suddenly plunged back into the analytics. Davies was right. The tincture would work – he knew it would work – but he did not have half the substances on hand. Some of them were extremely rare. And in the quantities he would need ...

They were startled from the issue as they heard the lock pop at the window. It raised, and the thief-boy Ethiere dropped into the room. Kashif tensed, Ethiere had an axe ...

"They were my friends," the thief said coldly. "Those children that you experimented on were my friends. I hate you for what you've done." Ethiere raised his head, and Kashif comprehended there was nothing to fear. The boy's countenance was void of violence. The thief stood, visibly grieving, and pled. "They have Kari – they have my friends. Please, help me! Please, I don't know how to save them."

Seeing Ethiere – it all made sense.

He knew exactly why the Banding had included a thief.

"I will need your help," Kashif answered. "Without delay."

The commitment was immediate. "Anything. Anything you need if it will save my friends."

The Arcan smiled and reached for the ledger.

57.

There had been a game of Tens going when he and Sarah had finally left the landing for their beds. It came as no surprise to see another game was already underway in the common room when they woke up.

Dom hated the game of Tens. It was the means by which his benign curse had been turned to evil use – to cheat and to steal. He hated what the game – and his father's demands – had made him become. But he couldn't look away. He couldn't stop reading the players. Each hand, each roll of the dice, each bluff and call – he was drawn to it. From the landing, he couldn't hear a word being said, couldn't see a single card, but he could predict the winner. Just by seeing their reactions, he knew who had the better chances.

Sarah seemed to be doing a little better. At least she wasn't openly sad this morning. He'd not known what to say when she'd started crying last night. He'd had a perfect view of her emotional disarray – but seeing the grief was a far cry from knowing why it existed. He felt bad for her – for his friend. It was still odd to think Sarah was his friend, but she'd not allowed him to hide himself away, barricaded within emotional walls much like he buried himself in the brown coat.

The Banding was breaking them. Dom could see it breaking them. But it was breaking none of them as hard as it was Sarah.

For a girl that couldn't feel physical pain – she was certainly making it up in the emotional variety.

As the gamblers shuffled the deck, Dom surveyed the room – and his eyes came to rest on Billick. He was still at the same table he'd sat at the previous evening – and Dom was willing to wage that he'd not moved from the seat the entire night. Dom had been surprised earlier to see the unapproachable murderer sharing his table with another man last night. And the way they'd talked – the way they'd gestured – it seemed impossible, but the man may have been Billick's friend.

Did murderers have friends?

But looking at him now, sitting alone, drink in one fist, Dom saw something even more improbable.

There were stirrings of emotion in the murderer's heart. They were faint, weak pulses in the hauntingly empty void of his soul – but they were there. Their flash was so muted, that Dom couldn't quite decipher them. It was extraordinary ....

He was watching a soul relearn how to feel.

Dom nudged Sarah, awakening her from her introspective trance. "You aren't going to believe this ..." he started, and then felt his entire body freeze.

"What?' asked Sarah. When the reply didn't come, Sarah looked over to him. "What am I not ... Dom? Dom, what's the matter?"

Standing at the barman's nook, conversing with the keeper, was his father. As if he could read Dom's thoughts, he looked up to the landing, and Dom knew he was found out. The onslaught of panic overcame the petrifying fear. Dom scrambled to his feet. "Run, Sarah ... run!" he whispered hoarsely. His feet pounded down the long hallway and he pushed open the door to the room. Sarah was several paces slower, and the seconds that elapsed as he waited for her seemed eternal.

He was coming. He would find them. He would hurt them.

The moment Sarah entered the room, Dom slammed the door. His anxious fingers tripped over themselves in a mad attempt to turn the lock. His mind played vivid premonitions of his father pushing through the door, catching him by the coat ...

The lock clicked and Dom scampered towards the bed. He secreted himself on the side away from the door, where Sarah was already hiding. The girl was white in the face, and trembling as well. "The demon?"

Dom held a shaking finger to his lips and prayed Sarah would keep silent. His ears strained to hear boots on the stairs, to hear footsteps in the halls, to hear the turning of their door latch ... but there was only silence. And it dragged on and on, the incessant silence taking glee over the nervous dread it built in his heart.

It was sometime later – a half hour? Maybe longer? Just how long, Dom could not say – but long enough. Long enough that he should have come – should have been beating at the door ... but ... but he hadn't ...

"Dom?" Sarah risked in the softest of whispers. "What was it?"

He swallowed the knot in his throat. "My father," he whispered back. "He found me."

Sarah nodded in mute understanding – but after several more minutes passed dared a peek over the side of the bed. When she slid back into place beside him, confusion furrowed her brow. "So ... where did he go?"

Dom shrugged. If by some miracle his father wasn't coming, he would be the last person to question why. After so many prayers to Merciful Domus to divert his father's anger ... wouldn't one eventually be answered?

Sarah thought out loud. "Should we go look? Maybe he left."

Dom shook his head. "We should stay here." Sarah frowned, but Dom was adamant. "It's safer here."

"If something was going to happen," the girl pressed, "wouldn't it have ..." She stopped as the commotion erupted downstairs. The shouting was muffled through the floor, but the sound of marching up the stairs was unmistakable. Sarah dropped back down behind the bed, eyes wide, as the noise coursed through the hallway. The shouting was drawing nearer.

The latch at the door rattled. It was locked, Dom had to remind himself. He raised himself up on one knee, just to verify. *The door is locked.*

A thunderous boom shook the entire door in its frame – Dom could feel the vibrations in the floorboards. He mouthed a prayer to Domus. From behind the door, the voice of the innkeeper cried out. "You'll break my door! Stop!" To no avail, a second tremor shook the door, and wood groaned. A third attempt; and the frame around the lock fragmented into shreds. The door swung free.

The prayer died on Dom's lips.

Billick's wide-shouldered frame filled the doorway, his eyes cold. He stepped inside, dragging Dom's father in by his collar. The man's face was red and swollen, blood dripping freely from his nose and mouth. Billick threw him to the ground, and he stayed down. Only the ragged heaving of his chest let Dom know he still lived.

Peering through the doorway, the innkeeper grimaced. Billick scowled at the man, who disappeared, pushing past those who'd gathered upon hearing the tumult. Reed pushed to the forefront. "Stay out of this, Reed!" Billick threatened, and leveled a sharp kick to the prone man's ribs. His father grimaced and curled up. "This is between this man – and his son."

Dom stood; backing up until the window sill stopped him.

Billick's eyes locked on Dom. "Say the word, and I'll kill him."

Dom darted a glance at his father, and returned to meet the waiting stare of the murderer. "What?"

"Just say it! Say what we both know – that he deserves to die – and I'll take care of it."

A terrible weight settled on his shoulders. His father, who couldn't open his eyes past mere slits, watched him. The murderer watched him. The crowd at the door, Sarah ... it was the whole world watching him. Waiting for the words. Dom balked.

"He's ... he's my father ..."

"Some father!" Billick spat. "We had a talk out in the alley. He confessed what he did you, Dom. The beatings – for you and your brother. And your mother. Who do you think took your share of the punishment in your absence?" Billick jabbed another boot into his father's ribs. "Tell him what you told me." His father only groaned, which earned a sharper kick. "Tell him!"

His father raised his head just enough off the floor. "She helped you run away!" he seethed. "She ruined everything!" He paused to spit blood on the floor, his eyes shying away from his captor. "She fell ..." Billick's foot swung forward again, and he cringed. "I pushed her! I pushed her and she fell down the stairs!"

"Tell him!" Billick roared in warning.

Jaw trembling in fear and indignation, Dom's father was helpless but to comply. "She didn't get up ..." Dom reached into his pocket for the chain ... and his numb fingers searched in vain. He didn't want to believe – it couldn't be true!

Dom stepped forward – surprised to feel his fists clenched. His breathing went ragged, as the fury and mourning raced each other to the surface. "No!" It was the only thing he could say as the welling tears burned his eyes. He took another step towards his father. "No!" he yelled at him. "No!"

"He deserves death!" Billick reminded him. "He clearly deserves death! Just ask, Dom ..."

He dropped to his knees, the grief overtaking him. He buried his head in his hands.

"Dom ..."

"I can't" he yelled.

"Your mother!"

"I can't!"

"You can't deny he deserves it!"

"We all deserve it …"

The unexpected addition came from Sarah, still hiding behind the bed. Dom had forgotten the girl; she'd been so quiet. Hearing her now, Dom felt sick. Billick wouldn't kill his father in front of the girl? He had no soul … but he wouldn't be so cruel as to do it in front of Sarah!

The murderer had an even greater reaction to the innocent girl. All of the sting and venom he'd burst through the door with evaporated off him. Had he not expected Sarah to be here? Had he not seen her behind the bed? Perhaps the murderer would spare the little girl the depravity after all.

Billick's rebuttal was directed at Sarah. "He does deserve it. He confessed. You heard what he's done."

Sarah nodded her head. "You said it didn't matter. You said you didn't need to justify it." She met the big man's eyes, steeled for the next question. "When you've finished with him, what keeps you from killing the rest of us?"

Dom swung his gaze back to Billick, not sure why Sarah was tempting the angry man to contemplate such topics. The murderer and the girl stayed locked for a moment – and it was Billick that flinched first. He grimaced, and returned his attention to Dom.

"He deserves it," he tried again – but it lacked the demanding confidence. Billick was pushing the statement forward as if it was starving for validation. "You know he does."

Dom looked down on the vicious man groveling on the floor before him. His father was bleeding from the nose and mouth – he'd already taken a savage beating. But it was no more savage than the ones he'd inflicted on him and Joshua! Dom knew perfectly well the taste of blood in his mouth.

Only today, there was a difference. Today, Dom knew what it felt like to be on the other side of the swinging fists. His misguided sense of vengeance had caused him to attack Ethiere. He'd tried as hard as he was able to inflict pain on the thief – and as much as Dom hated to admit it, the violence of the moment had been intoxicating. Today, his father knew what it felt like to be the beaten son – and the beaten son knew what it was like to be the unjust tormentor.

Who was he to play the part of judge?

"You're right," Dom answered as he looked down at his fist, balled around his mother's silver chain. "You're right – he deserves it. He does. But if you want me to condone killing him – I can't. I won't." Dom's father looked up, and Dom felt disgust ring through his frame. "I hate you. I hate what you do to me. I hate what you've made me become, how you used me. I hate you for Joshua, I hate you for mother. I hate you – but I forgive you. You don't deserve it – but I forgive you."

Billick put a hand to his forehead and paced back toward the door in disbelief. Captain Reed shouldered past him – and the murderer put up no resistance. His father's eyes stayed attached on him, even as Reed roughly assisted the man to his feet. His father didn't say a word – not a word. Dom didn't expect gratitude. Not from him.

"Listen," Reed said directly into his father's ear. "The boy's mercy was better than you deserve and you know it. You get to live – you get to walk away. But hear me – you better walk far. Go back to your home, gather a few things, find passage on a ship, and leave Tollia. Get as far away as you can – because if I or any of my men catch you coming after Dom again … I promise you, I won't let mercy save you twice!" Reed pushed him towards the door. His father reeled, unsteady from his injuries, but he stayed upright. He moved cautiously past Billick before fleeing down the hall.

Emotionally exhausted, Dom sunk back down beside Sarah. They both sat, staring into the nothingness before them, lost to their thoughts. In the periphery of his senses, Dom heard the others conversing mutedly as they shuffled out of the room. When things grew quiet again, he looked around the bed corner at the stain of sticky blood that had pooled from his father's face.

"I know what the Deacon's teach," Sarah said. "They'll say you did the right thing."

Dom nodded. "Those that seek for mercy seek to impart mercy," he quoted. He believed it, he did. But he contemplated the blood pool and wondered if he wouldn't regret his choice in the morning.

58.

Malcolm staggered through the morning streets with his broken gait, fueled by anger and indignation. His body ached – especially his ribs. He was sure the side-burned man had broken a few. It made breathing excruciating … and it only intensified his rage.

Boil them if they thought he was just going to walk away! Sail away on a ship – leave his tavern behind? It wouldn't happen! So the boy had a thug and a few swordsmen looking over him – but for how long? Whatever Dom was involved with would eventually end – the boy would be left to himself, and then?

Retribution.

How dare he leave! How dare he upset their profitable scheme! Without Dom, his advantage disappeared – he had no way of reading the saps he played against. He was just as oblivious to their bluffs as they were to his! After years and years, the boy finally showed some worth – they were pulling in considerable wealth – and he leaves! He abandons his family! And that woman – his wife! – helped him escape! Helped him leave! She deserved what she got – she deserved to fall!

Dom would pay for leaving! He would pay for his self-righteousness! Dom forgave him? Forgave him? He'd make the boiling boy plead for forgiveness! He wiped the blood from his mouth with the back of his hand. Yes, his useless, pitiful excuse for a son …

Reaching his inn, he slid the key into the lock. He had connections in the city; he'd find a place to hide for a few days. Maybe a few weeks. Just until Dom was on his own and vulnerable again. And then …

"Malcolm?"

The other man was standing right behind him. He recognized the voice.

"Hennessey?" He spat blood onto the street again as he turned back to the door. He twisted the key and it came unlocked. "What do you want?"

The devious contractor approached and patted him affably on the shoulder. "You don't know how much I regret seeing you this morning."

The words sounded strange; there was no time to contemplate them. His breath caught in his throat as the knife slid into his back, and Malcolm wordlessly slid to the cobblestones.

*　　*　　*　　*　　*

Hennessey wiped the blade on the dead man's shirt before tucking it back into his boot. He pouted angrily at the bleeding corpse before him. This was not his task to perform! He was the arranger – he was the intermediary! He was not the boiling knife-man! He rummaged through Malcolm's pockets, removing anything of value. He took great care to leave the linings pulled out; it would lead the constables to the indelible conclusion of a robbery taken to an extreme.

Boil Billick! What had happened to the man? Hennessey had seen it, clear as day, as he'd sat across from him in the Crescent Head. The once cold and competent assassin had been … what? Thinking? Questioning himself? With all of the blood on his hands, with all of the completed jobs under his tally, what could possibly make a man like that question himself? But he'd seen it! He'd not wanted to admit it – he'd have never believed it possible, Billick growing reluctant. And over a man such as Malcolm? Who was Malcolm to win the pity of a man who had never – never! – shown pity to anyone before?

But he'd seen it – in his face, in his eyes! Even when Billick had said it wouldn't be a problem, that he'd take care of the contract, Hennessey had heard it. Boil him, he'd waited the entire morning outside of Malcolm's tavern because he knew Billick would fail. But why? What could have happened?

Hennessey knew he'd not get an answer. The questions were just part of the mourning process. He was losing one of his greatest assets – the most efficiently ruthless killer in the city. Building up another to match Billick's reputation would take years. This was a major, unexpected set-back.

Reflexively, he found himself pushing open the door to the Eight Flagons. It was much too early for the regular crowd but he needed a strong drink, anything to take the edge off his nerves. He passed the barman's nook, giving the obligatory nod of the head to Janns as he went by. The taciturn keeper tapped on the bar to get his attention. Janns tilted his head towards the private back room. "Waiting on you – several hours."

"Do you know who?" Hennessey asked.

"Didn't ask." Which was par for Janns. The keeper of the Eights made it his business to not know what transpired within his tavern.

Hennessey didn't feel like meeting with a client in his current emotional condition. But nothing sang like a sum of money ... if there was anything likely to cheer him up it was the promise and prospect of another contract. He patted the bar – a gesture of thanks to Janns – and headed towards the private room. He stopped at the door – checking his coat for any splatterings from Malcolm – and allowed himself inside.

The man seated at the table was not a stranger.

"Master Rice," Hennessey said, acknowledging his patron. "How is our Lord Baron?"

Rice shrugged and changed the subject. "Busy morning?"

Hennessey pulled in a deep breath. "Regrettably, yes."

Rice moved straight to the point. "I have a contract for you." He tossed a roll of paper across the table. "It's of the upmost urgency." He watched as Hennessy fought the ribbon tie. "I dare say you might not like it."

"Is that so ..." Hennessey answered, distracted. The ribbon off, he unrolled the paper. His eyes immediately picked out the target. Or, in this case, targets. He looked away from the sheet, and aimed a bemused smile at Rice. "Honestly? The whole Band?"

"All six, yes," Rice confirmed. "They were specified. From what I'm hearing, though, you'll not eliminate the Band without cutting through some of the crew adjoined to them. I'm told they've got some of Lord Baron Cahill's swords with them." Rice leaned forward. "You've got a man on that list."

Hennessey bobbed his head. "It's true."

Rice cocked his head to the side. "I need to know if it's a problem. I do understand the finer ethical points that exist in our unethical crowd. You don't take a contract on one of your own– and so on." Rice tilted his head to the other side. "You and Billick have a history together. Understand, my coming to you was an act of courtesy – a showing of appreciation for our past dealings. But if I need to look elsewhere ..."

Hennessey grit his teeth, but his heart was decided. "It won't be problem."

The corner of Rice's lip slid up to a curious smile. "And the ethics?"

"Not an issue," Hennessey assured. "Billick and I do have a history together, but he has made it clear he is no longer one of my own." He took his seat at the table, and felt the flood of familiar excitement. Negotiation. Now this was his venue! "I see no mention of a price."

Rice laughed. "Billick's on the list. I assumed standard rates wouldn't apply."

"A wise assumption," Hennessey confirmed. He took the pen from the inkwell and wrote a number onto the contract. A very large number. He turned it and pushed it towards Rice.

The agent whistled. "That much?"

Hennessey folded his arms, brimming with confidence. "Trust me, you'll not find a man in Hollingston willing to go against Billick for a copper less."

59.

The afternoon slipped towards evening with little to comment on. Sarah and Dom had stayed in the room they shared the entire time, despite the horrible events that had happened earlier that morning. Dom had sat motionless at the foot of the bed, lost within his brown coat, staring at the pool of blood on the floor until a maid arrived to clean it up. Their door hung limply in its shattered frame – it seemed as somber as they were.

The entire world felt broken.

Sarah spent most of her time sitting on the bed looking out the unlocked window. It was past a full day now since she'd last seen Ethiere. She was beginning to think that maybe he wasn't coming back. Maybe he was dead; or maybe he'd just abandoned them. Sarah remembered the hopeless look in Ethiere's eyes when they'd found him yesterday morning on the Alben roof. Ethiere was already broken too. Perhaps he was already too lost to come and save her.

She knew she should probably say something to Dom. He was her friend – and he needed her. Sarah had to believe the crisis of decision was replaying over and over in his mind. For one singular moment he'd had the power to destroy his tormentor. How tempted had he been? How close had he come to giving Billick the permission he'd sought? Sarah knew she would never ask such a question, and she knew Dom would probably never tell.

It was Billick that occupied Sarah's thoughts. She didn't understand the man. In the wagon, he'd plainly described exactly why he could do what he did. There had been no doubt or hesitation in what he purported as truth. She'd believed him. The Deacons often spoke of good and evil – painting the world in shades of brilliant white and empty black. Sarah had always seen herself firmly planted in the ranks of the pure. Such a view had been consistent with the world she'd watched from behind her window-panes. But being outside now – and interacting with others …

Everyone and everything was touched by at least a tinge of gray.

Billick's actions bothered her. He'd brought in Dom's father – a man who went far beyond gray. This was an atrocious man – one who had beaten his own wife and children. Why let him live?

That question eventually pulled her from the room. From the landing she spied the side-burned murderer eating an early supper at one of the tables. Resolving to get some answers, she walked to the table and sat down across from him.

"Why didn't you kill him?"

Billick found something immensely interesting in his soup and delayed his answer. "The boy made the choice. You heard him."

Sarah shook her head. She wouldn't let him put this solely on Dom! "He deserved to die," she argued. "You said so yourself – multiple times. And you were right." Impulsively, she reached over the table and pulled the bowl of soup away from him. The act surprised Billick, and his eyes flashed angrily – but at least she had his attention. "Why did you bring him up to the room?"

"Sweet little girls don't talk like this …"

"Answer me!" she demanded. "You know he deserved to die! What happened? Why make Dom face that? Why put him through that? You could have finished him in the alley and have been done with it." The release of anger on Dom's behalf began to subside. Billick looked away – unwilling to answer. "What's wrong with you?"

Of all the questions, the last was the one she'd least expected a response to. She'd intended it as a barb – and it had worked. Billick's eyes flashed back towards her, and he growled his response. "You are."

It caught Sarah off-guard. She was? Was he really trying to pin it all – what he'd made Dom face – on her? Before she could announce her objection, Billick launched his own tirade.

"Why you, Sarah?" he asked, thrusting a finger out accusingly. "Out of the hundreds and thousands of people on this boiling island, why did the Banding have to choose you?" He sat back, daring her to answer, seething at her silence. "A purpose, right? The wizard spoke of purpose?" He rocked forward in his chair again, startling her. "I nearly cleaved the demon in half with my axe, and I barely survived. Hartley's magic only incites the creature – he's dead. Reed's men went down as fast as the demon cared to dispose of them. So tell me, Sarah, why you? Why bring a little girl who can't feel anything? What's the point?"

She swallowed the trembling in her voice. "So I can die."

Billick pounded the table with both fists. "Boil you! You accept that?"

"I deserve it!" she shot back. There were others in the common room watching them now, but Sarah wasn't about to back down.

"Why!?"

She concentrated on holding the tears back in her eyes. She wouldn't cry in front of him. "Because of everything I've put my father through. Because of all of the hardships he's faced on my account. He didn't deserve the burden – and Merciful Domus is finally granting him some peace." Despite her efforts, a drop escaped and rolled down her cheek. She rubbed it away in irritation. The murderer just sat there frowning. The fire was gone from his face. "What?" she demanded of him. "Why are you looking at me like that?" She swiped another teardrop. "Everyone deserves to die!"

"Don't parrot my words back at me ..." Billick warned.

"It's true! Everyone!"

The murderer shook his head. "Not you."

His excluding her from the universal list was a crippling blow. She'd accepted it, she had! She was guilty! She finally understood – had come to grips. Why in the name of Merciful Domus would he deprive her of that? Why take it away? "Why not?" she pled.

There was no belligerence in his silence. She saw his eyes dart, his brow fold in genuine regret. "I don't know," he admitted. It was not an answer she could accept. She angrily pushed the bowl of soup back at him, splashing some on the table.

Billick's hands shot out as if trying to strangle the elusive answer. He shook with frustration. "Boil me, I don't know! You think I don't want an answer – for myself? For years I've been just fine knowing everyone stands guilty and doing what is required of me. I've never needed justification. I've never needed to ask questions. Justice was doled out at the end of my blade, and that was the whole of the matter." His finger jabbed at the air in front of her, accusingly. "But you – boil you, you just being here – it isn't fair. And boil me, when have I ever cared about what was fair?! You've got me dwelling on why in Domus' name you have a part of this – because it isn't right! It shouldn't be that way." He ran his hands over his face in perplexed agony. "You deserve to live."

"What?"

Billick looked her in the eye, and Sarah saw a soul embattled. A soul that Dom claimed didn't exist – but she saw the turmoil inside. "You haven't done anything wrong yet," he whispered. "I wouldn't be able to kill you to save my own life." She could see the words shredding him – they were a betrayal of who he was. But she could tell he'd spoken them genuinely.

He shook his head, still fighting for words that were not easy to come by. "You represent an innocence I made myself believe didn't exist in the world. You being Banded – for the first time, I asked myself why someone should have to die."

Billick pushed his finger into the spilled soup, expanding the size of the mess. "Questions are contagious. Doubt spreads like a disease." He stopped, and rubbed the excess broth's residue between his fingers. "You want to know why I brought Malcolm up to the room; why I made Dom confront his abusive, degenerate father? I needed validation. I needed someone to silence the questions in my mind. I needed to have the last fifteen years and everything I've ever believed in justified." He laughed – a short, chagrined laugh. "I placed an irredeemable man in front of the one who had suffered the most under his hand. I thought validation was a foregone conclusion."

Dom had elected for mercy. She understood now, what she'd seen in his eyes. Like a drowning man desperate, reaching for flotsam ... only to find it is sinking as well.

Billick had lost himself.

"You've ruined me – you know that."

Sarah bent her head. "Another thing I'm guilty of ..." she pointed out, and he shook his head. He was lost – another of the Band broken. But it didn't mean she was. "We both know I'm going to die, Billick." She tried to let him hear she was being genuine as well. "It's okay."

"No ... it isn't."

She tried again. "There isn't a thing you can do ..."

"Boil me if I'm not going to try," he cut in. He sat forward again, dwarfing her. "I know why I was Banded. I'm to wield the weapon. Whatever the Arcan has been cooking up in his room all day, however it works against the demon, I'm going to be the one facing it. It's meant to be me. It's who I am. I kill things – and I won't need validation from anyone to kill a faceless monster."

He held his finger out in front of her again. She recognized it – her father did the same thing to her when discussing her limitations. "You'll stay behind me," Billick said. "You'll keep away from it. You'll hide if I tell you to hide." He licked his drying lips. "Don't go looking for death."

She slid away from the table.

Boil him. He was broken – but Sarah wasn't about to let him pull her resolve apart too. "You play your part, and I'll play mine," she said as she turned to retreat upstairs. "Whatever part it ends up being."

60.

"I want to eat in the common area."

Greer had memorized the soldier's rotations – and she'd bode her time to make the demand. It wasn't so much to corner Neald – far from it. If it was a matter of bullying someone, young Sperry would have been the choice. No, Neald's rotation aligned directly with the one Reed slept during. She'd waited until now to have Reed conveniently out of the picture.

Neald ran a finger through the thinning hair atop his head. "Captain Reed warned me you might try this."

Boil Reed! Thorough as always. "Then you should have an answer prepared."

"Reed says …"

She stood. "I don't care what he said …"

The soldier held his hands up in defense. "Yes, but I answer to him …"

"And he answers to me," she reminded as she meandered towards the door. "I've spent every moment since we arrived at the Crescent Head within this confined space. I've memorized every chip in the paint and counted every nail in the floorboards. I need a change of scenery. Now."

He wouldn't meet her eyes, which was a good sign. But he wasn't budging from the doorframe, which wasn't. "You're safest up here."

She threw her hands in the air as she stalked away. "Because everyone in the common area is assuredly out to kill me …" She bit down on her tongue. She'd not win the man over by making a fool of him. She let the sarcasm out of her voice and tried again. "We both know that isn't true. Look – I'm not saying I'd want to be on my own. You can keep Reed happy and stay right by my side. Invite Bostitch to come as well, we can all have lunch together."

Neald reached for the doorlatch; Greer thrilled at the victory. "Alright," he relented. "But I get to choose the table. I get to choose where you sit at that table, and I get to choose where I sit at that table. No arguing about any of it!" Everything about him gave off an uncompromising air. "Do we have a deal?"

A trip to the common room was hardly a grand escape, but Greer reveled at leaving the boxy room behind. It was the dinner hour, but the common room had only a few other patron. Neald stared one of the older gentlemen down as they passed – leaving the poor diner visibly troubled. Sperry watched them from his post at the front entrance – until he saw that she was watching him. After that, it was all jaw-set, shoulders-square, back-straight business.

Greer sat where Neald directed her – at the most isolated table in the room – and the serving girl was quick to run by. "It's soup today, my Lady. Some greens, too. Shall I fetch a bowl? I could see if the kitchen could work up some fish if you'd rather …"

"The soup, please," she told the girl, who immediately set about to retreat. "And he'll have one as well." The girl paused to look at Neald, her brow furrowed, and she ducked in to fetch the meal.

Turning to the soldier, Greer saw Neald perched on the edge of his chair in the exact same stiff pose Sperry was in. She frowned. He was actually facing more *away* from her than he was *to* her ...

"Must you do that?"

He looked at her sideways, but did not relax a muscle. "Do what?"

Greer sat back in the chair. "The vigilant statue-like pose?" She watched as Neald's eyes popped back forward – but not before she saw them roll. "Come on, Sperry's waiting at the doorway – nothing is coming in without him aware of it." The soldier didn't budge. Greer snorted in disgust. "Do you know how annoying it is having one of you acting like this in my presence all the time?"

She drew his eye once more. "Acting like this?"

She gestured towards him. "Not talking! Not looking! Pretending you're some piece of highly-focused human furniture." She was doing it again – losing her temper – embarrassing him. This isn't what she'd intended. Greer drew a breath and leveled her voice. "Look – I know I'm making you uncomfortable. I'm sorry. I'm supposed to just forget you're there, right?"

"I'm just a soldier, my Lady."

His response came in time with the serving girl, bearing two steaming bowls on her tray. She set them out, dipped a leg to curtsy, and disappeared again.

And here it was. "For the moment ... could you not be?" Neald's head turned briefly. He looked at her, and then down at the soup bowl. "Can't we just share a meal – you being you and me being me? No titles. No traditions. Just us and the soup. Can you do that for me, Neald? Forget who I am, just for lunch."

He was frowning, but statuesque he was not. His hand came up, and took hold of the spoon. He shifted his body, ever so slightly, but it was enough. He was still sitting at an angle, but it was an angle closer to her than it was not.

Now? She picked up her spoon as well. Now came small talk. She had no expectations Neald would start on his own accord; she'd have to pull him into a conversation. But about what? What did soldiers talk about? Women? She looked at the man across from her and spoke the first thing that came to her mind. "I've just realized I really don't know anything about you besides your surname."

He disguised his dithering between loaded spoonfuls of soup. "Not really much to tell ..."

She gritted her teeth on hearing the formality in his voice. "... That would interest a lady?" she interjected. "Come on, Neald. Please?" She racked her brain for a subject – any subject. "Your family! Everyone's got a family. Tell me about yours."

He dipped the spoon in and out of the soup while he spoke. "My mom, my dad. Got a brother and two sisters, all younger than me." He looked up and she gave him an encouraging look. "All of them still live out in Lower Brooking. Elder of the sisters got married two years ago – and the younger is awfully jealous." He smiled at the last bit, and she prompted for more. "My father is a Deacon at the Lower Brooking cathedral ... third generation of Neald ..."

"The family calling?" She ran her own spoon over the soup, breaking the congealing crust forming at the top. "Not you though?"

"I thought I would when I was little," he shrugged. "It's what granddad did and then my father – it was what they talked about at supper, every night." He laughed. "I'm telling you – Domus would plead for His own mercy if he had to listen to those two debate scripture at every meal."

"So how'd you end up in uniform?"

"The war talk with Arca was just building when I came of age. You should have heard the propaganda ..." Neald took a bite. "The Lord Barons' did a fine job selling that war to the common folk. Bost and I, we got enamored with the idea of heroes and glory. And the way the girls fawned over the boys all dressed for war." The smile faded as the memory changed. "My father was not pleased when I told him. He didn't understand. The men of our family, he told me, were men of religion, not men of blood."

Neald set the spoon down gently by the bowl and he turned to face her squarely. "He was right about me. Truth be told, I've been lucky to this point. Made it to Jauda, but never set foot on Arca. Seen my share of scraps out in the hills – but never a full-blown battle. To be honest, I offer a prayer of gratitude every day I don't have to draw a sword. I plead for mercy for each of the men I've killed over the years – that Merciful Domus will have pity on them. And on me." He looked up at her, resigned. "I'm not a man of blood, my Lady. As it turns out I'm just a man of religion in a terrific uniform."

Greer could not get a read on his feelings. "You regret your choice then?"

He shook his head immediately. "No." He smiled, chagrined. "I ask myself that question often, late on the coldest nights, sleeping on my sword as a precaution. I think about the little cathedral in Lower Brooking, can picture my father and me sitting in the glow of an ebbing fire, debating some minute point from some obscure passage ..." He sighed. "I can see it, and although it's probably where I should be, I don't regret taking the road that's led me here."

"Why?"

"Because," he explained, "had I never been a soldier, I could have never been able to enjoy being a Deacon. I would have sat at that fire, as my father made his next point, and I would have wondered if there wasn't something better out there for me. I would have wondered, just because I would have never known." He smiled again and scooped up the spoon. Greer watched him take a few bites, before he paused. He pointed the spoon at her as he swallowed. "Who knows," he said as his mouth cleared, "I might retire from soldiering someday. Perhaps the Lower Brooking congregation and Holyday sermons are ahead for me yet." He leaned in, as if sharing a great secret. "If this uniform was the price to know where I really belong – to know who I really am – I'm glad to have paid it."

Who I really am. Greer swallowed, his words sinking deep. *Who I really am.*

When it came down to it – that was her problem. That was what consumed her. She had no answer to that simple yet boilingly complex question. *Who am I really?* There was a price, and Greer knew that she would pay it gladly. For

Neald it had been stepping into a uniform – away from everything familiar and comfortable. For her? Was the price the same for her?

"Your soup is getting cold," Neald pointed out, and then raised an eyebrow. "Have you even tried it?"

Embarrassed, she hastily scooped a spoonful to her mouth. It was richer than she'd expected, and a tad cold – but she had only herself to blame. She savored the mouthful, rolling it around on her tongue, and found it as fitting as it was delicious.

The soup was tarragon – and it was not her father's recipe.

61.

It had taken them all afternoon. After freeing Hannah and Rissa, the three thieves had gone out it an effort to find those that had fled Hat's final trap. The girls were certain that a number of the Gang had managed to get away – but they were just as uncertain as to where to find the other children. So they'd split up, each taking a different district of Hollingston, each with the same goal.

They needed to gather in the remaining strength of the Gang. They needed to bring their brothers and sisters home.

Darkness was once again falling on the magnificent city outside of the Gang's lair, and Ethiere was able to look at the fruit of their efforts. There were only seven of them, but they would have to do. He looked on them – his friends – his brothers and sisters – his family. He had an audience – and they had questions.

"I know you want answers," he said. "I know you're scared – but you don't need to be. Not anymore." He turned his head, looking in the direction of Hat's office where his corpse still lay. "Master Hat betrayed us. The men he sold the bottles and powders to wanted more. They wanted us. They wanted children to experiment on." Ethiere stopped. These were hard words for children to hear. Ellis was only eight years old; Margeis only a year older. These were hard words, but these children had already known a hard life. "Many of our Gang suffered and died in these experiments. They were cruelly taken from us. I know one of the men who did it – one of the scientists. I've seen what his works have wrought. I've seen Pennie." He stopped as his voice faltered. "I saw what they did to her – what they've made her become."

He paused, looking again into the eyes of the forgotten children of society. "We all know what loss is. As a group – as a family – we experience it too frequently. We can look around the room – and our hearts remind us who our eyes no longer see." He clenched his fist. "But there is still hope that some of them might be alive. We can't give up on our brothers and sisters. If we don't rescue them, who will? Who else even knows they exist? We cannot give up! I will not give up!" He stopped, letting the words ring through the wide hall; letting the plea sink into their souls. "But I can't do it alone. I know what hopelessness feels like. I know what it feels like to have to accept fate. But this? I do not accept this. I intend to fight."

Hannah stepped forward. "What do you need us to do?"

"I have a list," Ethiere answered, drawing out the letter. "Items that we need to get from the apothecists – the bottle shops. It is a long list ..." Ethiere offered a crooked smile. "It will take a lot of effort and a lot of luck. Tonight we undertake the biggest, most coordinated raid Wellsford Park and all of Hollingston have ever seen!"

There were grins all around – some apprehensive – but most just anxious. Ethiere could see it in their faces. They'd been losing for so long; they were anxious for a chance to take something back.

"Now listen close, most of the items on this list are things we've already taken before – so some of them are going to be hard to find. But we have to find them all. Have to – or we've failed our friends. Take as much of them as you find – the more the better. If you think it might be on the list, take it just to be safe."

Ellis – an absolutely bone-thin boy with some of the deftest fingers Ethiere had ever seen – began to bounce on his heels in excitement. "I wish we could each have a partner. I wish we could watch each other's backs. But there isn't enough of us. There isn't enough time. The constables might catch on..."

"Not if we create a bigger distraction in the middle of Hollingston – something to draw all of the constables in?" suggested Javier.

"Maybe something with fire ..."

"... and horses if we can find them ..."

As the ideas bloomed, Ethiere stood back and just watched. Rissa disappeared from the group, heading around the corner to Hat's office. Ethiere wondered where she was up to but opted not to follow. Javier and Margeis were starting to lay out all of the shops they'd need to hit and were discussing assignments.

Hannah came to stand beside him. "You do realize how crazy all of this is?"

Ethiere nodded. "Yep. But we've got rocks in our stomachs."

"And candlewax for brains," the girl finished.

"And a head start," Rissa added. She rounded the corner with a box, laden with bottles. "There's another one back in Hat's office that's half full. It's the stuff he had us steal earlier this week!"

Ethiere picked up one of the bottles from the box and recognized the letters on the label. It was on Kashif's list. "These will help," he told his Gang. "Now let's figure out how we go get more."

62.

Billick awoke from a nap he'd not meant to take, and fought the momentary confusion. He sat up, felt the familiar pang of complaint from the stitches in his chest, and ran his hands over his face. He'd spent the early evening upstairs, alone in his room, hidden away from everyone and everything but his own thoughts. He felt like a rowboat being tossed around in the middle of the ocean – unsteady; every effort exerted to just staying above the waves. All his beliefs, drilled into him from his youth, were withering away before his eyes.

Show no mercy.

Decide why you can take a life.

Everyone is condemnable in the end.

Everyone in his life – from the time he joined the Lancers to the last job he completed for Hennessey – fostered that mindset. They'd mentored and molded him into the dispassionate, unthinking killer they needed him to be.

It had only taken four days with a naïve little girl to start him unraveling at the ends.

He needed a drink. Something hard enough to quell the gnawing reminder of the stitches and to commiserate the crumbling of the man he used to be.

What a time to grow soft! He'd have a second chance at the demon – after nearly dying from the first – and this time he'd go battling the problems in his own head.

Perhaps once he was away from Sarah, he thought on the way down the stairs. Perhaps once he was back at the Eight, surrounded by familiar faces who championed his devilish behavior …

At the bottom of the stairs, he noticed there was no one at the keeper's bar. It was strange to see it abandoned – the bar at the Eight Flagons was never unmanned. Janns was as much a fixture behind his bar as were the floors and walls. Billick paused thoughtfully at the bar. He drummed his fingers against it – sure if the barman were to hear the noise he'd perhaps …

Billick scanned the room. The dinner crowd was gone, only two of the common room's many tables were occupied. Captain Reed manned the post by the door. The soldier caught him looking, and he must have caught the concern written on his face.

There were no serving girls running around, tending the room.

No keeper. No girls.

Something was off.

Billick went straight to Sarah. She saw him coming and made it a point to ramp up her small talk with a disinterested Sperry. He cut her off. "Go upstairs," he ordered her.

She worked up an indignant expression. "I'm not done."

"Sarah! Go!" he growled. He looked around the room. What was it? He allowed himself two steps closer to a trio of men huddled at the far table. Their heads were bent low and they spoke in whispers, as if sharing a great conspiracy. The floor creaked under Billick's boot, and the noise caused the man closest him to peer around. It was the briefest of moments, but the man revealed his face.

Jovan.

Just by their sizes, Billick could put names to the other two men at the table. Black Foster and his younger brother. He knew these men. They were murderers.

They were Hennessey's men.

"Reed!" he bellowed, as the men at the table rose as one.

*   *   *   *   *

"Reed!"

They heard the resonating yell perfectly, despite their door being securely shut. It rushed through the floorboards; climbed the walls. Kashif looked up from the measuring board he was using to parcel out exact amounts of powdered antium. The thief had proven worthy of his title, and had brought a box laden with bottles each time he returned. It amazed Kashif how accurate the thief and his illiterate gang were turning out to be. Some of the bottles were useless to the concoction he was formulating – but the most were perfect samples.

Still, their haul had several shortcomings – the rarest of the chemicals were just not available in large quantities. Kashif had noted those elements they yet lacked, and Ethiere had disappeared back into the city streets.

There was a large crash and more shouting …. Kashif looked up to see Davies was no longer focused on the sulfates he was trying to dilute. His eyes were on the door, his curiosity killing his productivity. The Physician looked towards him helplessly. "Don't you think we should check?"

Kashif glowered and went back to scooting the antium into distinct piles on the board. "There are other things which should concern us more …"

Sadly, the sounds from the Physician's workspace suggested he disagreed. The man stood – and even without seeing his face, Kashif could envision the apologetic expression. "I'll just be a moment …"

With a crystallic ping, fragments of glass belched from the shattering window pane. Kashif threw his right arm up as a shield as the flying shards of glass tickled his exposed skin like sadistic rain.

He heard a rattling intake of breath, and saw Davies squirming on the floor, a solid steel dart lodged centrally in his chest. The Physician's eyes were wide, his face pale and bloodless. Kashif the scientist observed the situation quickly, assessing what could be done to save Davies' life. Kashif the human being watched in stunned horror as the Physician started his death throes.

The touch of the night breeze on his neck brought the Arcan quickly back to reality. A bolt – the window! Kashif dropped out of his chair and slid behind the bed just as the second dart whistled into the room and thudded ominously into the far wall.

Cowering behind the bed, Kashif felt the anger riding high on the cresting wave of his panic. His arm was lined with small rivulets of crimson, flecked with the powdery white antium. This wasn't how it was supposed to go! This wasn't right! They were on the edge of victory – they knew how to defeat the demon.

On the floor, Davies gurgled, his hand reaching out – pleading for Kashif's help. The Arcan watched the Physician – and every noble fiber of his being urged him to drag the man behind the bed. But he couldn't. He was frozen. The words of the thief rang in his ears.

Coward!

It stung, because it was true. Kashif felt his voice clench in his throat as he whispered his hollow justification to the dying man. "I'm sorry … I can't!" The next bitter words were an echo of his Master's last instructions. "I'm supposed to survive."

*   *   *   *   *

Having caught Billick's mood, Reed was already on alert when the men at the far table stood. As they drew daggers –he would have spotted anything larger on them when they'd entered – his hand took grip on the hilt of his broadsword. Between he, Billick and Sperry, the three enemies had only a momentary advantage – but that would last only as long as it took Neald and Bostitch to hear the ado of the melee and come running.

And yet, none of the men pushed their momentary advantage. Billick was unarmed, Sperry had been taken by surprise and was only now reaching for his sword, and Reed was half a room away from being a threat. The dagger-wielders could have gang-rushed the table in hopes of knocking Billick or Sperry out of the fight. But they didn't …

They waited. Although each held the dagger as if it was an extension of their own arm, not one looked comfortable with the situation. Each seemed severely reluctant to go after the side-burned murderer standing in their path …

Reluctant … or …

He caught the faintest of sounds from upstairs – and it confirmed his dread.

"Crossbow!" he yelled, his warning just beating the crescendo of glass shattering from the Crescent's large front window. The bolt whizzed into the room, and Sperry went down.

The dagger-men weren't reluctant … they were waiting for their opponents to stand and give a target to their fellows waiting in the darkness outside.

With surprising speed, Billick uprooted the closest table, turning it on its side – creating an effective, thick shield. He flung a chair towards the dagger-wielders – catching one square in the shoulders.

But the issue was the crossbow man. Billick would be forced to stay crouched or risk a bolt to the body. Reed knew where he was needed. He flung open the front door – and was immediately repelling the swing of a sword by the man who'd been waiting for him. The unexpected opponent pushed Reed back four steps into the Crescent Head before Reed reestablished his footing.

Reed heard Billick yell, but there was nothing he could do to help.

"Neald!"

Hopefully Neald would come quickly. But for the moment, Reed knew he and Billick were on their own.

*   *   *   *   *

"Stay behind the bed!" Bostitch yelled at Greer. Crouching to change his profile, he opened the door, ready in case anyone was waiting for him on the other side.

Someone was. Standing across the hall in his own open doorway, Dom almost got himself skewered. "Stay in your room!" Bost scolded the boy.

Then came the warning cry. "Crossbow!"

In one motion, Bostitch dove forward and pushed Dom to the ground. Seconds later, the window in the boy's room blew apart. The crossbow dart sailed through both open doorways and dove into Lady Greer's bedding with a small poof of straw.

"Stay down!" he bellowed back at Greer. Boil him, the noble girl better listen! Bost scooted forward on his elbows, dragging Dom by the shirt with one hand, until both were safely behind the boy's bed. He slid his own crossbow off his back and extended the bracing arms. The next door over opened, and Neald scurried through. His eyes were still squinting – he'd probably been sleeping when the attack started.

"Can you get him?" Neald asked. It was an important question. The trajectory of the darts … the bowman had to be on their same level, on the roof of the building across the street. Any attempt going after the man with a sword would mean a suicide dash across the street between the buildings.

"I haven't marked his location yet!" Bost grumbled as he fit a bolt in place and wound the crank. He blew out a short breath, and then risked a glance over the bed.

Another bolt flew through the opening of the shattered window, harmlessly planting itself into the hallway wall.

"Boiling, boiling …"

"Neald!"

It was Reed calling. Bostitch looked to his comrade-in-arms. Neald pursed his lips, and swallowed.

"Be careful," Bost told him.

Neald nodded, yelling back as he sprinted down the hallway. "Just get the boiling shooter before he gets me!"

*　　*　　*　　*　　*

Sarah could only stand, stunned, as the action broke out around her. Billick's second thrown chair didn't connect as cleanly as the first – but still managed to open an ugly gash on another of the men's forehead. With no more chairs in his immediate reach, the side-burned killer took hold of one of the table-legs with both hands and wrenched it free. It was not a clean break – the jagged, splintered end of the fair-sized club giving it a menacing effect.

"Come on then!" Billick yelled at the waiting men. "Cowards! Come on!"

It spurred them to action. Two charged forward, daggers at the ready. The first took a swing of the club to his midsection, and he stumbled backwards. The second's swipe at Billick drew blood before the club could be brought back around. The table leg caught the man across the back, and he splayed forward

He landed in front of Sarah – his dagger bouncing on the wooden floor.

Without thinking, Sarah reached down and picked it up. Its owner raised his head, shook away the haze; and looked up at her. Sarah panicked, her feet instinctively moved her backwards. The man rose to his knees and grabbed her leg. She fell, hit the ground hard, and felt the man grab for the dagger. She screamed and grasped the dagger with her other hand.

A sword flashed, there was a spray of blood and Sperry pushed the man off of her. The neck of Sperry's uniform was doused in crimson, and he looked only half aware of what was going on.

Strangely, he said to her what she was about to say to him. "You're bleeding."

The world started to wobble, and Sarah could not keep her eyes open.

*   *   *   *   *

He couldn't move away quickly enough. Jovan's dagger ran across his chest, swiping at exactly the opposite angle of the wounds the demon had left. By luck, Kashif's thick bandages lessened the depth of the cut … and Billick was struck with irony of being held together by the work of a filthy, dark-skinned Arcan.

Billick connected a sharp kick to Jovan's kneecap, and the man collapsed to the ground with a bitter curse. Before Billick could recover, Black Foster charged into him, knocking him from his feet. The man was a broad-shouldered bull, and his large hands snaked around Billick's neck. Billick tried to reach for his table-leg club, but Foster put a knee on his forearm, crushing it underneath his weight.

The shift in the man's balance did give Billick the chance to push off against the floor, and roll the man to the right. Foster lost his perch atop Billick but did not relax his vice like grip on his neck. Black specks of death began to dance across Billick's sight; his lungs demanded air. His left hand thrashed out, sweeping the floor, hoping to connect with …

It sliced his fingers, but he readily snatched it up. The large shard of glass from the window was already running with his own blood as Billick raised it. Black Foster saw it hovering above him, but before he could act, Billick brought the protruding edge down into the man's throat.

The grip waned, and Billick pushed away. His lungs welcomingly drew in a ragged breath – and the sudden influx of air left him momentarily light-headed. He heard the strum of the crossbow and instinctively fell back on his elbow. Sperry, ghost-white, did the same; but the shot was not targeted at either of them. At the bottom of the staircase, Billick saw Neald fall, his legs buckling.

Another man down.

He looked back to Sperry – and then he saw her.

Sarah. Motionless on the floor. Blood staining her face and hands.

"Sarah! No!"

Whatever inklings of mercy may have been growing in the murderer's heart exploded in violent indignation. Jovan was rising off of the floor as Billick set his eyes on him. Pushing the agony of his body aside, Billick stood to face his fellow murderer-for-hire.

All of the horrors of Oblivion rose up with him.

*   *   *   *   *

Ethiere felt his nerves rise with each roof to roof jump. The satchel firmly strapped to his back contained only three small jars, and the young thieves in the Gang had done their best to wrap each in soft padding. With every landing, Ethiere could envision them bouncing into one another. It would take only the smallest of cracks to start a leak; and the bottles were small enough even a tiny dribble would deplete the bottle in short order.

The Arcan was already concerned about their current quantities of some of the solutions – could they risk losing anymore?

Still, the rooftops were safest. The multi-site raid, which had begun with a horse pulling Davies' burning wagon down the main thoroughfare, had put the constables in a foul mood. They were out in the streets tonight in droves, determined to nab anyone looking the part of a thief. Getting these last three bottles had been risky … hopefully the Arcan would prove the effort worth it.

Two roofs away, Ethiere got the feeling in his stomach that something wasn't right. It was the feeling he got anytime something went sideways on a job. It was a warning – survival was on the line. Ethiere stopped, ducking into the shadows of one of the thin chimneys, and surveyed the quiet night.

There was movement, black against the black, on the roof. Not the Crescent Head roof – but the shorter one across the way. The thief jumped the next roof to investigate, keeping his profile as low as he could.

One building away and he saw the danger. A crossbowman lay prone on the roof. Across the street, only jagged fragments remained of many of the third story windows of the Crescent Head.

Kashif's window was an open, jagged maw.

The man fired again, and Ethiere saw the bolt streak in through what remained of the window of the room shared by Sarah and Dom.

This man was shooting at his friends!

Emotion trumping all reason, Ethiere took a direct line towards the crossbowman. His mind was solely focused on stopping the man; his body, acting on instinct, executed the unscripted course. As he touched down on the same roof as the shooter, his landing caused the man to look up.

It became a race.

The crossbowman rolled to his side and jammed his next bolt into his weapon. Ethiere's leather pads flew over the tiled roof. The man wound the crank; they both heard the spring lock into place on the bow. Ethiere saw he would arrive a second too late. He banked his body hard to the left, allowing his momentum to begin his slide down the roofway. The sudden change in angle took him out of the anticipated line of fire – and Ethiere was on him.

He had no plan – he'd taken no forethought into what he'd actually do when he reached the bowman. His feet were still slipping down the smooth rooftop tiles, so Ethiere did what he supposed was his last resort.

His hands shot out – one grasping the man's coat – the other entangling in the man's curly hair. Ethiere grabbed, and he pulled, and the man joined him in his slide down the roof – head first. Their combined weight increased their momentum; Ethiere felt his toes vibrating over the overlapping tile shingles. The bottles from his satchel worked their way out, each adding a distinct tonal chattering; music to accompany their fall. As the edge of the roof neared, he released the other man, who was scrambling madly for something to latch onto to slow his head-long descent.

Ethiere experienced a tingle in his extremities with the weightless feeling as the roof abruptly ended. He turned in the air and blindly reached for the gutter bar. His left hand slipped – but his right kept a tenuous hold on the cool metal bar shaking under the sudden burden of his weight. The bottles streaked by him, winking away sinisterly before shattering on the ground.

The crossbowman, arms flailing, somersaulted off the roof. The clatter of the crossbow on the cobblestones was quickly accompanied by a thud of a heavy impact.

Ethiere caught the bar with his other hand and allowed himself a breath. The bowman lay sprawled below him, neck at an unnatural angle with the rest of the body.

A movement caught his eye – he wasn't the only one taking in the view of the body. Another man down on street-level looked up in bewilderment, and his eyes focused on the boy dangling from the rooftop. The man scowled. He too had a crossbow.

He finished winding the crank and raised the sight to his eye. Ethiere knew the bolt was destined for his back.

*   *   *   *   *

Dom closed his eyes – and wished to just disappear. Sinking into the brown coat, tucked behind the barrier of the bed – it was like being back in one of his

365

old hiding spots – one his father hadn't discovered yet. He could hear the clamor of chaos around him, the yells and shouting. The whistle and hum of the incoming darts. If he slid into the coat far enough, if it enveloped him completely …

Dom knew he wouldn't disappear – but perhaps the world would disappear around him.

"Boil it all, I can't see him!" cursed Bost. The soldier had hunkered down just before the next bolt sped into the room. "He's on the roof, but I'm never going to spot him before he lines me up for the kill." The soldier was agitated – Dom didn't need his ability to see that. Bost was growing bolder with each attempt to locate the enemy crossbowman. Sooner rather than later, Bost would prove his synopsis of the situation correct. He'd risk a glance for a second too long … and then?

Dom was oddly detached from the situation. If Bostitch took a bolt, he'd die on the floor, not two paces away. Dom would watch the man bleed to death. But strangely, he was disconnected – as if he were buffered from the horrors of the world surrounding him. He felt safe. Even if it wouldn't last – for now, he felt safe.

Billick's roar pulsed through the inn from the common area below. "Sarah! No!"

Dom's heart stopped. Sarah – his friend! She'd gone downstairs for a late supper. His ears strained for anything additional – anything to clue him in on the fate of his friend. His one true friend! Was she hurt? Was she dead? The cocoon of protection tried to soothe his questions; tried to placate his worries. The coat seemed to pull in him deeper. But Dom resisted. Not everyone was safe. Until they were, his conscience would not let him idly wait.

There were things more important than safety.

Bost readied his crossbow and steeled himself. "Can't see in the boiling blackness!"

Tell me what you see!

His father's voice rose like a haunting specter, but Dom heard a different message in the demand.

"I can."

He stood – and turned towards the window. Everything was darkness – except the illuminations that radiated from the man on the roof. Dom heard Bost swear again, and felt the man's strong hands reaching to pull him down. But Dom stuck his finger out, pointing to their attacker.

"There!"

"Get down!"

"Shoot him!" Dom yelled back. Bostitch popped up beside him – leveling his bow – when a second figure darted across the roof. "Wait! It's Ethiere!"

Despite the dark sky, the two watched the thief slide into the man, grapple with him, and drag him down the slope of the roof. "Merciful Domus ..." Dom muttered. As both disappeared from view, both he and Bost charged to the broken window. His vision still active, Dom easily picked out the thief hanging from the storm drain bar.

Bostitch pushed by, snapped the crossbow to his shoulder, and fired downward. Dom crowded in next to the window just in time to see the light extinguish from the man that Bost had shot. Ethiere, still suspended in the air, turned to look backwards. The thief was awash with relief.

There were footfalls behind them – fading as Dom turned.

But Bost knew their source.

"Lady Greer! Wait!"

*   *   *   *   *

Greer crouched behind her bed, her arms hugging her knees tightly. The unforeseen attack had put her in shock. Reed and the others had talked about an attack on the Crescent Head. They'd planned a defense. But really? Greer had never believed them. She'd never thought it actually might occur.

And as the bolts continued to fly in, she wondered if their planning had accounted for crossbowmen.

"Get down!" she heard Sergeant Bostitch yell.

"Shoot him!" It was Dom's voice. Dom? Too curious, she glanced over the straw bed and saw both Bost and Dom running towards the window. It made her feel foolish – hiding like she was – when even the withdrawn abused boy was taking a part in the defense of the inn. As much as she protested Reed and the soldiers treating her different – at the very onset of danger she had immediately allowed everyone else to shield her from harm.

It was hypocritical. Why should everyone else sacrifice while she cowered in the shadows? Who was she to think she deserved better?

Her sanity shouted back an answer: *You are the daughter of a Lord Baron*! But its case was drowned out by the hurtful question asked by the one person she'd always thought to be her friend.

What did you do to deserve your status?

Nothing. It was a bitter truth – but she'd done nothing. Bridgette had been right – her infuriating words had been so maddening because they were so very accurate. She was painfully ill-suited for the life of nobility. She was as undeserving as possible of the luxuries her station had thrust on her. She was hiding – trembling behind the bed – because she was the Lady Greer of Cahill.

She crawled out from behind the bed because that wasn't who she wanted to be.

Neald had spoken of a price he'd paid – one that had led him into a life much more difficult and dangerous than the one he'd left behind. It had cost him ease, but had gained him so much more in perspective. Their conversion over a bowl of soup had resonated with Greer all evening.

She envied him. She envied anyone who knew who they were.

A price to be paid. Greer got to her feet and dashed from the room. Whoever she was, she was certain she wouldn't find out cowering in the back. "Lady Greer! Wait!" She heard Bost call for her, dread in his voice, but it only sped her flight down the corridor. She reached the stairs in such a rush her feet took them two at a time, always on the verge of falling forward …

She saw him, lying twisted at the bottom of the staircase. Neald. The ugly end of the crossbow dart protruded from his chest, wet crimson soaking into his uniform.

The life of a soldier had finally caught up with the man of religion who was just wearing the uniform.

She was able to stop her momentum before tripping over him. She didn't want to touch him – not for fear of the dead body – but out of reverence. This was a man who had been at peace with himself – even to the end. He was dead – but her envy of him did not wane in the slightest.

Instead, Greer felt compelled to pick up his mantle.

She loosed the broadsword from his yielding fingers. She'd never handled a weapon before – boil them all, she'd never handled anything more intimidating than the silver flute! A weapon was a coarse and vulgar thing – entirely improper for a girl – let alone a Lady! But she thrilled at holding it. The sword was heavier than she expected, and holding it aloft taxed protesting muscles in her arms.

She saw Reed, locked in a vicious melee with a towering man by the door. He'd called for Neald. Greer determined she'd answer the call.

She was not sure where the yell came from. She didn't recognize it as any sound she had ever made before – even though it emanated from her own throat. It was fitting though – a perfect cry into which she could pour her frustrations and her anger and her grief.

However, the yell did alert both Reed and his opponent of her approach – and of the two it was Reed who looked the more terrified. The brutish man was able to turn Reed away as she neared, and swept his sword directly into her path. The blow rang through the length of the blade, the vibration ripping through her forearms, and his strength sent her straight backwards. She landed roughly into the side of one of the common room chairs.

The enemy disregarded her completely, turning instead in anticipation of Reed's next onslaught. Greer saw Reed, crouched, holding his ground. The brute got into his stance and eyed the Captain suspiciously, before reeling forward and collapsing on the ground. Greer's eyes raced up to the landing of the stairs, where Sergeant Bostitch was just lowering his crossbow.

The grief was evident on his face.

"For Neald!" she whispered to herself. Dropping the sword, she cried into her hands.

*   *   *   *   *

Jovan swung his dagger with all of the skill his profession afforded him. Billick was oblivious to the blade. Whether it touched him or not, he couldn't say. He was past feeling – past caring about anything as trivial as pain. His anger consumed him; leaving nothing behind but the legendary, soulless killer of Hollingston.

With a vicious crack, Billick connected the table-leg club with Jovan's dagger-wielding hand, jarring the blade loose. The other murderer made a desperate grab for the thick table-leg and they wrestled the improvised weapon between them. Billick didn't blink – he made sure to look straight into the assassin's eyes. He wanted Jovan to see the awful black maw of Oblivion about to swallow his soul.

Jovan's feet began to back-pedal, but he didn't release his hold of the club. They turned in tight, contested circles, but it was always Jovan being forced backwards, weakening. With one last mighty push, Billick shoved Jovan towards the upturned table. Jovan collided with the jagged, splintered end where the table leg had been rent. The assassin's eyes flashed as the crude point dug in deep.

His grip on the club relaxed, and Jovan suddenly looked very tired.

"Who?!" Billick demanded of the dying man, lifting his chin to make him look into his eyes. "Who?!"

Jovan leered. "You know who," he said dismissively. Billick let him go, and he only stayed erect due to the stake in his back. "He said you'd weakened," the man said hoarsely. "Said you'd not put up a fight!" Jovan coughed – it came up mostly blood. "Boil him! Boil him and tell him I'll collect what he owes me in Oblivion." The assassin's head lolled to one side – and he would say no more.

The room descended into a somber quiet.

It was over.

Billick reached down and picked up one of the assassin's daggers.

It was just beginning.

63.

Captain Reed's first instinct was for Lady Greer. Nothing had unnerved him more than when she'd charged in, waving that sword. It had been rash and it had been stupid, and lucky for her, the man she'd attacked hadn't considered her enough a threat to finish her on the spot. He'd feared for her – but not out of duty, not because of the Lord Baron's charge. Even though it was something he could never rightfully express, he'd feared because it was *her*.

He stepped over the man's corpse and knelt beside the crying young woman. "Lady Greer?"

"Leave me be," she mumbled through her tears.

"Are you hurt, my Lady?"

"Leave me be!" she yelled at him in a sudden rage and pushed him away. She seethed; her eyes venomous. "I'm no more important than the rest of them, you hear me! Not a whit more important! So don't … just don't. Worry about those who actually took harm."

Her rebuke dispelled his singular focus, opening his mind to fully take in the destruction evident in the common room. He looked up to Bost, solemnly kneeling beside Neald's crumpled form. His most trusted ally saw him looking, and quietly shook his head.

Sperry stumbled forward in bewildered shock. "Captain?"

"You took a bolt!" Reed remembered, as he braced the younger man up. The collar of Sperry's uniform was awash with blood.

"Took it high, I think," said Sperry, wincing as Reed pulled at the uniform to get a look. Sperry was right – the dart had passed clean through – not even grazing the top of the young soldier's collarbone. Still, there was a chunk of flesh missing from his shoulder; it would need attending to by the Arcan or Physician Davies …

He caught sight of Sarah, motionless on the floor. Billick stood over her, face unreadable, a dagger clenched in his fist. Without explanation, the murderer strode towards the doorway.

"Billick? Where do you think you're going?"

"To finish this."

"We need you here ... we're short on men!"

Billick turned, eyes flashing. "I'm not one of your men!" He disappeared through the open doorway, leaving Reed and the others to defend alone. Three of them – assuming Sperry could fight through the pain. The Crescent Head was broken, but it was still defensible. They'd need to get everyone upstairs ... they could push the beds up against the exposed windows ...

A figure slipped in through the front door. Bost raised his crossbow. Reed spun, sword ready and he saw Sperry take his stance as well ...

The thief boy froze mid-step. He was very lucky to have not gotten a metal bolt to the face. "Ethiere? Get in!" Reed snapped, and Ethiere quickly complied. Reed crossed the room to shut the door. While he was curious as to where the boy had been over the last several hours, there were more pressing matters at hand. "Is anyone else out there?"

"Just Billick," the boy answered. "And the dead."

"Two crossbowmen," Bost reported.

The thief, gingerly cradling fragments of glass in his hands, cataloged the entire room. "Kashif? Is he ...?"

The Arcan! Had he and Davies survived the assault? Someone needed to tend to Sperry and Sarah – if the girl was even still alive? He turned to look at Bostitch.

"I don't know," he soldier shrugged.

The thief was already racing up the stairs.

64.

Reaching the end of the hall, Ethiere found the door to Kashif's room securely shut. He listened for the sound of voices, but heard nothing coming from the other side of the door. With trepidation, Ethiere shifted the fragments of the bottles into one arm. While broken, the glass was still coated with some of the compounds. Ethiere had gathered what he could in hopes the Arcan might be able to salvage even a little more of what he needed.

But if the Arcan was dead? What then?

There would be no hope for Pennie, or Kari, for any of the others. There'd be no hope for him and the rest of the Band. The Arcan was a coward – he'd run rather than stay and fight. He was amoral – he'd justified experimenting on and killing children. Ethiere still despised the foreigner, but he was mature enough to realize the Arcan was vital to their mission.

Without Kashif, the demon would win.

With a hand heavy with fears of what he might find, Ethiere pressed the latch and pushed the door open. His eyes immediately went to the jagged-toothed grin of the shattered window pane. He'd expected that – he'd seen it from the roof. Looking down, he saw Davies and the Arcan, both men frozen as if sculpted from stone. Davies was dead, a bolt planted high in his chest, but the expression on his face riveted the thief. The Physician's eyes were both wide, both focused on Kashif. One hand gripped the bolt futilely, but the other was straining in an attempt to reach for the Arcan.

Sitting with his back against the wall, shielded by the bed, Kashif sat in catatonic contemplation. His hands were on his knees, his fingers clutching his kneecaps tightly. He stared at the outstretched fingers of the Physician – no more than four steps from touching his boots.

"Are you hurt?"

Ethiere's question elicited a blink from the dark-skinned man. Had he only then become aware someone else was in the room? The Arcan lifted his right arm, turning it in self-examination. It was streaked with blood, though nothing appeared to still be running. If that was the worst of the man's injuries …

"I couldn't have saved him," Kashif said in a listless voice. Ethiere couldn't disagree – not with where the bolt had struck the Physician. "He still expected me to try." The Arcan shook his head slowly. "Nothing I could do – and I did nothing." He was still staring at the pleading, lifeless fingers. "I watched him die."

"But you're uninjured," Ethiere reminded him.

The Arcan skewered him with a stare. "I'm supposed to survive." How Kashif said it stood out to Ethiere. There was self-loathing in the statement; an admission of self-inflicted condemnation. "I am important to the eternal plans of the Master Architect. I have a purpose."

"You need to finish the poison," Ethiere prompted.

"I watched him die. I let him die. Him and thousands of untold others. Because of my purpose." The Arcan grimaced as if the words tasted bitter. "I should be proud."

Whatever the Arcan was dealing with, Ethiere needed it to stop. The man could spiral into his personal Oblivion of grief after he'd done what was needed. The thief set the glass shards down, crossed to the Arcan and tried to drag him up to his feet. "The poison – we need it. We can't destroy the demon without it. You need to focus and finish it." He was getting no help from the Arcan. "Davies would have wanted you to finish it!"

A level of alertness returned to the Arcan's eyes at the mention of the Physician's name. "He was a poor scholar, limited in his knowledge. His training was only on the basest of techniques and procedures. He lacked discipline, he lacked focus, he was easily distracted. He was sidetracked by his emotions. Those villagers that died in Alben – he sorrowed for them. They were *his* – *his* patients – he knew them. He'd served them. They belonged to him.

"I have been molded into the pinnacle of my caste – the perfect man of science. Everything I have done has been in the name of the Master Architect, for the perfection of my race. I have done much for which I have been lauded. I should be proud." He looked down to Davies. "But who is my race? A collection of nameless individuals? I do not know them – I do not care for them. I have not served them.

"Every good thing I have done – it has been for the benefit of the faceless masses of Arca. Every horror I have created – it has been for the destruction of nameless individuals, unidentified enemies. In every act I have taken, I have been shielded from the specific faces, the unique names." His haunted eyes turned to Ethiere. "I never had to watch their eyes as their life faded away."

Ethiere wanted to shake the despondent man. "You need names? How about Pennie! Kari! Ollie! What about Sarah and Dom! What about me!" Ethiere focused his face close so that the Arcan would be able to see nothing else. "You want names and faces? Look at me! We are dead – all of us – without that poison. Do it for us!"

Kashif eyes searched his, and a level of sanity returned. "I will still need assistance. Will you help me?"

Ethiere nudged the Arcan towards his door. "There are some people downstairs needing your help first. But when you are through, you will show me exactly what you'd like me to do," he said. As they exited the room, Ethiere took a fleeting glance at the strange looking equipment on the desk. "Lucky for us all, I'm an eager learner."

65.

As he pushed through the entrance of the Eight Flagons, Billick had the undivided attention of everyone in the room. There were fewer patrons in Janns' bar than usual – not surprising seeing as several of the regulars lay dead at the Crescent Head. Billick stared back at the rough lot. Did any of them know what had just transpired? Was anyone else in on Hennessey's assignment?

There was too little surprise in their faces; a lack of knowing fear. If any of these miscreants were involved in Hennessey's plot, seeing Billick in the doorframe should have caused them to squirm. As the drinkers returned to their hushed conversations over their steins, Billick went to the bar. Janns eyed him

head to toe, as if trying to divine the happenings of the last few hours through the cuts and the blood.

"Where's Hennessey?" Billick demanded in a low voice.

Janns' jaw clenched in an indecisive frown. Billick had no quarrel with Janns, but neither would he object to cutting the information out of the barman. He slammed the bloody dagger on the bar to help Janns with his decision and reiterated his question. "Where?"

The barman nodded his head in the direction of the backroom.

"Alone?"

Another nod from Janns, who offered further commentary. "He said you might come around for him tonight."

Billick slid the dagger off of the bar. So Hennessey expected him? Hennessey would have a plan – the contractor was too cunning not to leave himself a way out. "This is between him and me," he told the keeper. In five strides, Billick was to the door. He depressed the latch, and nudged it open – expecting the sound of a crossbow wire or the shuffling of boots on the floor. He heard nothing. He took a step inside.

The room was dark, the fire nothing more than dying embers. Hennessey sat alone at the long table, both hands wrapped around the stein he reflected over. He looked up as Billick entered with a note of resignation in his eyes. "You would think six professional murderers would be enough, wouldn't you? To take out one man?" To his credit, Hennessey wasn't denying what he'd done. "Between you and I, I wanted to send more. But those boiling fools – they'd not go after the famed Billick for anything else than a seventh share."

Billick walked to the table, taking no care to hide the dagger.

"How many did you personally kill?" Hennessey asked, still rooted to his seat. "Two? Three?" The contractor smiled. "Five?" He shook his head. "Boil me, but I bet you were brilliant to watch. I mean … look at you, Billick! You're back! You've got the look in your eye again – that's a good thing! I was worried you'd lost yourself, that you'd lost your footing … it's good to see that isn't the case."

"Why send men to kill me," Billick growled.

Hennessey held up a hand in defense. "It wasn't my idea, friend. After all you and I have accomplished together? No! I was contracted to send men …"

"By who?"

The contractor's eyes shifted away.

"Who!"

"By the one man you can't say no to," Hennessey snapped back.

A Northing, then. But not just any Northing. By what Hennessey implied, it was the Lord Baron himself. He pushed the revelation into the periphery of his mind. Hennessey had offered it as an excuse, as an avenue to shift blame for his actions onto someone else. Billick wasn't about to let the man escape.

"This is good," Hennessey assured him. "This is really good. You are you again – cold, exacting you! You have to understand, I thought you were lost to us. You were given every opportunity to eliminate Malcolm – and you didn't! You let him go! I had to clean up the mess for you myself. Do you see what I did for you?" The man had the gall to smile. "Your reputation is intact. Your instincts have returned." He laughed cruelly. "You've eliminated a large portion of your competition. This is good for us, Billick." He leaned in warmly. "We can continue on …"

"Like nothing ever happened …"

"Exactly."

Billick charged the table in a heated rage. He snatched Hennessey by his collar and held him aloft. "Something did happen!" he yelled. "You sent armed men in after a little girl!" He held the dagger uncomfortably close to Hennessey's face. "This is her blood. Look at it!"

The contractor's eyes narrowed.

"Her blood is on you, Hennessey." Billick grit his teeth. "And you'll pay for it with your own."

Hennessey tensed, but the carefully controlled malice was flashing in his eyes. "Now!" he screamed.

Billick felt his own body tense, as he waited for the blade or the bolt or whatever Hennessey had contrived as his fail-safe plan to act. But nothing came. There was no rush of boots, no twang of a crossbow string. The embers glowed steadily in the fireplace, but the rest of the room was absolutely still.

"Boil you, now!" Hennessey yelled again. Panic set in as he realized whoever he was calling for was not coming. "Janns, boil you!" The contractor looked at Billick, eyes desperate. "I have money. I can pay you. As much as you like! Whatever you like!"

Billick answered with the dagger, and dumped the man like refuse on the floor.

He hurt. The rage had fueled him and dulled the pain, but it was ebbing. Billick became aware of the cut and gashes he'd taken from Jovan's knife. His chest throbbed in agony – he was sure the wounds the Arcan had stitched together would be broken and bleeding again. As he exited the back room, Billick passed by Janns at the bar. The barman was pre-occupied polishing the crossbow sitting fully dismantled on the bar. He stopped long enough to give Billick a knowing look. "I don't get involved. I'm just the barman."

It was true about Janns. It was why there were never any stools at his bar. That fact had saved Billick's life. He nodded towards the back room. "I left a mess," he said as he turned to walk on. "Put it on my tab."

66.

When Sarah's eyes fluttered open, they were greeted by the sun. It seemed majestically white – and for a moment she wondered if this was the eternal embrace of Domus the Deacons spoke of. But as she blinked, the room came into focus. She was lying on a bed, in one of the identically decorated rooms of the Crescent Head.

She turned her head to the side and saw Dom sitting in a chair. He looked tired, but he was smiling.

"I waited with you the entire night," he said with deliberate mock-solemnity.

"Show-off," she teased. She tried to sit up, but her body was slow to respond. She reached to push the blankets off – and only then saw her heavily bandaged left hand. She eyed the wrapping curiously, and looked back to Dom.

"Yeah, be careful with that," he suggested. "And don't be surprised by the nice wrap you've got around your head either – ah, don't touch it!" She heeded his advice and lowered her arm. "Kashif's got everything in place to hold your brains in, so it'd be best not to poke around up there."

"My brains?"

Dom smiled again, unable to hold back. "Alright, so not brains. Said it was a concusser … or something like that. But your head really was bleeding in the back – they think you hit a mug or something when you got pulled down." He leaned in to whisper a secret. "Kashif said he would have shaved your hair off if he'd had time to spare."

Sarah harrumphed. "Numb and bald, can't get much worse than that." She waved her bandaged hand at him. "And this?

"You had a very tight grasp on the wrong end of the knife." Dom's smile fled. "He sewed you back up good, but he was worried. Said you might not be able to use some of them again. Or some might not bend as well as they should. Said we won't know for at least a week or more." He forced a grin. "We can pray for you, right?"

She leaned back against the pillow. "I think I've used my allotment of mercy this year," she opined sadly – but she too couldn't hold the ruse. "Merciful Domus already saved my hair."

They continued to talk, Dom filling her in on everything she'd missed while sleeping off the concussor. No other attacks had come in the night – though that hadn't stopped Reed and his men from sleeping on their swords. They'd found the owner of the Crescent Head and his serving staff hiding in the storeroom cellar. Apparently Reed had been forced to restrain Bostitch from killing the man, who admitted to taking a bribe. The owner kept his life, but hadn't been keen on being forced out of his inn.

But the best were the stories of her friends' heroics. She made Dom tell her those parts over again.

"So suddenly, Ethlere's there with him, up on the roof. He streaks in like he's being blown by a sea squall, and he latches onto the crossbowman by his hair – his hair! – and drags him down the roof ..."

Dom stopped as a shadow filled the doorframe.

It was Billick. The side-burned murderer looked ashen-faced, but he was standing on his own two feet.

"I'll grab you something to eat," Dom said suddenly, and he cut off her protests. "It's wonderful – with no owner or cooks, we've got full reign of the food stores. You'll love these peach preserves I found." Dom left, he and Billick giving each other an ample amount of space. As she watched him disappear out into the hall, Sarah was struck by the impression that something was different about Dom.

At the last moment, she recognized it.

He wasn't wearing his brown coat.

She smiled at the thought, before turning her attention back to Billick.

"You interrupted my story," she chided him.

"I heard you talking," he said. "I wanted to make sure you were okay."

"I feel fine," she reminded him. "I *always* feel fine."

He nodded, and the conversation stalled. She was being mean to him, she realized, which was poor of her. He was trying to protect her – just like her father had always done. She shouldn't be angry at the man for trying to help her out. "Thank you, though, for asking."

Billick nodded again, still very uncomfortable in the room. "Well, you're safe now. I saw to it, you're safe."

"For now," she clarified.

"For now," he echoed.

Sarah looked at the man – one she didn't understand and did not believe she ever could. The internal conflicts, the demons of his past, how strange a contrast to how he was acting right now. Who could have dreamt of a killer coming to check on the well-being of an insignificant girl?

She suddenly felt very sad for him. She knew why she was here – and he did too, even if he didn't like to admit it. "You're going to have a hard time when I die."

He looked away and slowly walked to the door. He paused with a soft grip on the doorframe, but still didn't look at her. "Let's see that doesn't happen any time soon." And he was gone.

67.

The end product looked remarkably similar to honey, both in coloring and in consistency. Kashif would have thought it the first thing one of the others would mention – but no one had. Were they thinking it? Or perhaps they were too focused on how little of the poison his efforts had produced.

"If we are careful to only coat the edges, I estimate we have enough for swords for Reed and Sperry, Billick's axe, two or three crossbow darts and a dagger or two." It would be enough to arm those that mattered. "Even dry, it will still be potent. Strike the demon, cut as deeply as possible. The poison should do the rest."

Bostitch snorted in derision. "Should?"

"Did you expect me to somehow test it first?" he challenged back. "What other choice do we have? What would you propose?" He knew he didn't need to convince the others in the Band. The compelling power of the Banding was already beginning to build. They'd been forced to move against the monster before the day was through. "If you have a better plan ..."

Reed's head was hanging. "If this fails ..."

"We're already dead, right?" No one had expected the cheerless comment from the thief. Kashif and the boy had worked through the morning – and the Arcan had been left impressed. He was ignorant, unschooled – but extremely bright and quick to understand. Had his circumstances been different, the thief boy could have been a great scholar. "This Banding isn't letting us go until it dies or we do. We're destined to face it ... we can only avoid it for so long." Ethiere moved behind Kashif, a show of confidence. "If the Arcan can't figure out a way to beat it – no one is going to."

"Assuming the poison does work," Billick stated, "we have other concerns to deal with. Lord Baron Northing. He hired the group that attacked us last night." Kashif had worked to stitch up those that had taken injury in the ambush the night before. While Sarah and swordsman Sperry's wounds had been significant, Kashif had been surprised by the sheer amount of wounds Billick had taken. It had been a wonder that the man had kept his feet then; it was a testament to his endurance that he was still on his feet now.

"Why would Lord Baron Northing do such a thing?" Greer wondered aloud. "Why would he try to destroy the Band?"

Not wishing to waste any time on a pointless debate, Kashif jumped in. "Lord Baron Northing is more involved in this than any of you realize. He was the one that hired my countrymen and me – and we created the demon."

He knew that the revelation would stun the group. Indeed, it seemed to suck the air out of the room. It was obvious by the varied reactions that Captain Reed had not distributed the information to any of the others. Billick recovered first, and mumbling how fitting it was the monster was Arcan-made, but Sarah voiced the first worried question.

"On purpose?"

Kashif shook his head. "No. At least not on my part. My mentor's experiment spawned the creature we chase. We sought to defeat death – and ended up spawning a self-sustaining demon made up of the corruptible side of magic."

Greer was still shaking her head. "Northing had you do this?"

"To beat death. He wanted a cure. He wanted immortality."

"That's wonderful," Sergeant Bostitch spat. "A demon – and Lord Northing's guards backing it up. I can't see how this could end badly for the … what now, nine of us?"

"Something is happening at the Northing estate," Ethiere reminded them. His crew of adolescent thieves had been employed to watch for another attack. A few had been given the assignment to scout the Northing manor to determine a possible route in. The latest reports spoke to an increase in guard activity – but all of it focused on something happening within the manor itself.

"The demon is loose, perhaps?" voiced Sperry.

"Perhaps," replied the thief. "There is rumor of a coup …"

"A coup?" Greer said in disbelief.

"It's not as if Lord Baron Cahill isn't experienced plotting coups …" Bost muttered.

"We need more than rumors," Reed said. "We need a plan."

"We need a boiling miracle!" Bostitch shot back.

"We're supposed to be the miracle," Dom answered. Surprisingly, he did not fold under the attention that suddenly came his way. "The six of us – the Band. We're the miracle. We were fashioned to be able to kill the demon in spite of all of the obstacles put before us."

Kashif looked at them – the Band of Six – and saw them anew. There was no longer a useless boy – there was Dominic. Not just a Numb girl – but Sarah. Greer was more than her money, Billick more than his axe. And Ethiere, surprisingly bright Ethiere … Kashif looked into their faces, finally seeing past the outer shells of those he was forged with.

There was fear in their faces, there was doubt in their demeanor, but there was a resolve in their eyes. They were six individuals – as unique a six as one might encounter – but they were one. They had names, talents, strengths – but together, they were so much more.

Billick crossed towards him, pulling the axe from his back. Without a word, he extended it towards the Arcan. Kashif knew the murderer would probably never extend a hand as a friend – but this unspoken vote of confidence was not something the Arcan looked at lightly. He smiled, recalling their confrontation that first night in the barn. "I thought you fancied running a sword through your problems."

Billick jostled the axe by its handle. "Close enough."

Kashif stood, rising to his full height. He was proud. He was proud to be numbered among them. They were preparing to run towards their deaths, and he would be proud to die with them.

"One way or another," he said, facing the group, "this will end today. Northing has had the demon for more than a full day now. Marooke and Djemal will have studied the girl's physiology in rich detail. If we do not hurry – I fear Lord Northing may get his wish …" He eyed the vial of poison – the much-too-small vial of poison. "… and we'll be forced to face two monsters."

68.

Dom didn't know why he wasn't more nervous. He certainly felt like he should be more nervous – and wondered if he wasn't being truthful to himself about the dire nature of their circumstances. The others were certainly on edge – he could see it painted all over their auras. None of their fighters – not Billick or Reed or any of his men – resonated with a tint of confidence. There was resignation, but resignation was a very misleading emotion.

Some men, when their backs were up against the wall, wilted. But others – feeling the finality of the wall behind them – found all the inspiration they needed for one final rally.

There were six of them waiting in the alley – Sperry and all of the Banded except for Billick. He, Reed and Bostitch were each making a lap of the outer wall of Lord Northing's compound in an attempt to find a way in. Ethiere's friends in the Children's Gang had performed a similar task earlier that afternoon – and their reports had been discouraging. The entire estate was locked down; each of the gates was closed and manned.

Reading the emotions off of Captain Reed as he returned to the alley, Dom could tell their outlook had not improved in the slightest. They were growing restless – and Dom knew exactly why. It was already a few hours passed midday. They were losing daylight.

None of them liked the prospect of fighting the demon at night.

Approaching the manor estate had eased the prodding from the Banding magic – for a time. Sensing their lack of progress, the pain was awakening in their shoulders again.

"All of the gates are locked," Billick assessed. "They're turning everyone away."

Bost harrumphed as he lit up his paper roll. "A lock-down seems a bit severe to keep out a little Band of Six, don't you think?"

"The guards are nervous," Reed agreed. "I don't think they know why."

"We're supposed to be dead, remember?" added the murderer. "I don't think the lock-down is aimed at preventing us from getting in."

The smoking soldier cocked his head. "You think those rumors of a coup are believable?"

Reed shrugged. "There's no way to confirm the coup. It's all conjecture."

Bost smiled grimly. "Life of a soldier – enough information to do your assignment, not quite enough to survive it."

"So what do we do?" asked Ethiere. "Can we take one of the gates?"

"It would become a contest to see which one of us gets closest to the gate before being shot down," Billick answered. "There aren't a lot of guards, but they'll be well trained." The murderer nudged Kashif with his knee. "You've stayed there. Are there other ways in?"

"Not that I was given to know," the Arcan replied.

"Ethiere could sneak in," Sarah suggested.

Ethiere frowned, and Dom could see his doubts. "It would have to get dark first …"

"… And we'd need to blot out the moon," Billick leered. "Those courtyards have no cover. Your dash would have to be something miraculous for you to survive. And then, you'd still have to manage getting the rest of us in. Unless you're keen to take on the demon yourself."

"My father is in there," Lady Greer offered. "He would assist us, I am sure. But we have no way of getting a message to him." The noblewoman shook her head. The group sat in silence – their ideas exhausted and their frustrations mounting.

"What if we asked?"

Sarah's newest suggestion brought a note of levity to the heavy situation. "Ask?" muttered Bostitch. "Maybe if we ask very nicely …" Lady Greer whacked him in the shoulder to silence his remark, but his smile showed he was still thinking it.

Reed tried to explain it to her. "Soldiers follow orders … they won't go against their orders because someone asks them to."

"Maybe they won't," Dom said. They looked at him; most still not used to hearing him voice his thoughts. Being unshackled from his fears was refreshing. "But maybe they will. Maybe if we explain the situation to them." There wasn't much enthusiasm echoing through the group. "We should at least try."

"We've not conceived of a better option," admitted Kashif.

As other heads nodded, Sergeant Bostitch emphatically threw the charred end of his smoke to the cobblestones and rubbed it out with the toe of his boot. "Boiling loony plan. Let's all remember to say 'please'."

As they neared the selected gate – the one that Reed said had the fewest guards – Dom wondered why he was suddenly in the lead. Talking to the guards – asking permission to enter – had been Sarah's idea originally, hadn't it? He'd only voiced his support for it – not thought it up! Besides, if anyone was going to win the sympathy of the guards, wouldn't it be the sad looking girl with the bandaged head and hand? The gangly boy would be the last person to lead the procession!

But leading he was. And maybe he wasn't the last person to be out in front. Billick and Lady Greer's soldiers were visibly armed. Kashif was an Arcan, which wouldn't likely garner him any favors. Ethiere still looked every bit the sly thief they'd met at the fountain.

So maybe there was some logic behind having him and Sarah lead the charge.

They had the attention of the three guards at a distance, who watched the group of nine people approach with a non-threatening gait. All had crossbows – and Dom's envisioned the frantic run across the barren courtyard Billick had described. Not even Ethiere was that quick.

"Turn around," one of the men at the gate called out to them.

Dom didn't know what he should say. No one had offered him suggestions.

Gratefully, Lady Greer spoke out. "Which of you is in charge?" she asked.

"Turn – around," the first soldier enunciated for them. "Now."

Greer managed a frown nobles must practice in the mirror. It warned they were displeasing someone they shouldn't be displeasing. "Who is in charge?" she repeated. "We have pressing business in your Lord Baron's manor."

"Gates are locked," the second soldier responded. "No one gets by. Turn around."

"But we're Banded!" This comment came from Sarah, and caught everyone off-guard. The girl stepped forward and pulled up the sleeve of her blouse, revealing the dark, welt-like ring marring the flesh of her shoulder. While Sarah's contribution to the conversation had seemed ill-timed – the soldiers guarding the gate both looked, and for the first time, no response was given for them to leave.

While others of the Band may have noted that too, only Dom could see a level deeper … into the recesses of their hearts and swells of emotion hidden behind their stoic, unbending facial-expressions.

And Dom knew why he was here. Why he'd been Banded. Why it was critical he'd been chosen.

"You are probably aware that something is going on within the manor," Kashif explained as he stepped forward. "The Arcans your Lord hired – I am one of them. My colleagues are responsible for creating a terrible monster – one that your Lord Baron brought back to the manor two nights ago."

"It tore through a unit of my best men," Reed added.

"The wizard we had with us was powerless against it," Billick added. "It bled him dry."

Kashif continued the joint petition. "It is a demon from Oblivion. Perhaps you have heard rumors of a shadowy, faceless thing? One that cannot be harmed by sword or bolt. Already it has killed; it will continue to kill – unabated …"

"Unless we let you lot in?" The first guard asked skeptically – and Dom knew that he and Sarah were the root of that skepticism. The others had just built the demon up into some unbeatable foe – and implied two children would be part of the assault team.

But looking into the hearts of the other two guards, watching their emotions, Dom saw doubt spreading. Not doubt towards what they were hearing, but doubts concerning their current decision to keep the Band out. Dom studied both of them before choosing his target.

He called a bluff.

"You," he whispered, pointing at the second of the guards through the bars of the iron gate. "You believe us. You think we should be let in." The man was immediately under the scrutiny of his two peers, and he grew nervous under the pressure. "It's okay!" Dom moved to assure him. "It's okay. As soon as you admit it, he'll agree with you!" Dom gestured to the third of the trio, whose aura was teetering with indecision. "Whatever you believe is going on within the walls of the manor, neither of you believe everything is well." Dom lifted his sleeve, bearing his Band like Sarah had. "When you saw the Band on the girl – you began to doubt …"

"Enough of that!" the lead guard declared, now eyeing his fellows with suspicion. "Last warning – back away from the gate! Crossbows at the ready!"

"You won't shoot us!" Dom yelled at the leader. "You're too boiling scared to give the order – I can see it in you!" The other two guards had only hefted their bows part way and were now watching their superior to see how he would respond. True to the reading Dom had divined, the man was impotent to continue.

"We sent the others to check and they never came back," the second soldier said quietly. "What if things are as bad as these people say?"

"We've been ordered to keep the gate secured!" the leader retorted.

"Against them?" argued the third. "Against a Band of Six?"

The leader spun to rebuke him, feeling as if he was being ambushed on all sides. "We'll be hung if we disobey!"

Billick harrumphed. "Would you rather wait to be ripped apart?"

They were close – Dom could see in their auras how close they were to breaking. But they were fighting it – the fear of deciding wrong outweighing their courage to do what they thought was right. It was like Captain Reed had predicted – they were soldiers. It was easiest for them just to obey, even knowing the orders were wrong.

"We could knock you out!" Dom blurted the epiphany.

"Boiling, what?" Bostitch cursed, and the three Northing guards looked equally perplexed. But Dom knew he was right. "You'll be punished if you allow us in – even though you know it's right. Well, what if your superiors find you unconscious? You could tell them we rushed you … that you put up a fight!"

"Are you a fool?" the first guard spat … just as the second swung the heel of his crossbow into the back of his neck. The first soldier folded to the ground. Everyone stood speechless. The third guard recovered enough to unlock the gate and stepped aside to let the Band through. "Thank you," Dom told him.

Surprisingly, he and the second guard fell in step as they headed towards the manor. "With the coup going on – who's to say who'll hang and for what. But there are rumors about a creature tearing people apart." The guardsman grimaced. "Whatever it is, I'd like to say I took sides against it."

69.

Northing's two gate guards seemed apprehensive as they entered the manor. "There should be sentries here," one said. The manor entry-hall, with its vaulted ceiling and impressive archways, seemed cavernously empty. Ethiere had never set foot in a place so magnificent – each nook and every corner seemed full of exquisite treasures. Normally he would have felt impressed to explore around a bit. But not today.

He took Kashif by the arm. "My friends?" he asked pointedly. "You promised me."

The Arcan nodded. "I did. I will show you."

Reed overheard. "Nobody splits off," he pronounced, "not until the job is finished."

Ethiere opened his mouth to argue, but the man of science did it for him. "Our part is finished, Captain. My role was to conceive of and create the poison. Ethiere's role was to gather the materials I needed. Without those efforts, the cause of the Band would have failed." He paused to see if Reed would argue. "I promised to take Ethiere to where his friends are being held. Please allow me to fulfill that promise."

Reed stayed silent and turned to the rest of the group for their input.

"Let them go," Billick opined.

"Go find your friends," Lady Greer urged.

Reed nodded, and reached to his belt. "Take this," he said, proffering one of the poisoned daggers. "Just in case."

"It shouldn't be necessary," the Arcan declined, but Ethiere took the blade forthright. He'd faced the monster once before – he'd known the terror of being defenseless then. This time, in the very least, he'd have a chance to strike back if he needed to.

Kashif pointed to a staircase visible down one of the halls. "The laboratory is up there."

They heard Sarah call after them as they sped to their destination. "Good luck."

* * * * *

389

Kashif took the stairs slower than the thief, but the boy didn't run off ahead. He'd get a half-dozen stairs ahead and then wait impatiently for the Arcan to catch up. Kashif couldn't describe the feeling in his stomach as he climbed towards the laboratory. While the thief was anxious to see if his captured friends still lived, the Arcan anticipated a far different meeting.

Marooke would be in the laboratory. Kashif would have to face his master and life-long mentor. Marooke had crossed the line; he'd gone too far. Had the wizened Scholastad realized his mistakes, had he rued his wrongful experiments with the Essen? Kashif prayed silently to the Master Architect it might be so. Because if not …

Marooke had made a monster once. The world could not afford for him to do so again.

He caught up to Ethiere on a landing. "Why didn't you want a dagger?" he thief asked.

He cleared a breath. "I am a man of science – not a man of war. Weaponry is considered beneath my station." The thief weighed the response, and seemed to accept it.

"So the small sample of the poison in your pack?" he asked. Kashif eyed the clever young man. Before they'd taken their work down to explain the plan to the others, Kashif had taken a thin vial of the stuff and hidden it in his pack. He'd thought he'd done so unobserved.

"I did not think you'd seen that."

The response was surprising. "I didn't. I found it – when I went through your pack."

The Arcan felt his irritation rise. "When …"

"While you coated the weapons." The thief smiled. "It was the first time since we've met you haven't been guarding it like a bulldog." The thief was not apologetic. "I didn't take anything. I just looked through it all. And I found the poison."

"So you did."

"What is it for?"

The Arcan felt his stomach roll again. They'd reached the top of the stairs; the laboratory door visible down the corridor. He felt it – his fate – waiting for him on the other side. The thief would not understand, so Kashif left his answer cryptic. "A last resort."

*   *   *   *   *

The workings of death greeted them as they continued further into the manor. Dead soldiers wearing Northing's colors littered the hallways in twos and threes. Greer did her best to avoid them, but her curiosity pestered her to look at them as she passed.

Empty, unseeing eyes. Ashen faces.

"This isn't the work of the monster," Sperry said to Reed. "Those are sword wounds."

At the next intersection of halls, Greer's heart froze mid-beat. Lying in the midst of four others, she saw Caleb. She broke from the pack to run to him, already knowing it was too late. His face was drained of color, his chest still. She dropped to her knees before him, heavy with grief. His lips that had kissed her so gently would never smile again.

"Merciful Domus," whispered one the gate guards. "That's Lord Owen's companion."

Armored men suddenly rushed down one of the hallways. Swords and crossbows were raised on both sides.

"State your allegiance!" demanded one of the soldiers at the forefront. His uniform, and some of those worn by the men around him, looked to be smeared with blood. "Which Northing?" another yelled. "Father or son?"

"Neither," shouted Reed; and Greer wondered if that was an acceptable answer. "We side with neither. We're here to slay the faceless creature! We lay no claim to the affairs of this barony."

The answer satisfied the newcomers. Their weapons lowered, but were not sheathed. "Then you side with the son – as we do." He approached Reed. "The

Lord Baron has gone mad. He ordered the slaying of Lord Owen, his council, and other nobles staying in the manor. He leads out in his slaughter. Lord Owen has been seriously maimed – though not fatal."

Greer stood – a new fear in her heart. "My father?"

The soldier studied her for a moment. "Are you a Cahill?" He shook his head with a tired smile. "I don't believe it – your father said you might show up."

"He's still alive?"

"Saw him not fifteen minutes ago, my Lady," he answered. "We've taken our injured to the courtroom and fortified it against counter-attack. The Baron controls the whole western wing; he and the few men still loyal to him press the assault from there. Your father has taken a lead in Lord Owen's stead."

"You're not going west," Reed pointed out.

"We're going for supplies. Food, water, weapons. Bandages for the wounded. There are several storehouse rooms on the floor below." He turned back to Greer. "Your father will want you back in the courtroom." He motioned up the corridor where his men stood waiting. "It's the safest place in the manor at the moment."

She should have expected no less from her father. She looked to Reed, and was surprised to see the Captain looking at her. "It's your decision."

He wasn't going to force her. She looked inside herself – and was surprised to feel something pulling her towards the courtroom. "My father should be with us," she told Reed. "You and the others are still responsible for his safety." She looked to the others of the Band. Would they feel she was abandoning them?

They nodded in understanding. "Go," said Dom.

"You and I will go fetch your father," Reed announced. He addressed Sergeant Bostitch. "That leaves you Billick's axe, Sperry's sword and your bolts."

Bost shrugged humorlessly. "Think that's enough? It's only an invulnerable, Oblivion-spawned demon." Behind them, the resistance commander selected two of his men out to accompany them back. Absorbing the gate guards, he and the rest continued to the storerooms. Greer started down the hall when she felt a hand on her shoulder.

Bost's head was turned away; he wasn't able to meet her eyes. In his other hand, he proffered the last of the poisoned daggers, tied around the hilt with a black thread. "Take it," he said. "It's was Neald's. You'll find it easier to use than his sword." She took it solemnly, and he drew in closer to whisper in her ear. "You find anyone who played a part in ordering his death – you see that Neald gets a parting shot, alright?"

"For Neald," she whispered back, and let Reed lead her up the corridor.

70.

Ethiere had never set foot in a laboratory before. As he and Kashif stopped in the doorway, Ethiere's eyes took inventory of the foreign room. Multiple tables lined the walls, on which sat fantastically complex-looking pieces of equipment. An oversized cabinet held more bottles than any of the apothecist shops he'd stolen from. There were papers – some bound into tight books like the Arcan's ledger – others loose and scattered on the tables and floors. If he had to describe it, Ethiere thought it looked like the Arcan's pack had expanded to fill a room.

Kashif moved in first. He was acting cautiously – as if expecting something. There was no one in the room with them, but Ethiere had the same heavy feeling in his stomach he'd experienced before seeing the crossbowman on the roof. Maybe it was just the Arcan's behavior making him jumpy – but the thief drew the dagger just in case.

"This was the area for our research," the Arcan told him. "The cells where we held … your friends … are through that door."

"You aren't coming?"

The scientist shook his head. "I need to find Djemal's latest notes. I need to determine what else they may have found – what else they might have done." Ethiere nodded in understanding, and trotted towards the door the Arcan had pointed out. "Ethiere!" he heard Kashif call from behind. He turned, and saw the man's head hanging down. "Whatever you do find … please know I am terribly, terribly sorry."

Ethiere did not know how to respond. He stood, facing the Arcan, and could not come up with a single thing to say. He lowered his head and retreated toward the other room. The door was slightly ajar, and Ethiere pulled it the rest of the way open.

The other side of the door was crisscrossed with deep scratches.

Something had tried to claw its way out.

"Ethiere?" He heard her voice and ran towards it. The room was dark, there were no windows and no lit lamps, but he could see it was lined, wall to wall, with cages. Kashif had said cells – Ethiere had pictured prison – but these were small boxes, not even large enough to stand in. They were stacked, three high to the ceiling.

There were unmoving bodies in some, and the thief resisted the urge to see if he recognized who.

Kari was in one of the lower cages. He dropped to his knees and extended his fingers through the small openings in the bars. Kari's fingers intertwined with his – and Ethiere felt like crying in relief. Kari already was. "Where in Oblivion have you been?" she asked through her tears.

"I came for you," he whispered to her. "I came as soon as I could." He retracted his fingers and set them on the brass lock on the cage door. "I'm going to get you out."

"Ollie is in the middle cage, over there," Kari told him. "He's really sick. I think they purposefully made him sick." She rubbed her eyes with her fingers. "I think the others are all dead." The lock was solid, and Ethiere was without a pick. "They put a monster in the room with us." Kari pointed, and Ethiere followed her finger.

The largest cage at the end of the room was in shambles. The frame was bent in several places, the metal bars crooked. The door had been completely ripped off the hinges. "They put Pennie in that cage, and they put out all of the lamps." Kari shuttered. "After that, people started to scream and die. I think Pennie ..." Kari had to stop.

Ethiere gave up on the lock, frustrated. "It's alright. I know, I know, it's alright. I'm going to get you and Ollie out of here." He held his fingers out to her again. "Please, Kari, do you know where the key is? Did you see where they kept the keys?"

"One of the dark-skinned men," she answered. "On his belt."

Ethiere scrambled to his feet and ran for the door. "I'll be right back. I promise, Kari, I'll be right back."

*　　*　　*　　*　　*

Kashif quickly went through the notes on Djemal's desk, and was disappointed at finding so few that were remotely current. It wasn't like the meticulous note-taker to not be keeping a record, so where was it? And where was Djemal? Where was Marooke? Why weren't they in the laboratory?

Both had Essen-rich blood. There was an obvious conclusion; Kashif tried to avoid jumping to it.

His ears picked up on a small sound – something tapping. It wasn't Ethiere – it was coming from the complete opposite direction from the cell room. It stopped, for just a moment, and started again. He focused on it – narrowed on its location. It came from the operating theatre. The door was cracked open, a teasing invitation.

Kashif pushed the door open wider.

Djemal sat at the scribe desk, back to the door, bent over the ledger he was working on.

But he wasn't moving.

In fives strides, Kashif was to him and put a hand on his colleague's shoulder. The body was rigid and teetered off-balance at his touch. Djemal's head rolled back, and Kashif could see the agony he'd died in written in his eyes. They were just like Davies. Large, in pain, and pleading.

There were bloody stains on Djemal's shirt. Four holes aligned perfectly with the man's arteries. Kashif did not need to look to know there would be two more on the torso.

"It couldn't be helped."

His master stood in the corner of the room, well-hidden in the abundant shadows. "Djemal had the highest Essen count among anyone in the manor."

"Excluding yourself," Kashif reminded.

"Excluding myself," his mentor agreed. "I was wondering when you might return. I found it ironic that you were compelled to leave to hunt the very thing we brought back to the laboratory. It appears you have managed to survive your ordeal to this point."

"Just like you required of me."

Marooke nodded. "You were always the most obedient of apprentices." The older Arcan took two steps around the central operating table. "It was why I couldn't include you in my last round of experiments. You were fully invested into the ideals of our society – the good of Arca and the perfection of the race. I could not tell whether you would condone or condemn my actions."

"How long ago did you lose those ideals, Master?"

Marooke smiled. "When I realized my race needed me far more than I needed my race. When I conceived perfection could be realized in my lifetime, and not through incremental genetic manipulation. I have not worked my entire life just to be another rung on the ladder to the Architect's ideal. I deserved to stand at the top."

Kashif nodded. His suspicions were confirmed. "Alone at the top. Without me, without Djemal. He was looking at you when he died, wasn't he. He was looking at you and pleading for a mercy he thought could be granted. He didn't understand that he was just a rung on your ladder, did he Master?" Marooke's face was a placid mask; Kashif could not see any remorse for his actions. "The experiments to conquer death – they were not just for Northing were they? He was just the patron for the work you'd already concluded to do."

"You were always bright, Kashif."

"Is perfection worth the monster you've become?"

The senior scientist thrust out a hand, and Kashif crashed into the wall, driven by an unseen force. Magic! The mentor grinned. "The girl could heal – the creature pulled so much Essen into her system that even unfocused, she could make her empathetic wishes reality."

He held up his hand, lightening crackling over his fingertips. "You see what a focused mind can accomplish? I have found no limits to the power." The electric display faded, and Marooke frowned. "It is a pity. Our Magistad have the power within them – and they do not exercise it! They have this power – and they withhold it from Arca! I shall have to ask them why."

Kashif staggered back to his feet. "You're going back to Arca?"

Marooke nodded. "It was in the final terms I struck with Northing. We both gain immortality. He gets Tollia and the entire world. I get Arca."

Kashif understood why. "Our programs of breeding. You'll propagate generations of Essen-blooded Arcans to feed the demons appetite!"

"Why our dear short-sided Lord Baron and experiment twenty-two proceed to rip unabated through the entire Tollian population – and then starve to death." Marooke paced forward. "Man has been perfected Kashif! Arca will rise to her natural place in the world! I will rule supreme!" The elder Arcan lowered his head, and darkness began to billow from the back of his neck like a cloud of steam. "Behold the form of ultimate perfection."

*　　*　　*　　*　　*

"We need to find the keys ..." Ethiere said as he returned to the main room of the laboratory. He was surprised to not see Kashif ...

Suddenly, the Arcan was in the doorway across the room. "Run!" he yelled, before he was pitched violently forward. The scientist slid across the floor before ramming into the thick legs of one of the desk. Kashif rolled onto his back and stayed down.

Coming through the doorway was the menacing form of the black monster.

Ethiere froze, feet rooted to the ground. It was just like Alben ... with nothing between him and the monster but a dozen paces ...

But this time was different ... the dagger! It was ...

Ethiere's fingers grew numb, feeling their own emptiness. The dagger ... he must have set it down when he tried to pick Kari's lock ... he'd not brought it back out!

His feet instinctively moved back towards the cell room door. Only his trained reflexes stopped him quickly enough as the chair flew by and smashed into the wall. The creature wrapped its long fingers around a second chair, and launched it.

Amid the spray of shattering wood, his body took over for his paralyzed brain. Ethiere's feet moved with a desperate purpose; his mind trying to catch up. His first foot landed on the closest chair, and he sprang onto the desk. A spray of white papers rose into the air as he jumped towards the stone wall, his fingers prepared for the contact. As they brushed against the rough-hewn stone, they found holds. Like a spider he climbed, escaping the reach of the long, clawed arms.

Ethiere found a corner of the wall, close to the high ceiling, where the grips were comfortable. He craned his neck, and saw the demon looking up at him. The glossy blackness of the monster slid away from the Arcan's mouth to reveal his amused smile. "Do you think you are safe from me up there, little spider?" Sparks of lightening crackled from the demon's long, lean fingers.

Behind the monster, Ethiere saw Kashif stir. The scientist shook his head, trying to clear it. Kashif looked up briefly, their eyes met, before the Banded Arcan's eyes strayed towards his pack. In that moment there was an epiphany – a simple clarity of what needed to happen. And Ethiere knew his part.

The demon-Arcan must have seen something of the exchange – its attention reverting back to Kashif. "That is correct. I should kill you first, my apprentice," he said. "I have nothing to fear from the spider."

Ethiere jumped from the safety of the corner – immediately in a dead sprint for the tall cabinet full of colored bottles. As he ran, his eyes scanned the shelves. The names of the chemicals flashed through his ears – but more than just the names. The lessons of the night before, as he'd worked with Kashif, flowed freely through his memory. He knew not only what they were called – he knew how they could be used.

His dash caught the attention of the demon, whose swipe barely missed the racing thief. The creature turned fully just in time to catch the first bottle as it shattered into the man's exposed face. Bosoric acid, Kashif had called it. Never touch it, he had warned.

It burns flesh.

The skin of the Arcan's face began to boil like a hot cauldron, and he screamed at the pain. But even as he burned, the scream changed from a howl of agony to a sadistic laugh. The monster straightened as the flesh fell away from the cheek and jawbone … and Ethiere watched as the muscle and skin began to grow back.

"Among all of those bottles, you happen upon the bosoric acid," the Arcan mused. "A lucky guess, thief? Or has my apprentice been educating you on your journey together." He laughed, and Ethiere could still see the man's tongue through the closing gap in his cheek. "What would the Magistad say to about that, Kashif? You would be whipped for imparting knowledge to a boy of this status? Educating a lowly Dynad! What of order, my apprentice? What of keeping everyone in their correct place? It seems to me that we have both lost our ideals!"

Ethiere kept both eyes on the madman, but kept his fingers moving in a sightless inventory of the bottles. There was nothing Kashif had taught him more powerful than the acid … but the other Arcan didn't know the extent of his education. For all Ethiere knew, there was something even more dangerous on the shelf … he only hoped the Arcan's eyes would betray it when Ethiere touched it.

This was all just a distraction anyhow. He just needed to give Kashif enough time …

Jaw completely healed, the older Arcan smiled before his face disappeared behind the faceless hood of sheer blackness.

"Ethiere!" Kashif's hands emerged from his pack, and he rolled one of his shiny silver instruments across the floor. It raced towards his waiting hands with a sweet, shrill hum. The monster located the sound, but was too late to stop it from going on by into Ethiere's waiting fingers. Clutching the new weapon, Ethiere realized he recognized it.

It was the scoping tool Kashif had used on Dom's wrist.

The tool was small and slender, but Ethiere didn't hesitate. In three rapid steps he reached the hulking demon and slashed the tip across the creature's ebony chest. The blackness ripped apart at the contact, but immediately reformed itself, like water returning to glass after the stone's ripples subside. There was a moment of waiting from both sides. Hope waned as the moment stretched … and fled …

With a massive balled fist, the demon knocked the flat-footed thief towards one a cabinet filled with equipment. Ethiere could not regain his balance, could not stop his momentum, until the tall cabinet stopped it for him. The instruments rattled angrily at the disturbance – but no sooner did he find his footing than the monster was towering before him. He held up the scoping tool, as useless as it was …

They'd failed. The poison didn't work. Sarah, Dom, Greer, Billick … they would all die.

Instead of the fatal blow Ethiere expected, the massive clawed hands reached around him, gripping onto each side of the cabinet. The inky blackness bulged under the strain as the whole shelf rocked forward. Ethiere tried to duck aside – get out of the way – but was too late. The cabinet caught his leg, pinning him under the heavy wood as Arcan equipment crashed onto the floor.

The silver tool rolled in a slow loop, just out of reach, until a massive, black shrouded foot stepped on top of it. The demon's face subsided again to reveal the mouth of his tormentor. "You should have stayed up on the wall, little spider." The fingers of the monster's hand stretched until the brushed the fabric of Ethiere's shirt and the thief tensed. "A shame – your blood has nothing to offer me. I shall save you, I think. I will show you the acids in my collection." The mouth curved to a hungry smile. "First though, I'm going to feed."

71.

"I don't think Lord Baron Cahill will be keen on leaving," one of the accompanying soldiers told her. "With Lord Owen down, he's directing our forces. He's the best strategist …" They rounded a corner – right into three other armed men. Both groups looked similarly surprised to see the other – but weapons were already drawn and ready.

Recognition came to the other group first. "Boiling traitorous dogs!" Swords began to crash into one another. Another of the loyalist guards began to shout for reinforcements. Greer looked down the corridor and saw men charging towards them.

Reed saw them too. "Which way to the courtroom?"

"Down the hall!" answered one of the rebels, pushing away from the opponent he was locked in combat with. "To the right!"

Reed slugged the man nearest to him in the face. "Go!" he yelled to her, and threw himself into the path of three more incoming men. "Run!"

She obeyed – the dagger looking pitifully short compared to the incoming blades. She ran, only risking a glance as she turned the corner to see no one chasing her. She entered the courtroom – anticipating safety.

She found it strewn with corpses.

The primary position of defense for the opposition was a graveyard. Perhaps it should have been obvious – the doors being ajar – there not being faces of men watching for the attack. There had been guards, but they were lying dead at her feet.

A chill sunk deep into her bones. The lifeless bodies before her were not like the ones they'd passed earlier in the corridor. These had been savaged.

The faceless demon, skin a polished black, rose to its full height. The fingers of one hand were still extended like thirsting tree roots into the body of a man on the dais. Greer's hand petrified around the hilt of the poison dagger; she felt very small and defenseless all the same. Merciful Domus, where was Reed? He should be here – he was the fighter! He was supposed to protect her …

Who was she to deserve protection?

She held the blade before her, and was dismayed at the way it uncontrollably shook.

The monster on the dais faced her. Eyeless as it was, she nevertheless knew it was watching her. Mouth-less as it was, she knew it was smiling. Suddenly, the oily blackness began to pull back, receding like an ebbing tide. Human features became visible, clothing, skin. The creature billowed inward, collecting itself behind the form of its host.

And Greer was staring at Lord Baron Northing.

"Not who you expected?" he asked her, putting forth a gloved hand to motion around the room. "To their credit, it was well defended – as well as could have been expected. They could have held off a force three times their size in the position they took." His appraisal fell silent, and he focused a leer on her. "But they couldn't stop me. All of them together, and they couldn't stop me."

"Where's my father?" she demanded in a quailing voice.

Northing pursed his lips and his head glanced around the room as if replaying the combat in his head. "Ah, yes," he said at last, pointing to a motionless mass,

"He ended up over there."

Greer felt weak on her feet. "You killed him!" she said, voice rich with venom.

Northing smiled. "It was bound to happen eventually."

"You killed him!" she repeated, her mind frozen on the thought. Her father – whom she'd fought and pushed against all of her life – was dead.

"If it is any consolation," the Lord Baron offered, "we both lost family today." He reached out with his boot and turned the face of the man he'd been draining. It was the pale, gaunt face of Owen.

"Merciful Domus," she whispered, and looked up to Northing with disgust. "He was your son! He was your heir!"

"True," the Lord Baron replied. "But as it turns out, I don't need heirs. They are quite obsolete, considering I'll live forever. Live forever and rule forever – which you may suspect, was difficult for Owen to accept. He's been anticipating his succession of the barony since his mother died – grew quite attached to the idea. Keeping him alive would have only delayed the inevitable confrontation. How long would it have taken him to raise an army against me? Before he sails back with a legion to wrest the kingdom away from me by force? Easier just to settle it now."

"Others will rise up."

"Undoubtedly, yes. The other Lord Barons must have come to an uneasy peace with the idea of a Northing ascending to claim the old throne. I could have had myself coroneted years ago – thankfully I didn't. Me, your father, the others – we were the original insurrectionists. How long before they began to plot to depose of me, just like we did the king so many years ago?" He let the question hang. "Your father was a good man – shrewd. Our rebellion wouldn't have found success without him. But he and the others are ambitious. They are power-hungry. I'll be settling my affairs with the others as shortly as time permits."

"You will get no rest. Bands will be formed."

Northing threw his hands wide. "Let them come!" he challenged. "I'm immortal now! Have them bring their swords and their shields, their bows and their wizards!" He laughed, and pulled down the open collar of his shirt. His chest was dotted with crossbow bolts. As he walked towards her, he grabbed one of the shafts, twisted, and wrenched it free. As Greer watched, the flesh around the hole in his chest mended before her eyes. Northing tossed the bolt mockingly at her feet. "I have defeated death – tell me, what fear can my enemies ever think to hold?"

Emboldened, Greer rushed forward with the knife. Just a scratch, she told herself. Just a boiling scratch! Northing's eyes brightened with amusement, and he caught her arm deftly as she reached him. He was strong and he bent her arm backwards, causing the sinews in her arms to scream in agony. Her fingers convulsed. The dagger dropped harmlessly to the floor.

The Lord Baron relaxed the angle he held her arm at – but he did not let go. Greer found herself face to face with him. "That was very un-Lady-like," he told her. "Your father would have died again had he seen the look on your face while you ran towards me just now ..." He leaned in closer. Greer pulled back, but could not escape his grip.

"I have no need of heirs, but I will have other needs," he said thoughtfully. "Death robbed me of my Queen – and while I do not expect I'll take another ... I will still have need for entertainment. I still wish to surround myself with the best that existence has to offer."

His suggestion repulsed her. She raised her other arm, but he caught it cleanly as well. "Your father spoke highly of you." Northing looked over to where her father lay. "That man! Shameless! All the subtly of a street-merchant hawking fruit or bolts of cloth. Ever since my house rose to the position of power among the Lord Baron's, your father has been trying to sell you – to me." He looked her over. "Are you everything he claims you to be?"

"I won't ..."

"Even for your life?"

"I'm Banded. I will never stop trying to kill you. You know that."

Northing laughed, and pushed her away. Greer steadied herself against the courtroom table. "That – I imagine – will be half the fun – watching you try, every night, to kill me." He paced as he fantasized. "Will you try to choke me while I sleep? Exhaust your strength with your hands at my throat? Fall, weeping into my bosom when your arms no longer can support your weight?" The Lord Baron bent down and picked up the poisoned dagger. He walked back towards her, waving it in her face. "Think of it – every day, every night, the

Banding forcing you to try to kill me again. Every day, every night – until either it breaks you – or I do." He pressed up against her. "That will be entertainment fit for a god!"

Greer felt her lips tremble.

"Think about it, Greer. You were bred for nobility. You will stand behind the most powerful man in the world. What more could a woman of your station want?"

Northing smiled, and bent in to touch his lips to hers.

His words stirred the demons in her soul.

She tilted her chin down, denying him. Defying him. She was able to look directly into his disbelieving eyes. "What do you know of my boiling wants?" She reached out with both of her hands, fighting for a grip on the dagger he held between them.

Northing butted his head against hers. The lights in her eyes flashed, and her knees buckled, but she held on to the dagger. He smirked at her. "Anyone else would have taken my offer."

She knew that. She did. It was why it had had to be her – why the Banding had taken her.

"I'm not anyone else."

Northing smiled cruelly, and his eyes lolled back into his head. Blackness began to snake around him, wrapping itself around his flesh. "You are all the same. Goodbye, Greer." The smile disappeared as the oozing ebony coated his face. The creature's arms flexed from the Lord Baron's back, independent of the man's arms still holding joint control of the dagger. The pointed fingers extended, drawing out into needle-like claws.

Bracing herself against the table she was pressed up against, Greer put every bit of strength she had into pushing the knife upward.

The move had not been expected.

The dagger shot upward, impaling the black faced monster through the neck. It reeled, as if stung, and Northing stumbled back. Greer, off-balance, pitched forward and fell to her knees. The demon steadied itself and raised a clawed hand to strike her …

The hand sagged, misshapen, as if it were too heavy for the arm to support. The monster shuddered, trying to swing the other arm, which dragged along the floor … and fell off. Greer watched, mesmerized, as the black ooze began to melt away from the Lord Baron's face. The dagger dropped to the floor, as the creature sagged away, and Northing's hands went to his punctured throat.

He could not breath, the creature no longer sustaining him.

The sweet gall of revenge raced through her veins. "You think you know me?" she laughed. "I don't even know me." Northing's eyes flashed towards her – anger, confusion – it was beautiful. She walked towards him. "If you could only see your face, Lord Baron." She bent down and picked up the dagger.

Neald's dagger.

She held it in front of his face, to let it be the last thing he saw.

"For Neald," she told him. "For Caleb." She reached out and put a steadying grip on his shoulder. "For my father."

72.

Marooke bent and picked up the scoping tool, and turned towards him.

"This was your best attempt?" his Master asked, his disappointment evident.

Kashif recalled his observation, several nights ago. *No one ever died from a scoping tool before.* He chose not to answer. It was all he could do to keep his

head up. The fall … he'd crashed into the desk so hard … he wouldn't be able to rise to his feet if he tried.

Marooke approached on a steady amble. "Poisoned, was it?" he mused. "The right idea, Kashif. Djemal came to the same conclusion. He got further along than I thought he would – before I fed on him. I knew if Djemal could conceive of a poison – you would as well. I expected it." Marooke hovered over him, pinching the thin tool between two fingers. "That you failed – well, you did not have your equipment, or access to the various compounds you might need. Your failure might be justified. Perhaps I gave you too much credit – I expected you to succeed." The elder Arcan bent down and slid the scoping tool back into the pack. "You've never failed before … of all the times to fail …"

The oily blackness oozed out of Marooke and built itself around his left arm. It twisted in snaking sinews, forming into the massive hand with the long, precision-sharp fingers.

Marooke flexed the fingers, admiring them. "The girl from the experiments – she fights against the demon inside of her. She resists the creature's power – seeks to contain its awesome force. In her sympathy she has rejected the full measure of what she might become. Sympathy – it is a weakness I do not share."

The mentor refocused on his student. "Let us begin your final lesson on the subject of pain," Marooke said. "I want you to concentrate, Kashif. Focus! Control your breathing. Djemal could not. He died screaming, begging for relief." The right arm grew and solidified, matching the left. "As your last conscious choice – choose to die with dignity."

Kashif raised his chin in defiance, and Marooke brought his hands into position.

He felt each of the extended fingers distinctly as they burrowed into his chest cavity. The pain was intense – more intense than anything his Master had ever inflicted on him during their hours of lessons. Kashif fought against the urgent commands from all of his instincts. It was everything he could do to keep his body from squirming, writhing on the floor. But he kept still, jaw tensed, eyes locked with his mentor's.

A new feeling flooded his body; starting with a numb tingling in his extremities. The creature was tapped into his arteries … he could almost feel his blood being siphoned off.

"It is a slow process," Marooke noted solemnly. "You are doing well."

The fogginess in his head continued to increase, and his vision began to dance with spots of nothingness. He could barely feel his hands …

"Good, Kashif," Marooke whispered. "Good! Fight it! Fight to stay awake for as long as you are able!"

He could no longer keep his fingers clenched, and he felt his grip relaxing. His left hand dropped first, and he heard the sound of the empty poison vial as in tinkled lightly against the floor. Marooke's head turned to the sound, but there was no look of concern. Kashif grit his teeth, and using all of the strength he had reserved, he raised his right hand towards his mentor.

He could only lift it only a few widths away from his body – his arms felt so heavy – but it was enough. Marooke saw the movement – Kashif had his attention …

The fingers on his right hand became unresponsive …

The empty syringe dropped harmlessly to Kashif's chest.

The serenity disappeared from Marooke's face, as the wizened scientist comprehended what had been done. In a panic, he tried to pull his hands free – but the long, arms of the demon were already drooping, bending to the forces of gravity. The blackness was sagging off of him like oversized skin.

The demon was dying.

It would take Marooke with it.

"What have you done?" the elder Arcan rasped, struggling to draw in air. "You poisoned … your own blood!"

Kashif fought to expel the breath he'd held in his lungs for this very moment. "I … die … proud …"

*   *   *   *   *

Greer could not say how long she'd sat on the bottom step of the dais before Captain Reed stumbled in through the courtroom doors. The lifeless body of the Lord Baron Northing lay at the bottom of the steps – but he was only one more corpse in a room thick with them. The courtroom was so quiet, so tranquil, time had vanished. It was just her, the dagger in her hands, and an eternity to ponder.

Reed was holding his side as he took in the room, before focusing on her. "Lady Greer?" he said weakly.

"Yes, I'm alright," she said automatically, her mind barely registering the words. Everything seemed so unreal. With all of the dead men, it seemed strange to have a living one in the room again. She held up the dagger. "I killed him," she said – and was struck by an odd realization.

Stabbing the Lord Baron through the heart had been a very un-Lady-like thing to do.

Reed's eyes panned the room once more, as if still expecting monsters to pop out of the corners. "I'm fine, Reed. I'm not hurt."

The Captain nodded in relief, and collapsed backwards. Greer sprung off of the step and ran towards him. She knelt beside the man, and was relieved to find him still conscious …

If but barely.

Close as she was now, she could see the wounds, she could see the sickly flow of blood that stained his uniform. "Merciful Domus, Reed!"

"They kept coming," he told her through pain-clenched teeth. "But I kept them from getting through." He attempted a smile. "I kept you safe."

"Be quiet, you're bleeding to death," she chided. He raised his head to give a retort, but his neck wobbled and his head fell back to the floor. "You need a Physician," she told him as she stood. "I'm going for help."

Reed feebly shook his head. "… Dangerous …"

"Stop me, then," she told him, and she took a step towards the door.

An unearthly pain exploded in her chest. Her knees buckled at the shock and she found fell to the ground, back arched, arms convulsing. It felt as if she was being ripped apart from the inside-out. She tried to scream, but the agony was too great to lend it any breath.

"Lady Greer!" she heard Reed shout in alarm … but she could not answer.

She was sure she was dying.

*   *   *   *   *

408

Neither Kashif nor the elder Arcan slumped atop him were moving by the time Ethiere pulled his leg free. His knee didn't feel right – it complained nastily each time he tried to put his full weight on it, but he limped over to the two men. He'd not heard everything the two had said, they'd talked so softly, but he'd heard enough to know what had happened. He took the gray-haired Arcan by the shoulders and shoved him aside.

Kashif's eyes were staring into the distance, as if he were in deep meditation. But they focused on Ethiere, and the Arcan's head rolled slightly towards him.

The thief found the syringe. "You injected the poison into yourself?" Ethiere said in accusatory disbelief. "Why not the silver tool! I could have done it!"

"… couldn't … risk it …"

"But you risk this?" Ethiere demanded, his cheeks felt hot, and his eyes burned. He found trouble speaking again. "You're not going to make it, are you?"

"… no …"

The tears welled in his eyes, and he threw the syringe against the far wall. "Boiling, boiling, stupid …"

"… Forgive me …" the Arcan said urgently, abruptly ending Ethiere's cursing. "… your friends …"

Ethiere could only nod. The corners of Kashif's mouth curled in the smallest of smiles, but a look of peace filled his eyes … before they quietly shut. The thief boy, bowed his head, and tried to fight the racking sobs.

"… Ethiere …"

He looked to see the Arcan staring at him through heavy-lidded eyes.

"… burn … everything …"

And he was gone.

Ethiere stood, trying to balance without using his hurt leg. He looked around the room – at the wooden desks and splintered chairs – at the stacks and stacks of papers – at the flammable chemicals waiting on the shelves. At the half-dozen oil lamps that hung on the walls above.

Kashif would get a proper blaze – a burial by fire.

But first things first. He found the key ring on the elder Arcan's belt and limped to the cell room. Kari was clutching the bars, and cried at the sight of him.

"I was sure you'd died," she told him.

He shook his head. "Not yet," he told her as he stuck the key in the lock. "Not yet."

As the lock clicked open, a wave of intense torture overtook him. His entire body convulsed, and his head slammed into the bars on Kari's cage. She screamed and fearfully took refuge in the back corner. He saw the terror in her eyes, and knew it must mirror the terror in his own.

His chest was going to explode, his organs were going to burst … and he realized what was happening to him wasn't really happening to him.

It was happening to Dom.

73.

It made sense why Billick had insisted they stay with the pro-Owen faction of Northing's army on their run for supplies. With Kashif, Ethiere, Greer and Captain Reed all gone off, there were only five of them left. Sarah still wondered if it was really fair counting herself as one of the group. She was unarmed – there had not been enough weapons to go around – but she didn't know how to fight. She was only there because of the ring marking her shoulder – which hardly seemed like an excellent reason.

It was nice to see more of the manor, though. Sarah could not get past the idea that this was, of a truth, one gigantic house. There were so many hallways – so many doors – Sarah wondered if she wouldn't get lost in this place if she tried to run off. And would that be so bad? She felt like a prisoner inside the one-windowed room they rented from the Goodwidow – but here? …

It would take years to explore every corner of this place!

They followed Northing's men down a steep staircase, descending into the manor's cellar. Just a single level lower, but the air took on a whole new feel. It was cool and damp, and seemed to linger in your throat and taste different on your tongue. The lighting was dreary, but increasing, as the foragers lit small mounted oil lamps as they moved deeper into the storage area.

As her eyes adjusted, Sarah got a sense of just how big the room was. There were several large stone columns – wide enough around that four or five people would have to join hands to loop around them – staggered throughout the cellar, serving as a foundation for the floor above. There were no other walls ... no other barriers she could see. Sarah peered even deeper into the darkness – trying to see if she could make out where it ended.

"I don't like it," Bostitch said from the bottom of the staircase. The crossbowman had his weapon cradled in his arm and an unlit roll tucked into the corner of his mouth. "It's too dark down here. Too many blind spots."

In response, Billick stabbed the bulging sack nearest him. Kernels of grain sputtered out as he withdrew his sword. "The monster eats people – not wheat. It wouldn't have any reason to be down here." What he said made sense – but Sarah exchanged a knowing look with Dom. Just like in Alben, they could feel the creature was near – but how near, they couldn't say.

Each of the shadows Sarah looked into could have held three or four demons without her being any the wiser.

"We should keep up with our supply-gathering friends," Billick insisted. "We're more likely to run into the Lord Baron's loyalists than we are any monster – and our chances are better with them than without."

"Shouldn't we wait for the Captain and Lady Greer to catch up to us?" Sperry asked.

Now it was Bost and Billick exchanging the look. "He's not coming back," the crossbowman said.

"Not if he's half the soldier you both believe him to be, he won't," Billick agreed. "He'll recognize keeping Greer tucked away safely with her father, surrounded by armed men, is the absolute best choice to make. She's better off where there won't be fighting."

"And us?" asked Dom, pulling closer to Sarah.

Billick frowned at them – unspoken determination written in the expression. "Keep behind me," he instructed.

The murderer – axe poised in striking position, led the way deeper into the storage room labyrinth, angling them towards the tiny specks of lamp light marking the path. Sarah and Dom followed five paces behind – their shoulders bumping into each other as they walked. Sarah didn't fault Dom at all – neither one of them wanted to stray any closer to the plentiful shadows. Bost and Sperry trailed behind, forming a triangular shape with Billick at the head. The crossbowman, primed for action, kept playing with the unlit roll, moving it from one corner of his mouth to the other as he walked. Sperry – well, Sperry was acting brave…

Something stirred in the dim light nearly twenty paces in front of them. Billick widened his stance defensively, and Sarah heard the sound of the crossbow lock into position against the shoulder brace.

"Is that you Cahill lot – with the children?" asked a man's voice. It sounded like the leader of the soldiers they'd followed down.

Billick relaxed as the man approached. As he drew into the light, Sarah could see the concern on his face. "Got something you'll want to see," the man said. "We've found bodies."

*   *   *   *   *

Morbid curiosity forced Dom to peer over the large barrel to look at the bodies. Billick was examining them with the leader of the opposition. There corpses were increasing the murderer's distress, but he kept was keeping the emotion locked down and suppressed.

"Some of the Lord Baron's faction …" the soldier was saying. "Not any of ours …"

"Looks like they had the same idea as you, though," Billick observed. "Coming for the water."

The commander of the opposition crossed his arms. "The thing you're hunting … it did … this?"

The carnage was the reason the adults had shepherded him and Sarah behind the water barrels. There appeared to be four bodies – but with the dim lighting, and the severed limbs – it was hard to count for sure. Something had torn the men apart –

"… There is surprisingly little blood …" the commander noted.

"That's our demon then," Billick acknowledged. "Where are your men?"

"In groups of twos and threes, going for various supplies …"

"We need as many of them back here, together, as possible," Billick directed. "Your weapons won't do against the creature, but the more eyes we have watching and the fewer gaps in our formation …"

The commander nodded and pointed to one of his men. "Go to the medical supplies, recall Teagarten." He selected another. "Valsing and Myers went for the hams …" The second man ran off. "I've got another three going for medicinal supplies, but they should be heading this way by now …"

Bost snapped the crossbow into place and took a step outwards. He immediately had everyone's attention. "Oil lamp just went out!" he said tersely. The direction he was looking at was dotted with lamps … and half way down it was one of the men who had just been sent as a runner. He too had noticed the light, and was only a good fifty paces from the water stores. His sword was out, and Dom could see the nervous fear pulsing in his aura …

The next lamp in the row went out … casting everything before the lone swordsman into complete darkness. He took one step backwards … then a second before turning on a dead run back towards the group. Something swept across the way, intercepting his path, and his scream echoed in the cavernous space before being cut short.

That something had glowed brilliantly in the darkness for the brief moments it had been visible. "It's the demon," Dom said. "I saw it."

Sarah was standing, clutching at his arm tighter than was comfortable.

"You saw it?" the commander asked, incredulous.

Billick ignored the question and redirected Dom's focus. "Keep your eyes open! You point it out the moment you see it!" The murderer planted his feet between the two closest stone pillars – staring in the void they'd last seen the monster disappear into.

Never lifting his head from the sights on the crossbow, Bostitch moved to a supporting position behind the side-burned murderer. "Told you there were too many blind spots," he said dourly. "Sperry, take our backs, lad."

"Fan out," the commander told his remaining men – just him and two others now. "Reynolds, watch between those two pillars. You, that one there." Very gradually, the soldiers were forming up with Billick and Greer's men in a loose semi-circle around the water stores. The stacked barrels formed a nice back barrier, but not a perfect one. There were enough crevices in the stacks to leave plenty of room …

"Just lost another boiling lamp!" cried out one of soldiers, and the darkness crept in closer. The vanished lamp was at a right angle with the last position they'd seen the monster … and Dom had not been quick enough to catch sight of it this time.

"Keep watch on your own gaps!" urged the commander, who couldn't keep his feet still as he watched.

There was motion, and Dom saw the illuminated figure run across the gap between Sperry's pillars. Sperry and Dom raised the warning in unison, and just as rapidly Bost turned and fired off a shot. "It's a miss!" someone called out, and the crossbowman set to reloading amid a fury of muttered curse words.

"Watch his gap!" shouted Billick, taking two steps back in an attempt to cover both angles. The massive pillar ten paces before him blocked most of his view. "Watch his gap!"

"There!" shouted another man … and Dom turned to see … a lamp blossom with renewed light. Two faces could be seen in reflected in the growing radiance.

"That's Valsing!" the commander cried out. Evaluating the gulf of darkness separated the two groups, he looked to Billick. "We could use two extra men!"

"If they can make it back to us …" the murderer muttered.

"We could advance towards them …" the commander offered.

Bost rejoined the formation with a reloaded crossbow and a deep scowl. "You want to be first to walk into those shadows?" he asked.

The commander took an angry step in their direction. "I should abandon them? Is that what you'd have me do?"

Dom's attention was drawn away from the conversation as a new light sprang up … back in the gap where the commander had been watching. Dom felt his blood chill in his veins when he realized … there were no lamps in that direction …

He turned and saw a frail girl with long hair, leaning weakly against one of the nearby barrels. Her aura was near-blinding. Dom's throat tightened, and as he tried to remember how to scream, the girl lifted her head.

Her eyes were filled with a knowing terror. "Please!" she begged in a hoarse whisper. "Please, run away … I can't hold it …"

Her form grew, the brightness swelled. The demon emerged and the two of them intertwined.

Dom stood frozen in place. He could only think to utter a simple plea.

"Domus, save me!"

*　　*　　*　　*　　*

Just a scratch. All it would take was a scratch. Billick choked the handle of the axe, feeling the wood rub warmly against his calloused hands. The demon had no fear of steel during their first encounter. It had charged heedlessly into groups of armed men, knowing their weaponry held no danger. Billick watched the shadows, and only hoped the monster hadn't grown more cautious. If only it would charge at them … sure of its invincibility. Billick almost wished the creature would attack through the gap he was watching.

Yes, he'd be the first man standing in its path. Yes, the demon's claws would rip him open again in the encounter. But he'd be able to clip the glossy black flesh with the axe blade. Billick pained to take the monster down; even at the expense of his own life. And he knew it wasn't the Banding magic that was causing these thoughts.

Billick was resigned to the idea Oblivion awaited him. He expected to boil in the depths for the crimes he'd committed. But if he could save Sarah – protect the life of the girl who presumed her own death? Billick knew it would not redeem him, would not deliver him from an eternity of torture. But knowing the innocent girl yet lived?

It might make Oblivion's tribulation bearable.

A pleading whimper. "Domus, save me!"

A cry of alarm. "There! Behind you!"

Billick could not turn his body fast enough. Boil it all, how had it flanked them!? Billick saw Bost react in a similar manner. The crossbowman rotated the encumbering weapon, seeking out the target.

It loomed by the barrels, towering over a stunned and petrified Dom. Seeing it again caused the sirens of death to sing in Billick's ears. This creature had left him for dead once. And now, it appeared to have grown. Was it an illusion of the darkness, or did the creature stand two full heads taller than it had in Alben?

The creature was in motion. Oversized hands wrapped around the circumference of the water barrels, lifting them without effort. Bost's crossbow sang, the taut wires vibrating. The bolt sailed true – but was intercepted by the wooden barrel the monster held. In retaliation, the barrel rocketed in their direction. Billick dove to the side – but the crossbowman was still frozen in his shooting stance. The barrel hit him square; the force of it laying him out.

As Billick got to his knees, the creature was already slashing through the commander of the rebel Northing faction. The other hand was grasping at another of the barrels. The Northing men stood terrified at their assigned gaps, watching as their leader died at the hands of the shadowy behemoth. It mattered little – their weapons would have no effect anyway.

"Sperry!" he called out, and caught the Cahill soldier's eyes. It would be on them, and only them, now. "Charge it together!" The young soldier looked spooked, but nodded anyway.

There was no time to waste. Billick rushed forward and only hoped the other man would do the same. Another barrel flew – in the direction of Sperry – and the murderer risked a glance. The men of Northing had started forward as well; the creature's projectile had been aimed at one of them. The barrel burst against the man's shoulder and he flailed backwards. Sperry was forced to his knees amid the shrapnel of wood and the spray of water.

Billick hesitated six paces away from the demon – his coordinated attack with Sperry ruined. The man was getting to his feet; they'd be able to resume …

Clawed fingers extended and snaked towards the paralyzed Dom. Billick knew the exact moment the pointed fingers penetrated the boy's chest as the indescribable agony resonated in his own. The boy cried out, but the shock of pain was too overwhelming for Billick to do the same. All at once, Billick lost control of his body. There were no legs and feet, no arms and hands. There was nothing but overwhelming excruciation.

Billick fell on his face, unable to do anything to brace against the impact. His head hit the cellar floor, and stars flashed across his eyes – but in truth, he didn't feel it. There was nothing – absolutely nothing – except the feeling of those fingers digging deeper into his chest.

He couldn't breath – couldn't force his lungs to unconstrict long enough for a breath. Billick raised his eyes to the monster, and realized he would die here. The pain was too much. Their only hope was Sperry ...

The creature, still latched onto Dom with the right hand, took a step with the left foot in Billick's direction. The left hand reached out, the clawed fingers stopping an arm's length from Billick's face. The demon shuffled forward again, stretching its arms. The fingers elongated, straining for contact with the murderer's skull.

There was movement from behind the monster ... a small figure bending down ...

Sarah.

His body already breaking, Billick felt his heart snap as well. *No*, he wanted to yell to her. *No, just run!* But his throat was locked, words were vain.

He could only watch.

*   *   *   *   *

Sarah had stayed hidden behind the barrels when the alarm was raised. What was she to do – the useless, weaponless girl of the Band? The low barrier of barrels before her blocked off all view of the demon, but she had a near perfect angle for watching the soldiers moving for the attack.

She saw Sergeant Bostitch go down – the barrel knocking the heel of the crossbow backwards into his neck. He'd not moved since. The soldier next to Sperry took another barrel – Sarah was close enough that several drops of water rained down on her skin. She saw Billick race in … and then Dom screamed, and the murderer collapsed in a writhing heap to the floor.

Sarah watched in horror as the murderer twisted and convulsed on the ground. Peering over the barrels, she saw the cause. Dom was leaning backwards as if falling. The only thing keeping him upright were the demon's fingers tethered to his chest.

The monster was feeding on Dom! It was debilitating the rest of the Band. Somewhere in the manor, Ethiere and Kashif and Greer were experiencing a pain more intense than even Dom was enduring. Of them all, she was the only one not incapacitated – because she was the girl who could feel no pain.

She knew what she needed to do. She could not commiserate with their suffering – but she could stop it.

Sarah hopped the barrels and found herself behind the monster. The demon was stretching itself wide – trying to keep one hand embedded in Dom while the other reached to claim Billick. Sarah found the weapon closest to her – the sword of one of the men murdered earlier, and hefted it up. With the bandages on her hand, it was difficult to grip the sword, but she managed to rest it against her shoulder.

It wasn't poisoned. But it didn't need to be.

She staggered forward, the sword compromising her balance as she neared the demon. It didn't see her – didn't sense her – its focus entirely on Dom, Billick and the two remaining soldiers. The sword slipped from her bandaged grasp, the tip hit the floor, and the creature's head turned in alert surprise. Sarah didn't wait. She swung the sword in a high arc, bringing it down on the exposed right forearm.

The blade passed cleanly through – severing the oozing arm. Dom collapsed backwards to the floor – the detached hand and fingers already losing definition. Immediately, the creature was growing a new right hand, the fingers emerging from the stumped arm.

But it had been enough. For the moment, Dom was free.

The creature pivoted on its hips, the left, fully formed arm being brought around. Sarah saw it coming, too late to react other than to know what was going to happen. She felt her feet leave the floor – she knew she was airborne. The stacks of barrels embraced her like a hero and greeted her with tumbling applause.

*　　*　　*　　*　　*

The pain abruptly ended as Dom's head hit the floor, the impact relieving the boy of consciousness. Billick sucked a desperate breath of air into his welcoming lungs, and lifted his head …

… The demon's powerful left arm swept into Sarah – throwing her into the wall of stacked barrels. She hit against them, limbs flailing awkwardly like a child's rag-dog, and disappeared as the stacks collapsed into disorganization.

Domus, no!

The murderer pushed himself up onto shaking legs, took hold of the axe handle, and jumped towards the menace. His legs threatened to give out at every step, but anger drove him forward. The creature was just pivoting back when Billick met it – his axe blade meeting directly at the shoulder of the left arm.

The boiling arm that had catapulted Sarah.

Billick cleft it off cleanly, just as his left leg teetered and gave way. He fell to one knee, but his focus did not falter for a second. He dug the blade into the creature's exposed side – and the monster lurched away. Already Billick could see the poison working; already the monster was struggling to stay upright. The legs were wilting, the knees lowering into the feet.

Billick stood once more, pulled back the axe, and swung. He connected with the creature's neck, and the misshapen, faceless head flew off. The black body fell backwards with the momentum. The glossy black flesh melted away rapidly, leaving only a girl in a dingy white nightgown behind.

The girl raised her head with a look of relief and mouthed a last message. *Thank you.* Her eyes closed in a long-awaited sleep.

The cellar fell into silence. A warm tingling overtook Billick's right shoulder, and he reached for it. It was the exact spot the Banding magic had branded him. It was too dark to see, but Billick knew what it meant.

He knew the mark was gone now.

The hunt was over.

He dropped the axe and ran to the collapsed pile of barrels. He worked like a man possessed, throwing and pushing barrels aside as he dug deeper. He found her, small body shattered, her eyes open.

She was still smiling. His eyes burned; it was unfamiliar. He could not remember the last time he'd wept.

"I told you," she told him in a peaceful whisper. "I told you you'd take it hard." Then she already knew. She knew she was dying.

"It's okay," she reminded him. "It doesn't hurt, remember?"

He rubbed at his eyes, and could only nod in response. He'd failed her. He clutched her hands and held them tight.

"Do something for me," she requested, and he nodded again. "Tell my father what I did…" and she stopped as tears crept from her eyes. "… tell him, it was all for a purpose."

"I will," he said, choking on his own words. "I will."

 She smiled up at him again, closed her eyes, and her small body released its last breath with a gentle, relieved sigh.

74.

The wait was killing Greer. It was morning again, light slipping in through the windows of the Northing Estate. The coup was over – both father and son dead in the fighting. The soldiers who had survived had begrudgingly joined forces to scour Hollingston for physicians and put out the blaze that had started in the eastern wing.

As the attending physician opened the door and slipped through it, all eyes went to him for the latest update. "Its good news," he assured them. "They are all through the worst of it now. The first boy – Dom – lost a fair amount of blood, but the wounds to his chest were small enough and seemed to have closed well. I've sedated him again – I think it best to let him sleep and recover his strength."

The next comments were directed to Ethiere and the young girl thief who had not left his side. "Your friend Ollie has been poorly treated. I will not know for certain what chemicals were introduced to his body – but his condition has improved in the last few hours and I am optimistic whatever it was will exit his system given time."

The man turned to her. "Your Captain Reed is a very stubborn man, Lady Greer. He absolutely refused to die on me, though Domus knows I didn't hold much hope for him when we began."

"But he's going to live?" Sergeant Bostitch sought to clarify.

The physician nodded. "He will make a full recovery – given time." The man adjusted the spectacles on his nose. "But I doubt the Captain is a man who'll give himself the time." He sighed and his eyes met hers again. "He's asking for you, my Lady. First thing when he revived – he demanded to know if you were alright." The physician stepped away from the door and smiled slyly. "Might I suggest you all go in to visit the man before he crawls out here to visit you?"

"Thank you," Greer said. "We are in your debt."

The physician nodded again, and went to stand before the thief. "Four weeks – minimum – before you remove the brace," he instructed. "No weight on that knee – do you hear me? And at least eight Holydays before jumping across any roofs, understood?" The honest grin returned. "Not that you do that sort of thing, I'm sure."

The physician – for all he had done – had not asked many questions. He did not demand to know what men of Cahill were doing in the Northing manor, how Dom had gotten the holes in his chest, or why Ethiere and Kari reeked of acrid smoke. Never once had the Banding come up – and now that their shoulders were ring free, there was no evidence the magic had ever held them. He'd come to do his job, and had withheld seeking out more than he wanted to know.

He patted Ethiere on the shoulder and leaned in closer. "And make sure this girl gets a few good meals in her belly, alright?"

The thief turned a knowing eye to Kari, who clung lovingly on his arm. "Might be tough …" he dithered.

"… we've got rocks in our stomach," the girl finished with a mocking seriousness.

"Big, big rocks …" Ethiere agreed. "But I'll do what I can."

The physician knew he was an outsider to the joke the two young people shared, but he smiled graciously and didn't press the matter. Lastly, his eyes strayed to Bostitch. "I still think you should let me have a look at the ugly bruising on your neck …"

The crossbowman declined, and Greer wondered if the purplish mass wasn't a medal of honor in the man's eyes. It certainly looked painful – and Bost wasn't doing much nodding – but it was his choice whether or not to be treated. "Got to have something to show Reed," he said. "Can't let him think he had all the excitement."

The murderer stood. Billick had been very quiet the entire time. He'd said almost nothing since Sarah had died in his arms. "A word with you, physician?" The man nodded and the two stepped out in the corridor. Greer followed them out with her eyes, but they moved too far away from the door for her to hear what was being said. Sperry slipped by her, into the room where Reed was resting, and she decided to follow. Bost caught her arm.

"Apologies, my Lady, but there is something needs to be said."

"Go on."

The soldier's eyes darted towards Reed's door. "Was it eight men that they counted? That he cut down for you?"

Greer smiled. "There is a man that will not shirk his duty," she answered.

The Sergeant twisted his lips, as if trying to shape the words of his disagreement. At last, he spoke. "Duty might slay four or five. It takes a bit more of something to get all the way up to eight." The crossbowman looked her in the eyes. "With enough of that extra something, the entire force of Northing couldn't have gotten through to you … if you understand what I'm saying …"

Greer wondered if she did, because Bost seemed to be implying … She felt color rise in her cheeks. "Captain Reed?"

"I've served with him long enough and know him well enough to have seen it back at the Crescent Head," the crossbowman admitted. "I just thought you should know." His tight smile didn't extend to any muscle in his neck, and he excused himself through the door.

Reed? It couldn't be right! But not because of her title and his lack of one. Greer knew that titles were not nearly as important as the soul of the people that carried them. No, she couldn't believe it because she couldn't fathom Reed carrying anything more than dutiful compassion for her. What could the noble Captain have seen in her during this crucible that would have won his affection? She'd been terrible to him, most of the time on purpose ...

Greer did not know who she was, so how could Reed? How could he possibly have affection for someone so pitifully undefined?

She puzzled on the suggestion for a few moments more before entering into the secondary room. The two boys – Dom and Ollie were both sleeping soundly on beds against the far wall. Captain Reed was propped up in another bed, his eyes looking more alert than what Greer would have expected. He was looking at her – looking at her for what? For any sign of distress, any indication of pain?

"I'm fine, Captain," she assured him, and she saw his shoulders relax. "I'm ... I'm grateful that you are too."

Bostitch cleared his throat. "So ... eight men ..."

"I'll have to tell you the story sometime," Reed answered. "But I'm more interested in how Lady Greer managed to kill Lord Baron Northing." Greer dropped her eyes to the floor. Reed saw her reaction, and coughed nervously. "Or perhaps not." Heavy silence filled the room before Sperry piped up.

"Rumors say the Lord Baron's cousin is claiming the barony. With Owen and most of the other Northing's dead in the coup, he's next in line for succession."

Greer had already thought of that – she'd hoped it wouldn't come up. Reed made the connection. "That is the man you are betrothed to." She looked up at him, wondering if it was more than just a simple comment. Boil Bost – seeding these ideas in her head! She didn't answer, and Reed went on. "You'll be the Baronessa of Northing."

Her father's dream – his daughter in a position of influence in the most powerful family in Tollia.

Before she could say anything, a knock sounded on the door. Billick slipped in before anyone could invite him. The murderer looked them all over, and stopped at her. "I want to say something," he said. "If anyone asks what happened here today, tell them I didn't survive. Tell them I died."

"Why?" Reed asked.

The murderer stood like stone, but Greer could see the softness in his eyes. "Because I did," he answered. "A little girl killed me; murdering what I was once. I can't go back to it." He fought the emotion in his voice. "I'm going to find a ship. I'm leaving Tollia. I don't know where I'm going ... but I don't want any part of this life finding me in whatever my next might be." He looked over his shoulder. "I've spoken to the physician – I've asked him to do the same. The thieves ... I've made arrangements with Ethiere. If you will all agree ... I'm going to cease to exist."

Reed looked to Greer, and she nodded.

"If I may, Captain," Bostitch said as he stood to attention, "I would like to announce I didn't make it either."

It stunned Reed. "Bost?"

"I've got something to take care of," the crossbowman answered. "A man named Rice ..." Greer saw Billick nod knowingly. "It is something I need to do for Neald."

"Be careful not to walk too far down that road," the murderer advised.

Reed starred at his right-hand man, but he nodded. "Be careful." The Captain's head swung to look at Sperry. "How about you?" he teased. "You dead as well?"

Young Sperry shook his head in immediate denial. "No, sir."

"But I am." The words popped out of Greer's mouth, which shouldn't have surprised her as much as she'd been thinking them. The room went still. She met Reed's incredulous eyes, and grew in confidence. "I died too."

Reed shook his head. "But ... you'd be a Baronessa ..."

"That's not who I want to be." She watched him, hoping he wouldn't ask the next question. She didn't have an answer. She did not know who she wanted to be. Like Billick, she could only hope she'd find something over the next horizon.

It was Bostitch that spoke. "Sperry, lad," and he pointed to the door. "A word outside with you." The confused young soldier frowned at Bost as he passed. "You've got to paint a lovely picture of my heroics when you get back home, and I've got a few details you shouldn't leave out …" The crossbowman smiled to Reed, bowed his head stiffly to Greer, and disappeared through the doorframe. Billick watched them go before turning to her.

"Good luck," he told her.

"I hope you find what you're looking for," she told him.

He nodded, turned, and offered a smart salute to Reed.

Reed grinned. "You aren't one of my men," he reminded him.

Billick nodded thoughtfully. "Maybe that's why I turned out the way I did." He shrugged a smile, and he too left the room.

Leaving her with Reed and the two sleeping boys. Greer found she could not meet his eyes, and the silence grew more and more pronounced.

Reed broke it. "Where will you go?" he asked her.

She looked into her own empty hands, as if the answer were written somewhere on her palms. "Away," she said, knowing it wasn't an answer. "Like Billick … I'll probably find a ship. There are lots of islands …"

"It's a big world," Reed agreed. His eyes wavered and Greer saw him struggling with his next words. "I could come with you …" He trailed off, trying to determine how it was received in her expression.

She blushed, and cursed herself for blushing. Greer forced her head to shake. "No, I don't think so. I think Billick has the right idea … a clean start somewhere. Somewhere where nobody is going to think they need to bow, or offer me the best of their plate, or treat me like a title …"

"Greer." He spoke her name. It was the first time she heard anyone say it as he had. "I can call you by your name. I can call you Greer."

She didn't understand why her stomach felt all queer, or why her skin suddenly felt so warm. She tried to laugh off the feelings, laugh off Reed and the silly things he was saying. "Could you, Captain? Could you really?"

"I believe the Captain is dead," he told her, and he reached out his hand. He held it out for her– inviting. "My name is James," he said. "Please – call me James."

75.

It was a bright collection – white daisies, marigolds and a pair of velvet bramble roses – all neatly bundled and tied around with green ribbon. The man lowered the bouquet with quiet reverence, and stood back away from the newly hewn headstone.

"She liked green," Sarah's father shared. "She'll appreciate that the ribbons are green."

It was just the three of them – Ethiere, Dom and the father – a trio reflecting on the headstone before them, and the brave, little girl whose grave it marked. Ethiere could see Kari sitting on the fence that ringed the cathedral cemetery, content for the moment to give him some space. Perhaps she sensed this was a hallowed moment – one Ethiere needed to experience in the company of those who shared his loss.

"I owe her my life," Dom said. It seemed hardly fitting to call him a boy anymore; the one terrifying day in the Northing manor aging him beyond his years. There was a calm maturity to him now, and Ethiere could only look proudly on the poised young man who had emerged from the cocoon of the brown coat. "The monster would have finished me, without a doubt. Any longer, and I might not have had enough blood to pull through. She risked her life – she came out of hiding. She didn't need to, I would have never asked it of her …" His words failed, and he was forced to swallow.

Sarah's father wrapped an arm around him supportively. "It was the kind of girl she was," he agreed.

"She was my friend," Dom added. Hearing him speak the word – it was clear Dom thought there would never be a greater title anyone could ever aspire to.

Ethiere shifted his weight on his crutch and cleared his throat. He'd not wanted to interrupt, but he had a message to deliver. "She wanted you to know something," he told her father. "Her last thoughts – last words – they were for you." The thief felt tightness in his throat, and fought down the raw emotions.

"She wanted you to know it was all for a purpose, her being in the Band. It couldn't have been anyone else. She was important ..."

"But it was more than that," interjected Dom. "She was the soul of our Band. She was the bind that held us together. The magic – it forced us to walk the same path, but Sarah – she forged us into one." Dom lowered his head, and took a tear off his cheek with his finger. "You know, she worried so much that she was a burden on you, that you'd suffered so much on her account ... I told her that I saw how much you loved her. I told her she shouldn't have any reason to doubt your love."

The father nodded, and smiled through his mourning. "I thought perhaps she would be angry at me. I've kept her locked up safely in that upstairs room for all of her life – never let her experience what most young girls her age take for granted. But what you are saying makes me glad. I'm happy both of you had the opportunity to know my little girl – who has been the single greatest blessing and joy in my life." He ran his hand lovingly along the curve of the headstone. "Our little room seems so empty now ..."

Ethiere became aware that they were no longer alone in the cemetery. Two others had joined them, waiting a respectful distance back. The nearest was easily recognized – white beard, amethyst stole and sage, knowing eyes. The wizard Algius nodded a greeting to Ethiere, but did not speak until both Dom and Sarah's father had also noted his presence.

"Do not let us interrupt," the wizard said, which was no longer a possibility. Seeing he had their attention, he continued. "The news reached the college doors. I have come to pay my respects to the heroes of the Band. Those surviving – and those who have earned their rest." The wizard ambled forward and laid a strong hand on the father's shoulder. "The world grieves with you, my good man, for it knows the secret beauty and strength she carried in her special frame."

As the wizard spoke, Ethiere watched the other man out of the corner of his eye. He stayed back, in obvious subservience to his Master, but carried the aura that resonated from those with wizard training. The other man's eyes were fastened on Dom, and he moved forward apprehensively, waiting ...

Dom saw him. His face contorted with wonderful confusion that quickly flooded with elation. "J-Joshua?" A laugh blurted out. "Is that really you? Can it be?"

A smile broke the young wizard's placid expression. "My goodness, Dominic, you've gotten taller!" There was no time wasted as the two embraced. Dom winced at the contact – but it was evident he wasn't going to let go.

"I thought you'd gone away – that we'd never see you again. You left that night without warning – without even a goodbye. Mother was always praying that you'd …" he stopped, and the two brothers released one another. Joshua was nodding, knowingly.

"I heard about mother. And father." The elder brother could not make the news any less heavy. "Yes, father is dead too. There isn't an easier to say it." Dom looked pained at the news, but not surprised. "It's the reason that Wizard Algius wanted me to come along." Before continuing, Joshua looked to the old wizard, who nodded approval. "We've come to take you home with us, little brother. You've got the makings of a fine wizard, I've been told."

Dom looked wary, and Ethiere was surprised to see the young man turn to him. "What should I do?"

Ethiere smiled. "That's up to you."

Dom's brow furrowed and he turned a questioning eye to his brother. Joshua shrugged. "Wizards aren't as scary as dad made them out to be …"

Algius smothered a secretive smile. "Hush … you'll ruin our advantage …"

Dom kept his eyes on his brother, and his face slowly lit up. "Okay, then. I'll come."

"Wonderful!" The elder wizard's exclamation lacked all hint of surprise, leaving little doubt he'd expected any other answer. "That just leaves the tavern, then." A key appeared in his hand, and he tossed it to Sarah's father. The man stood dumbfounded. "Ever run one before? No? Well, that's no bother. I'm sure you'll be able to figure it out." Algius took the new owner by the shoulder and gave him a reassuring jostle. "Just charge an honest rate, don't water anything down, consider giving a discount to wizards …" He grinned at his own joke.

Sarah's father shook his head in wondering disbelief. "I don't know what to say …"

Dom stepped forward. "I think Sarah would have wanted it this way. She told me as much. You know, she just might sneak away from Domus' embrace to watch you laugh with your patrons from time to time."

The wizard clapped his hands. "We're settled then. Dom with us, you to the tavern ..." He turned to Ethiere. "I'm afraid I've nothing for you, my thief. But something tells me you won't have any problem taking care of yourself." He leaned in for a muttered secret. "I must say, a pity only two of you that survived ..." Ethiere pulled away just enough to see the knowing look flash through the wizard's eyes.

Was it possible? How could the wizard have divined their secret?

"I, personally, would have expected a few more to live ... but you can never tell with these Bandings!" He winked. "Everyone's ship sails eventually, so they say ..."

He did know ... or was he just guessing extremely well? Ethiere tried not to let his face give anything away. He looked to Dom. Would wizard training make Dom this fascinatingly cryptic as well?

The young man saw him looking. Thankfully the wizard had hushed his voice enough that Dom wouldn't sense anything deep in the words. Dom wasn't aware the others weren't dead. "Ethiere?" Dom was able to close the distance between them faster than Ethiere could hobble on his mending ankle. "I almost feel like I can't leave you. We're Banded. And I know it's over now – but ... it doesn't seem right to just be able to walk away ..."

He sensed Kari behind him, and was not surprised to feel her fingers trail down his arm – her hand finding his. Ethiere had a feeling he and Dom would meet again. "I'll be alright, Dom." He looked at Kari – and he knew that he'd be more than just alright. "But you'll come find me in the city sometime, right? Show me a few tricks? Mix me into your wizard's business and what not?"

They embraced. "If you're ever up by the College ..."

Algius coughed into his sleeve. "We'd have to have him empty his pockets before leaving ..."

Ethiere laughed as Dom walked towards his new life, talking animatedly with his brother every step of the way. Sarah's father still stood graveside, and Ethiere tugged on Kari's hand. They'd leave him in peace to share the news about the tavern with her.

Their ambling pace was slow, but there was much to ponder as he and Kari left the cemetery. So the old wizard knew about the other survivors? It didn't seem to matter too much; Algius didn't seem to be of a mind to let the secret slip. But Ethiere was captivated with how he'd figured it out. And his comment – about not having a problem taking care of himself – it seemed he knew about Billick's last secret as well. The secret he'd given with the charge to share Sarah's last words with her father.

Not even Kari knew about the murderer's cache of coins, hidden under the floorboards of Billick's small room. The murderer had horded his share of numerous rewards – and appeared to have never spent a single thin copper. Ethiere had already used a stack to purchase Sarah's headstone – donated anonymously to the cathedral.

He hadn't counted his new found fortune yet – he wasn't sure he could count that high. But he would – soon enough. He and the rest of the Gang – they'd enroll in school. They'd learn to do sums and to read. They no longer had to be at the mercy of their circumstances.

They could create whatever they wanted to out of their lives. He stole a glance at Kari. Create whatever life they wanted – with whoever they wanted it to be with.

He would become a Physician. Or perhaps a scientist, like Kashif. He could picture it now …

"What are you thinking about?" Kari asked with a whimsical smile. She saw his face and shook her head. "Do I even want to know?"

Ethiere laughed at her bemused dismay. "Boots," he told her.

"Boots, again?" she chided. "You can't dance in boots remember?"

He did. But he could picture the boots. Black and shiny, with silver buckles that ran down the length of them. Exceptionally fine boots. It would be terrible

trying to dance in them, but he'd buy them one day soon. He took Kari by the hand, and entwined his fingers with hers.

He'd need proper boots to get married.

FROM THE AUTHOR

I grew up reading fantasy novels that had an eclectic group of heroes – often of diverse races, nationalities, genders and skillsets. While having such a varied cast made for exciting stories, I was often left wondering how such a dissimilar group would ever manage to form in the first place. This fantasy trope would eventually lead me to the concept of the Banding – a built-in deus ex machina for the formation of a group that could solve the problems the plot puts forth.

As I began to write the novel, I soon found that the Banding was not only the central plot point – but was the protagonist of the novel as well. Though I have six main characters, I attempted to write this novel so as to not make the story solely about one or another of them – but a story of them as a whole.

This novel is heavy on flashbacks – also a conscious choice on my part. I was intrigued by the story-telling concept of the television show "Lost", which explored a character's current motivations by giving the audience a window into their past. I wanted this to be a story about who these characters are – and why they are the way they are – and show the personal demons that each was having to fight.

I want to thank all of those who had a hand in getting this novel from my head into the form you are currently reading it in: my wife, my family and my friends. A special thanks is extended to Kayelyn H. for her assistance in editing, to Kevin S. and Mike S. for their input and critique and all others who offered the motivational pushes that I needed.

And thanks to you, reader, for allowing me to share this work with you. I would appreciate and encourage you to share your impressions of the book by offering a review on Amazon or Barnes&Noble.

ALSO BY BRETT KELBERRY

AURIC THE GREAT

Auric the Great is a hero of legends. Strong handsome, brave ... everything except punctual. When he fails to show up for his quest, it is up to a scheming history wizard, a blind bard, and a replacement Auric – the broom-toting store clerk – to finagle their way through the predestined adventure in his behalf. What could possibly go wrong?

Praise for *Auric the Great*:

"The conversations have those funny little details that make it feel like real people talking." – Lirulyn (Amazon review)

"Great unexpected twists, and I actually laughed out loud several times! I can't wait to read it again to pick up all the subtle nuisances I didn't get before." – harrypotterfan (Amazon review)

"Packed with humor and references to popular fantasy themes. I would recommend it to anybody!" – SunGirl (Amazon review)

Available as an e-book on Amazon and Barnes&Noble. Also available as a paperback through Amazon.

www.ingramcontent.com/pod-product-compliance
Lightning Source LLC
Chambersburg PA
CBHW051435260626
47162CB00001B/100